Praise for

Echo Six

"Readers of Jeff Shaw's established Blood Line series will be delighted by *Echo Six*, his stellar foray into the world of Science Fiction. A tale of time paradox and haunted dreams, Shaw skillfully ponders the future and the repercussions of altering our fate."

—**Robert Gwaltney, award-winning author of** *The Cicada Tree* **and Georgia Author of the Year**

"Jeff Shaw's *Echo Six*, is a fast paced, edge of your seat, action packed, sci-fi thriller with romantic intrigue. In it, Echo Six falls to earth bleeding profusely with his telemetry suit torn. Six learns to improvise quickly as he struggles to orient himself in his new surroundings, seek help for his injuries, and create a livelihood to survive. He befriends a woman, yet she has trepidations about his past and is afraid to move forward as he fights for his life hunted by the military and the NSA."

—**Jo Lovejoy**
Author of *Terminal Lucidity*

"Jeff Shaw leaves the streets of San Francisco to journey through space and time. However, his talents remain the same. With *ECHO SIX*, Shaw once more engages readers hard with relatable but complex characters, fast thrilling action, and like all the best sci-fi tales, exploring the flaws of humanity, yet showing all the best qualities we can manage."

—Brad Watkins
Author of *Legend of the Kellashar Knights*

Echo Six

Other Books By Jeff Shaw

Who I Am: The Man Behind the Badge, 2020

The Bloodline Series
Lieutenant Trufant, 2022
LeAnn and the Clean Man, 2023
Broken, 2024

The Echo Class
Book One

Echo Six

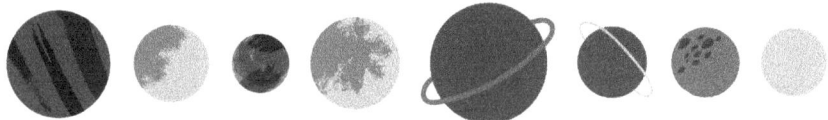

Jeff Shaw

BOOKLOGIX®
Alpharetta, GA

This is a work of fiction. Names, characters, businesses, places, and events are either the products of the author's imagination or are used in a fictitious manner. Any resemblance to actual persons, living or dead, or actual events is purely coincidental.

Copyright © 2024 by Jeff Shaw

All rights reserved. No part of this book may be reproduced or transmitted in any form or by any means, electronic or mechanical, including photocopying, recording, or any information storage and retrieval system, without permission in writing from the publisher.

ISBN: 978-1-6653-0946-2 - Paperback
ISBN: 978-1-6653-0947-9 - Hardcover
ISBN: 978-1-6653-0948-6 - eBook

These ISBNs are the property of BookLogix for the express purpose of sales and distribution of this title. The content of this book is the property of the copyright holder only. BookLogix does not hold any ownership of the content of this book and is not liable in any way for the materials contained within. The views and opinions expressed in this book are the property of the Author/Copyright holder, and do not necessarily reflect those of BookLogix.

Library of Congress Control Number: 2024921113

♾This paper meets the requirements of ANSI/NISO Z39.48-1992 (Permanence of Paper)

1 0 1 4 2 4

*For my fellow Science Fiction fans,
I hope I have done the genre justice.*

Chapter 1
Six

Echo Six stood in the hatch of his crippled ship and stared into the vastness of space. The darkness was cold and absolute and the stars offered no hint of what lay below. Blood pooled at his feet and staying with the ship meant death.

It was a simple step, and the fall to Earth was short. Landing face-first in the hardpacked soil knocked the wind out of him and intense pain shot through his left arm. A new torrent of warm blood ran from the jagged holes in the sleeve of his flight suit. He wanted to scream, but couldn't utter a sound.

Shutting his eyes, he tried to slow his breathing. He was hyperventilating and each breath sucked sand and acrid dust into his mouth. Choking on it, he rolled onto his back.

The specks above him became stars and each watched him suffer. He tried to name a few hoping the distraction would help ease his agony, but their names proved elusive.

Taking another deep breath, he sat upright. The grit, bitter and abrasive ground between his teeth. He tried to spit it out, but his mouth was too dry.

Through the holes in his flight suit, the torn mesh of the telemetry suit underneath glistened with blood. Whatever had blasted through the ship had punctured clean through his left arm.

Pushing himself up with his good arm, he stood and looked back at the ship. It was difficult to see in the dark, its silhouette a shade darker than the sky around it. The hatch was open though, and the dim light of the view-screen grew dimmer as he watched.

It's dying.

Damaged beyond his ability to repair, he sealed the hatch and started walking. The feeling of deserting a faithful companion was powerful and troubling.

I'm sorry old friend.

Twenty meters from the ship, he tripped, stumbled and fell. On his back again, he looked at the ground around him. In the starlight, he could pick out loose rocks and dead brush at his feet.

He listened hoping to hear signs of civilization, some sign of life, but heard nothing but his own heartbeat and a dry rasp coming from his chest.

"Let me live," he whispered.

Somewhere close by he heard a soft tapping sound, like water dripping from a faucet. He reached for the sound with his right hand and found a sticky pool of warm blood.

He needed a tourniquet. Pulling at the sleeve of his flight suit, he tried to rip the cloth with his good hand, but the material was tough and he didn't have the strength. Standing, he felt his knees shake but took a step, then another propelling himself forward.

Another hundred meters and he slipped again and almost fell. He looked back toward the ship fearing he was walking in circles, but there was no sign of it.

Turning three hundred and sixty degrees left him disoriented. He was tempted to lie down, to rest but fear kept him moving. Each breath and the sound of his boots dragging through the soil were signs of progress.

Just before his forced landing, he passed over the lights of a small town to the east. He looked for its glow on the horizon.

If I can reach that town, I can find help, but which way is east?

Above the horizon, the constellation Orion floated silently. If he had ever known which way the hunter's sword pointed, he couldn't remember.

The horizon in front of him did look brighter. He walked and crawled towards it for another hour and collapsed again. This time the pain left him.

He was in a dark room, and although it was pitch black, he knew he wasn't alone. It was a dream, but knowing it was a dream didn't help. Something silent was in the room with him. It was intelligent and it was studying him.

The pain returned, slow at first and then like a hammer pounding a nail into his flesh, he was awake.

What happened to the stars? Are my eyes open or am I blind now too?

No, he wasn't blind. The pinpricks of light floating above him became the constellation Pegasus. He could name a few of its stars now, and knowing their names gave him hope.

He had been out of deep sleep for several hours and he would need food and water soon. After a long trip and months in deep sleep, pilots often spent a full day in recovery.

Touching his left sleeve again, he rubbed his thumb and forefinger together. The blood was tacky now, the bleeding had slowed and the pain wasn't as sharp.

Will I die of thirst or will it be blood loss?

Walking until his legs grew weak again, he sat, laid on his back and let the dream continue.

He was in his ship's flight seat, the view-screen in front of him flashing red warnings. An alarm blared behind him, Warning! Warning! He ignored it.

The feeling of being watched was strong now. Whatever it was felt close, and curious. It reached out to him—was it trying to speak?

A steady, dull thumping sound drowned out the blare of the ship's alarm, and the sensation of being watched faded.

He opened his eyes and Pegasus, the winged horse was an hour closer to the horizon.

Taking deep breaths of cool dry air, he thought if he could

stand, he could go a little farther. Then the thumping sound that penetrated his dream returned. Something was behind him.

Circling on the other side of a small dune, a bright beam of light illuminated his ship.

They've come for me!

Rolling over, he pushed himself up and stood, waving his good arm. "Here, I'm over here!"

It was hard to focus on the searchlight, but as his vision cleared, the steady green and red flashing light sharpened. The craft's dark silhouette turned. For a moment, he thought he was still dreaming. Then horror struck him.

A twenty-first century helicopter was circling the ship.

"Oh, God!" He lost all feeling in his body, including the pain, and collapsed back into the dirt.

As a child, he had seen a similar helicopter on display at a museum, a relic from a long-forgotten war, Afghanistan maybe. How long had it been since the last of its kind had flown—a hundred and fifty years? Probably more.

It wasn't unusual to lose or gain a few hours or even a day when traveling faster than light, but during his two longest trips, he had returned more or less within hours of the correct time. He tried to think of a logical explanation, but couldn't. There was an ancient machine from a long-gone past circling over the ship.

Through the damaged telemetry suit, he reached out and touched his ship. He had been linked to it for more than a year now, and he could feel the last of the systems failing. Life support and navigation were off-line, and now the core itself was dying, and it felt as if part of him were dying with it.

He tried to link with the helicopter, but sensed no electronics. Either it was too far away or just not transmitting anything he could understand.

Above him, his emergency beacon floated in orbit. He launched it when he knew he was in trouble. It was up there somewhere, and he looked into the night sky wishing he could see it. It had all the ship's mission data, along with his distress signal. He could sense it, even communicate with it if he had to, but should he?

As a young student at the Institute, he and a few of the other cadets watched *The Day the Earth Stood Still*. It didn't work out well for that pilot, they shot him as soon as he walked out of the saucer.

What will they find on my ship? Not much. Sixty percent of it is organic and with a dead core, the rest was useless framework. How much technology will they recover? I don't know—but they will be looking for me!

He had to keep moving. He wasn't ready to explain who he was or why he was here until he had time to think this through.

He stood, felt pain in his leg and touched the back of his calf. His pant leg was ripped and wet—more blood. Something had grazed the muscle deep enough to bleed.

The crescent moon cleared the eastern horizon, giving him enough light to see. The blood on his sleeve and the clear mesh of the telemetry suit looked black in the weak moonlight.

I need water.

There were a few plants growing in the hard packed soil. Most looked like dried weeds, but he picked some of the healthier ones and chewed them. They were bitter and dry and he spit them out.

Heading toward the dim light and away from the ship, he hoped that small city would be just over the horizon. If he was lucky, he could make it before dawn.

Hours passed. The moon was well above the horizon now and he could see out to twenty meters. He was in a dry creek bed. The bed was smooth, the dirt under his boots was packed like hardened clay and the same dried shrubs and grasses grew along its edges.

Something moved just ahead and two eyes peered back at him.

A small animal, possibly a rabbit panicked and ran headlong into the underbrush. He could sense its fear through his suit. Then somewhere to the north, an animal howled—a coyote or a wolf—and several more answered farther away. Wolves would not be good, and it sounded like there were a lot of them.

Can they smell my blood? Probably, even I can smell it.

The horizon was growing brighter—definitely city lights—and he hoped he would see them when he crested the next hill.

The animal howled again, closer this time.

He kneeled, listening. Something was creeping through the dried weeds to his left. It paused and was close. He waited, hoping it would run off like the rabbit, but it stayed motionless. Right in front of him something feral—a predator—was deciding whether he was a worthy prey. He stood and faced its direction, ready for it if it came at him.

"Here I am, do your best!"

He was tired, but he would fight. Bleeding to death was better than being killed and eaten by an animal.

He waited, trying to sense the creature like he had with the rabbit. There was a vague feeling of curiosity and adrenalin. It crept closer and two silver orbs appeared, moonlight reflecting in the animal's eyes. He pointed at it with his good arm and stepped closer.

"I see you! What are you waiting for?" he whispered to the beast.

The eyes blinked, and as if the animal understood, it too stepped forward and out of the shadows.

It was bigger than he expected, long and low to the ground. It sized him up, still curious but no longer thinking like a predator, more like an equal. The wolf turned and trotted off, the soft sound of its paws padding through the underbrush, followed by a strong smell of urine. A message.

He saw me, and he let me live.

With the glow of the lights as his beacon, he set off again. Another few meters or another kilometer and he would rest.

Chapter 2
Croft

White Sands Missile Range, New Mexico

Colonel Robert Croft sat in his overstuffed recliner staring at the bottle of Knob Creek. The bottle said the whiskey was nine years old, but it was older than that. He remembered the exact day he brought it home, the day he buried his wife four years ago last week.

It had been a rainy day, a perfect day for a funeral and Big Daddy's Liquors was on his way home. He stopped, not sure if he wanted a drink or if he was delaying the inevitable fear of walking into the townhouse knowing it would always be empty. He drank four shots from the bottle that night hoping to numb his anger and grief, but the alcohol only made them worse.

Anger was the first and easiest emotion to let go of. The driver was only eighteen and on his first leave from boot camp. Drunk and on his way home from a night of celebration, he hit Sara head-on. She died instantly, and the boy died a week later. There was no one left to hate.

Grief was more difficult, but it eased over the years and left him with only the loss of his best friend and lover. For four years, there were times he didn't think he could endure living without her, but the alternative was not an option. So the bottle was still just four shots shy of full.

His cell phone vibrated on the end table next to him, creeping across the table like a living thing. He picked it up before it slid off the edge.

"Yes?"

It was Lieutenant Burton again, his second call in the last hour. The first call was just after ten o'clock. A high altitude, supersonic radar contact was descending over Texas and then minutes later vanished over New Mexico. Ground stations reported the contact was not using a transponder and not in communications with any military or civilian controllers.

"Sir, I think you need to come over here," the lieutenant said. "The Apache we sent out is on station and over some type of object. They're waiting for orders."

"What do they think it is?"

Burton paused. "They said that it was round, possibly a satellite."

Croft was the commander of a special operations unit based at the White Sands Missile Range in New Mexico and acting commander of the base while General Bowman was on leave.

"Alright, Lieutenant, get me a Blackhawk and another Apache ready to go. I'll need a few men too, so wake up a squad of Rangers and tell them to pack light. I want to be in the air in twenty minutes."

Putting the phone down, he reconsidered the bottle and the stack of boxes against the wall.

His mother-in-law had dropped the boxes off just after the wedding. Photos mostly. Everything from Sara's birth to report cards, even a few scrap books with school projects. Things only a mother saves watching her child grow into an adult. He feared leaving them in a storage unit with the rest of their furniture, so there they were, sitting in a corner for four years. One day he would open them—but not today.

Dressed in a clean ACU, he checked himself in the mirror. The Army Combat Uniform was tighter in the waist than it had been; something he would have to work on soon.

At the main gate, the whine of a turbine and the navigation lights of a UH-60 Blackhawk told him his team was ready. Six soldiers dressed in standard desert camo standing outside the rotor wash, turned and watched him park.

The cool night air pulled at the weight riding on his shoulders, it was refreshing. The earthy smell of desert sage was replaced by the acrid odor of jet fuel drifting in the wind.

There were two rows of AH-64D Apache Longbows inside the chain-link fence. As he walked toward the idling Blackhawk, a second turbine started, and the rotors of one Apache began to turn, the glow of its instrument lights illuminating the crew finishing their checklists.

Croft took the jump seat in the Blackhawk and adjusted his harness. As the whine of the turbines increased, he could feel the adrenaline kick in, and the fatigue and thoughts of his wife washed away. The helicopter lifted off, pitched forward and the two rows of Apache helicopters disappeared behind him.

There were no city lights, no sign of the terrain below, just a complete absence of light. For a moment, he felt vertigo and forced himself to stare at the pilot's instrument panel until the feeling passed. Both pilots navigated through the darkness using AVS-6 night vision goggles, and other than the whine of the turbines, there was no sound.

The Rangers sat in the dim red light, loaded with everything they could carry. Each had a semi-automatic pistol, extra magazines, first aid gear, tie wraps, and canteens. Some sat with their eyes closed while others stared straight ahead.

They were young, just kids, and he remembered his feeling of invulnerability at that age. They had no idea what they would be up against, yet they had no fear. They would rely on their training and each other, and that was all they needed.

"Sergeant Sanchez," Croft said through the Blackhawk's intercom, "when we reach the site, we are going to relieve another Apache. It's orbiting something I need to check out. Could be an aircraft or space junk that fell out of orbit. I want your people to stand by and assist if anything comes up. It's probably nothing, and we'll all be back at the base in a few hours."

The Ranger nodded and checked his men.

"Five minutes," the pilot said, pointing to the Apache's lights in the distance.

The Rangers began a final check of their gear, and Croft unbuckled himself from his jump seat. At six-foot-one, he had to stoop to reach the pilot.

"Captain, patch me through to the Apache."

He heard a few clicks through the speaker in his helmet, and then he heard a thick southern accent. "Lieutenant Jimison here."

"Lieutenant, this is Colonel Croft with Special Ops out of White Sands. We're five minutes out. As soon as we arrive, you're clear to return to base. When you get back, report this as a routine training mission with us. Your commander will probably have a problem with that. Have him get with me and me only. Everything you've seen and heard is classified until further notice. This is probably nothing. If it is, you won't hear any more about it; if not, well you won't hear anything then either."

"Roger that, sir."

As Croft and the two helos approached, the Apache pitched forward, and headed home.

"Captain, have our Apache light that thing up please."

The Blackhawk had ARDIMS, or Airborne Radiation Detection Identification and Mapping System. It circled twice over the illuminated sphere below them picking up only normal background radiation, and Croft had the pilot set down.

"Keep your men on board for the moment, Sergeant," Croft said and stepped out as the rotors slowed.

He walked forward and then stopped. In front of him, illuminated by the pulsating beam of the Apache's searchlight, was a dull gray sphere.

At first, Croft thought it was perfectly round and then noticed it was wider at the bottom where it sat in the desert sand. He stood close to it, trying to guess its dimensions. It was tall, seven or eight feet, and just about as wide.

He backed up and looked around its base. Something was

wrong. If this was a satellite, there would be an impact crater, gouged earth, debris, or parachutes, but there was nothing, and whatever it was, it appeared undamaged from its re-entry.

He ran his hand over its surface. It was warm and smooth, a flawless surface void of any technology—no antennae and no access hatches.

This is not possible, he thought.

It looked like a marine buoy, but he was a thousand miles from any ocean. If it was a satellite, what was its purpose, and how did it get here?

The orbiting Apache interrupted his thoughts, and he realized he had been staring at it for several minutes. He looked back at the Blackhawk and saw the Rangers in the doorway watching; he motioned for Sergeant Sanchez to join him.

"What do you think, Sanchez?"

The young sergeant walked halfway around the sphere and said, "Creepy is what I think, sir. What is it?"

"I don't know. Have your guys check the perimeter, look for tire tracks, footprints, or anything out of the ordinary."

It wasn't wreckage. He stepped in closer and put his hand on the hull again. It was warmer than it should have been for an inert object sitting in the cool desert night. Instinctively, he pulled his hand away and noticed the lighter gray honeycombed texture on its dark surface.

He walked around it. There must be an access panel or a hatch, but even with the searchlight, the surface was hard to see, like the hull was absorbing all the light. He gave up and returned to the now silent Blackhawk and called Emil Fischer.

Fischer was a civilian member of his special operations unit put together when a Russian satellite crashed in a California desert thirteen years ago. It was a military reconnaissance satellite that had failed to reach orbit, and the Russians assumed it had gone down in the Pacific. Most of the systems and cameras were cloned US designs, and after they determined it had no military value, they reduced the whole thing to scrap.

Fischer worked at the Jet Propulsion Laboratory and lived in Rosemead, California, with his wife Catheryn. Croft knew Fischer could respond on short notice, and he picked up on the first ring.

"Croft, it's almost midnight here. I just got to sleep." His voice cracked from having been woken up, but Croft could hear some humor in it.

"Emil, get your ass up, get yourself on a plane, and meet me in the desert ASAP," Croft said with as much humor and urgency as he could mix.

"What is it?" Fischer was now alert.

"I'm not sure, and I don't want to guess until you get here. Call Burton and make the arrangements. I'll be waiting. Hurry."

Next, he called Burton and told him to find the closest CH-47 and have it on standby. The Chinook can fly at speeds of over a hundred and seventy-five miles per hour with a payload of over twenty-six thousand pounds, and he would need one to lift this thing and take it back to the base.

"And I need Fischer here ASAP. Find him transportation."

Croft ended the call and looked at the sphere again.

"Is this a weapon?" he whispered. "Jesus, it looks like the Fat Man bomb.

Chapter 3
Six

The whisper of his soft soled shoes scuffing the dirt quickened. The pain was bearable now and the bleeding had slowed. In this last hour he felt more alert, more alive.

"Just another few steps, Six. Another few minutes."

A structure loomed out of the darkness right in front of him. He might have missed it if not for the glow of the city lights behind it, and there were more all around him. The signs of life he had been praying for, and he had walked right into the middle of them.

The closest one was small with no windows and a single primitive door. He couldn't sense anything inside it with the telemetry suit—but something was racing towards him. It sounded like thunder. Not one helicopter this time but two, and they were coming fast.

Burning heat raced through the telemetry suit as powerful radar waves swept ahead of each aircraft. The neural pathways along his spine pulsed with electricity as the aircraft approached. Pressing himself against the wall, he felt the aged wood snagging his suit. He moved around the corner, praying they hadn't seen him already.

The heat peaked and then dissipated as they passed overhead. The building shook and the downwash blasted dirt and dead vegetation into the air.

His suit locked on to the lead craft's electronics, and he watched the pale green optical image of buildings racing by, including the one next to him. Then a transmitted radio message: "White sands …

training mission … classified …" Static blocked the rest as both helicopters vanished over a hill. The ground images lasted a few more seconds and then they too stopped.

Training mission, training for what?

It was a farm. There was a barn, a silo and a corral, but there were no animals, crops, or vehicles. It had been abandoned years ago, weeds and trash littered most everything he could see.

The door next to him was secured with a rag wrapped through the handle and tied to a bolt in the doorjamb. Pulling the cloth free, the door swung open revealing a storage room with empty shelves, a few cans and empty buckets.

Unzipping his flight suit, he eased it down to his waist trying to avoid moving his arm. Still holding the strip of cloth, he wrapped it around his bicep as tight as he could. Using his teeth and his good hand, he tied it off.

The main door of the barn was unlocked. He opened it, listened for a moment and stepped in. The interior was darker than the night outside. He hit his shin on something that clanged like a heavy piece of metal. Touching it, he ran his hand along its surface feeling the rough and pitted steel. Backing away, he sat in an empty space, leaned back against the wall, closed his eyes and prayed.

Please, not that black room again.

Hours or minutes later, he opened his eyes. He had slept dreamlessly this time. Refreshed, he walked back outside. There were no signs of dawn and he could still hear the distant drumming of a helicopter's rotor blades. They were less threatening now, but soon they would be searching for the ship's pilot.

Kicking at the hard clay, his footprints were difficult to see. In daylight though, it was possible he was leaving a trail the soldiers in those helicopters could track.

Far away, the wolves howled.

The amber haze of city lights marked his destination, the low hills flattened out making it easier to walk. He touched the wet sleeve of his suit, it was tacky this time, the blood was drying and his makeshift bandage was working.

Individual lights began to reveal small homes scattered to his left; he avoided them not wanting a chance confrontation in the dark. He was thinking about how and when to approach someone when he saw the roadway running parallel to his path and toward the city ahead. He stopped and listened. There were no sounds now, the helicopters too far away and the wolves were quiet. Walking on the road would be the easy choice, but he would be exposed. The road faster, the river bed fraught with unseen perils. He chose the road.

The asphalt highway rose towards another hill and his pace slowed. Breathing hard, he stopped and sat on the smooth surface to catch his breath. There was a new sound, not helicopters this time. This was the steady, dull moaning of an engine. Peering back down the road, he looked for lights, but there was nothing to see. It was a vehicle still several kilometers away, but was coming.

In the old black and white movie, the spaceman had found a suit and used a name that helped him blend in with those around him. He thought of his flight suit and wondered how the operator of the approaching vehicle would be dressed.

It came a few minutes later. The roar of a diesel engine, straining as it pulled the big truck up the incline, then the glow of the headlights casting his shadow in front of him like a stick figure. He stepped off the road just as the blur of the big semi roared past, its red taillights fading in a swirl of dust over the hill. Cresting that same hill, he saw the sign. *"Portales pop. 12,335"* and under that, *"6 miles."*

When had the US switched to metrics? Middle twenty-first century? He hadn't thought of miles since his early years in primary school.

Nine kilometers, a longer walk than he had hoped.

Below the hill, a building stood just off the roadway. Surely there will be some source of water he could tap into. He was desperate. He wanted to run, but already out of breath, he settled for a quick shuffle down the sloping highway.

An electric sign towered over him, ten meters off the ground. It was dark, the electrical current switched off and Texaco was the only word on it.

The business was closed, its interior as dark as the sign, its doors locked, but lights from machines outside illuminated the building's front. He listened for any sounds or signals and then approached the closest of the machines.

"Coke."

The telemetry suit read the machines simple circuits, its small processors and servo motors. The device offered refrigerated fluids in plastic bottles. He could see them inside the glass, but couldn't touch them.

He ignored the rest of them when he saw a hose attached to a faucet on the wall. Turning the handle produced the sound of air escaping, he waited hoping water was just seconds away, but the sound died without offering a drop.

Two white vehicles with "Tommy's Garage" painted in red letters were parked in the back and he forgot about his need for water. These could provide him with transportation eliminating his nine kilometer walk to Portales.

The older of the two had a layer of dust and grime covering its roof and windows and one of its rubber tires was flat. A raised access panel in the vehicle's front exposed an eight-cylinder internal combustion engine. He felt no energy in this vehicle. It was as dead as his ship.

The other looked as if it had been used recently; it was clean, and its battery was charged with twelve volts of DC current. This close, the damaged telemetry suit easily read the truck's small computer, and he visualized its simple binary programming. Its main purpose was fuel management for the engine. There were other secondary functions, a braking system, entertainment, security, and a type of travel data recorder. This vehicle had no data transmission capabilities, but it could receive FM radio waves through its entertainment system. Opening the door activated an interior light, and he examined its controls. There were two foot pedals, a steering wheel, and some other levers he wasn't sure about.

With his hand on the instrument panel, he followed the circuitry until he heard the starter motor turn, then the engine fired, raced for a few seconds, and then settled into a smooth idle.

With both hands on the steering wheel, the thought of driving such a vehicle on the roadway was appealing, but too risky and there were too many unknowns. He killed the circuit and listened to the engine die, smelling the unique odor of gasses emitted from its exhaust.

A basket of laundry sat on the seat next to him, dozens of red shop towels and folded neatly on top were several jumpsuits similar to his own. He took the first one and held it up to the light. It was dark blue or black, and the name Sandy was stitched above the left pocket. It seemed the right size, and it smelled clean. His own suit was stained with blood and had smelled better a few months ago.

Hoping that Sandy wouldn't miss this suit, he stripped off his flight suit and put the new one on. It fit well, a little tight in the shoulders, but it felt good. He dropped his own suit in a barrel of refuse, forced it down deep, and covered it with some of the trash.

Back in front of the business, he peered through two large roll-up glass-paneled doors. The glass was dirty and it was dark inside, the only illumination coming from a clock on the far wall.

A small vehicle sat raised on a lifting device, two of its tires lying on the floor underneath it.

"This is a maintenance facility for their vehicles."

The digital clock indicated it was five-thirty and sunrise could be any minute now. A sign on the door showed the business hours as eight to four, which meant Tommy or Sandy or someone else could arrive at any time, so he headed back to the front, turned the corner and froze. Pointing right at him, was a small box with an optical lens.

"Hello," he said, and waited for a response.

There was no answer. The device was inoperative—broken or

just switched off, he didn't know, but no one was watching him. He turned his attention back to the machines near the entry door.

The fluids he needed to survive were right in front of him, but he needed currency, or did he?

He shook it, hoping one bottle would fall out, but it only made his arm ache. Instead of shaking it again, he studied its processor for a moment and sent a signal activating the machine's circuitry. Small servo motors whined and with a loud thump, a brown plastic bottle fell into the slot below.

Twisting off the cap, he smelled it first—some type of sweet fruit drink. It smelled harmless, and he swallowed as much as he could.

Fire burned in his throat, he belched, gagged, and dropped the bottle. It rolled away spewing foam and brown liquid as it went. He couldn't breathe; each breath reignited the ache in his throat, sending spasms of pain from his chest down to the wound in his arm.

Once the fire in his throat eased, he checked his makeshift bandage. There were no signs of fresh blood and it felt no worse than it had before. He picked up the bottle and tasted it, letting the cold liquid lie on his tongue and then swallowed it—carefully. It was good.

I should have sipped the wretched stuff first!

The machine next to it, the most complicated of them all was labeled, "First United Bank ATM.

Powering up its programming, he found it would send and receive data based on its transactions through a small dish antenna mounted to the roof of the garage. There was a functioning optical lens in the front, and it would activate once a transaction was in progress. He stood off to the side and sent the first command.

The camera activated immediately, but the processor was waiting for user information, he searched for its last transaction and duplicated it. The machine hummed for a few seconds, and a small stack of paper currency slid out of a slot. Then the machine shut down, along with its camera.

Five slips of thick paper, each printed with the words "Twenty

Dollars" and the portrait of someone named Jackson on the front. He held them up to the light and rubbed his thumb over the man's face. There was a sharp smell of chemicals, they felt crisp and recently printed.

One hundred dollars. It seemed like a lot, but was it? The drink machine required two dollars, so he could purchase fifty of them. Maybe one hundred dollars wasn't much at all.

Back on the road he turned and looked at the service station again. There was something sad about the place, maybe during daylight and open for business it looked more alive, but here and now, it looked … like failure.

The second truck passed him fifteen minutes later. Like the first one, it roared by, pelting him with dust. "Walker's BBQ" glowed in this one's taillights.

Walker! The truck is mocking me.

The sun inched its way above the horizon, the ball of dull orange accenting a bright pink contrail of an aircraft moving east to west. He watched the tiny plane moving across the sky and wished he were on it. He was tired and still thirsty, and the road seemed to go on forever. He stopped, looked out at the horizon and turned in a circle.

Desolation! There was little life to see, even the few living plants looked like they were fighting for their lives. The plane's contrail faded, and the only clear sign of life now was the road in front of him.

The magnitude of the empty landscape was crushing, but he had seen the helicopter, the buildings, and the passing trucks.

My future is down this long road.

Chapter 4
Croft

A second Blackhawk settled near the first and Emil Fischer, one of the best aeronautical engineers in the country stepped out of it.

At fifty-one, he was a year younger than Croft and in better shape. Dressed in a loud Hawaiian shirt and jeans, he looked even younger. Ducking under the spinning blades, he joined Croft in front of the sphere.

"Morning, Emil. How was the flight?"

Fischer didn't answer. Standing next to it he let his fingertips brush the surface, caressing the smooth shell. He walked around to the opposite side and stopped.

"What the hell is this thing, Bob?"

"I don't know. I was hoping you could tell me?"

"You were dramatic on the phone, but you always are. Now I understand why."

Croft had known Fischer for years, and Croft had insisted that he be included in his Special Ops team. Fischer had worked on everything from the Voyager program to the Curiosity rover, still sitting on the surface of Mars.

The engineer backed away and looked at the ground around his feet. The constantly changing light from the orbiting Apache made a close inspection difficult.

He bent down and pulled a small herb out of the ground.

"Something's wrong here, Bob. Except for our footprints, everything is flattened ten feet out from the base. Look at this sage, it looks like it's been crushed in a hydraulic press."

Croft had missed it. Something with intense pressure had crushed everything around the sphere, and everything outside of the circle was untouched.

Fischer dropped the herb and ran his hand over the surface again.

"I'll tell you this," he said. "It's not ours. It's not Russian either." He pointed to the honeycombed surface. "Looks like a new Nomex composite. Like carbon fiber, but I don't think it is. I haven't seen anything recent from the Chinese, but that would be a long shot. It's too damn clean, Bob. Re-entry would leave burn marks on the surface. There are no signs of thrusters or steering jets either. I don't think it flies on its own and I don't see how it could have been dropped off here; there would be tracks."

"Maybe it was part of something else, part of an aircraft," Croft said.

"Like what?"

"I have no idea. There was a single radar contact that stopped here and nothing left. Could it be something private, another billionaire trying to make it to space?"

"Not from the U.S., we would have heard something."

Looking east, Croft saw the first hint of dawn. "I want it out of here before sunrise. A Chinook is on the way; it should be here soon. We'll put it out at a safe distance, at least five miles and have it scanned. I need to know what's in it before we bring it in close."

The Chinook was late, the sun already an inch above the horizon and casting the ship's long shadow across the landscape. They were getting their first look at it in daylight and it was getting warmer. In the distance, he heard the distinct chopping sound of the twin rotor Chinook echoing off the low hills.

"Holy shit, look at this!" Fischer said, pointing at the ground. "Blood. It looks fresh, but I'm not touching it to find out, and… are these footprints?"

Mixed in with the blood wherever the dry clay allowed were shoe prints. Croft followed them and found another pool of blood, this one larger than the first.

"Whoever came out of that thing fell here, bled some more and then walked away, east towards Portales."

Croft pulled out his satellite phone and made another call.

"Look here," Fischer said, tracing his finger across the surface of the sphere. "I didn't see it earlier; it's the hatch. Christ, Bob. This is a manned ship!"

In the sunlight, just visible in the honeycombed surface, Croft saw two dark vertical lines. He traced them upward and saw a horizontal line crossing them, forming a rectangle not much different than the door on a pressurized airliner. He ran his hand along the now visible seam and could feel its edge.

The Chinook set down a hundred yards from the Blackhawk, and as the dust settled, the three-man crew stepped out and began the long walk over to Croft.

"What is it?" the pilot asked.

"We're not sure," Croft said. "I want to take it back to White Sands and scan it. Take it to the far south end of the missile range; there's a concrete test pad there. I have a CX2500 scanner on its way there now. Once we're sure it's safe, I'll need you to move it again to our hangar."

The Chinook copilot and loadmaster were trying to estimate the ship's weight by rocking it; it wasn't budging, but the loadmaster was confident he could get it in the sling and lift it.

An hour later, Croft watched another helicopter set down between his Blackhawk and the first Chinook. The desert was getting crowded. Looking south, he saw a few trucks on US 70 a mile away and wondered if they could see him.

Major Tristan Flórez stepped out of the Chinook, and his men rolled a Humvee down the helicopter's ramp.

Flórez was the military police commander assigned to the traffic homicide investigation involving his wife Sara and the young soldier. Over the years, he and Croft had worked on several projects together and had become friends.

"Morning, Tristan," Croft said as they shook hands. "This," he said, pointing to the ship, "came down about 2200 hours last night. There's blood and footprints heading toward Portales and I need you to find whoever came out of it. Also, can your guys collect enough blood for a sample before we lift it out? We're too close to the highway, and I'm afraid we're going to attract sightseers, so I'm moving it onto the base in a few minutes."

Flórez looked down at the blood and then east. "Portales is just a few miles over the horizon; what if he makes it to town?"

"I want to keep it low key. I haven't alerted anyone in law enforcement yet. If you need their help, tell them as little as possible."

Flórez nodded and Croft said, "Tristan, I'm pretty sure this isn't ours, and I have no clue whose it is, so be careful."

The major nodded again and walked back to his men.

The Chinook crew finished with the harness and lifted off, hovering overhead as the loadmaster winched up the slack in the cable. Croft heard a slight increase in noise as the Chinook took on the added load and the pilot lifted the ship a few feet off the desert floor. It was flat on the bottom, as he had guessed. The helicopter lifted it another hundred feet and made its way west until it disappeared.

Croft, Fischer, and the Rangers boarded the Blackhawk and followed the Chinook back to White Sands, and they spent the two-hour trip catching up on their personal lives.

"I'm retiring soon," Croft yelled over the whine of the turbines. "Whenever we figure this one out, that's it for me."

"What the hell are you going to do, Bob? You have no skills!" Fischer said, and laughed.

"I'm fifty-two years old, Emil. I've been in the Army now thirty-one years and a colonel for six. I don't see any advancement on the horizon. Maybe I'll just put my feet up and relax."

"I know what you mean. Teaching is getting old, and I don't feel like getting back into aeronautics. It's all kids now and they call me a dinosaur. It seems like just a few days ago I was one of those kids. Damn, it's just not right."

They cut the conversation short when the Blackhawk decelerated.

It circled the landing pad once and Croft watched the Chinook below them lowering the ship. It reminded him of Oppenheimer and the Trinity test that occurred not far from this very spot.

"Manned or not, there could be a bomb in that thing, Emil."

"If it blows, Bob, you and I will never know it."

Chapter 5
Six

Another truck passed him, this one bigger than the last. It blasted him again with grit and the stench of exhaust, 'Earnhardt Trucking' painted in bold red letters on the back.

Traffic was increasing, people were waking up and soon he would have to speak to one of them. Contact was inevitable.

I want to hear them speak before I engage them in conversation, he thought. Will they speak English or Spanish … will I sound strange to them?

A small silver two-person vehicle like the one inside the garage drove by next, its driver slowed to look at him, then accelerated. At the top of the next hill, it turned off the highway and stopped in front of a yellow building. Three large trucks, including the one that just passed him, were parked in the lot. He watched the man from the small vehicle look back at him again before he went inside.

Blue-gray smoke from the building drifted towards him, and the intoxicating smell from a kitchen rode with it. His stomach cramped and the first pains of hunger rocked him.

The cramping eased as the fear of first contact and hunger battled. Hunger won and he found himself moving forward, unable to think of anything but the need to eat and hydrate.

"Good day, sir. I would like some water please," he said, practicing on the cactus standing sentinel just off the highway. "Perhaps some food as well."

Over and over, he repeated those two sentences until they sounded casual.

I need to survive this first hour, maybe two, and I'll worry about the rest of the day later.

From fifty meters, the man walking from the silver car wore clothing similar to his borrowed jumpsuit, so he walked into the parking lot and watched the men and women inside the restaurant.

There were a dozen people seated inside. Three men sat on separate stools along a counter and several more men and women sat in booths near the windows. Two women and another man appeared to be the employees. One man was cooking over a grill, and the women were delivering food. One turned and looked at him. He took a breath and opened the door.

A bell jingled. An alarm or sensor had somehow detected him. Startled, he backed out just as a woman holding a glass of water said, "Good morning, welcome to Edna's Waffle House."

He looked into her eyes, and then at the water. She did not appear frightened, or threatening.

"Thank you, madam."

His words seemed appropriate. She turned and set the water down at an empty table, then gestured for him to sit.

Too many things here are out of my control, too many variables.

Cold sweat ran down the small of his back. He was terrified and was about to leave when the woman stood next to him, blocking his exit.

"I'm Haley, can I get you some coffee?"

"Yes please."

Haley was in her early twenties, she filled his empty cup, gave him an odd look and walked away.

Her voice had been pleasant, but the look she gave him was one of curiosity.

Something I said was unusual to her.

He replayed the conversation and felt his words were correct.

Looking around the room and those eating near him, he studied everything. The closest man, the one driving the silver car was eating waffles that looked similar to those served onboard the *Constitution*.

"Waffles, please," he said as Haley returned. Watching her face as she wrote on her pad, it seemed whatever had concerned her must have passed, and she left him alone.

Condensation rolled down his water glass. It was cold, clean and delicious. He drank half the glass and prayed he could keep it down, unlike the Coke an hour earlier.

The bell jingling behind him announced another customer, and Haley repeated the greeting, "Welcome to Edna's Waffle House!"

He looked close at the bell and then at the new customer, a woman. She walked past him and sat in the next booth. An aroma followed her like the dust had behind the big trucks, but this was a pleasant smell. He inhaled it, savoring the rich floral scent.

When was the last time I smelled something like that?

Her back was right in front of him and he studied every square centimeter. Blonde hair brushing her shoulders, the clasp of a fine gold chain visible on the pale skin of her neck. She turned as the server filled her cup, and he saw a spray of tiny freckles across her cheek and nose.

She looked familiar, an impossibility, he knew, but still …, she turned and looked at him. She had caught him staring and was uncomfortable. His face flushed with heat and he turned away, bringing the coffee cup to his lips, hoping she didn't notice.

Coming inside this cursed place was a mistake. He allowed the prospect of nourishment to overpower his common sense and now everything was going wrong. But part of him knew he would be that much closer to death without food and water.

He replayed the memory of the woman walking past him. She was wearing a uniform, a beige pantsuit with epaulets on the shoulders, and a gold brooch that may have been a pair of wings above her chest. She walked with an elegant grace. He suspected she may be in the military, a pilot perhaps. Was it possible the government was already aware of him?

No, he would have sensed the threat. Even damaged, the telemetry suit would have picked up something this close.

He scanned each patron, an older man in the corner was speaking into a handheld device, conversing with a woman … something about the purchase of … a new home.

There was nothing else, if he felt any emotions from these people, it was contentment.

He brought the coffee cup to his lips, sensed the temperature, inhaled the scent and took a sip, and then another. It was the best he'd ever had and he stared into the cup.

"Is your coffee okay?" Haley asked.

"It's wonderful."

"Oh, that's a good one," she said and laughed. "I think you are the first person to ever call our coffee wonderful."

"Is it real coffee?"

"You mean is it decaf? No, it's regular."

"No, I mean, is it organic, made from actual coffee beans?"

"Yes, of course. What else would it be?"

The new woman had turned to look at him, and he knew he had said something odd that drew her attention. She quickly turned away as the server refilled his cup.

The coffee did taste organic and must have been grown nearby. Looking back outside at the arid landscape though, it seemed an impossibility. Pouring sugar into his cup, he watched the white crystals spin and dissolve. This was real sugar just like the coffee, he was sure of it. It tasted foreign compared to the synthetic sweetener served in the station's commissary.

Stirring the brew and watching the tiny whirlpool in his cup, he tried to relax. This was going to work, then the woman turned to him and spoke.

He watched her lips move, heard the words, but he couldn't speak.

Was it a question?

"Can I borrow your sugar?" she repeated. He stared for another awkward moment, then passed her the jar.

"Thank you," she said and turned away.

Was that it? Should he say something else? Hopefully she would offer it back to him, and he could try to speak to her then.

His waffles arrived, and he let the thought go. The moment had passed and anything he said now would be a red flag, pointing him out as a stranger, a possible threat.

Margarine melted on the waffle, filling each grid with the amber liquid. His stomach ached, and his mouth, so parched just a few minutes ago, was watering. He smelled each bottle of syrup and chose the maple. It had an earthy, sweet smell, and it too was probably made from a nearby grove of trees. As far as he knew, no real maple trees grew on Earth when he left. Agricultural land was too valuable to grow something so inefficient as trees for syrup.

Twirling the piece of the waffle on his plate, he replayed the image of the woman speaking, listened again to her words and watched her eyes as she spoke. She had brown eyes with a touch of hazel in them. He thought she may be thirty but had the look of intelligence that suggested she could be older—and she was beautiful.

She reminds me of someone, but who?

Without thinking, he put the small bite in his mouth and almost choked on it. All the rich, succulent flavors surprised him.

He must have made a noise because the woman looked back at him again, making eye contact, and then turned away.

She saw me choking on a mouth full of food? Oh no!

He ate the rest of the waffle in silence, savoring each bite and hoping she would turn again. He ran one finger through the remaining syrup and sucked it dry. It seemed a shame to waste it.

The woman was eating now, her head down reading something on her table. She would not turn again.

What's wrong with me? I need to get out of here!

Finishing the last of his water, he stood leaving only the syrup on the plate. The slip of paper the server left on the table was unreadable, but he could see 7.93. One of his twenty-dollar bills would be enough.

A man at the counter stood up and gave Haley his bill. The exchange looked simple enough, the man left his change on the table and walked outside. It was his turn now. He handed her his bill and one of the twenties and waited.

"Thank you, Sandy," she said, offering him the change.

Sandy? The name surprised him, then he remembered the jumpsuit.

"Keep that and good day to you, Haley."

Giving the blonde woman another quick glance, he walked out the door.

Chapter 6
Croft

The three million dollar CX2500, a self-contained mobile X-ray machine was designed for the inspection of vehicles, tractor trailers, and shipping containers. Today it sat soaking up the morning heat far from any port or border crossing.

Fischer paced in the scanner's small air-condition control room as Croft relaxed outside on the trailer's steps. Both men were waiting for the first scans to finish and download.

"They're ready, Bob."

Staring at the black-and-white image, Fischer pointed at the ship's outer shell.

"Bob, the framework is all honeycomb. It could be titanium; it's hard to tell for sure. It seems to be the main structure, and there's a second spherical frame within the first, separated by several inches of ... liquid, or gel. Insulation maybe."

"Look at this section, Emil, three anomalies in the outer skin. They look too random, like something tore through it. Look here, there's three more matching holes on the opposite side.

A technician told them the next scans were done and would be on the monitors in a few minutes.

"I hope the next one shows more of the interior," Croft said. "Let's go look for those holes."

Fischer found them first. "Right here and here. They've been filled in with a clear resin."

Running his fingers over the surface, Croft could feel the difference; it wasn't as smooth or as perfect as the rest of the ship. "It's been repaired," he said. "I think these are exit holes, and the ones on your side are entry holes. They remind me of shrapnel damage on my Humvee in Afghanistan. Maybe now we know why our missing man is bleeding."

"It has to be old damage, it would be an impressive repair for a wounded man, Bob. Let's look at the new scans."

The second set of scans focused on the interior, and the exterior honeycomb was now transparent.

"There's the seat, right square in the center," Fischer said, tapping the monitor. "This is flooring, about three feet up, and it's shielded. No telling what's under it."

"The big box in front of the seat is shielded too. Storage maybe," Croft said.

"Here's the hatch. I don't see any sign of hinges or a latching system, and it seals with both the inner and outer shell. How does it open, or should I say, how do we open it?"

"Good question." Fischer said, leaning in closer. "Maybe a remote transmitter like a garage door opener. I don't see anything else in there. No power source, no engine, and no flight controls. A few things under the flooring maybe, but it is a manned vehicle not a weapon. I say we move it to the base and put it inside the big hangar."

Chapter 7
Six

The sun was higher in the sky and the heat radiating off the blacktop road was brutal. He was soaked in sweat and the restaurant was only a half kilometer behind him.

I didn't drink enough water, he thought. Have I ever been in heat like this? At the beach maybe, with Mom and Dad.

Just off the road, the white skull of a small animal stared at him. He kneeled next to it. The rich stench of decay had long passed and he wondered if it had died of thirst or been caught by wolves.

"I feel your suffering my little friend."

No doubt the wolf and rabbit he had seen during the night were sheltering from the savage heat now, their destinies waiting for nightfall.

Two more hours and he would reach the town of Portales. It would get much hotter as the sun peaked, and he began questioning his ability to last that long. At least he wasn't bleeding any longer.

His own flight suit might have been cooler than the borrowed one, but it was in a rubbish bin now. The telemetry suit was the real problem. It was thin and elastic as it needed to press tight against his skin to contact the data transfer, or DT nodes along his spine. The material didn't breathe, trapping his body heat inside.

He reached under the mechanic's cotton jumpsuit and pulled the zipper of the telemetry suit down to his abdomen. *That's better!*

He thought of taking it off, but that often resulted in nausea as it disconnected from the nodes.

And I might need to use it!

Learning to use the suit with the artificial neurons had taken years.

"Think of it as an antenna, just like the hull of your ship," the technician had said. "The mesh in the suit acts as both a transmitter and receiver and is powered by your own electrical impulses."

There had been so many procedures at the Institute he lost track of when the first nanorobotics were injected into his bloodstream. He remembered the pain though, and the DT nodes had been the worst. As they created new pathways of artificial neurons, they destroyed the old ones, and heavy medication was required after each trip to the lab.

I am done with that though. Never again.

The nanorobotics were also unpredictable. He and his classmates were given the newest version, and there had been problems. One of his classmates suffered partial paralysis, and another went insane and never spoke again. "It's very rare though," one tech said. But she admitted, "No one knows what happened. On the plus side some students have reported extraordinary positive results!"

One of the side effects he discovered soon after reaching puberty was the dreams. Dreams and the precognition of actual events. "Déjà vu," his psychologist had called them. It was all his classmates talked about, the increased vividness of the dreams—but with the dreams, there were also nightmares.

Most of his early dreams were pleasant and involved genuine memories of his parents, but as he aged and those memories faded, the dreams changed too. Some were frightening. The psychologist assigned to his class said, "Six, you're replacing actual memories with your fears and imaginations, and in those dreams your parents always suffer horrible deaths."

Other nightmares involved the lab, or The White Room as the cadets called it. Strapped face down on a gurney, the nano-robotics were injected by a frightening machine with long slender steel arms, and in the dreams, it was alive. On those nights the terrors and the pain seemed real, he would wake up in a cold sweat, and fearing he had cried out in the dormitory.

Walking down the road, he thought of another one of his recurring dreams. There was a woman, he could never see her face or hear her voice, but somehow he knew her. In the best of those dreams they were in a city park, strolling down a gravel path, floating bird-like between enormous trees, the smell of fresh flowers in the air. He could smell them even now. Other times they sat at a picnic table just holding hands.

Holding his hand out in the sunlight, he envisioned her long slender fingers entwined in his. The deep red nail polish, and the thin gold ring on her little finger glistening in the light. The thought of her, that simple memory always comforted him.

"You're dreaming of your mother," the psychologist said. "In your dream, you know she's passed on. That's why you can't see her face and your mind is still coping with her loss."

"She is not my mother," he screamed at a passing flock of crows.

Angry now and sweating heavily, his legs trembled. This heat could kill a man, as it had killed that dead animal. The fear of bleeding to death or being eaten alive had passed; now it was just him and the sun, still threatening to bake him alive.

A vehicle approaching behind him decelerated. Stepping off the road, he watched it pass. It was the blonde woman from the restaurant. She looked at him, smiled and pulled over.

Cold, paralyzing fear overwhelmed him and he couldn't take another step. Every mistake he made in that restaurant screamed, *You're not ready!* He wanted to run, but there was nothing but desert as far as he could see.

He willed his legs to move, they refused until her subtle floral perfume drifted from the open passenger window—releasing him. He walked to the door and peered in.

She was nervous, but also unafraid. The suit didn't allow him to read her thoughts, but he could sense basic emotions, and anxiety was one of the easy ones.

"You're Sandy, right?" she asked, as he looked in through the open window.

The morning sun behind her turned her blonde hair into a fiery halo of gold. He wanted to answer her, but each response seemed inappropriate, then a breeze caught her hair, adding to the illusion of fire.

"Yes, I am."

"I'm sorry, I couldn't help but hear the server call you Sandy and it's on your uniform. It's going to be near a hundred degrees soon. Do you need a ride? I'm heading to Clovis, and I can drop you off anywhere along the way."

"Yes, thank you." He opened the door and got in. The interior was cool, and he felt air blowing out of the vent in front of him. Her perfume was stronger in the car, and he hoped he didn't smell as bad as he imagined.

Talking to her would be difficult. The brief time in the restaurant taught him these people spoke differently. It was English, but their syntax and accents were all foreign to him.

"I've never picked up a stranger on the side of the road, but it's too hot to walk and you don't look dangerous."

She pressed her foot on the right pedal and the car accelerated, not unlike the carts on board *The Constitution*. The tires hummed on the asphalt as they drove in blissful silence, and cold air from the vents cooled his face. Then she touched a knob on the dashboard and music surrounded him.

"Do you like country?" she asked.

She glanced at him, the same look from the restaurant, waiting for his reply.

"Yes, I do."

He had taken a class at the Institute that included music history as far back as the tenth century, but he couldn't remember country. The music was pleasant though, and he stretched out to relax, which triggered a jab of pain in his arm. He winced and reached for it, but that only made it worse.

She was staring at his arm and he sensed the first trace of fear.

"What's wrong with your arm? Were you in a fight?"

"It's nothing. I injured myself trying to fix my vehicle," he said, as she looked back at the road in front of her. "What does one look like?"

"What?"

"Someone dangerous."

She laughed. "I don't know. So what, your car broke down, is that why you are walking?"

"Yes, a few kilometers outside of town. It was an accident."

"Kilometers, where are you from?"

"I'm from Atlanta, but I was raised in France. My mother was French."

"I love France, I want to go to Paris one day. Are you a mechanic?"

"No, why do you ask?"

"You're wearing a jumpsuit. The mechanics at the airport wear them. I'm Susan by the way."

He wanted to tell her his name was Six, or Echo Six as they called him on the station, but that would be hard to explain now.

"Thank you for offering me a ride, Susan."

They rode on in silence and he stared out the window, listening to the words of the song. *Whiskey and dying, what odd lyrics they find entertaining.*

They passed Roosevelt General Hospital. The car jolted over a pothole in the road, and it felt like a knife cutting into his arm. The rag wrapped around it was dry, but it would need to be cleaned soon. *Do they seal wounds yet or still stitch them?*

"I need to have my arm examined," he said. "Can you let me out here?"

"Sure, but do you need an emergency room? Is it that bad?"

"I'm not sure. I know I lost a lot of blood, but I have limited medical training."

"Well, I'm heading to a clinic in Clovis. My roommate works

there. It will be a lot cheaper at the clinic than an emergency room."

"If you think that's best."

They were in downtown Portales now. Residents were going about their daily routines, businesses opening, shopkeepers sweeping sidewalks, trucks making deliveries. One business stuck out. A line of customers stood outside the front door and more were sitting outside under green umbrellas.

"What is Starbucks?"

"It's a coffee shop, everything a caffeine addict could want. How can you not know of Starbucks? They're everywhere."

"I have never heard that name, but I like your coffee."

"You're lucky you haven't had to drink my coffee, Sandy."

"I meant the coffee at Edna's Waffle House; it was very good."

Speaking to this woman was a mistake, maybe a serious one, I don't know anything about her. She could alert the authorities.

Wishing he could spend the rest of the drive in silence, he watched as the town of Portales, the one whose lights guided him through the night, disappeared behind him. The air was still clear, and he could see for miles, although there wasn't much to see, just a few hills on the horizon, still pink in the bright mid-morning light. The desert looked different now, sitting in the cool interior of the vehicle speeding down the highway.

"Is it a car or a truck?" she asked.

"What?"

"Your vehicle, is it a car or a truck? People around here don't call them vehicles."

She glanced at him and then back to the road. "And where did you say you were heading?"

"I was hoping to reach Atlanta, and it is a truck."

"Oh," she said, and paused. "I've been to Atlanta, but I'm originally from Savannah. I live in Clovis now."

He didn't want to tell her that no one lived in Savannah anymore.

"This is a fine car, Susan," he said, studying her as she drove.

"Thank you. She's starting to show her age, but she has never failed me."

"She?" he asked.

"Yes, I call her 'she.' I've never given her a name."

"Interesting," he said.

Twenty minutes passed according to the car's time piece in front of him. Twenty minutes of uncomfortable silence.

"How much farther is it to Clovis?" Any moment she would realize something about him was wrong and the ruse would be over. He hoped to sense that before it happened. So far, the last of her anxiety had faded and she seemed relaxed.

"Just a few more minutes. You can see some of it ahead." A moment later, they passed a road sign, "Clovis, 5 Miles," and then another, "US 70."

"I will stay there overnight, at least until I secure a new vehicle."

"You talk funny, Sandy. I like it."

She laughed, so he laughed along with her. "Anyway, there are several motels near the clinic that are decent."

"Thank you, a motel will be fine, and I will work on correcting my speech while I am there."

She stared at him, it was awkward and he laughed again.

"I was trying to be humorous, Susan."

He listened to her breathing, slow and regular, but caught her steal a few quick glances at him.

A blast of energy passed through the car, he jumped as heat radiated across the telemetry suit.

Radar again!

"What is it, Sandy?"

This radar wasn't as powerful as the ones in the helicopters, but someone was scanning them. Adrenaline pumped into his system, time slowed, and he tuned out everything happening inside the car, including Susan. The radiation was coming from in front of them.

"Radar," he said.

Two vehicles parked side by side were behind a "Welcome to Clovis" sign, each with a man in uniform.

"The cops are pretty tough on speeders here in Clovis," she said. "When you get your truck fixed, be careful driving through here."

The men were talking to each other through open windows, and neither man seemed interested in their car.

It was over in seconds, but the rush of adrenaline took longer to dissipate. He looked over at her and saw she was waiting for him to speak.

"I will have to get a new vehicle … a new truck." He turned and watched the police through the side mirror.

Cops. Civilian police, not the military, but like in that old movie, they could prove to be a problem if I had to explain myself.

As they drove through the main section of Clovis, Susan pointed out a few places of interest.

"That's Norman Petty's recording studio. Buddy Holly recorded 'Peggy Sue' there in 1957."

He nodded as if he understood.

"You've never heard of Buddy Holly have you, Sandy?"

"The name sounds familiar," he said as he read the next road sign. "What is Cannon AFB?"

"It's an Air Force base. A lot of Clovis depends on it. Good for the economy and all that."

Through the fencing, he could see the gray tails of several aircraft above the rooflines. The military was searching for him, maybe people from this very base, it was transmitting a lot of energy, but nothing he could decipher. He turned and looked at her and then at her uniform and tried to read her emotions. *Was this her plan all along, to bring me to this Air Force base?* Everything he could sense—said no.

She drove past the base entrance into downtown Clovis and parked in front of the Hillcrest Urgent Care, an adobe brick two-story building.

"I'll walk you in, Sandy. I need to tell my roommate something."

A blast of cool air greeted them as the automatic doors opened and a woman behind the counter looked up. "Hi, Susan," she said.

"Annie, this is my friend Sandy. He needs some help with his arm. Oh, and I didn't get in until almost six this morning. I'm beat, and I'm going home to get some sleep. Can you wake me when you get off? I have another flight at seven tonight."

"Sure, no problem."

"Great, I'll see you then. Good luck, Sandy. I'll leave you in good hands." She smiled and walked out. He watched her until the doors closed and then turned to Annie.

"Have a seat and fill this out, and I'll need your ID and insurance card, Sandy."

"I am sorry, would you please repeat that?"

"Your ID and insurance card."

"All my identification is in my vehicle."

"I'll need your insurance for the billing. How will you be paying for the treatment?"

"I have some currency, and I can get more if needed."

"Okay, cash works," she said. "Fill these out, and I'll get you into a room as soon as you're done." She handed him a clipboard and pen and motioned for him to sit in one of the nearby chairs.

A large fish tank sat in the center of the floor, and two small boys sat in front of it watching tiny yellow fish as they swam in slow circles. A middle-aged woman saw him looking at the boys and told them in Spanish, to get off the floor and sit next to her. They obeyed, and she gave him an odd look.

Next to her an older man sat with his eyes closed, his head leaning back against the wall. Every other adult in the room had their eyes on him. It was unnerving and he fought the urge to stand up and leave. One by one they looked away and went back to their own thoughts.

A view-screen on the wall in front of him was an entertainment system. A purple cartoon dinosaur chased a mouse across the screen. There was nothing else in the room, and he looked back at the clipboard.

"First Name"—the first line on the form. He hesitated and then spelled it out— "Sandy." It was official now. He scratched through

"Middle" and looked at the next line, "Last Name." He thought of the big truck blasting dust and grit in his face and the long walk in the night and wrote, "Walker."

The rest was quick except "Zip Code." It was in the address section, but he did not know what a zip code was. He drew a line through it and stepped back up to the counter.

"I have no phone; I disabled all my phones when I left Atlanta. I hope that is not a problem." He smiled and handed her the clipboard.

"No that's fine. Have a seat, it shouldn't be long."

He sat in a plastic chair and studied each person in the lobby again, hoping to learn what he could from them. They were all dressed different and most spoke in Spanish. One woman said a few words in a language he didn't recognize and he thought she may have been a Native American. He loved the sound of her words, a lyrical type of speech, and he tried repeating them, "Ayoo … Ayoonishishnee." It didn't sound right and he quit trying. He looked back at the yellow fish as they made their endless repetitive circles around the tank. *What a life they live.*

"Sandy Walker!"

He jumped hearing the name. He turned and saw Annie standing behind the desk looking at him. The woman's glossy black hair reminded him of the ravens outside of the restaurant, thick and iridescent in the light. She had a pleasant smile, showing perfect white teeth, and except for her black hair, she reminded him of his classmate, Echo Two.

"Come with me, Mr. Walker. Just a few quick things, and then we'll check out that arm. Step on the scale, please." A minute later, they were in a smaller room and the doctor came in.

"Mr. Walker, I'm Doctor Snyder. Let's look at your arm, shall we?"

He stood and unzipped the top half of the jumpsuit and slid both arms out of the sleeves. Both women looked at the rag tied around the telemetry suit.

"That is disgusting! I can't believe you put that on an open wound," Annie said.

She untied the rag, and he saw it for the first time in the light. He had to admit it was bad. It was yellow now, but it had been white at one time and there were stains on it he knew weren't his.

The telemetry suit was next. "What is this?" Annie asked, touching a clean section. She picked up a pair of scissors, preparing to cut the sleeve off.

"Please don't cut it." he said, unzipping it. Both women helped him out of it one arm at a time. Nausea and vertigo washed over him as the suit lost contact with the nodes under his skin.

"Are you okay?" Annie said.

"I'm fine."

"You have some odd scarring on your back, Mr. Walker. Was this surgical?" the doctor asked.

"Yes, I was a child and remember little of it."

The mechanic's jumpsuit and the telemetry suit now hung at his waist, and he hoped he didn't have to stand nude for the exam. The jagged holes in his bicep were bleeding again and he felt his knees weaken.

"This is a serious wound, Mister Walker. How did you say this happened?" the doctor asked.

Both women looked at the bloody telemetry suit as a fresh drop of blood fell, splattering on the tile floor between his legs.

"It is a long story. I damaged my vehicle, and a piece of metal went through my arm during the collision."

The doctor was wary. What was wrong with his story, it was true?

"And you say this happened yesterday?"

"Yes, just outside of town on the desert road."

"It's remarkable. These edges have already healed some, and I'm surprised it's not infected. We'll clean it up and stitch it, and I'm giving you an antibiotic."

She wiped the wounds with Betadine and injected each with lidocaine. The first injections stung worse than the wound itself, but the pain eased and the doctor put in the first stitch.

Thirty minutes later, the doctor stepped back and examined her work.

"Okay, that's it. Twenty stitches and you'll have some nice scars to remember. The wound on your calf is minor, no stitches, but I'll give you a few samples of Neosporin. Use it several times a day, and use it on your arm as well. I want you back in a few days for a checkup. These wounds in your arm are serious, Mr. Walker, and I worry they can still become infected."

"Thank you, Doctor."

"It's a little unusual," Annie said, walking him back to the desk, "but if you bring me your insurance card later today or tomorrow, I'll file it then. And don't forget to fill the prescription for the antibiotics. The Walmart will do it; it's right down the street."

"Thank you, I will. Everything I have is in my vehicle, so I will need to purchase a few things. I am going to stay at a hotel until I get new transportation."

"The Saguaro Inn is right across the street—it's not bad—and the Coyote Deli is great for lunch."

"Thank you, ma'am. I will see you again soon."

The Saguaro Inn was across the street, but he walked next door to the Coyote Deli and stood at the entrance. The sign on the door said, "Internet Café and Espresso Bar," and in smaller letters, "Free Wi-Fi. Students welcome."

The amount of data flowing from the café was overwhelming. Separating them into individual communications was the hard part. It was like being in a crowded room full of screaming people. "You just have to concentrate on a specific voice," his instructor had told him.

It was just past noon, and the lunch hour was in full swing. Most tables were full of college students working on computers while they ate. There was a single empty table in the back and he made his way to it watching the customers as he went.

A single ultra-high frequency Wi-Fi router connected several dozen devices: handheld phones, computers, laptops, two entertainment systems, and more.

He watched the girl next to him, and like the vehicle's computer at Tommy's Garage, her computer used a simple binary code. He tuned everything else out and concentrated on her computer. She was logged into the Clovis Community College's library and was researching an economics paper. A man sitting in the corner spoke on a wireless phone and was ending a relationship with his girlfriend. An audiovisual signal was streaming a rebroadcast of a baseball game played in New York last night; he looked up and saw the flat panel view-screen on the wall showing the game.

An employee made his way to his table with a menu and said, "Good afternoon, my name is Enrique. Our special today is a tuna fish sandwich and a cup of fresh tomato basil soup."

"Thank you, Enrique. My name is Sandy and I would like the special and a large glass of water please."

Enrique smiled as if something he had said was amusing, but he walked back to the kitchen.

He turned back to the view-screen in front of him, a simple flat screen monitor with the word "Windows" moving randomly across the screen. He pressed "Enter" on the keyboard, and the screen came to life. Keyboards had remained unchanged over the years and by the time his sandwich arrived, he had logged onto the *Clovis News Journal*.

The date shocked him. *Tuesday, June 10, 2025.* He had left Earth's orbit on February 9, 2376. More than three centuries! What happened? The young girl next to him looked over, he must have said something aloud.

The date staring at him in black and white, was too much to process. He knew he had lost a few years maybe more than just a few, but three centuries?

What happened in the ship? How did the mission go so wrong?

It had been a simple assignment: scan and collect data from a void thought to be a small black hole drifting through space. That was it, a simple scan.

Two years before his departure, a probe had been sent to examine the void, and one of its two beacons returned with data inconsistent with a black hole. Like his ship, the probe produced its own faster-than-light drive field. It had taken four months for the probe to reach the void and another four months for its first beacon to return. The probe itself never returned.

A second probe was sent and neither it nor its two beacons were heard from again. The void continued its slow drift and was expected to reach the outer fringes of the solar system in twenty-six years. More than three hundred years from now.

The young girl typing furiously at her keyboard would never know the simple pleasure of a mentally driven interface. He let his telemetry suit lock onto the computer's Wi-Fi signal, and images and texts flashed across the screen as fast as he could absorb them. He went back several months, scanning the front pages of the local papers, then *The New York Times*, *The Washington Post* and finally the French *Les Echos*.

Reaching for his water, he saw the girl looking at his monitor. *Christ!* She had been watching him racing through hours of information in just the last few minutes.

"I think something's wrong with this one," he said.

She looked back at her own computer, then grabbed her things and walked out, her lunch still half-eaten on the table.

The crowded cafe thinned out and he was alone in the back of the room. He needed identification and a driver's license seemed to be the most common form of ID.

The Windows operating system was frustrating. It was slow and cumbersome, but soon he was in the New Mexico Motor Vehicle's database and creating a driver's license. Using the deli computer's webcam, he photographed himself, typed in his new name and the Saguaro Inn's address and had his new license mailed to the motel.

Transportation was next. He would need to buy a vehicle and learn to drive it.

The crash of breaking glass and shouting interrupted his search. He looked up to see an angry man arguing with the server, a drink glass shattered on the floor between them. Sitting next to the man was a woman trying to calm him down. The man shouted something at the server, then reached across the table and slapped the woman in the face, knocking her out of her chair. The brutality shocked him.

The man said something to her in Spanish. He couldn't hear everything, although *puta* was plain enough. *He's calling her a whore!* He had never seen or heard such violence.

The man stood to leave, his heavy boots crunching on the remains of the water glass.

He was a brutish man, tall and muscular with tattoos over both of his bare arms. He threw something at the server that looked like a twenty-dollar bill, grabbed the woman by the arm, and shoved her outside.

The two of them walked across the street and out of his view. He wondered if this was a routine event, noticing all the remaining customers had stopped watching.

The incident passed, and he logged back in to the *Clovis News Journal*. An article on page three reported a search and rescue mission just outside of Portales during the night. The Air Force was looking for a downed aircraft and had sent a search plane out of Cannon Air Force Base. The aircraft located the remains of an old satellite that must have reentered the atmosphere and crashed into the desert west of town.

I am sure they are smarter than that!

Then another article caught his eye.

"Iranians still seeking peaceful nuclear energy."

He looked at the date in horror and remembered sitting in a world history class at the Institute. It had bored him then, but he remembered the event.

Was it 2025 or 2026? *I should have paid attention to that professor.* It all started when an Iranian scientist defected to France. He had proof that Iran had violated a United Nations-sanctioned treaty and had completed a nuclear warhead. The US responded with sanctions but deferred all action to the UN.

He could still picture his professor pacing in front of his classroom, shouting at the cadets in front of him.

But he did remember one thing. Several weeks after that defection, Iran detonated not one but two nuclear warheads, one in Tel Aviv and another in the port city of Haifa. The death toll was estimated at 1.2 million people with twice as many injured.

He looked again at the date in front of him. *How long do I have?*

The Israeli government never recovered, and most surviving Israelis immigrated to other countries while the Palestinians and Iran assumed control of Israel.

It was the beginning of the end for the United States.

Supported by supremacist groups like al-Qaeda and ISIS, the once powerful Muslim Brotherhood was resurrected and a large section of France seceded, declaring themselves a caliphate.

"More water, sir?" Enrique asked.

"No, thank you, I'm almost finished here."

He remembered the date of the next major event; every student memorized that day.

On May 11, 2026, a nuclear device was detonated by a suicide bomber just outside of Washington, DC.

Five years after the blast, the United States was nearing total economic collapse and Canada, Mexico, and several Central American countries merged governments and became a single entity: North America.

As a child, the last vacation with his parents was a trip to Washington, DC, the capital of the old United States. They had stood just outside the prohibited area and much of the city's damage had been preserved as a historical site.

The attack on Israel and later the United States, began the chain of events that led to the death of his parents many years later. The attack in Paris occurred on Bastille Day, July 14, 2352 when a toxic agent was released in the city's water system.

He was eight years old when one of his instructors had come to his room with the news. He remembered every moment of that visit, every word, the powder blue color of the room, even the spiced scent of the man's cologne—his parents were dead, murdered.

He pushed his chair away from the table. *Is there anything I can do now that would save them, or avenge them?* He paid for his meal and walked outside.

Across the street, the angry man from the deli stood in front of an ATM, still shouting at the woman next to him. She said something, and he raised his hand as if to slap her again, she backed away cowering on the sidewalk.

Watching them in the reflection of a glass window, the brutality of this man replaced the thoughts of his parents. *I may not be able to save them, but I can avenge this woman!*

Focusing on the ATM, he separated the data stream from everything else flowing around him and memorized its transactions with the man.

Stuffing cash into his pocket, the man pulled the woman off the sidewalk with one hand, then shoved her into a red convertible. She looked back and saw him. There was unmistakable fear in her eyes, the sensation was strong and acrid, like the smell of burning plastic. He tried to reach out and calm her—it was all he could do—but it seemed to have no effect. The car sped off down Grand Avenue, leaving him alone with the ATM.

Replaying the images of the woman and the scene inside the deli left him angry. There was nothing he could do for her now. He was too late!

He pushed the image aside and looked at the ATM. It was an exact copy of the machine at Tommy's Garage and one thing he had learned, was that a hundred dollars would not get him far.

There were no active surveillance cameras on either side of the street, and few people braved the afternoon heat outside. He stood out of the camera's view and brought the machine to life.

First, he shut the camera down and bypassed the maximum withdrawal restrictions. The angry man's name was Ricardo

Caride, and he had nine thousand, one hundred seventy-five dollars in his account. The machine hummed and spit out twenty-dollar bills faster than he could pull them from the slot. He stuffed them all into every pocket of his jumpsuit until the machine was empty. The angry man's balance was down to two thousand, five hundred seventy-five dollars. He would withdraw the rest of it another time.

Chapter 8
Flórez

Portales

Major Flórez knelt in the coarse sand, gathered up the blood-soaked earth and sealed it in an evidence bag. "Diaz, run this over to Cannon Air Force Base, tell them I want a complete DNA profile and to screen it for everything else they can think of, then send the results to Colonel Croft."

The Chinook lifted off and Flórez rejoined his men to start the search. In the first fifty yards they came across a few more drops of blood and impressions that might have been boot prints too shallow to make a casting. Using a measurement marker for scale, he took two close-ups of the print with his phone. They were odd prints; a boot or shoe with no tread pattern, most likely a man's size ten or eleven.

Another twenty yards and they lost the trail, but looking forward the blood and boot prints led straight to Portales.

"This is a single person, and he or she is wounded, so let's take it slow for another hundred yards; I don't want to miss anything of value. If we come up empty, we'll use the Humvee and make better time."

"Major, I have more blood here."

Three hundred yards from the ship, impressions in the dirt looked like someone had collapsed in a clearing. More boot prints, and this time handprints were mixed in with smaller drops of blood. Flórez took more photographs and followed the trail as the drops grew farther apart, and then stopped altogether. The trail ended, but looking east, he saw the top of an old grain silo.

Dead brush and trash lined the wood-fenced corral. Endless droughts had destroyed this farm and most of the others in New Mexico. This one looked like an old dairy farm and the cattle farmers had suffered the worst. Most gave up and moved east to Texas.

"Let's start with the barn."

Flórez pointed to a footprint and a single drop of rusty brown blood in front of the barn's side door. It was ajar and Flórez drew his gun and pulled at the latch. It protested with a screech as the rusty hinges gave way, but it opened revealing old empty feed bags and an overturned five-gallon bucket.

Pointing to the blood, he whispered, "We'll get that later, lets move to the front."

The main door was wide open exposing the remains of an old tractor. The rest of the barn was empty.

"I think he slept here," his sergeant said, pointing to a clean spot on the concrete floor. "There's at least an eighth of an inch of dust and crap everywhere except right here, and look at this," he said, pointing at a brown smear.

"He's not bleeding as bad," Flórez said. Looking east, he saw a truck heading toward Portales on the highway. "Let's get the Humvee."

An hour later, Flórez was talking to Tommy Harper, the owner of Tommy's Garage.

"Major, I had just opened up, and the only thing I noticed was a Coke bottle on the ground. It was still cold, and I threw it in the trash barrel out back."

Flórez found the clear plastic bottle lying on top of an open fifty-five-gallon drum. Next to the bottle, blue fabric stained with blood was mixed in with the trash.

"Sergeant, I need a pair of gloves and a few more evidence bags."

He poured out the last of the Coke and put the bottle in one bag, then pulled the jumpsuit out of the barrel. Holding it full length in the sunlight, he saw the ragged holes in both sides of the left sleeve.

"That's a lot of blood, Major," the sergeant said.

"Yes, and I bet it hurt like hell."

On the left pant leg, the fabric was torn horizontally, and blood had run down the length of the leg.

"This wound is superficial; it looks like a bullet grazed his calf. That arm wound though, that one might kill him. Sergeant, help me with this."

"Major Flórez," Tommy Harper said, "my mechanic thinks one of his jumpsuits is missing. We picked up our clean laundry yesterday—you know, shop towels, rags, and our uniforms. It was all in a basket in my truck, and now one of his uniforms is missing. It's dark blue and has his name embroidered in yellow across the left side."

"What's the name?"

"Sandy."

The desert-camouflaged Humvee looked out of place in the empty parking lot of Edna's Waffle House. It was two in the afternoon, and the lunch hour was over.

"Miss, did you see a man in a blue jumpsuit this morning?" Flórez asked one of the two servers.

"Just one," she said. "Haley! These men want to talk to you about Sandy."

"He came in not long after dawn, about seven I reckon," Haley said. "He was tall, six foot two, early thirties, dark blond hair with hazel or blue eyes and good-looking; easy on the eyes if you know what I mean." She grinned and winked at the other server.

"Did he speak English?"

"Yes, he did. Why do you ask?"

"We're trying to figure out where he came from. Did he have an accent?"

"Well I know he wasn't from around here, I couldn't quite tell from where though, Canada maybe."

"Anything else, Haley?"

"Well, he looked like he had had a rough night. He limped, and he had a little dirt in his hair. He paid cash and walked east toward town. It was odd you know, only a crazy man would be out there walking in this heat."

Flórez and the MPs drove through Portales checking all the hotels, clinics, hospitals, and even veterinarians looking for a man with an injured arm. On the way out of town, they stopped at the police department and left a description with Chief Tully.

"Call me if you come across him or anything unusual," he told the woman.

He phoned Croft and gave him the bad news. "Without some fortunate stroke of luck, we've lost him."

Chapter 9
Croft

White Sands

Croft stood in the cavernous hanger, staring at the ship's hull as technicians strung lights from above. The sight of it sitting alone, so quiet but with so much to say, chilled him. His phone rang, he looked at the caller ID and answered.

"Yes, Tristan."

"Colonel, I have some good news and some not-so-good news. I'll give you the good news first. We tracked him to an abandoned farm a few miles farther east. I think he slept in the barn. We found more blood inside and I bagged another sample. Then he made it to a service station on the highway and then Edna's Waffle House just outside of Portales."

"And that's the good news?"

"Some of it. The garage is owned by a guy named Tommy Harper. We found an odd type of jumpsuit in a trash barrel and he said one of his mechanic's uniforms was missing, a dark blue jumpsuit with 'Sandy' embroidered above the pocket. It looks like your guy ditched his bloody suit and took a clean one."

"Anyone see him?"

"Not at the garage," Flórez said. "The owner opened at eight, and our man was long gone. I bagged the suit, a Coke bottle and took some prints and they are on their way to the lab. The wound is on his left upper arm, a through and through similar to a gunshot. He lost a lot of blood, Bob. There's another minor wound on the lower left leg. There are no markings or labels on the suit.

"And the restaurant?"

"It seems he's recovered enough to eat breakfast. The server said he came in just after dawn, sometime between seven and eight. She estimated he's six foot two, which matches the suit. He's good-looking, dark blond hair with hazel or blue eyes and spoke English with a trace of an accent, possibly Canadian. He paid cash and walked east toward town."

"Did she see the wound or any blood?"

"No, she didn't notice the wound, but as she put it, "He looked like he'd had a rough night."

"Any surveillance cameras?" Croft asked.

"None at the restaurant, and the one at the garage doesn't work."

"So what's the bad news?"

"He could be halfway to Canada or Mexico by now."

"Okay, thanks, Tristan; keep me advised."

The hangar was built in the late 1940s and had been used to maintain and test the first of the B-36 Peacemakers, and the ship looked tiny sitting alone on the huge open floor.

The new spot lights spaced around and above it eliminated all the shadows but were adding to the hangar's heat. It was still cooler than being outside, Croft thought. He watched the technicians as they packed their tools, they avoided looking at it, or getting too close and with good reason, its dark gray surface gave the illusion it was sucking the light out of the air.

Alone now, Croft and Fischer stood in front of it. He felt Fischer's anxiety, and felt it himself. From twenty feet away, the ship seemed dangerous, as if it was intelligent and watching him. He wanted to back up, but he also wanted to get closer, to learn its secrets.

"Bob, do you feel it? There is something wrong with this, something about the ship I can't put my finger on."

"Yes, I do. I was thinking the same thing."

Fischer was reluctant to get closer, but took another step. "Bob, we need to figure out how to open this hatch. A random frequency generator might work. What do you think?"

"It's not my expertise, but I'll make some calls. In the meantime, let's deal with the outside. What is it made of, and can it fly? If it can, it must be able to communicate so how does it transmit a signal?"

"I thought of that too. I'm thinking the metallic honeycomb could be both the receiver and transmitter antennae, like a radar dish. The honeycomb is embedded in this resin or ceramic material, but it's not like anything I've ever seen. I want to get a scraping and see what it's made of."

The two men were quiet, and Croft asked, "So it's not ours, or the Russians or even the Chinese. Could it be the NSA's or the CIA's, maybe some deep black project?"

"No," Fischer said. "And it's not that billionaire you mentioned either. This is totally foreign."

"I want to know why it's here, Emil, and more importantly, what it is. Let's just say someone sent it up in a rocket, it orbits, the man has some mission to complete, and something goes wrong. Or worse, nothing goes wrong, and he intentionally lands in New Mexico. Why? What is his mission, and is he a threat?"

"You're forgetting about the damage and the blood. I think something happened up there. And there is no way this thing came down by itself. It landed somehow," Fischer said.

"Chutes maybe?"

"They would be huge. I guess after it came down the pilot could have stored them inside, but I doubt it. Think of a wounded man trying to pack them up, and why bother?"

"Damn it, Emil! I need answers."

"We're not going to get any until we get inside it or find the pilot."

"Alright," Croft said. "How do we keep this to ourselves until we know more? If the NSA or anyone else gets wind of this, we may never see it again."

"You're right, Bob. Those bureaucratic bastards will take it and run."

Croft's phone rang. "It's Flórez."

"Colonel, the lab called me. The preliminary results are back on the blood. It's human, O positive, and the tech asked if this was a prank or a test. She wouldn't say more, but a copy should be in your inbox by now. We'll keep looking around Portales."

"Okay, thanks."

"DNA results are in, Emil."

Croft's printer came to life, and the two of them fought over the first page. Croft won.

"Damn it! Read this, Emil. It's confusing as hell. What I can understand is bizarre."

Fischer went through all four pages and then started on page one again.

"I'm no biologist, but these numbers are off the charts. And the tech's comment at the end says it all, 'Abnormal Genetic Markers. Either this sample was contaminated or there was an error in the testing.'"

"We need Jon Stephens here now," Croft said, dialing the number.

The call connected, and he listened to the recording, "This is Jon Stephens at Caltech, I'm probably at the lab right now, so leave a message."

"Jon, it's Croft. I have a problem and I need your expertise in a classified matter. Call me as …"

"Colonel, sorry," Stephens said. "I had my hands full of chemicals and I couldn't touch my phone. What problem?"

"Some odd blood test results. I don't want to say more over the phone, but I'm going to send you the results. Look them over and I need you here today if possible. I'm sending them to you now."

Chapter 10
Six

Walmart's automatic doors opened as he walked through the store's passive motion detector. Surveillance cameras inside mirrored domes along the ceiling were active, but only one was being monitored and it was in the far corner of the store.

Walking along the aisle, his fellow customers were reluctant to make eye contact. Socially it was odd, but suited him fine.

In the men's section, he picked out a pair of sturdy pants that appeared the right size and realized he would need a cart. The first one he tried clattered, one of its wheels was missing a large chunk of rubber. The irritating noise caused a man to turn and look at him.

"I've picked a defective cart it seems."

The man nodded and moved on.

The next cart was almost as bad. He tried a few others and settled on one that made the least noise, then returned to the men's section.

He walked every aisle, picking things up out of curiosity and smirked holding a bottle of the foul brown Coke that almost killed him. He had to admit, it had a pleasant taste once he stopped gagging. Replacing the bottle, he selected a six pack of bottled water.

Once the cart was full, he had everything he needed including the antibiotic. Now he stood over a display of twenty first century computers.

Putting his hand on each one and with just enough voltage, the telemetry suit allowed him to probe the hardware inside. Most were similar, but they were all faster than the ones at the deli. He chose a laptop, the one with the most memory and the fastest processor, then stepped up to the cashier.

The security camera above him activated. He could feel its servo motors turning the camera. A gray scale image superimposed over his own. Without looking up, he traced the signal back to a small room. A woman sat in front of a bank of monitors, and the largest monitor was focused on the customer right in front of him. He could see part of his own shoulder on the screen.

The camera view shifted to the customer behind him and then to the cashier.

I would like that first computer," he said pointing at the display. The woman unlocked the cabinet behind her and scanned the code on the box.

"I'll take care of this," she said holding the laptop, "but you'll need to take the rest of that up to the front of the store."

The image of the cashier shifted, and now he saw his own face. It remained there for a moment and then powered off.

With a sigh of relief, he pulled out a wad of twenties and counted out nine hundred and sixty dollars, forty-eight bills with Andrew Jackson's face on the front. The pile of currency on the counter must have amused the cashier, as she made a show of counting each bill.

"You should get a Visa card," she said.

"I shall."

The items in his cart totaled another ten bills and his pockets once full of currency, were thinning. At the exit, another ATM sat unattended. The temptation of withdrawing the balance of the angry man's account was powerful. He wanted to punish that man further but thought of all the cameras and decided it could wait.

Pedestrians on the sidewalk gave him odd looks as he pushed the shopping cart toward the Saguaro Inn. There were too many bags in the cart to carry with one good arm. *Let them stare.*

The inn was right in front of him, he was tired, his arm ached and he wanted to get out of the heat, but he turned and crossed the street, reentering the Hillcrest Urgent Care Center.

"Well, hello again, Mr. Walker! You've been shopping I see. How are you feeling?"

"Much better, thank you. I was able to get some cash and I thought I would settle my account if that's okay."

"Sure, but you may have trouble getting your insurance carrier to reimburse you."

"That will not be a problem."

"Let me pull up your account. Here it is. The total is two hundred and twenty-five dollars even. Your insurance may cover most of that though."

"Thank you. I'm going to check in at the Saguaro Inn across the street. Could you tell Susan I said thanks for her help? I would still be out there walking if it wasn't for her."

"I will. I'm off in forty-five minutes, and I'll let her know."

Halfway to the door, he turned and asked, "Does Susan work for the military?"

She laughed. "No, she works for Midway Airlines."

He wasn't sure why that was funny, so he laughed too. "Thank you. I will see you again."

The lobby of the Saguaro Inn was empty; the decor looked old and smelled old, but appeared clean. The desk clerk wore a uniform not much different from Susan's but without the golden brooch wings. He sat with his feet propped up on the desk and watched a small view screen under the counter.

The clerk stood, making a facial gesture that said he was annoyed at the distraction. "Garrett Teller" was printed on his name tag and underneath, "Assistant Manager."

"Yes?"

"Mr. Teller, I apologize for interrupting your entertainment, but I want a room for at least three days."

"I'll need identification and a credit card please."

"My identification is in my vehicle ... my truck," he added remembering Susan's remark. I'll be paying cash if that's okay."

The man's attitude changed at the word 'cash.' He was going to keep the money for himself.

"That will be two hundred and ten dollars in cash then."

"I'm expecting something from the DMV in the next day or so. Please make sure I get it as soon as possible. And I may need to stay a few more days after that."

The clerk counted the cash and put a plastic card and a map of the hotel on the desk.

"That's your key card to room 124, which is on the first floor, near the end of that hall by the ice machine."

The hallway was long and dark. Behind one door he heard a man arguing, but the voice faded as he neared his own room. The six bags he carried with his good arm included the heavy laptop, and the two lighter bags pulled at the wound in his arm. He dropped them all at the foot of the bed.

The bed was twice the size of his bunk aboard the *Constitution*. There was a television, a bathroom, and a view of the parking lot. He looked out the window and saw two large trucks, one of which he had seen twice earlier, "Earnhardt Trucking."

He stripped off the mechanic's uniform and then the telemetry suit and stepped into the warm shower. Tiny grains of light brown sand spun in a small whirlpool and then vanished in the drain. He stood letting the water run down his back, easing the aches and pains and imagined the water carrying the memories of last night into the sewer and out of his life.

Without the telemetry suit, the room and its surroundings were dead silent. No annoying signals were playing in the background of his mind. He was free to think, alone and without the intrusion of personal conversations.

The warm water began to cool. He rinsed the blood out of the telemetry suit as the water went from cool to cold and toweled himself dry.

The stitched wounds were hot to the touch, and fresh blood

seeped through the sutures on both sides. He dabbed them with the towel and spread some of the Neosporin over them. They were healing at least, and he wrapped them with fresh gauze. Tomorrow, or maybe the day after, he would pull the stitches out.

For most of his life, he had worn issued uniforms and for the last few years that uniform was a dark blue flight suit. This would be a new experience for him. He put the heavy cotton jeans on first. They were stiff and had an odd chemical smell. With luck, the hotel had a laundry service.

Wearing a striped polo shirt, he studied himself in the mirror and imagined himself traveling through a nostalgic dream or dressing for a part in an old movie.

I look like one of them now, and soon I will be.

"Good evening, sir. I would like to see a menu," he said to his reflection.

It didn't sound right; that was not the way they spoke at the diner.

"Hello, sir, I wish to see a menu."

His face was wrong, too formal, perhaps. He tried it again.

"I want to see a menu."

That will do.

Loose cash covered the bed. He had never needed any type of currency, he had never needed anything, and the thought of taking something even from a stranger like the angry man was appalling and morally wrong. There was no way to return it now, and doing so would put him at risk.

The conflict frustrated him. He wanted to punish that man, and he needed currency.

The dining room was empty and dark, just like the hallway. He chose a small table near the bar where he could monitor the door, fearing he was a wanted man now.

A musty smell of cigarettes permeated the dining room's air. No one smoked on the *Constitution*, the station's air was purified and odorless, but he recognized the smell from his days in Paris. Everyone smoked in France.

"I would like to see a menu, sir," he said to the waiter.

When his cheeseburger arrived, he could smell every part of it: the onion, the pickle, and the ground beef. He savored each smell, then added ketchup and mustard. The french fries were next, and he sipped his red wine. The burger was at least colorful, but the more he ate, the less he wanted it.

The fries were cold and greasy now, and he pushed them away. He enjoyed the pleasant effect of the red wine and ordered a second glass. Those effects were short-lived as his metabolism burned through the alcohol.

Behind the bar, dozens of liquor bottles of all shapes, sizes and colors looked appealing. He had tried vodka and tequila once after graduating flight school and remembered the headache the next day. It had been a glorious night of celebration, and now here he was, alone. His friends, the entire Echo class wouldn't be born for several hundred years, if ever.

The view-screen, or television over the bar was on, but the volume was off. He tried to concentrate on the woman speaking, to read her lips, but his mind wandered back to the desert. That feeling of desolation gnawed at him, weighing him down like a heavy cloak. This empty and forlorn hotel with its threadbare carpet and faded wallpaper mirrored the bones and the dead and dying plants in the desert. Even the server seemed hollow and worn out.

His entire life had been centered on traveling through space, and he knew he would never fly again. He was stuck here in this strange and tragic period in history.

Looking at the remains of his cheeseburger and again at the empty dining room, he felt the first signs of a panic attack. He knew the symptoms well enough. The pulse in his carotid artery pounding against the fabric of his collar, each breath shorter than the last. His nerves were on fire and he needed oxygen. He exhaled and took a slow deep breath, let it out and took another—and the anxiety eased.

Swallowing the last of the wine, he ordered a third glass.

The military will find me, just as they had in that old movie. I should give up. Just find that Air Force base and walk through the front door. Here I am! Do your testing, ask your questions, cut me open if it's your will. But I've survived almost twenty-four hours now. I can make it another day, and maybe another one after that, but then what?

What can I do here? It is not possible to get back where I belong and there is no one I can trust. But I have nothing to lose!

"It's the wine talking," he whispered.

The sensation of having nothing to lose was both frightening and reassuring. Back in his room, he stepped into the still damp and cold telemetry suit and eased his bandaged arm through the sleeve.

Locking onto the hotel's Wi-Fi, data cascaded across his vision as he sat in the darkened room.

Where do I start?

Computer security and technology he decided, and spent the next several hours memorizing everything he could, from protection programs to fraud investigations and then moved on to banking, wireless transactions, tax laws, and even the workings of Wall Street. Memorizing what he felt important, he stored the rest on the laptop's hard drive.

First United Bank had a branch within walking distance of the Saguaro Inn. Their encryption was a level above that of the DMV, and its firewall was excellent, but after several trial-and-error attempts, he was into their system. Using the same information he gave the clinic, he created his own personal checking account, then thought of the angry man at the deli. The crack as the man slapped the small woman still shocked him, the brittle glass shattering under the man's boots just as vivid.

His own anger spiked as he paced the room, listening again to the hushed whispers coming from the other diners, their eyes and faces blank and uncaring.

Why didn't anyone help her ... is this the way of the people in this era ... and why didn't I?

Replaying that memory several times, he froze the image of the woman's face. There was a dark circle under one of her eyes—an old bruise perhaps—and he could see the shiny wet track of a tear as it fell, still suspended in midair.

As the tear hit the deli's greasy floor, he opened the man's checking account and transferred the remaining balance into his own.

I will never sit silent again!

He stood, fists clenched, and he could taste rage, the overwhelming fury. Was he angry at the man, or at himself?

The angry man was Ricardo Caride. With his new laptop, he entered the name in the Windows search engine, saw his picture and read, and the more he read, the angrier he got and guilt became less important.

Caride was born in Bogotá, Colombia, and he was forty-nine years old. He had several arrest records in New Mexico, Nevada, and California, most for minor drug violations, running prostitution rings, and gambling, but there were two arrests for aggravated battery charges and one for homicide. The three serious charges were all dismissed when witnesses either disappeared or refused to testify before his trials. There was also a pending deportation hearing scheduled in August.

Using aliases with variations of his name, Caride had two open arrest warrants for drug possession in Santa Fe and Albuquerque. The Clovis Police Department's website offered an anonymous tip line, and he left a detailed summary of Caride's aliases, the arrest warrant, and Caride's current address.

An article in the *Phoenix New Times* identified Caride as the leader of a large prostitution ring and the owner of Red Hot Escorts operating in Arizona; there was also an arrest photo of a younger Caride.

Why is this man free?

Next, he searched Red Hot Escorts. Caride was the listed owner, and he had a business account with a bank in Phoenix. With a few keystrokes, he transferred all of Caride's funds into his own account, leaving Caride penniless.

Covering his tracks took longer than cracking the bank's firewall, but when he was finished, any investigation would show that Caride himself had drained the accounts.

He sat back in the recliner, expecting to feel gratification. It was an odd feeling, judging other people. There was little hope of helping the woman, but this man needed to be judged. He needed to be punished, and taking his money would hurt him, and that seemed right. *Justified. Then why does it make me so uncomfortable?*

He logged out of the bank and never thought of the angry man again.

Thirty-two thousand dollars was a substantial amount, but to live, he would need a steady income.

What can I do? What do I know how to do?

Everyone he had met so far had a profession: truck drivers, clerks, doctors. He had no skills. He looked at his laptop and then sat on the bed. Computer technology seemed to be the fastest growing profession, and although his specialty at the Institute was astrophysics, he knew as much about computers as anyone else in this era.

I can make a much faster computer!

Chapter II
Croft

Emil Fischer ran into the room holding a glass vial above his head looking like he had just won the lotto.

"Bob! The hull is not ceramic, it's not resin either."

"Calm down, Emil."

"I knew it wasn't ceramic, at least not the ceramic we're used to dealing with. It's organic, closer to tooth enamel or bone, but I think it's also part synthetic. It has all the heat dissipating properties of ceramic, and I think they grew it around that honeycomb."

Croft looked at him. "They grew it, like algae? How is that possible?"

"I don't know, Bob. I don't think it is possible, but someone did it, and I'm hoping Stephens will know how."

"He should arrive soon. I'll head to the field and pick him up."

The Gulfstream V set down just after seven o'clock and Jon Stephens, the plane's only passenger, stepped out.

"Good flight, Jon?"

"Yes, thank you. This is some interesting shit," he said, holding the blood test results.

"Let's wait till we get to the hangar. There are other things we need to discuss."

The White Sands Missile Range was like every other military base;

security checks, guard gates, and drab buildings. Croft parked next to the hangar, and two MPs stepped out of their Humvee and checked Stephens' identification.

"Christ!" Stephens said, looking at the ship. "What is this?"

Like Croft and Fischer, Stephens was reluctant to step too close.

"What are your impressions?" Croft asked. "I need some fresh opinions on what it is."

"Well it's damned odd," he said, walking around it. He stepped up close to the hull and knocked on it. It made a dull hollow sound, and he stepped away again.

"Other than the structure itself, I see no signs of technology. What I see is a structure whose purpose is to protect the man inside from an outside environment. And I know that much because you told me someone came out of it. He looked closer at the texture and stroked his fingers over its surface.

"Spacecraft are not my thing, Bob—but this is," he said shaking the report. "Can we sit down? I have a lot to say.

"This DNA report is incredible," Stephens said. "I thought it was bullshit, but now I don't think so. Listen, we all have negative genetic markers in our DNA, some of us more than others. They show an inherited risk for common diseases like cancer, Alzheimer's, etcetera. It doesn't mean we will develop any of them, but they are in our DNA, and from what I can see this man, and we know he's a male, has none—not a single one—which is an impossibility.

"But what's more puzzling is he has every marker known to indicate positive traits—all of them. He could have extreme intelligence, strength, stamina, and who knows what else. I don't think this man could catch a cold! If you wanted to engineer the perfect human being, this guy is it.

"One last thing," Stephens added. "Normal DNA markers can give a pretty good indication of where a person's ancestors came from, his genealogy—European, African, Asian, and so on. This man's DNA is not as defined, as if it's been watered down. Imagine taking DNA from someone in Italy before Columbus sailed to America. His markers would show Western European much stronger than someone in Italy today because people are immigrating everywhere. Most of us are just mutts, but this guy has taken that to an extreme. I can't tell you where he's from."

The silence hung in the room a moment and then Croft stood up.

"I'm starving. Let's go over this at the Officer's Club."

They found a table near the back of the dining room and ordered.

Croft, shredding the label of his Corona Extra said, "Jon, this has been at the back of my mind all day so I have to ask, could this thing be alien?"

"The ship, or the man?"

"Both, I guess."

"Well, not if you're referring to some other race. This man is human. Everything I see in the DNA says he's from Earth, but he is different. He's not like any man I've ever seen or heard of."

"Then there's the ship," Fischer said. "It has an organic shell that can survive re-entry for Christ's sake. Who could do that? The scrapings from the hull are similar to marine microbes, like a coral reef. Lawrence Berkeley has been researching a metal-ceramic composite that has some bone-like structure. One day they hope to use it for bone transplants, but they're *years* away from even trials."

"There are too many facts here we can't explain," Croft said.

Their dinner arrived, and they tossed around ideas while they ate.

Croft watched his two friends arguing their opinions. So consumed in the technology, neither seemed to remember the pilot. Frustrated, he slammed his empty bottle on the table.

"Listen! I'm not interested in the mechanics of the damn thing; it's about the man! What is he doing right now? Who is he and why is he here? Those are the questions we need to focus on. Remember, he could be a threat! He's been here for almost twenty-four hours, and I think if he wanted to be found, we would have heard something. Don't forget that!"

"You're right, of course," Fischer said, "but we have nothing to go on. We need to get the thing open."

"Then that's our priority! Just remember, I don't care what it's made of. I want to know why it's here!"

They were civilian scientists, he had to remind himself, and *he* was the soldier. He took a long swig from a new bottle and looked at Fischer.

"Emil, I think you're right about the remote entry. I'm going to brief the general when we get back and see if he can recommend someone with that kind of skill. Scott is a guy I can trust, at least to a point. If he feels we need to go to the NSA, he will be the first to say so. But I want at least a week or two without Washington getting their hands on it. We'll give it a day or so and then we'll cut the damn thing open!"

Dropping the two men off at the base's hotel, he drove back to the hangar alone. He knew sleep would be difficult tonight. There was a nagging feeling that if he wasn't careful, the investigation would spiral out of his control. That reminded him of Scott. The general was retired, but he had connections all over the country and Croft trusted the man's instincts. He called him knowing it was after midnight in Washington.

"General Scott, it's Croft. Sorry to call so late, but I want to brief you on something important."

He kept it short and expected more questions from the man than he got. "Keep me informed," was all he said.

He moved a chair in front of the ship and sat watching it. It was like a living thing, sitting in silence under the lights, like it was waiting for the right question. It was a feeling he couldn't shake. The damn thing had a story to tell, and he just needed to figure it out.

He shut off the lights, leaving it alone in the dark, and locked the door.

"See you guys in the morning," he said, passing the MPs.

He was right, sleep did not come easy. Just before dawn, he sat up and looked around the small bedroom. The soft green light from his digital alarm clock told him he had slept four hours. Stumbling into the bathroom, he washed his face and studied his reflection in the mirror. A few more lines, a few more wrinkles here and there, and the gray in his hair had overtaken the brown.

"Who gives a shit?" he whispered to his reflection.

He grabbed his keys and went out the door, then dialed Flórez's phone.

"Hey, Tristan, anything new?"

"Nothing new, Colonel. I've done all I can in Portales and spoke with the local sheriff and asked her to call me if anything unusual comes up. I sent my guys back to the base, and I'm just heading out alone now to check Clovis. It would be his next stop if he hasn't bugged out already. If he caught a ride with a trucker, he could be anywhere by now."

"Okay, thanks. This guy worries me. Be careful."

The air was still cool, and to the west, small, pink clouds hovered over the horizon. Maybe it would rain later and wash some of the damn dust back into the desert.

He drove through the last guard gate and parked next to the Humvee with two new MPs inside. The driver stepped out and said good morning, glanced at Croft's ID, and saluted. Croft punched in a four-digit code on the keypad and heard the soft click in the lock.

The putrid smell of decomposing flesh hit him as soon as he opened the door. He had found the rotting body of a pilot still strapped into his plane years ago, and this was just as bad. It seemed his first priority of the day had been determined—the ship's hatch was open. He stepped back outside and got on his phone.

The hazmat team arrived at the hangar just ahead of Stephens and Fischer. Croft met them at the door.

"I walked in this morning and found the hatch open. I think something's dead inside. I want them to check it out before any of us go in. Better safe than sorry."

The three-man team went inside wearing DuPont TK555T suits,

a closed system that protected them from any toxic gasses, bacteria, or viruses. Two carried handheld gas sensors, and the third rolled a small cart through the door and into the hangar.

"I can smell it from out here," Fischer said, and stepped farther from the door.

Croft looked at his friend and remembered his aversion to the smell of death. "Trust me, Emil. It's worse inside."

The two civilians talked privately while Croft paced the length of the hanger doors.

The hazmat team walked out. "All clear, Colonel," the captain said as she stepped out of her bulky suit. "Whatever that stuff is, it stinks like death, but there's nothing that will kill you, just simple decomposition. What is it, a pressure chamber?"

"Something like that, Captain."

She took a small blue jar out of her gear bag and handed it to him. "Vicks—it will help with the smell. Just put some around your nose."

"Thanks!" Fischer said, snatching the jar from Croft's hand.

"Take these too," the captain said, handing them a dozen Nitrile gloves.

With the large hangar doors opened for ventilation, Croft walked up to the ship and looked through the open hatch. The interior of the ship was dark gray, like the outer shell. High-density foam that reminded Croft of a gym mat covered some of the curved wall surfaces. In other areas, he could see the honeycomb structure embedded in a layer of what looked like amber.

He had to crouch to get through the hatch, and Stephens followed him, leaving Fischer standing outside. The menthol smell of the Vicks around his nose helped, but he saw Fischer was still hesitant to get closer.

"Emil, I'm going to need a flashlight," Croft said.

"You're going to miss out, Emil," Stephens called back with a laugh. "Man up, buddy!" Fischer edged inside the hatch, and the three men squeezed into the cramped interior of the ship.

The seat was the most striking thing inside, a cross between a dentist's chair and a Lazy Boy recliner. It looked comfortable yet high tech. The frame appeared to be titanium or stainless steel and carbon fiber, upholstered in something like leather over memory foam. Each armrest had a steel-gimbaled joystick, which were the only flight controls visible. Croft thought of moving one of them, then thought better of it. On the left armrest, he saw ripped fabric and a reddish-brown stain that ran off the side and pooled on the floor.

"Careful there," Croft said, shining his light on the stain.

"This is high velocity blood spatter," Stephens said. "The pilot was sitting in the seat when something came through the hull there," he said, pointing to the wall. "This is from his arm wound. It hit him and then exited out the far side. The rest of this is just passive drops and smears as he bled."

The two uprights they had seen in the earlier scans were in front of the seat. Fischer leaned over and knelt. "This may be the pilot's optical display screen, like a hologram. It's right at eye level for anyone sitting in the seat."

"It's no doubt a single person craft, no other seating and too small for anyone else," Croft said.

The shielded box they had seen in the scans was a cabinet made of the same materials as the seat and ran the entire length of the far wall.

"More blood here," Croft said, stepping around a brown pool.

Stephens squatted next to the bench and touched it with his gloved finger. "This is different," he said. "This yellowish fluid separating from the pool doesn't look right."

Croft kneeled next to him and pointed a finger at the small holes in the bench. "It's coming from inside this." He stood up and ran his gloved hand along the padded top, then lifted it free. Underneath, he found a single faded photograph and a small glass cube.

In the photo, a man, a woman, and a small child stood in front of an elevated train. The boy appeared to be seven or eight years old and the couple in their mid-thirties. The train had no visible tracks or wheels and looked to be hovering over a metallic rail that stretched across the photo and out of view. In the background, the Lincoln Memorial stood partially submerged in a sea of water, and in the foreground, the jagged white base of the Washington Monument was just visible above the surface. Missing from the picture was the US Capitol. Beyond that, the landscape was barren.

"Jesus, half of Washington is gone," Stephens said.

He handed it to Fischer and picked up the small glass cube about an inch square. There were thousands of small reflective metal specks suspended just below the surface. Etched on one side was the word "Motorola" in small letters.

"This changes everything," Croft said.

Underneath the padded top was another panel with the words "DO NOT OPEN IN FLIGHT." Looking down inside the cabinet, he reached for a strap-like handle on the panel and pulled.

Croft fought the urge to gag. Fischer snatched the jar of Vicks from Stephens, twisted it open, and held it under his nose.

"Shouldn't we have masks on or something?" Emil exclaimed.

"Too late now," Stephens said with an uncomfortable laugh.

Forty-eight clear canisters in four rows of twelve took up every inch of the cabinet's interior and reminded Croft of a "Prego" display at the grocery store. All but three of the canisters were cracked, and the red matter inside the canisters had leaked out into the compartment. The bench itself contained most of the coagulated mess, but they could see some had seeped out around two jagged holes just above the flooring.

"This is what brought the ship down," Fischer said.

"Whatever is in these jars was vital to the ship," Fischer added. "He could patch the outer hull but couldn't fix the damage in here."

"Or maybe the ship healed itself," Stephens said. "This was living material twenty-four hours ago. This yellow gel mixing with the stuff in the canisters looks like cerebrospinal fluid; it's what protects our spine and brain from trauma and infection. I'll send a sample to the lab, but I'm pretty sure that's what it is. If I'm right, then this red stuff is cerebral tissue. It's brain matter."

Croft looked at the broken canisters in the cabinet. The putrid smell was worse this close, and he saw the tissues in the broken canisters looked darker than the intact ones.

"We need to refrigerate this as soon as possible. We need to stop its decomposition."

"Can we step out for a minute?" Fischer asked. "I need some air."

Fischer was paler than normal and edged past Croft and out of the hatch.

Outside and in fresh air, they studied the photo.

"You thinking what I'm thinking?" Croft asked the two scientists.

"I'm afraid to say it, Bob," Stephens said. "It's crazy, but put it all together, the man's DNA, the technology of his ship, and that," he said, pointing to the photo, "and somehow, he traveled here from the future."

"Shit on a stick!" Croft said under his breath. "Could he be responsible for this? If he wasn't, he knows who was."

"Just a guess," Fischer said, "but I think that boy is our pilot and this is a family photo, maybe on a vacation, and whatever happened to Washington happened long before this picture was taken."

"This is why we need to focus on the man!" Croft said.

He passed the photo to Fischer and held the cube in the sunlight.

"Motorola! This is a storage device, I'll bet. Like the ship's log or maybe some personal data."

Like a DVD, Bob. It would need a reader though, and I see nothing like that in there."

"Why did the hatch open? And did you notice there are no visible electronics? No radios, no instruments, and no computers." Stephens said.

"Maybe it's all under that shielded flooring."

"Yes, good questions," Croft said. "But let's get this stuff on ice ASAP, and I want this whole hangar cooled. I'll make some calls."

Fischer looked relieved. "Great, I'd like to wait for the fans to get here before we go back in."

"Colonel, if you don't mind, I want to take a sample of the tissues in those jars back to Caltech this afternoon. I can't examine them here, and I'll be back by morning."

"That's fine, Jon, but don't involve anyone else. We can't let word of this get out. I don't want any more of a paper trail than we already have. I have plenty to do here, and I want to document what we know so far."

Chapter 12
Six

Just over twenty-two thousand miles above Houston, Texas, a small satellite floated in geostationary orbit. On its surface, a red LED flashed, and three people on the ground took notice.

Walter Price was the first man to recognize the encrypted signal. Price was a senior analyst at the NSA's Fort Meade headquarters in Maryland, and all encrypted messages like this one, along with messages containing certain keywords or phrases, were flagged and sent to an analyst on the fourth floor. Price saw this transmission matched two others received Monday night. He wrote a quick report, forwarded it to his deputy director, and went to lunch.

At NASA's White Sands Tracking and Data Relay Satellite ground terminal near Las Cruces, Cookie Martin's computer terminal flagged the signal also. The TDRS system provided uninterrupted communications for both manned and unmanned spaceflight.

Her computer flagged the transmission when the ground station rejected it for lack of a destination. The transmission was on a seldom used frequency of 14.0 GHz, the same frequency detected two days earlier over Texas and New Mexico. Knowing Colonel Croft was working on something related to those transmissions, she pulled out the base directory and forwarded the message along her chain of command.

The third person was Six. He was sound asleep when his beacon's signal woke him. Without opening his eyes, he reached out and tried to acknowledge it. He didn't expect a response, and he wasn't disappointed. Even if he had the damaged suit on, he wouldn't be able to transmit enough of a signal to reach it. The powerful little beacon could reach him though, and he wondered who else had heard the signal.

He thought of the implications, then ignored them; there was nothing he could do about it. The beacon was in a good orbit and would transmit a short signal every twenty-four hours. Without a response, the beacon would remain silent and try again the next day and every day after that for years.

The transmission had ended his dream however, one of the pleasant ones. He and the other nine students in his group were in their classroom. This was the Echo Class, and they were all still young. He had been assigned the number Echo Six and by a tradition started generations ago, they called him Six and seldom used his given name.

Tracy, or Echo Two, was the only girl in the class, and like his parents, her parents had died in an accident. The two bonded immediately, and they became best friends.

In the dream as ten-year-olds, they had run away and gotten married. Two was gone now.

Gone ... or was she?

He lay in the bed wondering if her time line would still be intact. Was her time line running parallel with his, or was this the only time line and she wouldn't be born for three hundred years?

Will she miss me? Will her parents still die?

Just walking down a sidewalk or talking to a stranger could change the time line, how much, he had no idea. The military had his ship and whatever technologies they may discover would have some consequence. The scientists working on it would have been elsewhere, and whatever they would have accomplished would never happen. He had disrupted their lives, and that alone could have significant implications.

There were other things too, but he thought they would be trivial. His brief interaction with Susan, taking money from the angry man—those would have little effect on any future events. But his ship, that was a different story.

A shaft of sunlight came in through the curtain and crept across the wall. He watched it until it dimmed and disappeared. Another new day—one that was going to be very different from the last.

He dressed in his new clothes and bundled the rest of them into a plastic bag he found in the closet. Garrett Teller was on duty again, and he handed him the bag and a twenty-dollar bill.

"I would like these cleaned and left in my room, please." He didn't wait for a reply and walked down the street toward the IHOP.

If there is a bright spot in this world, it's the smell of breakfast cooking—pancakes, waffles, and bacon. The smells are stronger here than they are on the station. Perhaps it's the climate?

He ate fast, maybe too fast, noticing the people in the next booth watching him. Ignoring them, he swallowed the last bite of pancake and was back in his hotel room by nine.

The telemetry suit was dry, he put it on and let it lock onto the Wi-Fi. The signal seemed stronger and faster today than it had been the night before. Opening Google Maps, he memorized everything around him: restaurants, a driving school, banks, and a car dealership.

If he was going to design a faster computer, one he could sell to one of the current manufacturers, he would start with the processor and it would need to work with the binary operating systems like Microsoft and Apple. It would have to be much faster and much more efficient. Last night, the battery in his new laptop needed to be recharged in just two hours.

By noon, he had the basic design in his head. Getting the design into the laptop took the remainder of the day. The work was time consuming. His inexperience with the laptop and its archaic operating system frustrated him, and he had to delete his work and start over dozens of times. The processor was difficult enough, but he needed to write the codes to make it work as well.

The night's dinner special was little better than the previous evening's cheeseburger. At least it was hot, and he decided this would be his last meal at the hotel.

By midnight, he felt he had mastered Microsoft Windows, and by three in the morning, the processor was ready for its first simulation. It failed. Again and again, it failed, showing no signs of life.

Frustrated, he lay back on the bed, feeling the clean sheets on his skin. He had survived another day after almost giving up that first night, and he was determined to survive the next one too. He slept peacefully, free of the nightmares until, like an alarm clock, the beacon woke him again.

Staring at a familiar stain on the ceiling, he thought of the anger and depression he had felt over his processor's failure. They were emotions he wasn't proud of, but like a fever, they had run their course and he was glad to be rid of them. Today he would learn to drive a twenty-first century vehicle and with luck, buy one of his own.

He stepped out of the lobby at eight o'clock, inhaled the cool dry morning air and looked east. The sun was up a few inches over the horizon and pink clouds were forming to the north. He turned left and walked the short block back to the IHOP.

The booth he was in yesterday was occupied. He looked around at the few open tables and saw Susan and Annie sitting in the far corner. They were leaning in close to each other as if sharing some secret and then laughed. He walked over and stood behind Annie, wondering if saying hello to her first would be inappropriate. Susan looked up and smiled.

"We were just talking about you. Would you like to join us?" she asked, moving over in the seat. She was wearing her uniform again, and he looked at her gold wings as he sat.

"How's the arm?" Annie asked.

"Much better, thank you. A little sore, but better."

"You'll need to come by in a few days so we can remove the stitches." She rose and added, "I've got to run. I'll leave you two alone." She winked at Susan and walked away.

It felt uncomfortable sitting this close to her, so he moved around to the other side of the table.

"Thank you again for everything," he said. "I could still be walking out there somewhere, or perhaps my bones would be bleaching in the sun if it wasn't for you."

"Well, I'm glad I saved you from that. You look better and I approve of your new clothes."

"Thank you," he said. As she sipped her tea, he looked at her uniform again.

"So, you're a pilot."

She choked and spilled some of her tea, and then laughed.

"I wish! I'm a flight attendant, Sandy. I work for a small commuter airline, but I hope to get on with one of the bigger ones soon."

"Do you enjoy flying?"

"Yes and no. I like the feeling of flying, but being a flight attendant isn't the same thing."

Looking into her eyes as she spoke, he had difficulty following along with what she was saying.

What is it about this woman? I feel like I have been sitting in this very seat, having this same conversation before!

He was sure he could predict what she would say next, but he was wrong. He was watching the freckles across the bridge of her nose, waiting to see what she would say when he realized she had stopped talking and was looking at him, waiting for an answer. He had missed her question.

"Oh, I am sorry. I'm in the computer business at the moment."

It was a half-truth, and as he said the words, he promised himself he would never lie to her again.

"Well, here's your breakfast, Sandy. I'll let you eat. I have to run some errands on my way home and I hope to see you again."

"That would be nice," he said, looking at her hands. She left, leaving a trace of the same perfume.

He ate, savoring each bite, replaying the memory of her at Edna's Waffle House and then again during the long ride to Clovis.

It was ten degrees hotter when he walked outside. Passing the Coyote Deli, a truck and several men were unloading a new ATM across the street. A Clovis police car was parked at the curb, the officer talking to the men as they worked on the machine. The officer turned, and looked right at him.

His new shoes caught the uneven concrete, he stumbled, grabbed a light pole and almost fell. The officer stepped off the curb looking his way.

He was sure the officer recognized him. He took a few more steps and glanced back, thankfully the officer was on the sidewalk again and talking to the workers.

The Creek Driving School was a small building on a lot next to the Ford dealership. Opening the door, he found a dark skinned middle-aged man sitting behind a desk. His hair was long, black, and braided in a ponytail, his face so lined and weathered it was hard to tell his age.

"Can I help you?" the man said.

"Good morning, sir. I would like to take driving lessons."

The man's face was stoic, there was no smile, if anything the man looked suspicious. Maybe coming here was a mistake.

"You serious ... you've never driven before?"

"Not in New Mexico. I want to familiarize myself with a car again; I have not driven a vehicle in a long time, and I will be paying cash."

"Do you have a driver's license?"

"Not exactly, I lost all my identification, but I am having a duplicate mailed to my hotel. It should be here before noon."

"Okay then, let's go outside. My name is Len, but my friends call me *El Guapo*."

"*El guapo*, the handsome one."

"Yes! You speak a little Spanish, I see." When Len eased out from behind his desk, he saw Len's prosthetic leg and the three missing fingers on his left hand.

"My friends call me Sandy."

They drove through Clovis and its surrounding neighborhoods for two hours. The first fifteen minutes were terrifying. Controlling the car was easy, but navigating through traffic as he learned what the traffic signals and signs meant was the hard part. He drove as slow as Len would let him, and it took another fifteen minutes to get comfortable with the controls. The next hour and a half he drove just for the pleasure.

Len was short for a Native American name Six couldn't pronounce. Born and raised on the Mescalero Apache Reservation just west of Roswell, he learned the carpentry trade from his father and uncle.

"What happened to your leg, may I ask?"

"When I turned twenty-one, I left home and joined the Army. On my second tour in Iraq, I stepped on an explosive device. There wasn't much they could do to save my leg. I spent three months in a VA hospital and then six months of private rehab funded by the Gary Sinise Foundation. They also gave me an interest free loan to fund my driving school. How about you? What's your story, Sandy?"

He tried to keep his own story as close to the truth as possible. "I learned to fly in Atlanta, then worked in the aerospace business. Now I'm designing computers."

"Me," Len said with a laugh, "I've never had any luck with computers. Give me a pencil and a piece of paper, and I'm happy."

He had never met a Native American with such a rich history. The man had even fought in a war and had the scars to prove it. As he thought of Len, he thought again of the United States and its great history and of its eventual destruction. He had no feeling of patriotism when he thought of North America, but living in the

United States appealed to him, and he wondered if he hadn't been born in the wrong era.

"I would like to come back one day and talk more with you, if you don't mind."

"Sure, Sandy, any time."

He paid Len eighty dollars in cash, shook his good hand, and set out toward the First United Bank.

The air inside the bank was cool. He stood just inside the door and watched the tellers and the customers doing business. The currency process was more complex than he expected.

"May I help you?" a well-dressed man asked.

"I need a debit card for my account, please."

"Right this way, sir."

The man showed him to an office and he sat in a chair watching a woman behind a desk talking on her phone. She looked over at him and lowered her voice but continued talking.

Her conversation over, she said, "Yes?"

"I need a debit card for my account."

"What is your account number, and may I see your identification?" The inflection in her voice was one of annoyance, and she seemed to want him to know it.

"Have I offended you somehow?"

His question startled her, but it also changed her disposition.

"No, sir, but I will need your account number and identification."

He *had* offended her somehow, but she sat straighter in her seat now, and he saw her looking him over, judging him and wondered what her judgment was.

He wrote his name and the account number on a card and handed it to her.

"I'm very sorry, but I lost my identification in a vehicle accident. I should have my new driver's license later today."

"Mr. Walker, if you could write down your address and your mother's maiden name, I can do this without your driver's license." Her tone had softened some and her thin lips formed a half smile.

He wrote the information down and pulled a roll of twenties out of his pocket.

"This is four hundred dollars. I would like to deposit it as well."

"I'll be right back. The debit card will take a few minutes, and I'll take care of your deposit as well."

A few moments later, she returned with two small envelopes.

"One is your debit card and a receipt for your deposit and the other is your pin number; we don't recommend you keep them together."

Banking was an annoying process, he decided, one he hoped he could do online in the future.

The smell of talcum powder coming through the open door of Roosters Grooming triggered a pleasant memory of his father. He walked in and an older man motioned for him to take the middle chair. As he sat, he saw the worn leather was riddled with deep cracks from years of use, and although it was old, it was comfortable. He leaned back and absorbed the smells of the shop, the talcum powder, the aftershaves, and the hair gels.

The barber was in his early seventies, and like Len, he had deep wrinkles around his eyes and mouth, but his hair was white. He had a deep voice and spoke English with a thick Spanish accent.

"Mi nombre es Sandy, señor!"

"Ah!" The man's eyes widened, and he spoke in deep, throaty Spanish.

As a teenager, he had read Ernest Hemingway's *The Old Man and the Sea* and vowed he would travel to Cuba one day. As he walked out of the barber shop, he knew that day would never come, but still, the thought entertained him.

Next to the barber shop, two mannequins in a storefront window of Callahan's Fine Menswear stared out at him. One dressed in a dark gray pinstriped suit reminded him of a politician he had seen aboard the *Constitution*. He was a powerful man, and part of that aura of power came from the suit.

He stepped inside, felt the cool air, and knew he would soon need that look of power.

Chapter 13
Croft

Croft looked up as Stephens walked into the hangar.

"Learn anything, Jon?"

"Yes, indeed! The tissues are close to normal human brain tissue, except it's almost all gray matter. In the human brain, gray matter is associated with processing and cognition, while white matter affects how the brain learns and functions. It's closer to an even mix in humans."

"So you think it controls the ship?"

"I'm not so sure. I'll bet it can function somewhat on its own," Stephens said. "But I think the pilot is in charge. That would explain the lack of white matter in the tissues. However, they must communicate with each other somehow. Also, I had a few thoughts last night. Remember how we were wondering about the hatch? I think it's possible the tissues in the canisters produce enough electricity to power some of the ship's systems and store it somewhere. But like any battery, it died, and the hatch released."

Croft thought for a moment and nodded. "I like it."

"Let me show you something," Fischer said, leading Croft and Stephens to the ship. "Remember how we thought these columns were the instrument display? If you look close enough, right here," he said, pointing, "I think these are the lenses of a projection system. I'll bet the circuitry is in the floor and walls, and it's connected to the brain over there."

"Okay, so what's next?" Croft asked.

"I'd like to bring in someone I think can help," Stephens said.

"Who?"

"Carol Vones. I've worked with her at Caltech. Her field is neuroscience and mapping the human brain; this is what she does, and she's the best in her field."

"Okay, she will need clearance though. I'll see if I can expedite it."

"I'll call her now and see if she can get out here as soon as possible."

"The general will be here in a few minutes," Croft said. "I want him to see the ship and brief him in person."

Retired General Ryan Scott had been stationed at White Sands for ten years as a colonel and transferred to Washington after his promotion. He retired three years later as a lieutenant general and now lectured at MIT. His last assignment at the White Sands Missile Range was the organization and staffing of the Special Operation Section, now Croft's team.

Croft met him at the hangar door. "General! Always good to see you."

The two large portable air conditioners had reduced the smell of decay down to a level that even Fischer could tolerate, and the hangar was now cool, almost comfortable.

The general gestured across the hangar where Fischer and Stephens stood just outside the ship. "You were right. Seeing it in person takes your breath away."

"I thought you would want to see it. I'm not sure how long I can keep this contained, and I'm going to need your help with Washington eventually."

The general straightened and spoke just loud enough for him to hear. "Speaking of Washington, I got a call from Marjory Hicks; she's the deputy director at the NSA. They intercepted the same signals you did. She knows something is going on out here, and she wants to be briefed."

"Damn it! That's what I was afraid of. If they get wind of this now, I'll never see it again."

"Be careful there, Bob. It's not yours. If this ship is what you think it is, once word gets out, it's going to be the biggest story in years, maybe centuries and sitting on it for even a day without alerting Washington could end your career. I'm not sure it's a good idea."

"I've thought of that, General, but I have the best people right here, and only three of us know what it is. And what do we know? What can we prove other than its technology is superior to what we think is possible? Remember that Soviet recon satellite? I got Washington involved in it, and they took everything from us and I never heard about it again. As soon as I can prove something, I'll write it up and let Bowman know immediately, he can advise Washington.

"You've had it almost a full week now, Bob. I wouldn't sit on it much longer than another few days at the most. The sooner the better."

"I hear you General. Stephens wants to bring in a specialist to help with this brain tissue. That might answer a lot of our questions. To be honest, we still don't have a clue of what this ship's purpose is."

Croft led him over to the ship, and Scott peered inside without saying a word, but his eyes never stopped moving, absorbing every detail.

"Can I see the photo?"

Scott held the old picture and shook his head. "It looks like something took out the east side of the city, and the rest of it is flooded. I guess they were right about global warming." He handed the picture back to Croft. "Interesting, it could be photoshopped I suppose, but it looks authentic."

He stepped inside, pausing a minute to examine the pilot's seat and pressed his fingers into the foam. He squatted to look at the damage near the floor, the blood and then the cabinet with the decaying material inside. The coagulated arterial blood, rich in oxygen had clumped together in different shades from bright red to almost black. If the smell bothered him, it didn't show. Croft and the general had seen worse and seen it often.

"You're right, Bob. Everything in this ship is beyond our current technology." He stood and stepped out into fresh air. "Do you have anything else on the pilot?"

Croft shook his head. "Not yet. Tristan Flórez tracked him to a restaurant just outside of Portales. His wound can't be that bad if he stopped for breakfast, but we alerted the sheriff and the local hospitals."

"Bob, be careful with this Hicks woman. I've heard stories of people who have gone up against her and didn't fare well. You can count on the NSA being into your phones and emails soon if not already, but remember, you may need them later to help track down your pilot. Don't offend them if you can help it.

"It's crazy, Bob. I'd like to know what happened to Washington. Keep up the pressure on finding him and let me know if I can help you further."

"Thanks, General."

Scott gestured to both the ship and the hangar. "You know, this makes me wish I had never left. Good work, Bob. See you soon."

Chapter 14

Six

It was the largest flag he had ever seen. Standing just outside the main door of The Big Country Ford dealership, he looked up and watched the flag rippling in the light breeze. "Old Glory," he whispered.

He sensed the man coming up behind him and turned.

"Afternoon, sir! Can I help you?"

He was a big man, tall and thick. His black hair looked unnatural and didn't match the gray in his eyebrows. Something about this man was irritating. He was friendly and informal, but the smile conflicted with the glint in his eyes.

"I want to buy a vehicle. A Ford Explorer, to be precise."

"Well, sir, I have just the Explorer you're looking for. My name is Sam, and yours?"

"Sandy Walker."

"Well, let's go inside, Sandy. It's hot as the dickens out here and the Explorers are on the other side of the lot."

"I would like one with four-wheel drive and in dark blue." He knew one was in the lot from his earlier research, and he knew what the dealer's minimum sale price would be.

"I have two in dark blue, Sandy. I see you didn't bring a trade-in, am I right?"

"Nothing to trade," he said, remembering the ritual of negotiation.

Looking through the glass double doors, he saw the Explorer in the second row, along with several others in different colors.

"I want that one."

"Let me get the key, Sandy and we'll take her for a spin."

He was anxious. Most of the comments on buying cars had a negative connotation, and it worried him. Looking through the glass at the line of new cars, he eavesdropped on the dealership's Wi-Fi conversations. Banking transactions, maintenance appointments, delivery quotas. Nothing interesting or nefarious. Still the feeling nagged him.

Sam returned with the key and they walked out into the heat. Wiping sweat off his face as he unlocked the door, he gave Sandy the key.

"Start her up, Sandy. Let's get that AC blowing!"

Sitting in the car, or SUV as Sam described it, the salesman explained the controls and options, but he had already tuned the man out and was concentrating on the electronics, the GPS, and the Bluetooth entertainment center.

"I'll take it."

"No test drive?"

"No, it will not be necessary."

"Well, let's go inside and start the paperwork," Sam said, wiping the sweat from the folds of his neck. Inside a small cubicle with glass partitions, Sam pushed a stack of papers off a chair and offered him a seat. The office looked ransacked. From a folder, Sam pulled out several documents and began reciting the manufacturer's suggested retail price.

"The MSRP is forty-nine thousand, nine-hundred twenty-five dollars, and dealer fees bring the total to fifty-three thousand, seven hundred fifty dollars, plus tax and tag." Sam smiled, "How will you be paying for the car Sandy?"

"I'll pay forty-eight thousand dollars even plus tax and tag. I want to put ten thousand dollars down and finance the balance for twenty-four months." He had done research and found his figures to be the lowest the dealer would take for the Explorer with its listed options.

Sam's smile faded for a moment, but returned just as fast. Dabbing at his face with a handkerchief, he chuckled and said, "We would all go broke selling cars that cheap, but we can take off the dealer fees and drop the price down a few dollars. How about fifty-two thousand dollars even plus tax and tag? Let me see what your payments will be if we finance it for sixty months."

Now he knew why so many hated the process of buying a car. He stood up and walked out of the cubicle, leaving the startled salesman following him out the door.

"I would like to speak to someone else."

The fleet manager's office was at the end of the hall, and he stepped in surprising the woman behind her desk.

"Can I help you?"

"I cannot do business with this man," he gestured to Sam who was coming down the hall. "I want to purchase the blue Explorer outside. The inventory number is one four seven six one, and I'll pay forty-eight thousand dollars for the car plus tax, and I'm not here to negotiate any further."

"I'll take it from here, Sam," she said.

He turned and looked at the salesman. The man's mouth was opening and closing, like the fish at the clinic's aquarium. He turned and left, dabbing at the back of his neck again.

The woman was everything Sam was not. She was polite and professional; where Sam's cubical looked like it was a storage room, hers was neat and organized.

"I'll sell you the Explorer for forty-eight thousand as an apology for Sam. It's the industry's average price for an Explorer. Let's start with your down payment and financing, shall we?"

He sat in the lot and looked at the instrument panel. Then through the windshield thinking of the open expanse of desert as the air conditioner cooled the interior. He had conquered all those fears, and now they seemed trivial.

He thought of the desolation that first night and looked around at all the life in front of him: the people, the traffic, and the green landscaping. The city was an oasis in a desert, and now this desert town was part of his life.

Purchasing a cell phone took longer than it did to buy the Explorer. He had expected to hand the clerk his Visa card and walk out, but there was an endless number of forms to fill out.

Now, in his hand, he held the most common means of communication, but he had no one to talk to.

His laundry was bagged and folded on the bed when he returned. There was no change from his twenty and no receipt, but there was also an envelope from the New Mexico's Department of Motor Vehicles.

He stripped, showered, and washed out the telemetry suit. As he dressed, he examined the wounds on his arm. Three days now and the wounds looked healed, but they were still tender. He decided to leave the stitches in for another day.

Tonight, he would work on the processor, and he would not sleep until the computer simulation succeeded. Three days later, at four in the morning, the processor came to life.

Chapter 15
Flórez

Portales was a small town off US 70 and for a population of just over twelve thousand, it had its share of crime. Police Chief Jennifer Tully and her eight officers dealt mostly with minor traffic accidents and domestic disturbances.

Sitting at her desk, she held a single-page report written by one of her officers several days ago. First United Bank wanted to document the loss of one hundred dollars from one of their ATMs out on the highway. Later the same day, another machine in Clovis lost several thousand dollars. She remembered the major mentioning Tommy's Garage and called him.

Tristan Flórez was on US 70 heading toward Clovis when his cell phone rang.

"Major, this is Chief Jennifer Tully, in Portales. You asked me to call if I came across anything unusual."

"Yes, ma'am?"

"A security officer with First United Bank reported money missing from one of their ATMs out of town on the highway, and I'll bet it's the one at Tommy's Garage. It was only a hundred dollars, and normally they wouldn't have bothered us with a report, but he said later the same day, an ATM in Clovis lost sixty-six hundred dollars and five minutes of the machine's video memory was wiped."

"Any suspects, Chief?"

"No, I'm afraid not. It just seemed odd, like maybe what you were looking for."

"It is. Thank you, Chief. I'm on my way to Clovis now."

By four o'clock, he was sitting behind a bank of CCTV monitors with First United Bank's chief of security, Lionel Garcia.

Watching the largest of the monitors, the chief explained, "The machine's camera is only active when it's in use. Any input will start the camera, and it ends fifteen seconds after the last command, which is the printing of the receipt. This twenty-second video was shot at 5:12 a.m. on the tenth."

They both watched the monitor for any sign of movement. Only the camera's time stamp moved, and then the video stopped.

"That's it. The data shows the machine dispensed a hundred dollars for no apparent reason. No card was swiped; no inputs of any kind. We replaced the machine as a precaution and thought nothing of it until the incident in Clovis."

"Any prints on this machine?" Flórez asked.

"No. No tampering of any kind. The incident in Clovis is even stranger." He started another video, and Flórez saw a tall, dark-skinned male in front of the camera. He was talking to a young woman on the edge of the camera's view. There was no sound and Flórez couldn't tell what he was saying to the woman, but it was an argument.

"A few seconds into the video, you'll see the man backhand the woman and she disappears from view."

Flórez winced as the muscular man knocked the woman down. Across the street, customers coming out of the Coyote Deli glanced toward the ATM and then walked away.

The man making the withdrawal reached down and pulled the woman back into camera view, then pushed her toward a red car. He couldn't make out the model, but it was a convertible. Then the car drove out of view, and the screen went blank.

"During the next five minutes, the machine was emptied,"

Garcia said. "Every dollar was taken. No signs of tampering other than five minutes of lost video. The last customer to use the machine was Ricardo Caride, the man you saw a moment before, and the missing cash was withdrawn from his account. He's mad as hell, and I think we'll have to refund his money.

"This machine is programmed to dispense a maximum of $600 per transaction, and every customer has a $600 limit per day, but somehow someone bypassed the programming. We rechecked the system, and the programming appears to be unaltered, so no one can explain how that's possible."

"Can we replay the video? I want to watch the people across the street again."

A man walking out of the deli glanced toward the camera and looked away like the rest of them. He was in the building's shadow, but it looked like he was wearing a blue one-piece jumpsuit.

"Freeze it right there. Zoom in on him."

The size of the image increased, but the resolution blurred, making him unrecognizable.

"Can I get a copy of this?"

"Take this one. I have it all stored digitally."

Chapter 16
Six

He ran the simulation over again several times, increasing the complexity of each test until he was sure the processor was perfect, and it was.

Probing the rough stitches in the shower, he saw the beginnings of pink scars on each side of his bicep. There were no signs of infection and just days ago, these wounds had almost killed him.

He cut the knot in each stitch with the scissors from Walmart and pulled the black sutures out. The wounds looked less dramatic now, but the scars would always remind him of that night.

Dressed in his new blue jeans, he walked out of the hotel and into the morning sunlight.

His favorite table was open and as he spread the napkin across his lap, he looked up and saw Susan walk in.

"Hello, Sandy. Are you expecting anyone, or can I join you?"

"Please do, Susan."

"How have you been?" It's been almost a week since I've seen you."

"Very well, thank you. I've replaced my vehicle—my SUV as I was told to call it—and the project I've been working on is complete."

"What is it?"

"A computer processor. I'm going to Chicago and I hope to sell it to Motorola."

"I don't know much about computers. Is that a big thing?"

"I think it will be."

"That's great, Sandy."

"You know, Susan, I've decided I've had enough of pancakes and waffles. Today I'm going to try an omelet."

She stared at him, and the look was frightening. He could sense the question she was about to ask.

"Susan, it's just that I'm used to eating in a commissary. We had a limited menu, so all this is new to me."

"Where was this commissary, Sandy, and where were you coming from?"

"That's hard to explain and something that I shouldn't talk about, not yet anyway."

"You were in prison, weren't you? It all makes sense now. You, walking alone in the desert, the jumpsuit, the way you reacted when you saw the cops that morning."

He watched her face as her emotions cascaded faster than he could interpret them. Fear, pain, and disappointment. Each felt like sharp knives cutting him.

She leapt to her feet. "I'm out of here!"

"Susan, let me finish."

Her face flushed and red blotches replaced the tiny freckles on her cheeks. Her anger was intense, but she waited.

"I was on a station, one similar to your Cannon Air Force Base, but I was not in the military. I worked there, I am not a criminal."

She moved back over to her seat, but didn't sit down at first, then collapsed into the booth.

"Okay then," she whispered. "I'm sorry, I'm sorry. I just haven't had much luck with men since I moved here. Sandy, something strange is going on with you and I want you to tell me what it is."

"I promise I will, but not today, not yet. I have a few things to work out first."

Glaring at him, her face still flushed, she waited.

"All right, but soon."

Something dark emanated from her and he wished he had worn the telemetry suit.

"Susan, can I ask, do you have plans this evening?"

"No," she said. "I'm off for the next three days."

Chapter 17
Flórez

Walking out of the First United Bank, Flórez saw the Hillcrest Urgent Care Center down the street. It was the last of the five clinics on his list in Clovis. He parked his government-issued black Jeep Compass in the lot and walked inside.

Two dozen people sat in the lobby, and half of them were waiting at the front desk. Mothers were trying to quiet their crying children. The men sat quietly staring at the white walls, or reading magazines. Several appeared to be sleeping.

A gray-haired woman behind the counter was speaking to an older man as he read one of several forms in his hand. The man had a fresh bandage on his left hand, and his arm hung in a sling.

Fifteen minutes later, it was his turn with the woman.

"I'm Major Flórez with the US Army, and I need to know if you've treated a man we're looking for. He would have been treated on the tenth or the eleventh of this month."

"Most of our patient information will be confidential. Maybe you should speak to Doctor Snyder. I'm filling in today and I wouldn't know anything about patients on those dates. Have a seat and I'll let her know you want to speak with her."

Every eye in the room watched him take the last remaining chair.

Staring through the clinic's plate-glass window, Flórez saw his next stop. The Coyote Deli, captured on the ATM's video. Then a woman wearing green hospital scrubs called his name.

"I'm Doctor Snyder, Major. As you can see, we are a little busy this afternoon, but come into my office and I'll give you a few minutes."

She sat behind an old but sturdy pine desk and gestured to the seat on the other side. "Are you looking for an AWOL soldier, Major?"

"Not exactly, Doctor. I'm looking for a man involved in an accident and I'm sure he needed medical treatment. This accident happened on Monday night and he would have had an injury to his upper left arm. That's all I can tell you for now. Has anyone come in here fitting that description?"

"I'm afraid I can't discuss anything relating to my patients. It's a privacy issue. You see, many are undocumented immigrants. We do pro bono cases for the local churches: the patient pays what he can, the churches pay what they can, and we write off the rest. They wouldn't come here if they didn't trust us. I'm sorry I can't help you."

The pilot had been here. He could read it in the doctor's facial expressions and body language as he described the man, and that was enough to tell him he was on the right track.

"Well, thank you anyway, Doctor. I won't hold you up any longer."

He walked across the street towards the deli.

Inside, each table was occupied. The crowd was young. Some were eating, but most were on computers, staring into the monitors. As far as Flórez could tell, there were three employees: a young woman serving food, another man at the register and an older man in the kitchen shaking the oil out of a basket of fries.

It's possible the pilot would have sat at one of these tables, even used a computer, but it was too busy to ask questions now. In opposing corners of the dining room, two surveillance cameras were mounted near the ceiling. If the man was here there may be an excellent video of him. He'd be back before the deli closed.

Chapter 18
Susan

Susan Matthews was on her second cup of hot tea, planning her long weekend and waiting for Sandy Walker to call. During the drive from Edna's Waffle House, he seemed like a nice man, maybe a little eccentric—and there was something about his eyes she couldn't quite put her finger on.

It had been a rough night, she remembered. A red-eye flight from Chicago to Santa Fe with passengers complaining about everything from the small seats to the peanuts. Then there was the long, frustrating drive from the airport.

That morning sun through her windshield was blinding and it felt like an ice pick digging into her skull. She was cursed with migraines, and this was going to be a bad one.

Edna's was a regular stop for her, a place to unwind and enjoy a cup of hot tea before the last leg of her drive. Then her table was missing the sugar jar and the server was busy. She had turned around to ask the man behind her if she could use his.

He stared at her for a moment as if confused. He was an attractive man, but there was something else, something familiar, something … eerie. She'd had to repeat herself. He never spoke but offered her the jar. She turned back around and was stirring sugar into her tea when a wave of heat washed over her. As that strange sensation dissipated, all her anxieties and the symptoms of a migraine vanished with it. It was odd. Frustrated and wanting to quit her job one minute and then—everything was good. Not just good, but great, like a switch had been flipped, and she couldn't understand why.

Then the pleasant drive to Clovis. He was quiet, but attentive and she liked that in a man. She hoped he wasn't married or an alcoholic like her last date. What a disaster that had been.

Clovis was a small town and there weren't many opportunities for a divorced woman, but after living in South Florida and Atlanta most of her life, it was an improvement. She lived in Miami for four years, never knowing the names of her neighbors. This town was different; she couldn't shop at the grocery store without running into someone she knew by name.

Monet's painting, *The Pont Neuf, Paris* on her wall reminded her of the promise she made to herself years ago. Travel to Paris, walk down the same streets as the artist, and have a cup of tea at a sidewalk café along the Champs-Élysées. Was it too much to ask? All she had seen with Midway Airlines was downtown Chicago and Detroit.

I should call American Airlines again.

Last month the airline assured her that her application was still on file, but she had been on that list for twelve months. She had hoped her experience with Midway would help get her foot in the door. Now she wasn't so sure. Then her phone rang.

Chapter 19
Six

As Flórez stood outside the Hillcrest Urgent Care Center, Six was across the street in his room at the Saguaro Inn. The picture on his driver's license showed part of the Coyote Deli menu in the background. How big a problem would this be?

With the laptop's camera, he took another photo making sure the solid white wall was behind him. He couldn't overnight this one to the inn though, he was leaving this wretched place in the morning and didn't want to see it ever again. Instead, he chose a hotel in Santa Fe, overnighted the new license to Sandy Walker and hoped it would be at the front desk when he arrived.

Showered and dressed in clothes appropriate for a first date, he looked in the mirror. Self-doubt was another new experience he added to the list. 'Jeans will be fine,' Susan had said. If only *Two* were here, he thought, she had a sense for such things.

The alarm clock on the desk said 3:30, and his two suits from Callihan's would be ready by four. It was time to go. Keys in hand, he looked at the laptop lying on the bed. Days of hard work was stored on that hard drive, and Garrett Teller was on duty. He disliked the man, grabbed the laptop, his suitcase, and carried it all out the back exit, passed the pool and put it in the back of the Explorer.

Traffic was light on Grand Avenue. With country music playing, he cruised east following the GPS and parked behind her red Honda. Beads of nervous perspiration dotted his forehead as he rehearsed his greeting.

An antique brass knocker hung at the door. Huge and intimidating, he feared it would deny him entry. Once used, he was committed and there was no going back.

Just knock on the door!

Then he looked down at his new denim jeans and knew they were not appropriate at all.

You are stalling like a rookie cadet. Just knock on the door!

Silently he mouthed the word "hello" several times and then reached out to knock, only to pull his hand back at the last minute—but the door opened anyway.

"How long have you been out here?" Susan said.

She was breathtaking. It wasn't the black jeans accenting every curve and the length of her long legs, or the beige sleeveless blouse with the small white buttons. Her perfume, as intoxicating as it was, paled in comparison to the beauty, wisdom and strength he saw in her eyes.

Before, he had considered her attractive—a woman of grace and confidence walking past him in her simple uniform. This was different. He knew at this moment, he was bound to this woman by something he couldn't understand.

"I was admiring your plants. They're ... beautiful." He had meant to say healthy, but beautiful came out of his mouth.

"Thank you. Come on in. I'm almost ready. Have a seat on the couch." She turned and disappeared into another room.

"How's your arm?" she called from around the corner.

"Much better, thank you. Where is Annie? She is a fair and honest woman. I wanted to thank her again."

He heard her laugh in the other room. "Fair and honest. I'll tell her that when she gets back. She drove to Albuquerque to see her mother, but she said to say hello."

The decor in the townhouse was unlike anything he had seen

since his arrival. This was a woman's house. The sofa and matching chairs were upholstered in a blue floral fabric and faced the television. A dark wood coffee table rested on an area rug that brought out the colors in the sofa. It seemed shameful to sit on anything so perfect.

On a side table sat several framed photographs. One showed Susan in her early teens sitting on a motorcycle. An older man, her father perhaps, stood next to her as she held a trophy over her head. Her hair was pulled back, and she was covered in mud from head to toe. In this picture, he saw the woman she would soon become.

The next photo was Susan in a cap and gown—a school graduation photo. She stood between the same man and a woman, and the proud look in their eyes was identical to his parents' eyes in the photo he left behind in his ship.

"Turn on the TV if you like."

He sat on the sofa and reached for the remote noticing a *Time* magazine on the table. On the cover was the portrait of a white-bearded man. If you didn't know him, you would have thought he was a gentleman deep in thought, but those who did, knew what he was. He was a monster. In small letters at the bottom of the cover was the caption, "Iran's Nuclear Threat."

Mahamoud Madine stared at him—and the nightmare of his parents' deaths played out in his head like an old movie. He was eight when they were killed by a faceless group of religious fanatics, and now three hundred years earlier, the man history blamed for starting it all was alive and well. His fingers trembled inches away from the man's face.

He couldn't breathe and pain radiated out from the center of his chest. All symptoms of a heart attack. He jerked himself upright knocking the rest of the magazines off the table. It wasn't a heart attack—it was rage.

His nails dug into the flesh of his palms. Pacing between the sofa and china cabinet, he tried to stop shaking. Don't let her come out now, he thought, I don't want her to see me like this.

Sitting on the sofa again, he reached for the remote control. As he reached, both the TV and the entertainment system switched on and he watched helplessly as the volume bar increased to its maximum level. The sound was deafening. He stood staring at the remote, still untouched on the table.

"Having trouble?" Susan yelled over the noise. She walked into the room, gave him an odd look, then picked up the remote and switched everything off.

"That thing can be a little confusing. Sorry. If you can help me with this, I'm ready to go." Handing him the backing of her earring, she turned.

She was close now. The perfume, the fine wisp of blonde hair running along her bare neck, the thin gold necklace—he was suffering from sensory overload. His heart pounded and his fingers trembled as he tried to fit the backing onto the earring's post. Just as he thought he would drop it, the post slid into place.

Who was he kidding? He wasn't ready for this kind of intimate contact. He had felt so confident leaving the hotel an hour ago, but now everything was going wrong.

"Thanks," she said, picking up her purse.

She set the alarm system and they walked outside. It was seven-thirty and still warm, yet he had chills. Was it the remote, the magazine or was it Susan? All of them, he thought opening the Explorer's passenger door.

"Nice car."

"Thank you," he said, getting behind the wheel. He took a slow, deep breath and exhaled.

"Are you alright?" she asked.

"I think so, Susan. I want to be honest, I'm nervous."

"That's good to know. So am I."

He turned on the radio, and as he backed out of the drive, she turned up the volume.

"*Beautiful Tonight*, I love this song."

"Your perfume, is it the same fragrance you wore when we met? It's very ... pleasant," he said, wishing for a better word.

"Yes, Red Door. It's my favorite."

She looked behind the seat and saw the new suits, bags and shoe boxes from Callahan's. "You've been a busy man; new car, new clothes."

"I have business tomorrow in Santa Fe, and I do not want to show up looking like I did that morning at Edna's Waffle House."

"You'll look fine," she said, and laughed.

It was a fifteen-minute drive to the restaurant and Susan did most of the talking, which was okay with him. He was learning, and listening was the best lesson.

She had several interesting stories about unruly and obnoxious passengers on her flights, one of which was a famous NBA player.

Days before, when she had picked him up in the desert, he had tuned her out, ignoring most of what she said and praying for silence. This evening, he listened to every word and absorbed every detail.

Chapter 20
Flórez

The Coyote Grill closed at four. It wasn't a dinner restaurant and served only breakfast and lunch. Their best customers were the students from the college and a nearby high school. A few office workers from the downtown area also came in, but once the local shops closed, this side of Clovis was a ghost town.

At a quarter to four, Flórez walked inside the deserted restaurant and rang the bell next to the cash register. He could hear someone in the kitchen, and seconds later, a middle-aged man in a white shirt and apron stepped out from behind the swinging doors.

"Hello, can I help you?" the man asked.

"I'm Major Flórez with the Army, and I'm hoping you can. Last Tuesday a man I need to speak to came in and left just after lunch, about one o'clock. Is it possible I could have a look at your security data for that day?"

"I'm sorry, Major, but even when those cameras worked, I could only store one day's worth of data. The monthly service to store it on the cloud was just too expensive, and now I can't get them to work at all. I struggle just to make ends meet, and I've had no real need to replace them."

A dead end.

Flórez walked outside and looked across Grand Avenue at the new ATM and then north as the shop owners locked their doors.

"Where would the man go from here?" he wondered aloud.

He has no transportation, but a lot of cash. Probably knows nothing about Clovis or even New Mexico.

Flórez walked toward the Saguaro Inn.

The man at the front desk was in his mid-twenties and had an overgrown mess of hair that may have been a mohawk at one time.

"Good afternoon. I'm Major Flórez with the Army's military police, and I'm looking for a guy that may have stayed here a few days ago, maybe as early as Tuesday. He may still be here."

"What's his name?" the clerk asked wiping something from his chin.

"He may have used the name Sandy. He's about thirty, dark blond hair, six feet, maybe a little taller. Sound familiar?"

"No. Just a lot of old people here."

The two men stared at each other for a minute, and the younger man blinked.

"That's not exactly true, is it Garrett?" he asked, looking at the man's name tag. "Did he pay cash? If so, I'm not interested in your personal business, but this could go bad for you if I find out he was here and you're being less than truthful."

The blood drained from the clerk's face.

"Well, there was a guy like that, but he left about thirty minutes ago. He didn't give me a name, but an envelope came for him. It was addressed to Sandy Walker."

"I'll need his room number and a pass key, Garrett."

Standing in front of room 124, he turned to the clerk. "I'll take it from here. Thanks for your help."

Once the clerk was out of the hallway, he slid the pass key into the slot. There was a faint click and a green light lit up on the lock. He cracked the door open an inch and listened, then stepped inside.

The room was empty, the bed was made, and there were no

personal belongings anywhere. Sandy Walker was not coming back.

The trash can was full of empty Walmart bags. He went through each looking for a receipt or anything important, but they were empty. At the bottom of the can, he noticed several bits of black string that looked like small spiders. He picked one out, it was a suture. The pilot had removed his own stitches.

Chapter 21
Six

The Yucca Restaurant was on the prosperous side of downtown Clovis. It was surrounded by older, restored wood-framed homes and storefronts built in the late nineteenth century. The city square wasn't a square at all, it was a roundabout and the restaurant was on the far side.

"Park in there," Susan said.

He pulled into the last parking space and hurried around to her side to find she was already halfway out of the door. He made a show of holding it open anyway. Earlier, he had researched dating etiquette, and opening doors on a date was a priority.

As they stepped into the restaurant, several men turned to glance at Susan, some more discrete than others. He couldn't blame them, remembering how he had stared earlier. She walked with such grace, leaving him feeling oafish and unworthy of someone so lithe.

The host sat them at a table next to a large window providing a view of an elegant, old Victorian style church, its tall white steeple and bell tower reaching up into the evening sky. He could just read a bronze plaque near its front door: "First Baptist Church of Clovis, est. 1858." There was more, but the lettering was too small even for him to read.

"I love this table," she said, running her fingers over the wood's coarse grain.

Thin cracks and weathered stains under the polished surface

gave the impression the dark mahogany was very old. Matching high-backed armchairs upholstered in a deep red, button-tucked fabric, and a candle flickering in a brass lantern gave the room a medieval castle appearance.

"Quite different than the waffle house."

She smiled and leaned back. "We can go back there if you like."

"No, this will be fine," he said, and picked up the menu.

He couldn't pronounce some of the entrées, and it left him wondering how many tasteless meals he had eaten at the institute's commissary. Onboard the *Constitution*, fish had always been listed as fish and chicken just chicken, baked or broiled. He never realized how generic those terms were. Choosing one was going to be difficult.

The server introduced himself and went through a list of the day's specials. Susan ordered one of them; broiled grouper parmesan and a glass of Sauvignon Blanc. "It's not always good to order seafood from a restaurant a thousand miles from the ocean," she whispered, "but I've heard that it's excellent here."

"I'll have the same and a glass of chardonnay please."

The salads came first. Mimicking Susan, he used the smaller fork and listened as she described meeting Annie on a flight from Chicago and how they became roommates and best friends. Both were divorced and starting over in new careers. Annie had been a secretary at a small real estate office and had just gotten her real estate license when the market crashed. Out of work and a new divorcee, Annie went back to college to study medicine at Eastern New Mexico University in Portales.

"I promised myself after the divorce that I would go back to school too, but right now, I just want to travel, to see more of the world, but all I'm seeing are small towns in the Midwest. I dream of walking down a street in Paris. I know that sounds silly, but it's important to me."

"I've spent a lot of time in Paris, Susan, and I believe dreams are important. You mentioned divorce. Is that a common thing?"

"I suppose so, now more than when my parents were young."

"I cannot imagine loving a woman, getting married and then divorcing her."

"Wow," Susan said. "Have you been living in a Hallmark movie?"

"Hallmark?"

"Never mind, it's a nice thought though. I'm sorry. I didn't want to mention my marriage, but," she stopped and then started again, "it's not something I want to hide from you either."

She held her wineglass but didn't drink from it. His skin prickled as the air around her grew cold and the brightness in her eyes dulled. She was thinking of what she would say next.

"I met Anthony Pistorius during my first year of law school at the University of Miami and we dated for six months. Miami was beautiful, we got married and I was happy. After the first year, we were struggling with tuition, so I dropped my classes and worked as a clerk at a law firm and waited tables part time until he graduated.

"Two months after getting his law degree, he filed for divorce and moved to New York. He left me penniless. Turns out he was on an expired student visa from Belgium. The marriage gave him legal status and once he got his law degree, he didn't need me anymore.

"I was such a fool. I had a lot of confidence issues after that, but that was six years ago. So, I guess I'm trying to apologize for my earlier outburst at breakfast. I'm sorry, Sandy."

"Please don't," he said. "I know how I looked that morning. I don't blame you."

"So what about you, any ex-wives you want to talk about?"

"No, I've never been married, but I guess we are both starting over. With my new processor, I hope to start a computer business and I'll be one step closer tomorrow if things go well. You worked in a law firm; maybe you can help me. I believe I'll need an attorney. That's why I'm going to Santa Fe. Do you know anything about patents?"

"Not really, but I know you'll need an attorney to help you.

Just make sure they specialize in business. You don't want to pick a criminal attorney for a patent. You'll love Santa Fe. Annie and I go there now and then and browse the antique shops."

"I hope to only be there for a few days."

"I wish you success, Sandy."

She smiled and reached out for his hand. Touching her fingers soothed the stress and doubts that had been building, just like the woman in his dreams. It could be her, he thought, but Susan's nails had a clear gloss, and the ring was missing. Still …

"Look," Susan whispered, nodding to an older couple at the next table.

The couple were celebrating their fiftieth wedding anniversary and were holding hands like newlyweds. The server brought them champagne and a small cake with a single candle, and everyone cheered as the wife blew out the flame.

"That is so fantastic," Susan said, watching them.

He looked at her hand in his, and pulled away. "That is true love, Susan. Look in their eyes. They will never leave one another."

He looked at her and tried to guess her thoughts. She smiled, and her eyes sparkled with wetness, but these tears were different, that icy sadness had run its course, and he knew she envied this couple. Even without the telemetry suit, he knew.

The thought of marriage or raising a family was something he had never considered. In fact, just the opposite. He was a pilot, destined to be alone, to live in the cold solitude of space, never thinking past the next mission. His parents, and then the Institute, had predetermined his life, but that life was over now and the possibilities were endless.

It had to be Susan in the dream. He looked across the table and watched the candlelight flicker in her eyes and remembered the earlier feeling of being bound to her.

The server brought their check, and he reached across the table for it.

"Oh my gosh! Sandy, your arm looks completely healed. It's only been a week, and I had forgotten all about it."

He pulled his arm back—and lied to her again.

"It feels better too and I have always healed quickly."

A birthday celebration at another table distracted her, and he stood to leave.

"Shall we go?"

On Prince Street, music played softly through the Explorer's speakers, and Susan tapped her foot as he drove through traffic. As he pulled into her driveway, something changed. Anxiety filled the interior, and he thought not speaking during the drive may have been a mistake.

They stood on the small porch, and she asked him, "Will you be coming back to Clovis?"

"Yes. I will be back in a few days, and I hope to look for a more permanent place to live when I return. Would you like to help me?"

She smiled, and the tension was gone. "I'd love to."

She kissed him on the cheek. "Call me," she said and closed the door.

The sun had set, and the oppressive heat was replaced by a cool breeze from the north. On the horizon, Venus hung in the deep purple sky above the low hills. He stood there a minute taking in the view, savoring the memory of holding her hand and that simple kiss. It seemed so familiar, another déjà vu moment, or another fragment of his dream?

The deep purple of the sky changed to black, and his headlights illuminated the scrub brush and cacti as he drove back to the hotel. Somewhere along the way, the memory of Susan's kiss left him, and reality crept back into his consciousness. He had been in that blackened desert just a week ago, suffering, and the feelings were still fresh and the pain still vivid. Everything and every person he ever knew were gone.

I need to let go of them. My life is here now and maybe Susan will be part of it.

But there was also Mahamoud Madine—and death was on its way.

Three dark green four-door sedans and a black SUV were parked at the front entrance of the Saguaro Inn. Military vehicles—and standing at the door, a soldier in uniform stood scanning the parking lot. He recognized the SUV, earlier it had pulled into the Hillcrest Urgent Care Center.

Without slowing, he continued along Grand Avenue. The military had finally tracked him down.

What do I do now, and what do they know? I have to leave this town now!

Clovis was a small town, and if the desk clerk knew what he was driving, finding him here wouldn't be difficult.

Heading west towards Santa Fe, he pulled into the Courtyard by Marriott three hours later.

"I'm sorry, Mr. Walker, but I will need to see your identification," the woman behind the desk said. She was insistent, and he knew this woman was not another Garrett Teller. He handed her his license, hoping she wouldn't look at it too closely, and put two hundred dollars in cash on the counter.

The driver's license alone could help the military track him. They could be here in hours, maybe minutes. Using his debit card would make it worse, financial records were the first thing law enforcement and the military used to track criminals. Were they already watching his account?

Garrett Teller only knew his first name, but the envelope from New Mexico's DMV was addressed to Sandy Walker. He could keep running, California was just another few hours away. But when and where would …?

"Mr. Walker?"

"Yes? I'm sorry, I was distracted."

"Here's your key card. Go straight down that hall to the elevator, third floor and your room is 309. Have a nice night and breakfast is served starting at seven."

"Thank you. I'm expecting a letter, probably tomorrow morning."

"I'll hold it for you, sir."

As the elevator door slid shut, the sensation of claustrophobia overwhelmed him. Confined in a two-meter square cell with stainless steel walls, his blurred reflection in the door was staring back at him.

Will they shoot me on sight? No. That was a Hollywood movie made seventy-five years ago. They will surround me though and transport me far away, and no one will ever know I was here.

In the new room, not much different than the old one, he undressed leaving his clothes in a pile. Sitting in his underwear, he logged into the hotel's Wi-Fi with the laptop. He hoped to find something about the military's hunt for him, but his search parameters must have been too vague. He thought of the telemetry suit packed away in his suitcase. It would make this faster, but the cold air on his bare skin was refreshing.

Deleting his file from the clinic's computer took three minutes, but the Ford dealership's computer was more sophisticated and took ten. That left just his bank, and he would worry about it later.

Exhausted, he collapsed on the bed. He needed to sleep and closed his eyes—and found the bearded man's face on *Time* magazine staring at him, taunting him. Fatigue fled, replaced by adrenaline. There would be no rest and no sleep tonight.

Splashing cold water on his face, he looked in the mirror.

I'm going to stop them, and I'm going to start right now!

Madine! The man's face reminded him of the remote at Susan's. How had that happened? Was it anger? Without the suit or even a conscious thought, he had somehow switched on the entire system.

Glaring at the television, he tried to turn it on from across the room. Nothing happened. He tried several more times, each time trying to channel different emotions with the command, nothing worked.

He unpacked the telemetry suit and looked at the damaged sleeve. The tiny, thread-like filaments were shredded and its continuity had been compromised. It may be possible to repair it one day, but for now, it was all he had. He put it on and felt the electronic signals in the room, not just in his room, but every signal in the hotel and even a few from the cars in the parking lot.

It was two in the morning, and there were two active devices using the Wi-Fi. The clerk's desktop computer and a TV on the floor above him streaming a movie. Several phones were connected to a cell tower nearby and an entertainment satellite overhead.

He started by reading everything he could find on Iran's nuclear weapons program: foreign news accounts, Iran's own internal reports, and he even found a copy of the Joint Comprehensive Plan of Action known as the Iran Nuclear Deal.

He read for hours, absorbing and memorizing everything he could find. In 2010, Iran's computers were infected with a virus called *Stuxnet*, which caused their uranium refinement and enrichment program's centrifuges to spin out of control, damaging them beyond repair. Their investigation showed the virus altered a software program controlling their centrifuges' RPMs, and they blamed Israel's intelligence agency, the Mossad.

The Mossad's computer system was impossible to find, if they used one at all. He switched to the Israeli's government system, including the prime minister's personal computer and found several generic emails referencing Mossad and the name of a commander, but there were no open links to any other personnel, and there was no link to the commander's computer.

The Israelis' systems were well isolated, so he switched to the Iranians' website. It took hours, but he found references to two North Korean–designed mainframe computers they used for their nuclear program.

He spent the rest of the night looking for them in vain.

"Damn it!" Frustrated, he looked at the clock on the desk and saw sunlight streaming through the curtains.

No point in trying to sleep now.

He wanted to call Susan, to hear that soothing voice again, but it was too early. The thought though reminded him of Anthony Pistorius, Susan's ex-husband, and what he had done to her. He sat back in the recliner and re-linked with the Wi-Fi.

Pistorius had done well for himself. He was a junior partner in a law firm representing Stewart Becker, a stockbroker accused of stealing thirty million dollars in a Ponzi scheme. Becker had fled to the Cayman Islands before his arrest and was being tried in absentia.

Two articles mentioned Pistorius. One announcing his engagement to the daughter of the law firm's founder and another detailing an ongoing investigation for insider trading on Wall Street. Pistorius made nine million dollars investing in an electronics firm just before they were awarded a contract with the military.

Leaning back in an armchair and closing his eyes, he let the images spread out in front of him, limited only by the hotel Wi-Fi's bandwidth.

Pistorius had two hundred sixty-thousand dollars spread out in several accounts, and by six in the morning, he transferred it all as a donation to the Gary Sinise Foundation. He thought of transferring some of it into his own account and remembered the distaste of stealing from Ricardo Caride. Pistorius split the rest of the nine million dollars between his fiancé's personal account and the down payment on a house on Staten Island.

Do I take money from the wife?

"Dammit!"

"I can't do it," he said, pounding his fist on the desk. "It's not right."

"She could be another clueless victim, just like Susan, caught up in another of his schemes.

He found something better. Two incriminating messages on a Hotmail account linking Pistorius to the stock fraud. He forwarded them to both the *New York Times* and the US Securities and Exchange Commission.

Satisfied, he leaned back in the chair, stretched and closed his eyes.

Anger and retaliation—yin and yang. Hurting Pistorius financially had somehow satisfied them.

He began to doze when the beacon's signal reminded him of the time. It was seven o'clock. A business attorney, Susan had said. He found one with experience both in business and finances. Eric Ridge. He called the listed number and left a message.

"This is Sandy Walker calling. I will be in at ten o'clock and I would like to discuss business with Mr. Eric Ridge. Thank you."

He ended the call and collapsed on the bed. He could close his eyes and get two hours of sleep, but he felt a thought forming—the Iranian mainframes. Someone uses them. Perhaps they were the key to getting into the computers.

Six scientists were mentioned working on Iran's nuclear program, all in Natanz, one of two underground uranium enrichment facilities, and one of them was online right now. It was a long shot, he had to admit, but it was a shot.

There was an old version of the original *Stuxnet* virus on the dark web, and he downloaded it. It needed modifications to ensure it would be undetectable, and once done, he uploaded it and waited. Twenty minutes later, the modified virus was downloading to a laptop thousands of miles away. Now it was just a waiting game.

Chapter 22
Croft

Croft's alarm woke him at 0600 hours. He had been dreaming of his wife again and this time they were sitting in wooden rocking chairs on the deck of his parents' cabin in Tennessee. This was a new version of an old dream. In this version, they were both much younger.

"Find him, Bob. He needs us."

"Who?" As he said the word, she began to fade. He tried to touch her, but as usual, she was just out of reach. The dream ended as it always did. He sat up in the darkness, trying to make sense of it.

Damn it. Who is he, and why does he need us?

"It was a dream you fool. She's been dead for four years."

Fischer and Stephens were waiting for him at the hangar with a box of Krispy Kreme doughnuts.

"Good morning, gentlemen. Is that my breakfast?"

The hangar was cold, and Croft watched his breath float toward the ship. Portable air conditioners had dropped the temperature inside to forty degrees. A single spotlight illuminated the ship from above like an art exhibit at a museum.

"At least it doesn't stink as bad," Fischer said.

"We're going to keep this room cold. The conference room is warmer, but we'll need these."

Six cold weather parkas hung on the wall, and they each took one.

One of the MP's announced Carol Vones had arrived. She was younger than Croft expected. Her dark red hair was cut short and she wore a pair of old faded jeans and a black Henley shirt. He watched her look the ship over, wanting to see her reactions.

She put her hand on the frame of the hatch, examining the texture of the hull, and then stepped inside and kneeled over the remains in the cabinet. She nodded as if agreeing with some silent thought and then stood.

"Carol, you understand everything you see and hear is classified?" Croft asked from outside the hatch.

"Yes, sir. Jon explained everything, and I've signed for my clearance."

"Well, what do you think?"

"It's impressive and it's hard to get past where it came from. What's under the flooring?"

"Hard to say. It's shielded and the scanners are useless. We could cut into it but we risk damaging something vital."

She looked back at the cabinet. "Jon briefed me on some of your theories so far. I need to know though, what are your goals here? What is it you want me to do?"

"My goal is to find the man who came out of it. I need to know why he is here. Your goals are to help us find out what this ship is, what its purpose is, and last, to learn from it."

"Okay, I'm good with that. I was reluctant when Jon said the military was running things here. I didn't want to be involved in any kind of weapons testing."

"I don't know for sure that this isn't some type of weapon. I need you to help us figure that out."

"Okay, so one thing you're stuck on is what powers the ship, and here's a possibility. The human brain generates roughly one hundred millivolts of electricity. I would think that your ship would need much more energy than that, but it's possible that its systems are so efficient, they can operate on voltage lower than we think. It's also likely its core produces more energy than we are estimating. It's highly engineered, so its capabilities are unknown. If it has twice the efficiency of our brain matter, the volume of material in those canisters could give the ship an amazing amount of power and, just as important, intelligence."

Croft nodded. It made sense, and it surprised him none of them had thought that the core, as Carol referred to it, could be the ship's power source.

He looked at Stephens. "Jon, any new thoughts on the pilot's DNA?"

"Nothing new. All the blood samples we've collected are from the same human male, so we're only talking about one pilot. No clearly defined racial markers. If I had to guess though, I would still lean toward Western European.

"Another thing, it's a myth that humans can only access ten to fifteen percent of their brain and that the rest is unused. We all use a hundred percent of our brain, but some of us use it better than others. There are so many conflicting studies right now on genetics and intelligence that it's impossible to know who's right. But if some of the studies are correct, and now I think they are, this guy's intelligence and how his brain functions could be phenomenal. I don't think we should underestimate him."

"Anything new on the search?" Emil asked.

"Flórez called last night. He just missed him at a hotel in Clovis. He's using the name Sandy Walker and thinks he was treated for his wounds at a clinic across the street. He's still looking around, but he thinks he checked out of the hotel. Dead ends so far, but he's hoping if he uses that name again, he'll find him.

"Another thing," Croft said. "We've had this thing for seven days now, and we're not getting anywhere. We're going to keep it under wraps a few more days, then I'll need to brief General Bowman. Once I do that, I think we will lose the ship. The NSA, or some other agency will come in, and we will never see it again. I want to figure this out—us, not some cloak and dagger bastard out of Washington. So, let's get to it."

Chapter 23
Hicks

Fort Meade, Maryland

Marjory Hicks stood in Walter Price's tiny cubicle listening to the printer spit out the last page of his report. She was a tall woman, six foot one and staring down at the analyst made him physically uncomfortable. She moved closer, trapping him behind his desk.

"I'll read all this later. Just tell me what you know, Price."

"There was a lot of activity last Monday night and all day Tuesday. It started with reports of a radar contact and the recovery of a downed satellite in New Mexico. At the same time, we recorded two encrypted radio transmissions.

"A colonel out of the White Sands Missile Range recovered something and had it transported to the base. This colonel oversees a small special ops unit. Twice they have been involved with the recovery of foreign satellites. I found nothing unusual except that several MPs were involved in a search in the town of Portales and then Clovis. Still, it could be anything, maybe a civilian took something from the crash scene. It happens."

"I know all this, Price. Las Cruces reported the transmissions too. I read the briefings each morning. Tell me something useful."

There was so much activity at first, but nothing since Wednesday. They've been quiet ever since, and …"

"And what, Price?"

"We're still receiving that signal, each morning at 0900 our time.

"So, whose is it and what's in the transmission?"

"We don't know, it's encoded. The satellite itself is tiny and difficult to see from ground-based telescopes."

"We have more computing power than any place on Earth, Price; how is it we can't tell what it's transmitting?"

"I don't know, Ms. Hicks. Nothing we've tried reads it as language. It might as well be static, but it has structure so we know it's not just random noise."

"Has anyone else noticed it?"

"If they have, no one's asking questions. China will see it first; it's in an orbit close to one of theirs."

"Jesus, Price. Why did you sit on this all week?"

"Ms. Hicks …"

"Stop right there. I don't like to be referred to as Ms. Hicks. You will address me as Deputy Director."

"My apologies. I sent the report to you three times. The last time I flagged it as urgent and also left a message on your phone. I assumed you were handling it."

The two stared at each other, and the deputy director spoke first. "I read that first report, Price, and it was very vague. I spoke to one of the director's army contacts, a retired general and he said he knows nothing about this, so who is this colonel you mentioned?"

"Robert Croft."

"Anything on him in here?" she asked, shaking the report.

"No, I'll pull his file if you want. Most of it's routine—the aircraft and crew assignments, et cetera. Croft is keeping the rest classified."

"Pull his file and the file of the MP supervisor that was involved as well. Are you getting Croft's phone records?"

"No, they're Army accounts. Are you sure you want me to?"

"No, you're right. Hold off on that for now. Anything else on that satellite? When was its last transmission?"

"Nothing new, but yes it transmitted that same signal at 0900 EDT this morning."

"All right. Make some calls. Keep it discrete, but let's see if we can at least find out who the damn thing belongs to. I'm pissed off, Price and I want some answers."

As she stood to leave, Price cleared his throat. "Ma'am, Deputy Director, one more thing: one tech in coding mentioned it might be a qubit system, but the other analysts disagree."

"A what?"

"A qubit quantum computer would be the holy grail for cryptography. It would use a qubit code, not a binary code. In theory, it could be very fast, faster than anything we have, but no one has produced one that works."

"Who's this tech?"

"Her name is Laurent. She's the new French woman."

"A French woman—here?"

"Yes, and I hear good things about her."

"I want her in my office tomorrow morning. You too. I want her to brief me on what she knows about these signals."

Upstairs in her office, she researched the quantum computer system Price had mentioned. Everything she read showed it was still experimental. Getting her hands on something like this would be a godsend to her stagnating career.

It had been quiet since the last presidential election, too quiet. She had moved up the chain and into the deputy's office quicker than most, thanks to the last president, but this new guy was not having anything to do with the appearance of workplace diversity.

The director had hinted at his retirement several times recently, and there were no rumors of his replacement, something she had not failed to notice. She wanted that office and the view from his window. *They will not screw me over!* She needed something, anything to grab this president's attention.

Desperate, she had thought of placing something compromising on the director's computer. She had his password, but it was risky. As good as she was with coding, somebody with far more skill might trace it back to her.

She picked up Price's report and went over it again. *Useless.* She slammed it down on her desk.

"Fucking Price," she said pacing, then sat in her chair staring out the window. "He purposely downplayed this. He wants my seat and I'm going to make him pay."

Opening the top drawer of her desk, she found the old scratched and dented Altoids tin and opened it. A dozen sticky mints, some with gray spots on them, were mixed in with several pills including a few ten-year-old antidepressants. She took one Xanax and chased it with a Diet Coke, then dimmed the lights and put her feet up on the desk. "That bastard," she whispered. She fished another Xanax out of the tin and swallowed it too, hoping the expired drug would ease the tension she felt clawing its way up her spine.

Price! How long had she known the man anyway? Maybe this was something else. "I've never trusted him," she whispered. Who else has he told and who is this Laurent woman? "A fucking foreigner—here in the NSA!"

She slammed her palm on the desk and scrolled through her phone's contacts until she found Special Agent Denning's number and called him. Denning had done internal research for her several times and she trusted him with the most sensitive of cases.

"Denning," she heard on the phone.

"Jack, I need a personal favor."

"Yes, ma'am, how can I help you?"

Cringing at the word ma'am, she bit her tongue and let the insult slide. "I'm worried about two of my people on the fourth floor, analysts working on a project out of New Mexico. I want you to pull their files, check them out, bank accounts, phone and credit card accounts, et cetera. I think they are dirty."

"I'll get right on it. Anything else?"

"Yes, be very discreet. Nothing in writing and report only to me."

She reached for her keyboard and heard, *Maybe they're testing you again, Marjory.*

Her fingers froze inches off the keys. She looked around the room, hoping someone was sitting in the chair behind her. But she knew better.

Maybe she's not really French but just speaks French, the voice said.

It was happening again, the voice she hadn't heard since high school.

Rising from her desk, she stood, went to the window and looked out toward the Patapsco River. She couldn't see the river, she was hundreds of miles away, sitting in her father's office with her mother beside her. She had been sent home from school again, an argument with a teacher this time. She could still feel her mother's hand on her shoulder, so soft and warm.

"It's schizophrenia, Marjory," her father said. She had never heard the word before, but she could see the tears in her mother's eyes. "It's a mild case, and we can treat it right here at home. No one needs to know."

And so it began: several types of drugs, some making her weak and tired, some leaving her with the shakes and insomnia. On the bad days, Thorazine helped, and she would miss a day or two of school. It was the tapes that worked best—tapes her father made as he read her favorite story, *Alice's Adventures in Wonderland,* written by Charles Dodgson under the name Lewis Carroll.

Her father had served in the VA clinic in Trenton, New Jersey as a psychiatrist since returning from Korea. He knew the stigma associated with mental illness and did all he could to protect his only child from it. There were no reports to her school, or anyone else for her entire life. She had learned to cope with the illness and hid it from everyone.

Her first proper job after graduating from Princeton was working in a field office of the Bureau of Alcohol, Tobacco, and Firearms. The drug tests never worried her, but the battery of psychological tests were terrifying. Every advancement required new tests, new interviews, and before each she spent hours listening to her father's voice.

Now she was the Deputy Director of the National Security Agency, and hopefully there would be no more testing.

She had carried the cassette tapes with her for years until she transferred them to digital. Now they were on her phone, a constant trusted companion. It had been more than a year since she had last listened to them. Just knowing they were close had been enough to keep her grounded, and the voice silent.

But there it was. Not the worst it had been, but the voice was back. If she wasn't careful, paranoia and hallucinations would come next.

Opening the Altoids tin again, she pushed the pills and the moldy mints around until she found what she was looking for: six orange tablets mixed in with the mints, as were several dozen other pills she couldn't name.

Thorazine. The orange pills were the antipsychotic her father had prescribed. *Just how old are they? Twenty years?* She took one and swallowed it, put on her headphones, started the recording, and closed her eyes, picturing the black-and-white illustrations. For the next hour, she was Alice, and she was in Wonderland.

Alice was getting very tired of sitting by her sister …

Chapter 24
Six

Santa Fe

Sandy Walker arrived at Eric Ridge's office at ten o'clock dressed in his dark blue, pinstriped suit with a white shirt and red tie. Wanting every advantage he could get, he wore the telemetry suit as a precaution. If he wasn't sure he could trust the attorney, he would walk out and find another.

The attorney's office was a modest two-story, red brick building that shared a parking lot with a realtor. Both were running separate Wi-Fis, and as he walked in, he scanned the attorney's hard drive and his recent search history.

A man in his mid-twenties greeted him at the entrance.

"Mr. Walker?"

"Yes, I am."

"Mr. Ridge is expecting you. Go right up."

The staircase curved ninety degrees and ended in a small landing that served as a waiting area. He found the attorney standing in the open doorway of his office.

"Mr. Walker, it's nice to meet you. Come in and have a seat."

Ridge was a short, powerfully built man with black hair over his ears and a goatee. His eyes were a light gray that matched the gray hair on his temples.

"This was rather abrupt, Mr. Walker. I seldom see anyone without an appointment. What can I do for you?"

"I have designed a computer processor. I want to market it, but I don't know how. All I do know is that I will need a skilled attorney."

"Well, you will need to apply for a patent. You will want to file for it under your business's name for tax purposes; I have some experience with patents so yes, I can help you. Have you created a business, an LLC maybe?"

"I am just Sandy Walker, Mr. Ridge. We will need to start from there."

Eric Ridge scribbled on a legal pad, only stopping to ask questions, and then he hit the first snag.

"What is your social security number, Mr. Walker?"

"Please call me Sandy. I don't recall the number. I was in an accident last week and lost most of my personal information. Can you give me a day or two to look for it?"

"Of course, and in the meantime, I'll be drawing up the paperwork for the patent application. Once it's filed, your processor will be protected. Show me what you have, detailed schematics perhaps."

"I have it all on this USB device," he said, handing it to the attorney.

"I would like to meet with someone at Motorola as early as Thursday, if that's convenient and I would like you to be with me."

"Thursday? That's not possible. You're talking about their office in Chicago? It will take me a week to get the paperwork ready, and I don't have any idea of what this processor is even worth. I want to be honest with you, Mr. Walker. I can handle the patent and the LLC—I do that every day—but I've never negotiated with a corporation as large as Motorola. I'll be dealing with an entire team of attorneys with much more experience than I have."

"Then this will be a first for both of us."

"I appreciate your confidence, Sandy, but meeting Motorola in three days is just not possible. I would need at least a week to prepare a simple contract."

"Friday then?"

The attorney, frustrated, pushed himself away from the desk.

"Sandy, do you have any idea how much research and preparation goes into something like this? I'm serious. It would take me a week to sell a concrete block to city hall."

"Mr. Ridge, I do not intend for there to be a lot of negotiation. It will be a take-it-or-leave-it transaction."

"I'll try for Thursday. That is, of course, if they can meet with us that soon. So Sandy, what kind of numbers are we looking at here? They will open with an offer, what is the minimum figure you'll accept?"

"I have done the research, Mr. Ridge. The current top-of-the-line processor retails for about one thousand dollars. My processor will power everything from home computers to cell phones and cars. It is one step above the processor they are designing right now, and it will take them a year to get that one on the market. They should be able to produce mine in half that time and once they see its potential, I believe they will accept whatever we ask. I think five million to sign, with another ten million once a prototype is finished, and after that, a percentage of their sales."

"Jesus!" The attorney's face paled. He pulled out a legal pad and scribbled notes.

"I've done the math, it is a reasonable amount. Do you think I'm wrong?"

"Mr. Walker. I have no expertise in computers, and to be honest, I should refer you to someone who does."

"I am confident in you."

"I can see that. Okay, back to your LLC; what do you want to call this corporation, Mr. Walker?"

He had agonized over this for days. Would he be rewriting his own history? Would he have the time to accomplish anything meaningful?

"I wish to call it Trans-Data. And is it possible to withhold my name? I would like this transaction to remain anonymous, if possible."

"No, I'm sorry, your name will be public record for the LLC.

It's the law. But I can make it difficult to find. Anyone doing a deep-dive into Trans-Data, however, will find your name."

"I understand, and I wish to approach Motorola the same way. Is that possible?"

The attorney looked at him for a moment before answering. "Is there anything you're not telling me, Mr. Walker?

Chapter 25
Iran

Natanz

Darioush Amiri was up early, humming a song and organizing the notes on his laptop from the previous day. Security at Natanz had installed an American antivirus program on the laptop, so the twenty one year old programmer thought nothing of connecting it to his apartment's internet system.

He was meeting with Director Aram Engeta at noon to discuss the completed warheads in the bunker in Tehran and the remaining six lacking their uranium cores. Engeta was a dreadful little man, and Darioush's nerves were already on edge.

He was almost finished with his notes when the song stopped. It started and froze a second time and then played normally.

The laptop was a Chinese copy of a Dell Inspiron and had been running slow the last several days as the hard drive neared full capacity. Today, if his meeting with Engeta went well, he would ask the director for an upgrade.

Darioush was the youngest programmer working on the software codes, something his mother bragged about at the dinner table each night.

"Mother, you shouldn't talk about my work even here at home. I told you what happened to Bardia's father. You never know who could be listening."

Three days earlier, two intelligence officers searched his fellow programmer's apartment and the man's father was taken away for questioning.

"Darioush, Bardia's family comes from the hills, all of them are untrustworthy. Never forget that."

Still, his mother crowed whenever she had the chance. He graduated first in his class at the University of Tehran and completed his master's degree at the Massachusetts Institute of Technology. Two weeks later, the Iranian Minister of Intelligence recruited him for the top-secret program.

He finished his tea, unplugged the laptop and left the apartment for his twenty-minute drive to work.

Traffic was light in downtown Natanz, the air was still cool and he drove his 2010 Tiba sedan with the windows down. He considered himself lucky as each day the oppressive heat baked his hometown, he was safely deep underground.

He parked inside the gates and walked to the first floor security entrance. Each morning, the security officers rescanned his laptop upon entering the building, it was frustrating, but he had read the reports of the damage done by the Israeli virus and understood the risks. He was third in line this morning and his knees were shaking as he pictured Engeta's dull eyes focusing on his report.

It was his turn. Stepping up to the security counter he handed the guard his laptop.

The guard glanced at him, looked at his ID tag and sneered. None of the guards liked the high paid, young programmers. The man plugged the laptop into the console as a second guard patted him down and led him through a scanner.

"Shoes," the second man said.

Darioush stepped out of his loafers and set them on the counter, a daily indignity he was forced to endure.

As the guard inspected his shoes, the American-Israeli-designed *Stuxnet* virus was downloading into the mainframe. It would remain dormant, disguise its own files, and upload any new data the next time it was connected to an external drive.

After several minutes, a small chime sounded, indicating his laptop was clean.

He retrieved it and walked to the elevator that would take him deep below the surface. Humming a BTK pop song, he waited for the doors to open and stepped out into the bright lights illuminating the concrete corridor.

The cool air smelled of the antiseptics left behind by janitors mopping the floors twice daily. Now the cold penetrated his heavy coat and his nerves began to twitch as he walked the dreaded Blue Line leading him to the administration section and Engeta.

The director was not a friendly man. His predecessor had been executed years earlier, and other senior administrators had been imprisoned for the damage caused by the cyberattack. The loss set the program back several years, and Engeta was determined not to suffer their fate.

He took Darioush's laptop and ran the same virus scan the guard above had run moments before. Both men sat in silence as the scan continued. Darioush had been in this same chair before, and like the last time, he was struggling with anxiety. Sitting cross-legged in front of the director, he clenched his foot with his right hand to keep it still.

Finally, the familiar chime sounded, and Engeta smiled as if Darioush had just entered the room.

"Tell me some good news, Dari."

"Sir, as you know, they transported the first six completed weapons to Tehran several nights ago per Minister Katami's request. The final six are waiting for their nuclear cores and we expect them to be finished within the next few days."

"Yes, yes, I know all this!"

Darioush was sweating despite the cool air-conditioned office. The technicians were shorthanded and months behind schedule and it was no fault of his. One of his partners had complained the delays resulted from interference from The Ministry of Intelligence, and the man was never seen again.

"I want to know about this latest programming, Dari."

Dari turned the laptop towards Engeta, showing him the updated test. "It's a self-diagnostic program. Every seven days, the weapons will upload their status via an encrypted satellite signal to us here. The status of the circuitry, its GPS location, battery strength, and integrity of its core will be checked for deviations. What you're seeing is the status of the first three devices in Tehran. The arming, triggering and failsafe software are already loaded."

"And the special programming for the other three Minister Katami requested?"

"They have the special triggering software, sir. As of this moment, only he has the final sequence that will activate the program and allow their detonation."

"Very well. Proceed at once and keep me informed."

Darioush grabbed his laptop, not wanting to ask about a new one and left as the director picked up his phone. The director had promised to have the final six ready and delivered in the next several days, and he was now back on schedule.

Tehran

One hundred and eighty miles away in the northern outskirts of Tehran, Mahamoud Madine rested his hand on one of three one-thousand-four-hundred-fifty-gallon propane tanks. It felt warm, but the engineers assured him it was safe. These seventeen-foot-long tanks would never hold propane. Inside each white tank was a nuclear warhead containing fifty kilograms of uranium 235. Three other warheads rested in wooden cradles several feet away. His scientist estimated each to yield a twelve to fifteen kiloton explosion, but there was no way to test one. If things went according to plan, the first test would be in Tel Aviv in the next few months.

This warhead … he thought, caressing the seams in the tank. This tank was destined for a longer journey. This one was going to the heart of America.

Mir Katami, Iran's Minister of Intelligence waited for Madine by the staff elevator.

"Sir, everything is in order," Katami said. "Both ships are in place and the crew of the *Andaman Sea* is preparing for departure. Captain Jazayeri is on board and reports he will be ready to sail as soon as the containers arrive."

"Very well, Mir. I want you to begin preparations for the next two. I want them in place when the Jews attack Natanz. That could be as early as next month. A scientist from Natanz will arrive in Paris in a few days. He has orders to defect and his information should set Israel in motion. We must be ready for their strike."

"Yes, sir. I'm preparing another two trucks now."

The minister saluted and said, "Allahu Akbar," as he turned to leave.

"Allahu Akbar, indeed," Mahamoud repeated.

Chapter 26
Six

Santa Fe

There were no government cars at the hotel when he returned. He circled the parking lot twice to be sure and then parked the Explorer near an exit door, avoiding the lobby entrance.

Dropping his suitcase at the foot of the bed, he switched on the TV and hung his new suit in the closet. Two CNN reporters were discussing a rift between the American president and Israel's prime minister.

The newscast reminded him to check the laptop and he found the *Stuxnet* program had uploaded a single entry. It was encrypted and compressed into a single burst that downloaded a few seconds later.

Sitting in the room's leather lounge chair, he studied the three-page file. It was a mix of computer code with a few notes in Persian. He found a free internet program that translated the Persian to English and created a new file. Minutes later he uploaded the file and three of the six Iranian nuclear engineers online downloaded it at the same moment. Once downloaded, his new program allowed him direct satellite access to the mainframe.

Hours later, he was scanning the new data. There was live video and hundreds of hours of archived video from every section of the Natanz facility, production figures, estimated yield figures, and more. Starting with the live video feeds, he found six canisters in an assembly room that appeared to be nuclear warheads, each hardwired into a console behind them.

He tried to find an access into the console, but the console was off-line or not part of the mainframe's system. As he watched, several technicians in white lab coats stopped in front of the camera, blocking his view. Finally, one of them stepped away and he saw they had removed an access panel exposing a keypad. Unable to control the camera, he was left guessing what they were doing and he switched to another camera.

This camera identified itself as "level 3 #11." The first camera had said level four and by switching from feed to feed, it seemed there were four levels: the first two were administrative, and they devoted level three to enriching uranium. Hundreds, maybe as many as five hundred, centrifuges were active, supervised by men wearing full protective suits.

He downloaded as much as he could and used all his flash drives and most of the laptop's hard drive. While it was downloading, he read the archived emails from the administrators.

Twelve hours later, he collapsed on the bed, too exhausted to undress.

Chapter 27
Croft

White Sands

Lack of sleep was affecting his judgment, his and probably the team's as well.

"Lord, let me sleep eight hours," he said and closed his eyes.

He was crouching in the corner of a large white room. Bright lights glared off the glossy tile floor, so bright he had to squint to see.

In the room, there was a small boy strapped face down on a table wearing a white hospital gown open from the neck down. As he watched, a machine with a long arm moved closer, humming as its arm rotated until it was centered above the base of the boy's neck.

Croft could see the young face through a round hole in the table. He was crying and tears dripped and splashed on the tiled floor below. The boy turned and looked at him.

In that moment, Croft was the boy, bound to the table and no longer the observer. He could feel heavy straps binding his wrists. Screaming, he twisted and pulled uselessly at them.

A deep thrumming noise reverberated off the walls, drowning out his screams ... and the room grew colder. He tried to turn, to see the machine but was held fast. Helplessly, he looked through the hole in the table and saw a man kneeling in the corner.

"Help me!"

His ears popped, the thrumming sound quit and the connection with the boy snapped. He was in the corner once more, watching the machine's arm inch closer.

"Echo Six, why are you crying," a metallic voice asked. "There will be no pain, and you will be smarter and stronger than you were before. Don't you want to be strong?"

Croft watched a thin needle slide from the arm of the machine and into the boy's spine. He screamed and arched his back, convulsing in pain.

"It burns!"

"It burns!" Croft screamed, thrashing in sweat soaked sheets.

What the hell!

He sat up, his stomach cramped and the bedroom spun like a carnival ride. He was going to vomit and fell trying to crawl out of the damp sheets. Grabbing the back of his neck, he felt a hot, swollen knot between two vertebrae.

This was real pain, not something he imagined in a dream. He felt bile in his throat again and raced to the bathroom not wanting to puke on the floor.

Kneeling over the toilet, he waited for the cramping to stop and tried to rationalize what was happening. It was a nightmare, a bad one and his body was just reacting physically to the dream. Nothing more than that, he told himself.

Once he was sure he would not vomit again, he stood feeling his strength return. The back of his neck itched, and the knot was still warm and … there was blood on his fingertip.

Cold sweat washed over him again, and he sank back to his knees.

Sweet Jesus, what is happening?

There was no chance of getting back to sleep now. He knew the symptoms of adrenalin and sleep was an impossibility—he also wanted no part of returning to that dream—ever, so he showered and was out the door as the sun peaked over the eastern skyline.

The wind coming off the desert was still cool as he drove through the grounds of the White Sands Missile Range and he hoped he would be the first to arrive.

Today, he was looking forward to getting into the ship's secrets.

He felt they were close, and maybe today was the day they could prove the ship's origins and most importantly, its purpose.

Stephens, Fischer, and Vones were in the parking lot waiting for him.

"Morning, Bob."

"You guys are here early."

"Carol and I flew back in last night. After examining the tissues in the canisters, we found some interesting things. First, it's definitely cerebral matter, but it's highly modified similar to the DNA of the pilot. Second, it's not human, and it's not completely organic." Stephens paused a minute to look at his notes. "It's living tissue but doesn't require blood for nourishment. All it needs is in the fluid we thought of as cerebrospinal fluid. The tissues get the nutrients from it, which regenerates them somehow, maybe like electrolysis. The fluid between the inner and outer hull is very similar to those fluids, but in a gel. There are also very fine, wire-like structures that run throughout the tissues. We first thought they *were* wire, but they are actually strings of nanorobotics, chalcogenides, and carbon nanotubes. They're artificial neurons, Bob!"

"Okay, slow down, Jon. Let's go inside. I need some coffee."

At the table, Carol Vones took over the conversation.

"Each canister is connected to each other and to the ship by a system of these strings. These neurons are important as we believe they allow the core and probably the pilot to control the ship and its electronics mentally. Caltech is experimenting with that idea and so far has provided quadriplegics with the ability to manipulate simple items within their environment."

"The composition of these strings is also important," Stephens added.

Croft could see the man was excited. He was pacing around the room like a professor teaching a seminar.

"Our computer systems use a binary code of zeros and ones because our processors work with switches that are open or closed or on or off. The chalcogenides allow a variable switch called phase-change memory: instead of ones and zeros, the variables are unlimited."

"The cerebral tissues transmit the power and data throughout the ship along these strings. And I should add, chalcogenides can store memory." Stephens sat, took a deep breath and pushed his notepad to the center of the table.

Croft asked, "Could the pilot use this same technology to hack a computer in an ATM—mentally?"

"Yesterday I would have said no, but this morning, I think it's possible."

"Sir," Carol said, "once we're sure of how the energy is transmitted around the ship, I think we should bring in an energy source of our own and basically hot-wire it."

"Would we risk damaging it?"

"Hopefully we will know more about it before we try anything."

"When?" Croft asked.

"I have a lot to look at before I'm sure."

Croft thought for a minute. "Let's look into that. I want to know what the risks are first though."

He rubbed the back of his neck again. It itched now and the swelling was worse. It felt like a wasp had stung him.

Maybe something bit me, and the dream was a reaction to it?

Chapter 28
Six

Santa Fe

He woke up in his hotel room and like Robert Croft he was breathing hard. Drenched in sweat, he shivered in the cold air. It was an old dream; one he had learned to live with.

Tonight though, it was different. A strange man was hiding in the corner. He wanted to call out to him, but couldn't speak. As he watched, the man's face changed into that of the boy he had seen before, then the machine came to life. The humming grew louder, vibrating the table as the needle moved closer, and it ended as it always did, with him screaming.

It was hours before dawn, but he was wide awake. He got out of the soaked sheets and started the small coffee maker, then checked the *Stuxnet* program. There was nothing new, so he sat in the chair, drank the coffee and thought about the White Room.

Will I ever be rid of this dream?

His parents told him that one day, he and his new friends would go into space and he would need special skills to survive. He was eight when they dropped him off at the institute, and he never saw them again. Two years later, the technicians took him to the White Room. That day was the first of many and he remembered them all clearly, the way he could remember every day of his life.

But who was that man?

Soon he would take his first flight in a twenty-first century aircraft, an event that both exhilarated and terrified him. There were no alternatives to the flight, and he put the thought out of his mind and slept in the recliner until the beacon woke him again.

As the shaft of sunlight began its daily march across the wall, he felt a cell phone signal pass as someone walked down the hallway. Seconds later, a door slammed and the signal ended.

This was the second time in two days he had felt a signal without wearing the suit. The beacon was one thing—it was calibrated to interact with the data nodes in his back—but a cell phone signal was different.

The telemetry suit was draped across a chair on the far side of the room. He sent a command to the television, but it remained dark. The remote control used infra-red light but the electronic receiver in the television refused to switch it on.

Resting his hand on the laptop's screen, it booted up and loaded the latest Stuxnet file. Now he watched in horror as a man thousands of miles away programed a nuclear bomb.

He watched for hours until his legs cramped and the shaft of light had completed its trek across the room. He still had much to do, but he needed to eat, to get out of the room and walk.

It was a pleasant temperature as he strolled along the street outside the hotel. He glanced into the different shops, admiring art in one, antique furniture in another and listening to conversations all around him, some through cell phone signals and others just from people close enough to hear. Cell signals were stronger now and without meaning to, he locked onto a Wi-Fi from the AT&T store in front of him.

Are they stronger because I'm changing?

He remembered one technician telling him the system can adapt. It is possible, he thought. I have never gone such long periods without wearing the suit, and now that it is damaged, maybe my body is compensating for it.

He stood in front of Las Delicious Café. Crisscrossed US and

Cuban flags were painted above the door and under that, "The best Cuban-American food north of Havana."

Cuban-American food. He had never tried any Spanish cuisine, so he walked in and found an open stool at the counter. Ordered a *media noche*, a midnight sandwich, and a cold beer and watched a soccer game between Mexico and Venezuela.

Soccer and baseball were still big sports in his time, and he enjoyed the game, even cheering along with the other customers when Mexico scored. He ate the sandwich, savoring the hot ham and Swiss cheese and ordered a second beer. It was dark when he stepped outside.

He stood in the shadows across from the hotel and looked for signs of the military. Looking up, he picked out his room and saw the lights were off as he had left them. There were several cars near his Explorer, but none looked unusual and all the transmissions around him were routine. He felt safe standing in the dark, but he had much to do and walked across the street and into the lobby.

On his laptop, a technician with his back to the camera stood next to one of the warheads. The access panel was open and a cable connected it to a port on the wall behind it. A few more hours of this and I will sleep he thought, but before I do I want to hear Susan's voice.

He called her knowing she was flying and that her phone would be off. He just wanted to hear her voice again.

"Hello, Susan, I have business in Chicago on Thursday, and I would like you to join me if you can."

Ending the call, he closed his eyes and slept.

The sounds of early morning traffic woke him; cars honking, a siren in the distance, a truck backing up in the parking lot. The ray of sunlight finally appeared on the wall and he knew it was almost seven o'clock, then the beacon transmitted, right on time. It was a growing frustration and he had to shut it down. Every previous attempt to contact it without the suit had failed, but he reached out to it anyway and—felt the signal lock on.

He sat up, listening to its command tone as it waited for his next response. He requested it play back the last hour of flight as a test, and the telemetry scrolled across his vision.

He stood at the window and looked down into the parking lot until he found the Explorer, and with a thought, he unlocked it and saw its lights flash. He did the same to a pickup truck farther out and then saw the traffic signal control box across the street. It was a simple system, and he cycled through several light changes until two cars nearly collided.

Turning his attention back to the beacon, he put it on standby and noticed how just in the last few minutes, its signal had improved—far from perfect, but any signal at all without the suit was an improvement.

Chapter 29
Hicks

Marjory Hicks sat across from Price and Renée Laurent while the young French woman squirmed, tapping her black suede loafers on the floor. Twenty minutes earlier, Marjory had taken her second dose of Thorazine of the morning and was feeling comfortably lightheaded.

"Relax, Ms. Laurent. I want you to tell me why you believe this transmission is so difficult to decode. I have some experience with computer languages, so spare me the history lessons."

The analyst looked anything but relaxed and started to stand.

"Sit down. This is not an inquisition, I just want an informal report."

"Yes, ma'am, I—I'm sorry. I did my doctorate at MIT on Theory of Computation and, more specifically on Quantum Computing. I studied all the old attempts at replacing binary codes or trinary codes. All those attempts failed as far as improving computational speeds. A quantum computer would use any variable of numbers instead of just zeros and ones. One of the qubit codes I saw resembled the signal Mr. Price asked us to investigate. It's more complex, but I think it came from a working quantum computer."

She took a deep breath and continued. "This image is a binary communication code, and this is the image of what we picked up from the satellite over Texas."

Hicks studied the two images. In the first one, she saw the cascading zeros and ones, but the second looked more like a Rorschach inkblot test. She nodded, not wanting to appear ignorant to this low-level analyst.

"Who has a working quantum computer?"

"No one. There are a few small models that simulate one, but none that can operate a complex code."

"Someone has one, Ms. Laurent!" She jumped out of the chair, startling both Price and Laurent. She went to the window and looked out at Maryland. She was seething and didn't want them to see it as a weakness.

Be careful now, she heard.

She spun back around to face Price. "What did you say?"

As the words came from her mouth, she knew it was a mistake. It was the voice, not Price. Both looked at each other, and she knew what they were thinking.

"We … I didn't say anything," Price said.

Be careful now, the voice repeated. It had been so loud. How did they not hear it? She needed to be alone. She needed to end this quickly before it got worse.

"I apologize; I'm not accusing you of incompetency, but something is generating this signal and it's over Texas right now!" She sat down and felt the heat on her face cooling. Hopefully she didn't look as out of control as she felt.

"Ms. Laurent, get back to me if you find anything new. You too," she said to Price and then rose, expecting them to take the hint.

"There's more," Price said.

"What?" Hicks screamed.

Laurent sank further into her chair.

"Something or someone communicated with it this morning," Price said.

Chapter 30
Iran

The two Fuso Super Great transports and their escort were cruising comfortably at eighty kilometers per hour when the escort in front braked hard. Mohamed Hadid cursed and hit his own brakes. He prayed his brother in the big Fuso behind him was paying attention; it would be the end of them both if they damaged their cargo. He watched in the mirror as Syed slowed. Another thirty kilometers and they would all refuel in Maku, and he would be rid of the cursed escort.

Crossing into Turkey was uneventful, just as the intelligence officer said it would be. The Turkish guards looked at the Bayegan logo on the trucks' sides and waved them through.

Six hours later and full of fuel, the two trucks passed through Hassa, then headed southwest toward the Kasab crossing. This would be the risky part his leader had explained. Bribes had been paid, but there were no guarantees. Corruption was rampant, but it was still safer than the direct route through rebel-held Aleppo. The remnants of ISIS and al-Qaeda still held much of northern Syria, and they were indifferent to anyone besides other Sunni.

As he approached the crossing, he slowed, allowing two smaller trucks to pass in front of him, then followed them through the gates, hoping the smaller trucks would hold the attention of the guards. At the last moment, just as he accelerated, two Syrian guards stepped out onto the road and waved him into a holding area. Syed followed him.

He set the brakes and reached under the seat for his silenced Makarov 9mm. With the pistol inside his jacket, he stepped out with his cargo manifest in his hand.

"Good day, my friend. Allah is good," Mohamed said to the senior guard and unlocked the cargo doors. The man ignored him, pulled himself up into the container, and inspected the two big propane tanks resting in their wooden cradles. The guard tapped on the first tank with the butt of his Kalashnikov rifle, listening to the tone, then he lifted the hood off the valve assembly. He seemed satisfied and moved to the next one. He tapped the outside again, then he moved all the way to the front of the container and looked underneath it with a flashlight. He jumped down and let Mohamed secure the container with the padlock, and they both moved to the second truck.

Mohamed took the key out of the manifest envelope, unlocked the padlock, and handed the manifest to the senior guard. The guard, a young sergeant, read over the documentation and handed it back as the other jumped up into the container and repeated the inspection. He tapped once on the first tank and they all heard the hollow sound. The guard moved deeper into the shadows and Mohamed tightened his hold on the plastic grips of the Makarov as the guard tapped on the last tank. The guard turned and started back toward the group but stopped as he realized the sound was different.

The sergeant heard it too and stepped forward. Mohamed's silenced Makarov popped and the guard in the container fell to his knees. His second shot hit the sergeant in the forehead.

"Help me get this one inside!"

Mohamed had the guard under the arms and his brother helped lift him up and drag him inside.

"Check that one. This one is dead."

Mohamed jumped out and picked up his two empty shell casings. There were a few drops of blood where the sergeant had fallen.

With his boot heel, he ground them into the sand. There was blood on the sleeve of his jacket too. Stripping it off, he threw it inside the container with the dead guards.

The two trucks had blocked any chance that the inspection had been seen from the border station, and Mohamed couldn't see anyone else. With luck, maybe these were the only two on duty. Eventually someone would come to relieve them though, and he wanted to be far away when that happened.

"Let's go. Another two hours and we'll stop in Tartus; we can dump them there."

Chapter 31
Six

Chicago

Six stared out the window of the Boeing 777 as it sped across Missouri. At thirty-three thousand feet, he could see most of the terrain was undeveloped; a few farms and an occasional town made up most of the landscape.

In his time, there was little undeveloped land as agriculture and overpopulation competed for every acre. The human race had explored all the planets in the solar system and even tried to establish colonies on the moon and Mars. All the attempts failed; it was too costly to supply or produce what man needed to survive. Humans had discovered many planets outside the solar system, but none were capable of sustaining life. That had been part of his mission, to discover a habitable planet. Now he was looking down on the Earth with a new goal, and he would not fail again.

Susan sat next to him, her shoulder brushing his as she watched a movie in the seatback. The attorney sat across the aisle in a window seat and appeared to be sleeping. The three of them were the only passengers in business class, but the rest of the plane was full.

He tried to watch the movie with her, but there was so much to see and too many things to experience. The plane was surprisingly quiet in flight, and through his window, he could see one of the massive turbines behind him. Closing his eyes, he relaxed and examined the plane's electronic systems one at a time.

So complex! It would take a great amount of time to learn how to control it without the computers, if it was possible at all.

One of the plane's pilots used a keypad to unlock the cockpit door and disappeared inside, and for a second, Six saw all the dials and levers and shook his head.

The whine of the engines changed and the plane began to decelerate.

"Ladies and gentlemen, this is Captain Muentes. We are beginning our descent into Chicago and should be on the ground at 3:25 local time. It's currently eighty-one degrees with a few light showers in the area."

The landing was smooth, but he realized he had been gripping the seat's armrest when Susan put her hand on his.

"Afraid of flying?"

"It's been a while," he said, feeling his face flush.

An hour later, they were in the lobby of the Wyndham Grand Resort. Eric Ridge had booked three adjoining rooms on the twelfth floor with a view of Lake Michigan.

"I made reservations for dinner at seven-thirty," the attorney said. "The hotel shuttle will pick us up at seven. I have some calls to make, and I'll meet you in the lobby then."

"Sandy, can we have a drink at the bar? I heard someone playing the piano."

"Yes, I love country music."

"Sandy, there is no piano in country music. Well, not much anyway."

Bubba Gump's was crowded, tourists mostly—and it reminded him of a vacation in Louisiana with his parents long ago. He was five years old that day and ate fried shrimp sitting across from his mother.

He picked a shrimp dish off the menu at random and ate as he watched Susan and the attorney sharing childhood stories. She was good with people, extroverted in a positive way, and it reminded him of his own awkwardness.

"What about you, Sandy?" Susan asked. "Tell us something embarrassing about your childhood. You were born in Atlanta, right?"

"Yes, I was. I don't remember much of my youth in Atlanta though. My parents died when I was eight. We were in Paris at the time. I spent most of my childhood in private schools, both in Paris and later again in Atlanta. There's nothing I can remember that was embarrassing."

He tried to read the look on her face. She had wanted something from this question, wanted him to talk about his past and he saw disappointment in her eyes. But he was afraid he would say something he couldn't explain, and he had promised himself he wouldn't lie to her again.

The attorney must have felt it as well, he pushed his chair back and stood.

"Susan, Sandy, I'm going to leave you two alone and head back to the hotel. I've got a lot to prepare for. We'll meet back in the lobby tomorrow morning about eight thirty. Does that sound okay?"

"We will see you then."

Alone now, he said, "Susan, I want you to sit in on this meeting tomorrow."

"What? Sandy, I have two semesters of law school and I clerked at a firm for sixteen months, and you want me to help you negotiate a contract with Motorola? Is Eric okay with this?"

"Eric will handle the negotiations and he did not object so I assume he is."

"Well, okay then."

They spoke quietly at the table for the next several hours. He talked about his mother and father, telling her what he could and listened as she described her parents and growing up in Savannah.

"We should go," she said eventually, and it was near midnight when they got back to the hotel.

He looked through the window at Lake Michigan while thinking of Susan and dinner.

Saying good night had been awkward. A quick embrace and another simple kiss. "Should I have said more?" he asked the silent sailboats rocking at the dock below.

The bed was comfortable and he was tired. But the thoughts in his head begged to be heard. Wide awake, he linked to the Wi-Fi.

She said she was on a list of applicants for both American and Delta Airlines, but hadn't heard from either of them. He found her on both lists. The lists were long, and at their current hiring schedule, it would be another six months before her name came up for an interview. He moved her up to the top of the list with both airlines, giving her the option to choose one over the other.

Were there consequences to this?

It was a moral dilemma, like taking the angry man's money. Moving her up on the two lists meant moving someone else down. His actions would affect other people's lives in ways he would never know.

But I don't know those people!

Opening the curtains, he looked out onto the massive lake and wished he could open the window and let the breeze pull at the guilt he was feeling. Susan was a good woman and she deserved a break and yet—it could change everything.

He pushed at the glass. He needed to smell the air, to hear the sounds, but all he had was what he could see, black water merging with the night sky, only a few stars differentiating the two. Looking up, the constellation Orion and its massive star Betelgeuse watched over him.

As he watched Orion, a Chinese SuperView-1 Earth observation satellite floated three hundred miles above him. Through its cameras, he could see the states of Illinois, Iowa, and Nebraska slowly passing through its field of view. He tried to access its computer, but the signal faded and then disappeared. There were others up there too. He could sense them, but they were too far away or their signals too weak to link with.

Fascinating! Days earlier he couldn't change the channel on the television without the remote, and now he could access a satellite in space without the suit.

The thought of space brought him back to the present. Out of curiosity, he accessed First United Bank's executive mainframe to see if there was anything new with losing money from their ATM. He sorted through emails and interoffice memos until he found an email from the bank's chief security officer detailing a meeting with Major Tristan Flórez.

The Army's military police server used a different type of firewall and security program, and after some trial-and-error attempts and several hours, he accessed Major Flórez's reports to a man named Colonel Robert Croft.

Flórez had searched Tommy's Garage, found his flight suit, and tested the blood on the sleeve. They had also discovered a missing mechanic's uniform with "Sandy" embroidered on the chest pocket, and an employee from Edna's Waffle House had given them his description.

The last entry detailed his visits to the Saguaro Inn and the Hillcrest Urgent Care clinic and his plans to follow up on a clinic employee named Annie Lavelle.

Major Flórez could be waiting for me at the airport when I return!

His dream of starting Trans-Data was collapsing and the military was too close already. Annie will know enough and this army officer will seize him, maybe even tonight unless ...

He deleted his New Mexico driver's license and had a new California license mailed to Eric Ridge's office. There were several hundred Sandy Walkers in Southern California alone, which should at least slow Flórez down. Thinking of the attorney, he needed a social security number and soon. This proved more difficult than he had hoped, but by midnight Sandy Walker, who lived in Irvine, California had a social security number.

The Saguaro Inn had no recorded history of him and he had already deleted his records at the urgent care center. They would remember him, but little else. Now the major had Annie, and soon he will have Susan too.

"I'll have to tell her the truth in the next few days."

All his money was still in his account at First United Bank. The balance accurate, but the account itself was flagged. There was a file attached to it with an added level of encryption he couldn't crack.

He was able to transfer his money out though and into a bank in Los Angeles using his father's name. He deleted the old account including the transfer, but the encrypted file remained.

It frustrated him. Pacing in the small room, he thought of the things in the file, "Why can't I delete it?"

"It is what it is," he said, then searched for everything he could find on Major Flórez. There wasn't much—yearly evaluations, promotions, and a few commendations—so he switched to Croft. There was a lot more information on Croft, and he sat back and read. Croft had graduated from West Point in the top ten percent of his class and had been in the Army over thirty years. He was considered an exemplary officer by his superiors and now commanded a special operations unit at the White Sands Missile Range.

There were several photos of Croft in the file, and the man looked familiar. He looked a lot like the man in his last dream, but younger. He walked back to the window.

"I've seen this man!"

In the window's reflection, he remembered. It wasn't the dream, it was a photo he had seen many years ago. As a cadet at the North American Institute of Science, his class had visited the Trans-Data headquarters in Atlanta. During the tour, there was a large photo of the original headquarters, and on the front steps were the founding members of what would become one of the greatest technology corporations ever.

On those steps, Robert Croft was visible in the front row. There were six others gathered around him, two women and four men, He looked closely at the women, one of them he had never seen before he was sure, and the last one's face was obscured. Her blonde hair covered her eyes, and in the sunlight, there was a tinge of red in her hair.

He tried comparing what he could see of the woman's face to Susan's and even thought of the woman in his dreams, but either his memory of the picture was poor or the photo itself lacked the resolution. There were names under the photos too, but he had never read them and in his mind they refused to focus.

How was it possible that Robert Croft would become a founding member of Trans-Data, a company that should not exist yet? Naming his corporation Trans-Data had been nothing more than an impulse. The thought of jumpstarting Trans-Data had occurred to him, but it was just that, a whim.

The most recent entry into Croft's file was a request for a security clearance for Carol Vones. *Vones!* He had heard the name several times at the Institute. A woman named Vones had made the genetic breakthrough that eventually led to the engineering of a cerebral core, the core that allowed faster-than-light travel.

Could it be the same woman? Have I already changed the future?

Carol Vones was now studying his ship, and that would lead to her discovery. The implications were significant.

Has my ship always been the source of her discovery? That would mean I have been here before. Would that explain the dreams and feelings of déjà vu?

He could wipe out Trans-Data right now with a few keystrokes and few people would ever know. But Croft and Vones were different. These were major changes in the time line, a paradox with rippling effects.

The possibilities made him sick—sick with fear and sick with choices he still had to make. But doing nothing now eventually led to what he knew was already happening. He had seen the weapons, and he had read their plans.

Sunlight came through the blackout curtains, another sleepless night.

Chapter 32
Croft

White Sands

Croft stepped into the hangar and found Carol Vones already inside the ship.

"Good morning, Carol."

"Good morning. I've traced four strands of cable-like structures that lead away from the two supports. Two of them appear to be grounded to the ship's floor and the other two lead toward the ship's cortex. I'm ready to run a small amount of voltage through them to see if we can get the display in front of the seat to activate."

Croft heard Fischer and Stephens come in, and Carol briefed them on the plan.

"Any chance we can damage the systems with the wrong voltage or amperage?" Fischer asked.

"I'm really not sure. I've run several different continuity checks on the cables and they seem to be complete circuits, but to be on the safe side, I'm going to start with one hundred millivolts."

"Okay. Let's try it."

The four of them crowded inside the ship as Carol kneeled in front of the seat. She had a small power supply on the floor, and two thin wires were hooked to each of the vertical supports.

"Jon, can you bring the camera in here?" Croft said.

Stephens stepped next to her with the GoPro camera on a tripod. "Okay, we're recording."

"Go ahead, Carol. Let's see what happens."

At first, nothing happened. She increased the voltage, and at five hundred millivolts, a two-foot-by-four-foot holographic rectangle appeared between the supports. In the bottom right corner of the screen, numbers and unrecognizable symbols scrolled faster than they could read them.

"It's booting up!" she shouted.

After a few seconds, the scrolling stopped, and the words "Trans-Data" appeared at the bottom of the screen. The screen then split in half vertically—the left side was dark, but the right side split again horizontally.

No one spoke. At the top right quadrant of the screen, they saw the interior of the hangar, the conference table, the coats hanging on the wall, and the new coffee maker. In the bottom quadrant, they saw themselves looking at the screen. There was a camera somewhere behind the pilot's seat.

Croft reached out to the hologram and touched his image. The view shifted to the right slightly. Touching the exterior image, he panned around the room three hundred sixty degrees until the table came back in view. "It's a touch screen."

They spent a few minutes trying to find the camera projecting the ship's interior without luck. Whenever they shifted the view, the camera angle shifted as well.

"It must not use a camera lens like we expect, a type of electronic sensor maybe," Fischer said, "and it's doing all this with five hundred millivolts. A single D battery could probably run this for," Fischer looked up doing calculations in his head, "roughly a week."

Fischer put his finger through the dark side of the screen. "This side must need the ship's cortex. The right side of the screen is showing the hardwired data. This left side must require an active data source." As he said that, the word "Beacon2" appeared at the top of the left side, and computer code scrolled across the screen. It lasted only a few seconds, then "Canceled" flashed in red.

"Whoa, did you all see that?" Fischer said.

Chapter 33
Six

Motorola

By ten, they were in the Merchandise Mart's elevator on their way up to Motorola's office. Six could feel and taste the anxiety in the small, wood paneled enclosure as they rose floor after floor.

He watched Susan biting her lip, probably wondering why she was miles from home. Eric Ridge stared at the indicator as the numbers announced each floor. He could read the man's emotions and felt that Ridge was up for the challenge.

As the doors of the elevator opened his ship's view-screen activated, superimposed over the long hallway stretching out in front of him. His stomach lurched and he lost his equilibrium and grabbed Susan's arm. Both she and Eric looked like they were leaning forty-five degrees.

"Are you okay, Sandy? You're white as a sheet."

"Just nervous I believe, but I need to use the restroom. Go on, I will meet you in their office in a few minutes."

In the men's room, he splashed cold water on his face and stared at his reflection in the mirror. In his mind, he saw three men and a woman crowded around the view-screen of his ship. The image was weak—not enough voltage and too far away, he assumed—but he could clearly make out each person. One man was wearing a military uniform. A patch above his left pocket said "CROFT."

He was definitely the same man as the one in the picture on the steps of Trans-Data.

Croft looked younger now and as he watched the man speak, the feeling of familiarity was strong, as if they had met once before. It was impossible and he dismissed it. The woman must be Carol Vones, and he saw she too was younger than he expected, but she was not one of the women in the photograph. The other two did not look familiar, but must be the Jon Stephens and Emil Fischer Croft mentioned in his report. It was an eerie feeling watching them. It looked like they were all staring at him, waiting for him to answer their questions.

He saw their lips moving and wished he could hear what they were saying. Then Croft reached out and rotated the view, and again he felt he would fall. Holding the sink for balance, he forced the two images to sync, and he was able to let go, even as Croft rotated the external view again.

His ship was in an enclosed room and seemed intact. He tried to control the view himself, but nothing changed. Then the beacon responded to the ship's signal, and he watched its transmission scroll across the display. He signaled the beacon to stop and saw "Canceled" flash on the view screen.

They were making more progress with the ship than he had expected. Another ripple in time, and a big one. What else will they find?

The beacon's data stream would be meaningless unless they could read its code which was impossible now, but one day soon they might. Attempting to access the ship's functions could be a problem though. The worst-case scenario would be activating the ship's drive field or the auto-recovery system in an enclosed space; the field would crush anyone close to it, and they would not survive.

He splashed more water on his face. *I can't deal with this now!* He stood up, stared at his reflection and walked out.

The Motorola team was waiting for him. A man in a black wool suit and a woman in a similar gray suit sat on one side of a long table. At the far end, two women sat quietly, eyeing him as he sat.

Eric introduced himself, then Sandy, and finally Susan, as Sandy's assistant.

The woman in the suit spoke first.

"Mr. Walker, I'm Sheila Cole, Vice President of Research and these are two of my engineers. When we spoke with your attorney several days ago, he said you had designed a new processor we may be interested in. The simple schematic he sent us is indeed interesting, and so we agreed to meet with you. We are always interested in new technology, but to be honest, we did a background search on you and haven't been able to turn up anything. We are usually aware of most of our competition's personnel. Can you provide us with any references?"

"Ms. Cole, I have worked and studied overseas for most of my life, and I was involved with a small firm that no longer exists. I can assure you that this processor is not a result of technology theft and that it is my own design. I assume that is your main concern."

He pulled the flash drive out of his coat pocket and handed it to one of the women at the far end of the table. "This is the full schematic and the code required to operate it. I have provided a simulator program as well that should prove the design will function as promised."

One technician used her laptop and the two of them conferred for several minutes.

"Another question, Mr. Walker," the vice president said. "Why us and not Intel? They lead the industry in processing chips."

"I think Intel has less to gain, and their offer would reflect that. And another thing, Motorola has been lagging in technology, and I have a vested interest in changing that."

"And what is your interest in Motorola, Mr. Walker?"

He thought about not answering her question, but he had led her to it. "My own future is at stake."

There was an awkward silence as both executives stared at him, even Eric Ridge looked confused.

"I researched both Intel and Motorola before arranging this meeting, and I chose Motorola. It's that simple," he said. That broke the silence and they all turned to the two engineers hovering over the laptop as the simulation ran. Fifteen minutes later, one technician handed the drive to the vice president and nodded.

"As Mr. Walker's attorney, I must advise you that all the data and technology on that drive is protected under a pending patent. Should we take a recess while you confer?"

Once back in the elevator, Six asked, "What did you think, Susan? What were your impressions?"

"Sandy, I don't know what to think, to be honest. They seemed interested, and I got the feeling they would be professional. I would probably trust them, but I don't have the experience for this. A few days ago, I picked up a strange man walking along the road, and now that man is negotiating a contract with Motorola. It's a lot to take in."

"That is why I have asked you to come with me. I trust your judgement."

"Those were my impressions too, Sandy," Ridge added. "I'm sure they will want to study it more before making an offer, but I watched those two engineers. They want it."

Marshall's Landing was the only restaurant in the Merchandise Mart and after a few minutes' wait, they were seated at a small table near the bar.

They had just ordered when Susan's phone rang.

"Oh my God, it's Delta Airlines!"

"Hello?" She stood and walked toward the lobby.

He was overjoyed seeing the excitement in her eyes. She deserved it and much more. Then the thought of her leaving him as she pursued her dream hit home.

"So Sandy, how did you feel it went, is it what you expected?"

"I think it went well. We will know soon enough."

It went exactly as he expected. Somehow, he knew as if it had happened once before in another life. Closing his eyes, the faceless woman in his dreams loomed over him and said, 'Six, I'll see you soon.'

He opened his eyes as Susan came back to the table. As she reached for her wineglass, he looked at her hand hoping to see red polish on her nails.

"I'm going to need another drink," she said. "Delta wants me in Salt Lake City on Wednesday to start training. I can't believe it!"

Susan's fingers were identical, long and slender, but there was no ring and her manicured nails were not red.

Eric Ridge raised his glass and said, "I'm happy for you, Susan. Good things happen to good people."

"I too am happy for you," he said, squeezing her hand.

"I have to fly back tomorrow and make arrangements. I'm so excited! I've been praying for that phone call for so long."

When the negotiations were complete, five million dollars was transferred into a new account Eric had set up for Trans-Data. Another twenty million would be transferred when the prototype was working and performing as promised. The Motorola executives estimated the final figure could easily exceed eight hundred million spread out over a four-year period.

"You should celebrate tonight, Sandy. You and Susan head back to the hotel. I'll be here until late in the evening signing paperwork."

The two of them stepped outside, holding hands like lovers, and he heard the distant thunder of a late afternoon storm. As they walked, the storm seemed miles away. He needed to tell her soon. She needed to know the truth. Her fingers tightened around his as if she knew what he was thinking.

Chapter 34
Lightning

Troy and Jeremiah Findlay were now homeless and broke. Troy had used the last of the rent money weeks ago for ten bags of powdered meth. It lasted two days. Then they slept in the ten-year-old Honda his parents gave Jeremiah for his birthday four months ago—until Troy sold it for scrap. The sale bought another six bags.

Jeremiah watched Troy going through the progression of addiction and withdrawals and knew his older brother was going to die, meth was slowly killing him.

It had been three days since their last fix and they were out of money and options. Jeremiah only used meth now and then, but it was days like this that made him long for the needle.

Troy had been addicted since middle school and now was deep into its destructive phase. It wasn't long ago he'd said, "Tomorrow I'm going to rehab. I'll get off this stuff." Tomorrow never seemed to happen though, and now missing so many of his teeth, it was difficult to understand him—when he was conscious enough to speak.

The two of them were sleeping in an alley behind the Merchandise Mart and eating scraps they found in the dumpster. At least it was food, and thank God it was summer because the cold of a Chicago winter would have killed them both for sure.

Crouching against the alley wall, he looked down at his sleeping brother. Troy was impossibly thin, his skin stretched across his ribs, and angry half-healed sores covered his arms and face. Like most big brothers, Troy had always tried to protect him, but that was years ago and now the rolls had been reversed. Now he had to keep Troy alive.

He was drifting off, then had the feeling something bad was about to happen. He struggled to open his eyes, but his eyelids felt like lead. If he could just open them, everything would be okay.

He heard thunder and Troy's voice. Troy's speech was clear now, so he knew it could only be a dream.

He woke with a start, sitting with his back against the restaurant wall. Troy had been lying in the dirt next to him, but was nowhere to be seen. Then he heard his brother's muffled voice, and Troy was angry.

He got to his feet and had to limp around the big green dumpster. His foot had gone to sleep, and the pins and needles shooting up his calf felt like his skin was on fire.

His brother was standing in front of a well-dressed man and woman. The man stood slightly in front with the woman clutching his arm. She was afraid, and Jeremiah knew why. The man, though, had an unusual look, like he was curious, like he was studying Troy.

"Fi dolla? Is tha all?" Troy said. "I nee more. I hah to fee my bro!"

"Troy, stop!" Jeremiah yelled. But it was too late.

Troy's switchblade snapped open and a glint of chrome flashed in his hand. The man saw it too. Lightning flashed nearby, lighting up the street brighter than the afternoon sun. A crack of thunder followed, and Troy screamed, "Gimmie all o it!"

The first few drops of rain fell, and the man raised his arm straight out like a cop trying to stop traffic—a strange gesture for a man being robbed, he thought—and then the buzzing started.

He had stepped on a yellow jacket nest once, and that was what it sounded like just before they stung. Then the hair on his arm rose. His next and last sensation was his front teeth cracking against the sidewalk as his face hit the cement.

Susan had seen the man first and had squeezed Sandy's hand. She squeezed it so hard she thought she had hurt him and then he saw the man too. She was horrified and unable to speak.

"I nee money to eat," the man said, and then she saw the knife. It was huge. As a second man approached, she felt the hair on her arms and the back of her neck rise, then both men fell. The cracking sound was awful, and she heard someone scream, then realized she was the one screaming.

"Oh my God! What happened?" she finally asked. "Was it lightning?"

She watched Sandy reach down and check each man for a pulse.

"I'm not sure, but let's keep moving. They will be okay."

They didn't look okay, she thought. There was a lot of blood coming from the second man's mouth.

Sandy had her hand and was leading her down the sidewalk, away from the alley. She turned to look back, and both men were still lying on the sidewalk, motionless. The small stream of blood was running away from the second man's head. She had heard the crack as his face hit the concrete and knew something had broken.

Rain pelted them in the face, and it was hard to see where they were going. The drops were big enough to hurt, and she saw hail bouncing in the street.

A yellow cab pulled into an Italian restaurant just ahead, and Sandy flagged the driver. Both were soaked by the time the car's door closed.

Sandy called 911 on his phone and waited.

"Chicago Police and Fire," she heard on the speaker.

"There are two injured men in the alley next to the Merchandise Mart," he said and ended the call.

Chapter 35
Susan

Cold, she held him close, shivering. It wasn't warmth she needed.

Leaving a trail of wet footprints through the lobby, they made their way to her room. Her hand shook as she pressed the keycard against the lock and the fabric of her wet blouse trembled.

"Stay with me tonight, I don't want to be alone."

She was frightened. The glint of the knife, the blade threatening Sandy and then the men, boys really, struck down by lightning. *Are they dead?* It didn't feel right to leave them laying on the sidewalk, but she had been so afraid.

They stood just inside the door of her room, their wet clothes dripping on the carpet. Clutching his arm, her fear drained away, like the fear was a living thing and Sandy was ripping it free. Her head spun, she was going to faint—and then he kissed her.

His mouth was open and warm. She pulled away and looked at him. His eyes were the brightest blue. She kissed back, this time harder, and began unbuttoning his shirt, fumbling with the buttons until she saw another layer of odd fabric underneath.

"What's this?" she whispered.

"Just an undershirt.," he said, unzipping it.

Fearless now, she ran her hands over his bare chest, feeling his warmth pulling the cold from her hands.

He tried unbuttoning her blouse. "Not yet.," she said putting his hands on her breasts, her nipples hardening at his touch.

"Let me." She unbuttoned the last few buttons, and the blouse fell to the floor. Her bare skin was warm now, and she watched his face as he looked at her. Her bra was pale blue and transparent, she knew he could see through the sheer lace and it excited her.

She pulled away again, "You have too much on, Mr. Walker."

"I may not be very good at this Susan, it's been a long time."

"I'll let you know."

They made love in the shower twice and may have stayed longer, but they were running out of hot water.

As she sat over him on the bed, it was hard not to look at anything but those eyes. They were an electric blue now, full of an energy she could feel.

"I thought you said you weren't very good at this. I think you lied, sir." She reached down, and he was inside her again. She rocked slowly at first, but soon her rhythm increased. She could feel her nails digging into his shoulders, and she saw the pain excited him. Then her thighs tensed and she bit down on the finger of her free hand afraid she would scream.

She relaxed and collapsed next to him. "You're incredible."

She curled up around him, all her terror and the fears locked away temporarily in some other part of her mind.

Room service brought them dinner, and they both ate in silence.

She picked at her steak and finally pushed the plate away. "Should we call someone and check on them?"

"Who would we call?"

"The police, maybe the hospital?"

"I don't think that's a good idea. They would have questions we can't answer, and what could we say? If you want, I will call and find out tomorrow."

"Please. I can't stop thinking about what happened."

The storm had moved on during the night and dawn's pale light was shining through the open curtain. She watched him sleep. He was warm; she could feel heat coming off his back.

Looking closely at his skin, she saw a small mole just below his shoulder blades in-between two vertebrae. There was also a small black line the thickness of a human hair just under his skin. The line traveled up through the mole and stopped just below his hairline. A scar maybe? How had she not noticed that before? As she thought about it, he rolled over and opened his eyes.

"Good morning, handsome."

"Good morning!"

"I have to get ready. My flight leaves in three hours."

"Then we should get dressed," he said.

She slipped out of bed and started to wrap the sheet around her. Then dropped it and asked, "Do we have time for another shower?"

Chapter 36
Croft

The clock on the nightstand announced another night wasted. Cursing the hour, he sat up in the darkness.

The day's events inside the ship looped continuously like a bad movie. He was missing something. Something important was right on the edge of his mind—just out of reach. Was it something he had seen on the ship's view-screen, a feeling, or was it the dream?

Unlike most of his dreams, the one with the boy on the table was still vivid. He could not remember ever dreaming of the boy or the white room, and yet it seemed familiar. His finger found the tender spot on his neck.

"Damn you! I'm losing my mind!"

Over the last few years when things had been rough, he could close his eyes and think of the better times, even dream of Sara when she was alive and life was good. It had always helped him sleep. But tonight ... *if I close my eyes again, I'll be back in that dammed white room.* His eyes burned even in the darkness. He closed them, just for a second ... and he was in a huge park.

It was Hyde Park in London. His new bride was humming a song and the birds were singing in harmony as they walked on a concrete path between magnificent oak trees.

Sara turned and held out her hand. No, he begged, this is where the dream always ends. But tonight, it didn't end.

He reached out touching her hand. Her fingers were warm and soft as they curled around his. She looked up at him, her eyes the soft caramel brown he remembered—and she spoke. "Find him, he needs your help!

"Find who, Sara?"

He jerked himself awake and saw he had slept three more hours. This dream was like the nightmare; so real, he could still hear the damn birds singing.

"Sweet Caroline, she was humming Sweet Caroline."

"Emil, I hope I didn't wake you."

"No, I'm up. I was just getting ready to head to the base. What's going on?"

"I'm not sure. I feel like we're missing something. Have you had any strange dreams recently?"

"No, none that I remember. Why?"

"Probably nothing. I'll talk to you about it when I get in. I'll be there soon."

Chapter 37
Flórez

Tristan Flórez walked into the Hillcrest Urgent Care and recognized Annie Lavelle from her driver's license photo.

"Can I help you?" she asked.

"I'm Major Flórez, and I'm hoping you can. I'm looking for Sandy Walker, he was treated here last Wednesday. He had a wound on his left upper arm. I spoke with Doctor Snyder while you were out of town. She couldn't tell me much about him, patient confidentiality she said. Do you remember him?"

"I do, but I can't talk about him either, is he in trouble?"

"Not really. The Army would like to ask him a few questions about an incident outside Portales. It's probably related to his injury. Do you expect to see him again?"

"No, I don't. I had never seen him before. He paid cash, and I haven't seen him since."

"Well, here's my card, Ms. Lavelle. Please call me if you see him again. Or have him call me, if he can."

"I will, Major."

As he walked through the clinic's small parking lot, he made a phone call.

"Hey, it's Flórez. I need a favor. I need phone records for an Annie Lavelle, lives in Clovis. Go back to the ninth of June, and I need any calls she makes today as well."

Annie Lavelle knew more than she was willing to tell.

Chapter 38
Hicks

Marjory Hicks was sitting at her desk with her eyes closed. She had wiped her desk clean of all its distractions. Even her office phone was on the floor and it was off the hook. An hour earlier, she had taken her last Thorazine tablet and was already feeling drowsy.

Pressing her palms down on the wooden surface of her desk, she imagined she was sitting behind the director's desk, looking through his window at the view of downtown Maryland.

It was "The View," as upper management called it. It wasn't much different from the view out her window four stories below, but the power of being the one behind the glass was unimaginable.

As a child, she believed if she wished for something hard enough, with every ounce of her mind, she could force her imaginations into reality. She just needed to press harder, to clear her mind of every thought except those dealing with her goal: to be the first female director of the National Security Agency.

Her forearms shook and her wrist ached, but she continued the pressure. *Just a few more minutes.*

Her cell phone vibrated inside her desk drawer.

"Damn it!" she screamed. "I was almost there!"

She listened to the phone vibrating, resisting the urge to open her window and throw the device to the street below. She visualized the morning traffic crushing it into shards of glass and twisted metal. The image brought her back to the phone, still buzzing in the drawer. It was the director's office calling.

Could it have worked? Is this the call I've been waiting for?

"Hicks," she said.

"Ms. Hicks," the assistant said, "the director has been trying to reach you. He would like you in his office right away."

"I'll be right up. Thank you."

She looked at her watch and realized she had been meditating for an hour and forty minutes with her door locked. Now she could feel her heart pounding in her chest, and the pulse throbbing in the veins of her neck.

Calm down, Marjory. You can deal with the director. He is nothing to you.

Putting the phone back on her desk, she replaced the handset and checked herself in the mirror. Her dark red hair was pulled tight in a bun, but several strands had come loose and were on her left shoulder. She took five long minutes to get them under control and then she was ready to ride the elevator to the top floor.

"Ms. Hicks," the director said. "Is everything okay?"

"Yes, sir. Is there something I should know about?"

"Well, for starters, I've been trying to get ahold of you for over an hour. Your assistant assured me you were in your office, but you were not answering my calls."

"I'm sorry, sir. I just realized the phone was off the hook. I'm not sure how that happened."

"Marjory, the reason we're having this conversation is your request for the personnel files of two of our people, Price and Laurent. You have also made a request for the files of several officers in the military. Is there something you haven't briefed me on yet?"

He's on to you, Marjory.

She ignored the voice but knew it was true.

"I'm still looking into something happening out in New Mexico, sir. It's probably nothing, but as soon as I have anything worthy of a briefing, I'll put it in writing."

He wants to take the credit for your work, Marjory. He's going to ignore all you have done for this agency. He thinks you're unworthy.

"Okay, just tell me, why Price and Laurent?"

There is a leak on your floor. The French woman wants you to fail, Marjory.

"I'm just curious about the new woman's background, and Price is her supervisor. I thought I would refresh myself on his qualifications."

"Okay, Marjory, but in the future come to me first if you question any of the people on your floor."

"Yes, sir."

"Oh, and Marjory, send me a detailed memo on what you think is happening in New Mexico."

"Yes, of course," she said and stood to leave. Taking a look out his window at *The View*, she said, "I'll have it on your desk tomorrow."

Riding down the elevator, she wondered who had ratted her out: Agent Denning maybe, or was it Price? Price had been at his current post for four years without advancement, much too long. It had to be Price, and what a coincidence for this new woman to know about a quantum code just as the agency picks up the transmission. The two of them are working together, either for a foreign government or for themselves.

You need to watch them all, Marjory. Trust your instincts.

"Yes, I will," she said aloud as she walked through the hallway, ignoring those who turned to see who she was talking to.

There were four new files on her desk when she returned: Price, Laurent, Croft, and Flórez. Downing two of the expired Xanax tablets, she opened Croft's file as her father read to her through the headphones.

Chapter 39
Susan

The hotel's shuttle stopped in the morning rush hour traffic and Susan looked at the dark clouds moving in from the lake. She thought again of the lightning and hoped Sandy called the hospitals. The thought reminded her she had missed a call from Annie.

"Hi, Annie, what's up? I saw your missed call."

"Susan, a man from the Army came into the clinic asking about your friend, he was with the military police."

"What?"

"He wants to talk to him about something that happened outside of Portales last week, probably the car accident."

"Okay, thanks, Annie. I'm on my way to the airport and I'll be home in a few hours. Tell me all about it when you get off work."

She ended the call and thought about the last few days. She was worried. Too many things were happening too fast. For the first time in years, she was interested in a man, one she barely knew. Who was he really, and why did she feel so strongly about him? She had slept with him, and now of all things, the police want to talk to him. She remembered her conversation with Sandy at the IHOP: 'Are you running from the police?' she had asked.

Am I that bad a judge of character? Am I that gullible?

Ninety minutes later she was in the air, the jet speeding south over

Kansas City. She stared out the window as the landscape crept along the ground below. She wasn't looking at the farms or the highways, it was the image of two young men on the sidewalk and the glint of the knife.

Sandy had raised his hand, then there was a crack of thunder ... or was it? Each time the memory replayed, she saw new details. The thunder was startling, and the flash of light was odd, there was a blueish tint followed by a chemical smell. Static electricity had raised the hair on her arms and remembering the feeling made her shiver. Then heavy rain pelted her face as they ran.

I'm an idiot, it had to be lightning!! A man had been trying to rob them. How did she expect to remember every detail? She was sure of one thing, though, the sound of the last one falling—the sharp crack as his face hit the sidewalk.

Chapter 40
Six

The chair in his room was uncomfortable, the desk too small and he was irritated.

She's in flight now, racing across the country and every second carries her farther from me.

Thinking of her helped. Her perfume still lingered on his flesh, but even those pleasant sensations paled with the anguish of leaving those boys on the sidewalk. He had promised her he would call someone. Reaching for his phone, he thought of the consequences. *What if they died, what if the police were involved?*

It was hard not to know their fate, but they could have killed Susan. He pushed his guilt aside and opened his laptop.

The black and white image of six warheads and six empty cradles filled the screen. It was a live security camera feed from the Natanz nuclear complex. Where were the six missing weapons? Soon, tens of thousands of deaths would trigger a chaos that would consume the Earth.

Four days earlier, a video showed nine warheads in this room and seven days before that, all twelve cradles were occupied. Today, the six he could see were cabled to the console behind them—and he could control them—maybe even detonate them. The missing warheads worried him.

Frustrated, he stood and looked again at Lake Michigan through the window. Another storm was coming in from the north, a jagged bolt of lightning striking the water miles away.

Raising his hand, he studied the lines on his palm. He had caused whatever happened to those men. He felt it, a discharge of power. It was nothing like transmitting a signal. He had released a form of powerful energy and it was like firing a weapon.

The image of himself in the reflection reminded him of Croft inside his ship, and the danger he was in. *No more deaths on my conscience.* He picked up his phone.

"Croft," he heard the colonel say.

"Colonel Robert Croft?"

"Yes, who is this?"

"My name is not important at the moment. What is important is that you must be careful not to attempt to activate any of the ship's other systems. I didn't think you would be capable of activating the viewer. That system is harmless, but the others may place you in grave danger. We will speak again soon, Colonel."

He ended the call wondering if he should have said more, but just contacting Croft was risky enough. Another ripple in the big pond of time.

As he packed, he thought of the picture of Croft and inevitably meeting him in person one day. Somehow Croft will help organize Trans-Data into what it will become … or will it? How much of the future had he already changed?

Chapter 41
Croft

Croft was in the commissary mentally preparing his report for General Bowman, a report he knew would make his life miserable, but it had to happen. He felt his cell phone vibrate in his back pocket, an incoming call. The caller ID was blank and he remembered Scott's warning about the NSA.

"Croft," was all he said, and listened to silence on the other end. Not complete silence though; he could hear background noises.

He was about to end the call when he heard, "Colonel Robert Croft?"

It was the pilot. He knew it immediately and listened to the man as he spoke. He wanted to ask questions, but the man ended the call.

He stared at the phone for a minute and thought of calling Fischer, but he was only a five-minute walk across the base. He walked out into the open field and decided to try calling Fischer anyway.

Fischer's phone went to voice mail. He tried to call Stephens with no success.

Something was wrong, and he jogged the next hundred yards.

"Grave danger," the pilot said, and he began to run.

Carol Vones was kneeling over the ship's exposed wiring while

Stephens watched. They had hit a dead end with the viewer and were ready to move on. Carol had the leads of the voltmeter in her hands and touched two of the fine strands of wire.

"Anything?" she asked.

"Nothing," Stephens said.

"How about now?"

Stephens was about to say no when he felt something. He looked down at Carol and saw several fine strands of her hair floating above her neck. The hairs looked like they were reaching out for him, and he backed away. He smelled something too, like the sharp smell of ozone after a thunderstorm.

"Something's happening, Carol."

"Warning" flashed in red on the viewer.

Looking back through the hatch, Stephens saw Emil Fischer enter the hanger. There was a look of horror on the man's face, and Stephens saw the air in the room shimmering like the heat off a blacktop road.

"Carol, stop!" Stephens screamed as the ship's hatch slammed shut.

Croft heard an explosion as he ran toward the hangar. He was winded and sucking air as he turned the last corner and saw the damage. The exterior steel siding was bent inward and two sections of the huge doors had collapsed on top of each other.

Inside, he found Fischer crumpled on the floor and sunlight coming in through a large hole in the roof. It lit up the hangar floor like a spotlight where the ship had sat moments before.

"Emil, what happened?"

Croft watched fine particles of pulverized concrete float around Fischer's face as he tried to speak.

"I—I can't hear you. I can't hear anything."

"What happened?" Croft screamed and helped him stand.

Fischer looked at the hole in the roof, then they both saw the hangar floor.

Where the ship had been sitting moments before, there was a

carved crater in the concrete flooring. The crater was deep enough it passed through ten inches of concrete and reinforcing steel rods and then into several feet of gray dirt.

Croft ran outside, hoping to find some sign of Stephens and Vones. It was unnaturally quiet at first, then he heard sirens and dozens of soldiers running in their direction. As Croft looked at the damaged hangar and the hole in its roof, he knew they were gone.

"Emil, what happened? What were they doing?" he asked as his friend staggered outside.

"Carol said she was going to run continuity checks on some of the other wires in the floor. I was outside when I felt something like static electricity. When I opened the door, there was some type of electrical field around the ship. They were both inside, and I heard Jon tell Carol to stop. That's all I remember until you came in."

A feeling of helplessness settled over him like a shroud, the same feeling he'd had when General Bowman broke the news four years ago: "Bob, I'm sorry. Sara is gone." More death. The feeling wasn't as intense as it had been with his wife, but it was still devastating.

There was an urge to shut down, to collapse and let someone else pick up the pieces. He turned to look at Fischer, whose face was covered in chalky white powder. There were tear streaks that left flesh-colored tracks on his cheeks.

"He warned me," Croft whispered to himself.

"What did you say?"

"He warned me. I had a phone call a few minutes ago. No caller ID, but it was the pilot, I'm sure. He knew we activated the viewscreen somehow. He warned me that experimenting with the ship could put us in danger, "grave danger" were his exact words. He said we would speak again soon and hung up. I was on my way back here when it happened. I just didn't get to you in time."

He was the acting base commander, and he needed to detach himself emotionally from what had just happened. "I'll need to call General Bowman and fill him in, and Scott too."

He watched as paramedics checked Emil. *Where could Vones and Stephens be?* He was pretty sure they were dead, if not the moment the ship vanished, then soon afterward. *If only I could ask the pilot.* He looked at his phone again and squeezed it, hoping he could get the information out of it. He wanted to crush something, but he relaxed his hand and looked at Fischer.

"This is going to be bad, Emil—really bad and really soon."

It was worse. By 1800 hours he had been relieved of command, and General Bowman was in route from Washington and expecting a full briefing at 0900 hours tomorrow. Someone with the NSA would be coordinating an investigation with the Army into the loss and presumed death of the two civilians. The death of civilians on a military base was bad enough, but he had chosen not to inform his chain of command of the ship, something he should have done once its uniqueness and origin were discovered.

The last page of his report fell from the printer. All data, all the observations and speculations the team had put together rested in a pile on his floor along with his statement about the incident.

He drove back to his apartment and sat in the overstuffed recliner staring at the whiskey bottle next to Sara's photo. He thought again of the tears running down Emil's dust covered cheeks, then the image of Carol's face as she looked at the ship for the first time. The lack of expression on her face said more than she knew. She was socially awkward and he wondered if she had learned to hide her emotions fearing she would be judged differently being a woman. He had learned to respect her and knew her death would haunt him no less than Jon's.

The first glass of Knob Creek went down fast and smooth. The second was slower. He never finished the third as the whiskey, the fatigue, and the depression battled with his consciousness. Fatigue won as the glass slipped from his fingers, and for a few hours he slept until he heard the warning alarm.

He jerked upright in panic. He was sitting in the pilot's chair.

In front of him, both sides of the view-screen were active; red warnings were flashing on each side and numbers and symbols he didn't recognize were scrolling across the screen. A woman's voice, sounding like the AI assistant on his phone, kept repeating, "Memory Failure," and he watched as his hands reached out and started touching the symbols on the right side of the screen.

Something bad was happening, and the source of it was in front of him, some intelligent being. It was draining the ship's memory, and he had to get away fast before he lost control of the ship.

Then the ship turned away. 'Faster now ... I must go faster.' There was no sensation of speed or acceleration, but he watched the numbers increasing on the view-screen.

His eyes opened, it was dark outside, and the clock said it was 0500 hours. Sitting up, he reached for his note pad. Notes helped him remember the dreams. This was a new one and he knew it was important.

In the dream, he had been asleep for a long time, and the ship woke him. He could still see the messages scrolling across the view-screen. Something powerful was in front of the ship, and it was why he was there.

He closed his eyes and still felt its presence. Whatever it was, it had sensed him somehow, and it was curious. There was no threat or malevolence, but it had somehow damaged the ship.

That's what happened to the pilot, and that's why he is here! The revelation made sense of the questions he had been struggling with. The man was here by accident, not with some plan or purpose. It was an accident.

It was no use trying to sleep anymore, so he showered and dressed as coffee brewed in the kitchen.

Dawn's light illuminated the edges around the curtain. A new day was beginning, one promising nothing but dread.

Chapter 42
Six

Santa Fe

Sandy Walker was back in Santa Fe, alone, thrashing in his sheets and mumbling words no one could hear. The television on the wall hissed as images appeared, then tore apart into random patterns. One of those patterns spelled 'Warning!' The word stretched across the screen, dissolving into black and white spots only to repeat itself.

"No," he mumbled. He was deep in a nightmare.

Susan was at his door, a squad of police officers in black uniforms behind her. The officers pushed her aside and rushed in. "You lied to her," one of them said and led him outside where his ship was waiting.

Then he was in space and stars were streaking across the viewer. He reached for the screen to rotate the image, but another man's hand touched it. The man's hand was bare and the gold watch on his wrist said it was two o'clock. He was looking through someone else's eyes. A stranger.

The ships speed was increasing. Ten, then fifteen times the speed of light. It was not possible!

The dream changed. The stranger was gone and he was back in control, far from the strange void and out of danger. But the ship was damaged, its memory files corrupted and dozens of non-critical warnings flashed on the viewer. The mission was over. He had failed.

He woke up in the dark remembering the rest. It was true, the mission was indeed a failure. Too many of the ship's sensors were off line. All he could do was return to the station and make his report. Something was out there, not a black hole, but something—something sentient.

Maybe the ships corrupted memory files could answer that. In several hundred years that sentience would enter Earth's solar system. Let the technicians and the scientist figure it out.

Setting the automated recovery system, the ship had begun the sequence of putting him into deep sleep. It was programmed to return him to the *Constitution's* dock, then the slow process of waking him would begin.

But the docking sequence never occurred. The view-screen should have shown him inside the landing bay of the Constitution along with several other ships and technicians, but all he saw was the blackness of space. Rotating the viewer, he saw Earth several hundred miles below him, and he realized the ship was in free fall over the Atlantic Ocean.

The ship's drive field should have at least kept him in orbit, but its failure was now flashing on the screen along with the others.

"Constitution, this is Echo Six, I have an emergency!" He waited listening to static and was about to repeat the message when another audible warning sounded, "Collision alert."

Metal fragments tore through the ship, setting off new alerts, and he heard the hissing as oxygen escaped through gaping holes in the hull.

He stared in disbelief at the holes, then at blood running down his forearm from tears in his flight suit. He screamed as the pain finally registered in his brain.

He was still screaming when another warning sounded and streaks of red-hot plasma filled the view-screen. There was no time to deal with the wound as he and the ship were seconds away from incineration.

Restarting the ship's drive field manually had saved him. He remembered feeling the static as it engaged. The glow of plasma on the view-screen vanished along with the sound of oxygen venting into space as the hull sealed itself.

In the dark hotel room, he touched the scars on his arm. The warnings echoed only in his mind now, the television dark, but the feeling of helplessness this far from home persisted.

I should have died that night.

It was five in the morning. The imaginary pain faded and he got out of bed.

It was too early to call Susan. He listened to her voice mail again. "Sandy, Annie said a man from the military came into the clinic asking about you. What is this about?"

She sounded angry. He promised himself he would tell her the truth, but in person. She deserved a phone call though, and he sat on the edge of the bed, thinking of what he should say. She deserved the truth.

Who was that man in my dream?

Chapter 43
Croft

Croft's phone vibrated on the table, rattling like a serpent. He didn't want to answer, only bad news could come from it. Answering anyway, he heard a familiar voice.

"Good morning, Colonel. I had a feeling you were awake," the pilot said.

"I am. Two of my people died yesterday. Sleep is difficult."

There was silence on the phone for a minute, and Croft thought the pilot had hung up, then the man spoke again, "I'm sorry." Croft heard the man inhale, then, "What happened?"

He explained what he could and then asked, "Do you know where they are? Could they be alive?"

"What were their names?"

"Carol Vones and Jon Stephens. Why do you ask?"

Croft listened to more silence, wondering why the man cared. He could hear the hum of a fan or an air conditioner close to the phone.

"I am not sure where they are. It depends on what they may have activated. Possibly the auto-return system, if so, there is no chance they are alive. There would be no power for life support."

Now Croft was silent as waves of anger and frustration came and went. He wanted to be angry, but the man *had* tried to warn him and in retrospect, it had been foolish to tamper with the ship.

The silence on both ends irritated him.

"I had an amazing dream just an hour ago," he said, wanting

to change the subject. "I was on your ship flying through space. I've had other dreams too that I think are related."

"They may be. You said Carol Vones was on the ship?"

"Yes, again why do you ask?"

"I think we should meet, Colonel."

"Yes, I think we should. What do I call you?"

"Call me whatever you like. As you know, I am using the name Sandy Walker. I need to trust you, Colonel. I have no choice. I have much to do in the next several days and weeks, and I would hate for my plans to be interrupted by Major Flórez. He is close to finding me."

How does he know about Flórez?

"Why should I trust you? Two of my people are dead, and I know nothing about you. Trust must be earned. If I knew your plans, it may help. There is a lot of talk among us about what you might be doing here."

"I assure you: I am not here by choice, and I am no threat to you. I will explain more when we meet. This Monday would be a good time. I will call you again with the details. I'm sorry about Mr. Stephens and Ms. Vones. Enjoy your coffee, Colonel."

Not even a click as the call ended. He put the cup down and looked around the room. His laptop was closed and on the kitchen table. The only other camera he could think of was on his phone. He looked at the camera lens for a moment and then put the phone upside down on the table.

"He wants to meet with me, well good, I want answers," he said to himself, putting his uniform on. "Maybe I'll just call Flórez and let the MPs pick him up. But Flórez will want to take him into custody, especially now with the two deaths and I'll probably never get to see him.

"I want to look him in the eyes and tell me where my people are. I need closure, a peaceful end to this mess. Then I can retire."

He looked at his watch and saw the second hand was moving around the dial a lot faster than he wished. In less than an hour, he would be sitting in front of General Bowman trying to explain things he could not.

Chapter 44
Hicks

As Marjory Hicks' plane crossed the Mississippi River, she listened to her father's voice. She was on chapter two now, 'The Pool of Tears, and Alice had grown to such a tremendous size that her head touched the ceiling.

How ironic she thought, comparing her own predicament to Alice's. Here I am flying across the country to uncover one of the biggest events of the twenty-first century, and I am the only one capable of carrying it out.

Turn that off and listen to me, Marjory. You must act now. People are conspiring against you, and you know it, the familiar voice said.

"No one but I can see the big picture," she told the voice, not seeing the flight attendant listening behind her. "And now even you are trying to take credit for all I've accomplished."

The French woman is involved, Marjory. She is envious of your position. She and Price are working with someone in New Mexico, probably Colonel Croft. Follow your instincts.

"I'm going to meet Colonel Croft face to face," she said. "I'm going to get to the bottom of this, and if it's what I think it is, it's going to be big."

You are the only one who can sort this out, Marjory.

"More wine, Director?" the flight attendant asked.

Finally, a woman who can address me properly. "Yes, please. How much longer till we arrive?"

"Another ninety minutes."

Ninety minutes. She listened to Alice talking with the Mad Hatter.

As the plane touched down at the White Sands Missile Range, she dug the tin out of her purse and took two of her new Risperdal tablets and washed the powerful antipsychotics down with her wine.

The flight attendant and the pilot watched her walk down the stairway and into a waiting limo.

"She talks to herself," the flight attendant said.

The pilot nodded. "I know, and answers herself too."

Chapter 45
Croft

At 0900 hours, Croft stepped into General Bowman's office. Bowman and a severe-looking woman in civilian clothing sat behind the conference table, leaving one empty chair.

General Bowman was wearing his dress uniform, which Croft knew was not a good sign. The woman's dark red hair was pulled back so tight her eyebrows were stretched, and her eyes looked like chips of blue ice tracking him from across the room. The empty chair left him sitting directly across from her. He tried to match her stare but failed; the look was too cold.

Bowman was the first to speak. "Colonel Croft, this is Marjory Hicks, Deputy Director of the National Security Agency. She will oversee the investigation of the apparent deaths of the two civilians and of the special circumstances of the craft your team was working on. You will turn over all materials and reports to her and be at her disposal until her investigation is complete."

He could see in the general's face that his heart wasn't in what he was saying.

"Colonel Croft," Bowman continued, "we have worked together many years, and I have nothing but respect for you and your career, but this has created a great deal of concern in Washington. What is in this folder is extraordinary and should have been brought to my attention immediately. Can you tell me why you didn't file a report earlier?"

"I had no definitive proof of what it was until just before the accident." As the words left his lips, he knew they were weak. "I was putting my report together just before all this happened."

"I see," the general said, then turned toward the woman. "Ms. Hicks?"

Croft saw a flash of anger, directed at Bowman, and then just as quickly, the cold stare fixed on him. She shifted her weight in the steel chair and then leaned forward. "Colonel, a manned space vehicle falls out of the sky, and you didn't think it worthy of a word to General Bowman?"

"I have answered that question and it's all in my report. Everything I knew was speculative, and much of it still is."

She had been tapping a ballpoint pen relentlessly on the desk, and her eyes had never left his. "There was a picture of Washington, DC, in the craft. May I see it, Colonel?"

He looked through the folder and pulled out a copy of the photo.

She studied it, still tapping her pen on the desk. "And you didn't think this photo was worthy of a report either?"

"What do you see in that photo, Ms. Hicks?" Croft said.

"It's 'Deputy Director Hicks, Colonel. What I see is a photo of our capital blown to shit. I think that is a pretty significant piece of evidence."

"If I showed you that photo last week, what would be your first thought? Mine was that it was edited, and by some amateur. Now, of course, in hindsight, we see something else."

There was an odd look on her face. It took him a second to know what it was. She was enjoying his discomfort. This would benefit her somehow, and the worse she could make him look, the better off she thought she would be.

In the military, they called people like her "fast movers," people with no real skills but who moved up the ranks by stepping on those who did, always gravitating to the right circles. Most eventually reached a rank where their incompetence betrayed them—it was the Peter principle—and the NSA was no different.

She stared at him, those ice-chip eyes trying to crack his calm demeanor. She wanted to see him squirm. He leaned in closer to her. "Anything else?"

He looked over at Bowman, saw him look away and knew the general would play by the book now.

"We need to find this pilot, and I want to know what happened here," she said, stabbing the picture with her nail. "That will be my first priority. Is there anything not in your notes that I need to be aware of, Colonel?"

"No, ma'am."

"General, I would like a word with the colonel alone, please."

Once Bowman was out of the room, she leaned in close, her voice just above a whisper. "Tell me about the satellite, Colonel."

"What about it?" He had forgotten about the report from NASA until now.

"Don't pretend you don't know what I'm talking about. Someone here at White Sands has been communicating with it!"

She had lost her earlier composure and now stood over him and the whispering was over.

"And you have been talking to someone in Santa Fe! Have you been communicating with this man, Colonel? Are you conspiring with him?"

"Have you bugged my phone, Ms. Hicks? Are you tracking me?" He was furious now.

"Deputy Director Hicks to you, Colonel!" she screamed. Croft could see a white crusty film forming in the corners of her mouth, something he had seen before with drug users.

He stood, now face to face with Hicks. "I don't care who you are. Don't ever speak to me like that again."

She held his stare for a minute, then looked over his shoulder and focused on something behind him, then sat. He could see she regretted the outburst. Was it embarrassment, or did she say something she didn't want him to know? Still silent, she tapped the pen again, her angry stare fixated on him. Then her eyes shifted to an empty place in the room, she cocked her head as if listening to something, and nodded.

"Yes," she whispered.

Something is wrong with this woman.

"You can go now, Colonel. I'll be in touch."

He stood and walked out. The fresh air felt cleaner outside, and he saw Bowman was nowhere around, probably wanting to avoid anything unpleasant.

He called Fischer and gave him the news.

"What are you going to do?" Fischer asked.

"I'm not completely sure. I didn't mention that the pilot called me on the phone twice, but I think she knew, or she was guessing."

"Bob, that's going to bite you in the ass, and you know it. When did he call again?"

"This morning. I'm going to meet him Monday."

"By yourself?"

"Maybe, Emil, but I've got questions and he has the answers."

Chapter 46
Six

Six sat in his Santa Fe hotel room. He reached for the telemetry suit, then stopped, wondering just how much he could do without it.

His connection to the hotel's Wi-Fi felt stronger now than it had in Chicago. He searched for "real estate." RealEstate.com opened, and a dozen office complexes spread out in front of him. Two looked promising.

He carried everything he owned down to the Explorer.

Dawn had come and gone as he drove southwest on Veterans Memorial Highway and the Pretenders were on the radio when the first drops of rain hit the windshield. By the time he found Buckman Road, it was pouring.

He enjoyed the rainfall, even the sound of it on the roof. He watched as streams of water flowed off the highway and disappeared, sucked up by the parched desert sands.

The office complex was just off the main road, and he found the guard gate open. A landscaping crew just inside the gate was sitting in their truck, waiting for the rain to stop. He waved as he drove by, and the men waved back.

It was larger than he had envisioned from the satellite image. There were three sections. The first and smallest section was an executive office building. He parked in front of the main door and walked around its perimeter. It was similar to the photograph of the original Trans-Data building he had seen years ago. This building had fewer steps and was only a single story, but he didn't think it would make any difference.

The storm passed, leaving a steady drizzle. Stepping around the puddles, he walked up the steps to the front glass door. He inhaled deeply, and the scent of wet dirt was refreshing after breathing dry desert air for weeks.

The door was locked, and no tricks with electronics would open it—it needed a key—but just inside, he saw the keypad of an alarm system.

It was a wireless system with simple programming, and seconds later, the red LED light turned green, but the door itself remained locked. He felt around the top of the doorjamb looking for a key, but found only dust, bits of plaster, and a dead insect.

Perhaps the landscapers had a key? He turned and saw a lockbox chained to a handrail. There was a phone number attached to the box, but instead of calling, he tried the combination lock with 1-2-3-4. Nothing happened, so he tried another combination. Still nothing. He turned the small brass wheels to 9-9-9-9, and the lock opened.

The lobby smelled like old paint and dust. Looking back through the glass, he saw columns of steam rising over the hot asphalt and the landscapers were back at work, none of them looking his way.

There were four executive offices in this building, each with its own lobby and bathroom that included a shower. A year's worth of dust covered most of the lobby, and cobwebs laced across a few doorways.

This complex will do.

He dialed Eric Ridge's number.

"Mr. Ridge, I found an office for Trans Data at 400 Buckman Road. It's owned by First United Bank of New Mexico and is listed at three-point-four million dollars. Can you take care of that for me?"

He listened to the sound of the attorney typing. "I'm showing that address as a foreclosed office complex, Sandy."

"Yes, that's the one."

"Did you want to make an offer on this property?"

"No, the asking price is fair. I would like the sale completed today if you can arrange it. Tell them I'll pay the asking price contingent on their ability to close today. Do you think that will be a problem?"

"I'm not sure, but I'll do what I can. I'll get started on it right away."

"And, Mr. Ridge, use Trans-Data as the buyer, please."

He ended the call and stepped outside thinking about the loss of Carol Vones.

Will her death change my history? Have I been here before? And Croft, where does he fit in?

Chapter 47
The Andaman Sea

Syria

The container ship *Andaman Sea* sailed out of Tartus, Syria as the sun slipped below the horizon. It was bound for Oran, Algeria, and if things progressed according to plan, it would leave two days later for the Florida coast under her sister ship's name, the *Dena Ann*.

The actual *Dena Ann* was undergoing repairs in the same port and would be in dry dock for more than a month. The *Andaman Sea* was registered in Syria, and the name would be a red flag when it reached its final destination. The *Dena Ann,* however, was registered in Panama and had been to US ports several times in the last year alone.

The ship's manifest listed twenty-three hundred shipping containers full of textiles and manufactured goods made in India and Pakistan. Fifteen of those containers were destined for Harper's Ferry Propane, a fictitious company in Blacksburg, Virginia.

Warhead 01 was in one of those fifteen containers, disguised as an industrial propane tank and only a close inspection of the valve assembly under the galvanized hood would draw attention. A keypad under the hood required a six-digit code for the weapon to be armed, a code carried by two weapons specialists from Natanz on board.

The ship's captain, Saleh Jazayeri, was born in Sakākā, Saudi Arabia, to an Iranian mother and a Saudi father. Looking forward down the length of the seven-hundred-seventy-four-foot-long hull, Jazayeri could just see the closed hatch of the number two hold. There were seven holds total, each one capable of holding four hundred of the steel containers. But it was just the one container in that hold he thought about now.

After the fall of Shah Pahlavi, his family immigrated to his mother's birthplace, Sardasht, Iran. In 1987, Saddam Hussein gassed the village, killing a hundred and ten civilians, including his mother. He joined the Islamic Republic of Iran Navy when he was eighteen, first serving on coastal patrol boats, and he eventually made the rank of captain, commanding the frigates *Sahand* and later the *Moje*. With Hussein dead and the Iraqi government collapsed, his rage shifted to the United States, and revenge had become the motivating force in his life.

Cruising at twenty-one knots through the Mediterranean Sea, Jazayeri rechecked his GPS navigation system and then looked around the bridge. The sun had set, and the steel deck and bridge were cooling, a relief after near record heat for the sixth day in a row.

The ship's normal twenty-man civilian crew was now fourteen sailors, handpicked from the Islamic Republic Navy, and a few of those had served with him on his last command, the frigate *Moje*. There were two civilians on board also, the weapon specialists from Natanz assigned to monitor the weapon.

At his current course and speed, he expected to reach Jacksonville in twenty-four days and off-load his cargo. Once unloaded, his part of the mission would be over and the ship and crew would return to Tartus.

Looking out the port windows, he watched the lights of El Hoceima, Morocco, silently slipping aft. The only sound or sensation was the steady throb of the engine ten decks below him. The sea was calm and he hoped to pass through Gibraltar and into the open sea in a few hours.

Israel

Moha Kattan and Aayan Nazari had been on the long coastal route from Cairo to Tel Aviv for eight hours now. Somewhere behind them, another pair of drivers were making a similar trip to Haifa.

The trucks were painted in the red, white, and blue logo of Amisragas, the American-Israeli Gas Company, and each carried two of the one-thousand-four-hundred-fifty-gallon liquid propane gas tanks with all the proper documentation to pass through the checkpoint at Nitzana and into Israel. Several test runs had been made with the same trucks in the last couple of weeks, and once again, Moha passed through with just a brief inspection.

His fear that the smell of fresh paint might alert the border guards eased as he watched the terminal grow smaller in the side mirrors. Ahead, all he saw were miles of desert sand broken by razor-wire fencing and a few concrete bunkers.

Both Moha and his friend Mohammad had been recruited from the Al al-Bayt University Mosque and trained with the Intelligence Unit of the Islamic Republic Army. Both had been born and raised in a small suburb of Amman, Jordan, and traveled throughout the Middle East. Learning to drive a large transport truck had been a challenge for the two farm boys, but they each logged a thousand miles before pulling this load.

Just after nine at night, Moha pulled up to the delivery gate at the Ramat Aviv Mall and showed his paperwork to the civilian guard. The gates opened, and the guard waved him through and directed him to the emergency generators. As he set the brakes, he heard the guard call someone on his radio. A moment later, a forklift operator arrived. He spoke for a moment and pointed to two similar tanks next to the generators.

Fifteen minutes after ten, Mohammed was behind the wheel and the big Mercedes was back on the freeway with two empty tanks heading for Cairo. Moha changed the SIM card in his phone and texted a single word, "Delivered."

Chapter 48
The Copper Penny

They walked into the Copper Penny at seven o'clock and sat in a booth near the bar. The sports bar was a lively place on the weekends, but tonight it was quiet. There were two couples near the exit and the rest of the lounge was empty. The bartender brought them a menu and wine list and left them alone.

"Susan, I promised I would explain why the military police want to speak with me. It's complicated and I hope you will be patient."

One of the two couples paid their check and left as another man walked in.

"Sandy, I want this relationship to work, but you need to open up some. No secrets. I was okay with it in Chicago, but I want to know more. So have a drink to loosen up, or whatever it takes." There was a smile at the end, but the look in her eyes said she was troubled.

"I know and I'm sorry, but there is a reason I have kept things from you, and I hope that after tonight, you will understand who I am. We're meeting someone here tonight who may help explain Annie's visit from the military, and I'll try to explain the rest if you will let me."

"Someone here?"

"Yes, but Susan, I need you to trust me. No matter what you hear, please trust me. Can you do that?"

"I think so, but what is it you want to tell me?"

"That man at the bar is Colonel Robert Croft with the US Army. He doesn't know who I am yet, but I'll introduce myself whenever you're ready."

She looked over at the man. "This should be interesting."

Croft ordered a Blue Moon on tap and tossed the orange slice on the bar. The lounge was nearly empty. Behind him, a couple in a booth held hands, and another couple at the end of the bar were watching the Rockies game on the television. He set his beer on a coaster and wished he had brought his phone, but he was afraid Hicks was tracking him.

He had taken a big chance coming here tonight. After his meeting with Hicks, he took no chances and flew commercial into Santa Fe, telling no one but Emil.

The pilot was late. He looked behind him, the one couple were still holding hands and talking quietly, the man looked over at him and nodded. He was probably in his mid- or early thirties and in decent shape. The woman was about the same age, maybe a few years younger. He envied the man. Sara loved the art of romance and he missed moments like that.

"Another Blue Moon, sir?" the bartender said.

"Not yet, thank you."

He watched the Rockies' second inning waiting for the pilot to show. He would give the man another hour, he had come this far and would wait.

"Two glasses of White Zinfandel, please," someone said behind him."

He turned and saw the middle-aged man was at the bar now, looking at him.

"And another beer for Colonel Croft. Colonel, please join us," he said, and gestured to his date. "Come, Colonel. I know you have many questions."

He stood, still unsure what to say and looked at the woman. How was she involved in this?

"This is Susan Matthews. Susan, this is Colonel Robert Croft."

It was a surreal moment as he shook her hand. It was warm and firm and she had a nice smile. He had envisioned many scenarios of how this meeting would play out, but this was not one of them.

"And I am Sandy Walker," the man said.

He sat next to her wanting to be face to face with the pilot. He looked for some abnormality, something genetically different, but the man looked like everyone else.

"Colonel, Susan is unaware of why you and I need to speak. She has many questions too and before I leave here tonight I hope to answer them, and yours as well. But first, I want to say I am sorry for the loss of your friends. Had I foreseen the danger, I would have contacted you sooner. Their loss may be greater than you know."

"Who are you talking about?" Susan said.

The pilot picked up his wineglass and took a long drink.

"Susan, I'll explain that in a minute. Colonel, I need for Susan to know exactly who I am and why I am here. Let me begin."

Croft thought the pilot's speech was odd, maybe foreign like Flórez mentioned. His clothes looked new, and he could see a pink scar on his left bicep. The scar looked to be months old, but he knew it was only weeks.

"Susan, Colonel Croft is investigating an accident just outside Portales, and I was involved in that accident. I was injured when some debris flew through my vehicle. You remember that I called it a vehicle, and I'll explain that too.

"After the accident, I was in great pain and losing blood, so I started walking. I must have passed out at some point, and when I awoke, the military had found my vehicle. I was afraid I could not explain myself, so I ran—well, I couldn't run; I walked."

"Why didn't you ask them for help?" Susan said.

"That is the hard part. It would have been difficult, you see I wasn't driving an automobile. It was ..." he stumbled for a second, and Croft finished his sentence.

"It was a ship."

"What do you mean, *a ship*?" she said and Croft knew the woman had no clue who Sandy Walker was.

The pilot leaned back and looked at his wineglass, slowly spinning it on its coaster. "When I was a child, Colonel, I watched a movie called *The Day the Earth Stood Still*, the original black-and-white version. Have you seen it?"

Croft nodded, but the woman hadn't moved. Her skin was whiter, paler than it had been, and her smile was gone.

"Susan, this is the difficult part," he said, then looked over at Croft.

Croft interrupted the pilot again and said, "Let me tell her. On June ninth, around nine p.m., military and civilian radar picked up something traveling at the speed of sound over Texas. It wasn't unusual—there are several military bases in the area—but then it slowed and disappeared around Portales. At first, what we found looked like part of an old satellite, but it wasn't."

He paused, watching her reaction. She was seeing where he was going, and she didn't want to hear anymore.

"It was a ship, a spacecraft actually, and Mr. Walker was on that ship."

She grimaced and laughed nervously. "What, is this some kind of joke, two old friends playing a joke on the new girl?"

"How old are you, Mr. Walker?" he asked.

"I am thirty-two. I was born on October 11, 2344."

"Okay, can you let me out? I've heard enough, and I'm leaving."

"Susan, wait. I wanted to say something before, but how would I even start? I kept trying to think of a way or a better time or a better place, but I knew that would never happen. Please wait one more minute. There is more, and I want you to know everything before you leave."

The pilot pointed to the televisions above the bar, and the baseball game was now an image of the ship in the center of both screens. That image changed, and now they were looking over Croft's shoulder at the ship's view-screen.

"I slept in that ship most of the last year, 'deep sleep' we call it. The years before that, I was in orbit on a station called *Constitution*. The station was built by the North American Institute of Science and is in a geostationary orbit over Atlanta—or it will be."

The bartender picked up the remote and pointed it at the televisions, but nothing changed.

"I was on a mission—I will explain more of that mission at another time, Colonel—but something out there damaged the ship and I was injured, and of course you know the rest. I do not know how, but I'm here now. I'm alone, and I need you both to trust me."

He watched Susan as she leaned back in the booth, her eyes focusing on something far away. He glanced back at the image of the ship and then at the pilot.

"I am sure that looks very impressive, Colonel, but I am simply streaming a signal from my phone."

Croft pulled the original picture of Washington out of his pocket and laid it on the table. The pilot stared at it and then picked it up.

"This is the last photo ever taken of my parents. They died two weeks later in Paris. May I keep this?"

"Yes. I didn't want Marjory Hicks to have it. She and the NSA are looking for you by the way."

Susan took the photo. "I've seen this boy in a dream … just last night. He was in a hospital, crying and he had wires connected all over him. His name was …"

"Yes, Susan, that was me many years ago, or many years from now. My name was Echo Six, a name they gave me as a child. The hospital was real and I dream about it all the time. But I must tell you both—something is happening I cannot explain. You and Colonel Croft are involved in it somehow, and maybe others I am unaware of."

"What did they do to you, Sandy?"

"Many things, more than even I know."

"It wasn't lightning in Chicago, was it?"

"No, I don't think it was."

"Lightning?" Croft asked.

"A story for another time, Colonel."

"I knew when I saw you that morning you were different. She was quiet for a moment, then said, "I want to leave. If you don't mind, I'd like to take a cab back. I'm going to need some time to think this through. I'm sorry."

She looked at Croft, and he stood to let her out. Both men watched her walk out into the dining room.

"Do you trust her?"

"I do. She knows now and I owed her that. She is a strong woman and I believe her part in this is not over.

"I want to be honest, Mr. Walker. I thought of having Major Flórez come with me and take you into custody, but I've been relieved of my command, and a court-martial could be in my near future. I am here for one reason—the dreams. One particularly vivid dream in which my wife is begging me to help someone—you, I think. I'm not sure how that is possible, but for that reason alone, I'm here tonight."

The pilot sat silent, holding his empty wine glass, then asked, "Colonel, does the name Trans-Data mean anything to you?"

"Yes, I saw the name on your ship's monitor."

"I promised to answer some of your questions, but I'm afraid I will leave you with many new ones. Trans-Data developed most of the technology you found on my ship. A few days ago, I started a corporation on nothing more than an impulse, and I named it Trans-Data. It was a noble thought. I wanted to jump-start the technology that I knew would be crucial in the future. When I saw you on my ship, I knew you looked familiar, which should have been impossible, but it came to me that night.

"When I was training as a cadet, we toured the Trans-Data headquarters in Atlanta. There was a picture in the lobby, a very old photo of the original headquarters, and on the steps of the building were the Trans-Data founders. You were one of them, and I believe Susan was in the photo as well."

It's not possible, he thought. I'm a soldier, what would I be doing…

"This is crazy, Mister Walker … or is it?"

"It's the truth, Colonel."

"Let me ask you, in one of my dreams, I was sitting on a white tile floor—a hospital floor—and you were there. I woke up in a sweat and I could have sworn I've never had that dream before, but now, I'm not so sure. Then the dream of my wife, it was so real. Can you explain any of this?"

"Colonel, that dream in the hospital, the one that Susan mentioned, that is over three hundred years in your future. I saw you there. You were a child, and I did not know that it was you until this moment. So, I can ask you, Colonel, how is that possible?"

"It's like I'm living in an episode of the Twilight Zone."

"Twilight Zone?"

"It's an old show I watched as a teenager. There are times, like right now, that I feel as if I have done this all before, and other times I am sure I have not."

"Colonel, many years before I was born, a woman named Vones was responsible for the technology that led to the development of the cerebral core. It's that core on my ship that allows for faster-than-light travel. If she died several days ago, how am I here? I am afraid her death has changed my past in ways I cannot imagine."

"What happened to Washington?"

"Chaos—the end of the world as you know it. But I think I can stop that from happening. I just need a few more days."

He looked into the pilot's eyes, trying to find something to help him decide whether he could trust him. The man reeked of desperation, but he was not a threat.

"You can stop it?"

"Yes. If I have a few more days."

"I'll get with Flórez and see if I can hold him off. I can't speak for anyone else though. The NSA is in charge now."

"Thank you, that is all I can ask of you."

"Can we have another drink? I have a few questions, thousands of them but let me start with the important ones."

Croft ordered another round for each of them, and they moved to the end of the bar where they could speak privately. "What did happen to Washington?"

"Destroyed in a nuclear explosion."

"When?"

"Will you be compelled to alert the government if I tell you?"

"I already have, more or less. They have seen the picture."

"The plan may already be in motion, but in my history, it happened on May eleventh, next year. And it isn't just Washington, Colonel." He told him all he knew about the radical extremist in Iran and the future of the United States.

Croft tried to envision all of what the man said, but it was more than he could take in. "That's less than a year from now. We need to act right now. Millions of lives may be at stake."

"They are, Colonel. Think of your government right now and the people making the decisions. Are you sure they will act and be able to stop it? In my history classes, I learned that governments all over the world ignored the signs until it was too late. When we meet again, if things have not changed you can do as you wish."

He had never been more conflicted in his life. A major event in world history may be in his hands and he had to decide now while drinking a beer in a bar, based on information from a man he just met. *Help him, he needs us.*

"I'll give you until Wednesday. Then I'm going to have to meet with the NSA and tell them everything I know."

"That's fair, Colonel. I have loaded several encrypted files into your phone. They contain a few events that you should be aware of, and they will decrypt on their own should something happen to me."

"How do you do that?" he asked.

"It's one of the benefits from what you saw in your dreams. We will discuss it more another day."

By midnight, they had gone their separate ways. He had a new opinion of the pilot, and he thought he could trust Sandy Walker, or whatever his name was—at least until Wednesday.

Chapter 49
Six

It was Tuesday morning, twelve hours after Susan walked out of the Copper Penny. He reached for his phone hoping to find a voice mail or a text from her. Good or bad, he needed to know what she was thinking. There was no message.

The sofa bed was the only piece of furniture in the new office. It was stiff and uncomfortable, and he hadn't slept well. Replaying parts of their conversation at the Copper Penny, he watched her reactions as she listened to Croft, and then at her hands the moment she reached for the photo. Her nails were not red and there was still no ring, but they had color this time: a pale shade of purple, mauve or lilac. Their shape was different too. Still …

He thought of making a permanent residence somewhere in Clovis, but Flórez seemed just a few steps away from finding him. If he was lucky, he may have a week, two at most before Flórez discovered Trans-Data.

He spent the morning searching the Iranian mainframe computer and the weapons stored there. His plan needed to be perfect; one mistake, one small detail overlooked and the plan could fail, or worse they could trace it back to him.

The laptop chimed with a new download from the Natanz computer and a second from the Sa'adabad Museum in Tehran. Now he was looking at security video from an underground complex hidden below the museum showing three of the remaining nukes still plugged into a panel on the wall. The mainframe identified them as 04, 05, and 06.

Numbers 02 and 03 had been disconnected from the mainframe for days. There were no files at all for number 01 and he wondered if it had ever been to Tehran. Was it already on its way to Washington?

He found numbers 02 and 03 using their GPS signal. A satellite view located one of them in a shopping mall in Tel Aviv and the other in a building outside the Israeli port of Haifa.

I'm too late, he thought. Either warhead could detonate at any moment. He had disrupted the time line, and now anything was possible. The weapons firing programs were complex, and he could not completely disarm them, but he could change the primary arming code to one of his own.

To keep the Iranians unaware of the changes, he set all the telemetry on a loop that should show the weapons were unchanged each time they uploaded their status. Anything more serious than a casual diagnostic though, could expose the new programming.

Switching to Natanz, the camera there showed the last six warheads sitting alone. Two were complete; the other four still lacked their nuclear cores. It was a black-and-white video, but the image was sharp. The warheads were glossy white with four crescents and a sword, the "Emblem of Iran" and the "Principles of Religion," emblazoned across each. In twenty years, The Muslim Brotherhood would adopt that symbol as their own.

Checking the systems login, there were over three hundred dayshift employees inside the building, most of them on the upper floors working with the centrifuges. There was a similar afternoon shift, but from ten in the evening until the day shift arrived at six, only a few security personnel would be at the facility.

The computer had archived the video feeds from all the cameras going back the last twelve months. He downloaded some of the old and all the current files to his laptop and backed them up on an external drive.

Now he had a plan, and with any luck, he would have the time to put it into motion. But he would have to wait until the afternoon shift left Natanz, he could not live with so many deaths.

It was time to go. He realized he had been stalling. Something was bothering him—a premonition or was it the dream?

In the old photo, Croft was standing on the steps of Trans-Data, but he was not. The realization meant one thing.

I won't survive.

He opened the laptop and typed by hand, adding more encrypted texts to those he had already sent, then called Eric Ridge.

"Eric, I have emailed you a file. It contains instructions I wish you to handle should I somehow become unable to manage my affairs. It is encrypted but will decrypt on its own if you do not hear from me within the next seven days.

"Sandy, is everything all right? Is there anything I should know?"

"Everything is fine. It is just something I wanted to take care of. I do not want to say more now. Just know that the instructions are in those files."

Outside, he scanned the parking lot looking for anything odd. The premonition was strong now. He could call it off now and let history take its course and hope that somehow things would be different, but he knew it wouldn't be.

The key fob was heavy in his hand as he pressed the Explorer's unlock button. He stood back and looked at the car, then walked around to the other side. The car looked and felt normal, no unusual signals and no sign of tampering. He started the engine and drove out into traffic.

It was a three-hour drive to Clovis, and he struggled with doubts and indecisions, thinking of the horrific images of Hiroshima, Tel Aviv, Washington, New Delhi, and the others. Mile after mile, he recalled the old black-and-white films of Hiroshima and Nagasaki taken in the twentieth century. Those taken in the twenty-first spared no details of the suffering and effects of radiation poisoning.

The street in front of the Coyote Deli was deserted. The lunch crowd had come and gone, and parking in front of it now would leave the Explorer exposed. If Flórez was around and knew what he was driving, it would be over quick. But there were plenty of cars at the Walmart, and he parked in the middle of them and walked back to the deli.

Flórez could be anywhere now, so he listened for any odd transmissions. The only communications he heard were cell phone conversations and all of them seemed routine. He was still early, he had timed everything to minimize the number of deaths and he didn't want to sit in the deli any longer than he had to. Across the street, he saw a small storefront with a jagged lightning bolt logo on the glass, Miller's Electronics.

The smell of burned wiring greeted him as he walked in. An older man was leaning over a work bench, and blue smoke from a soldering iron rose and curled around the back of his neck. He turned and said, "I'll be right with you. Feel free to look around."

Stacked from floor to ceiling were crates and cardboard boxes full of small electronic devices of every type. On one side of the room, musical instruments—saxophones, trumpets and guitars—hung from every available space.

In the back, a machine caught his eye; a sign taped to the glass front said "1946 Wurlitzer Model 1015 Jukebox." It was new or recently restored and "Not For Sale" was handwritten at the bottom of the glass. Inside were several dozen large black discs stored in a chrome rack. It was obviously a very complicated system for entertainment, but he appreciated the craftsmanship. He had just read the names of a few songs when he heard the man coming up behind him.

"I'm sorry for the mess. I'm a bit of a collector, I'm afraid. My friends call it hoarding, but it's what I do. I love the old stuff, and I can't say no when I see it for sale." He stepped over to a shelf and said, "What can I do for you, sir?"

"I was just trying to pass some time and wanted to look at your wares. Do you mind? I would like to see the jukebox work."

"Sure, let me plug it in. It's a real classic, and I spent several years restoring it."

Colored lights came on, accenting the chrome and stainless steel, and bubbles ran through a clear glass tube around the outside of the machine. Mr. Miller pressed one of the song selections, and a thin chrome-plated tray slid out from one of the two dozen others. The tray dropped a black disc on a spinning pedestal that rose and connected to another part of the machine and Jerry Lee Lewis' "Whole Lotta Shakin' Goin' On" filled the room.

The sound was rich and full, and in all the years in the future, with all the advancements in technology, man could not improve on the sound coming from this ancient machine.

He thanked the man and looked through the window at the Coyote Deli across the street, then stepped outside as a small dust devil formed in front of him. It flung trash everywhere and then disappeared. The street was clear now, and the few cars he saw were not military vehicles.

Would the Coyote Deli ever be recognized in its role in what was to come? He had taken a chance returning to Clovis and the deli, but it somehow seemed right. He had been drawn back here, and he would trust his instincts.

This time he was the only customer. He sat at his original table, and the same young man took his order. Enrique was just a kid, probably a student at the local college, or even the high school down the street. A simple life, but he was about to change it, change everything right here in this small town far from the battle of religion and politics.

His grilled chicken sandwich arrived, but he couldn't eat. He took a single bite out of one corner and pushed it away.

"Anything wrong with your sandwich, sir?" Enrique said.

"No, it is fine. I have lost my appetite, I guess, but more tea would be nice." As Enrique filled his glass, he switched on the deli's computer and plugged his flash drive into the USB port.

On the monitor, Director Engeta was sitting behind his simple metal desk at Natanz and talking to a man just out of the camera's view. He knew who the other man was; he had heard the man's voice several times from the archived videos. The man's high-pitched voice was unique and could only be Iran's Minister of Intelligence, Mir Katami.

In the live video feed, he saw Engeta wiping perspiration off his forehead. It was almost midnight in Iran and the security logs showed only Engeta inside the building. Four security officers were outside on the ground floor, and he found it odd that Katami was not on the list.

Two nights ago, while lying in the hotel bed in Santa Fe, he had looked through Engeta's personal computer and phone records and found an Instagram account. That account led to several other accounts Mr. Engeta no doubt thought were untraceable, and he learned Katami and Engeta had plans of their own.

The last warhead to leave Natanz would never make it. ISIS and the AQAP had offered Katami ten million dollars for a single working warhead, and Katami and Engeta would soon be wealthy men. That Katami was also in Natanz this night was a bonus.

Half a world away, he heard Katami say, "It's late, and I need to get back to my wife. When we meet again Friday, we will be wealthy men."

"What will you do with yourself, Director?"

"I may live in Paris, or maybe California, who knows? It's best we don't discuss this. We would not live long if Madine or Rouhani ever found out about our little plan. Let them think they forced me to resign; they will never see me again." Both men laughed, and he watched as Katami rose from his seat.

His finger moved toward the Enter key. The enormity of what he was about to do made him sick to his stomach.

I could cease to exist the moment I press this key. But Carol Vones is dead. Her research and her discoveries will never happen, yet here I am.

This was different and he knew it. This would be a catastrophic event in history. He saw his finger, closer now and thought of his mother dying on the subway platform, and then seven thousand two hundred ninety miles away, Katami and Engeta laughed.

He pressed the *enter* key.

The signal traveled first through the deli's Wi-Fi to a fiber optic cable, to a tower in downtown Clovis, then it uploaded to a satellite overhead, then through several more before it reached the facility's mainframe computer in Natanz.

One hundred and sixty feet below the computer, the remaining six warheads sat in their cradles. The red LED lights on the two completed warheads' interface lit up, and both warheads detonated.

Directors Engeta and Katami ceased to exist. They never felt the blast or saw a flash of light or experienced any other form of death. One second they were alive, and the next they weren't.

In the Coyote Deli, Sandy Walker watched the camera feed go blank and waited. Would he vanish, or would he simply fall to the floor and die some natural or unexplainable death? Neither it seemed, as he stared at the blank computer screen. Had anything happened?

He had expected something more, some verification, but all he had was the blank screen. He drank the last of his tea, pulled the sixty four-gigabyte flash drive out of the desktop and walked out into the afternoon heat.

He closed his fist around the drive. It felt toxic in his hand, and he wanted to be rid of it. He wiped the data from it and threw it in the trash bin.

In the small weapons chamber, the explosion was close to twenty kilotons—five more than the power of the Little Boy bomb dropped on Hiroshima. Although small when most weapons were measured in megatons, it had met the expectations of its designers.

The five-hundred-million-degree hypocenter consumed everything around it, including the rest of the uranium cores in the next room in the first picoseconds of the explosion.

The blast was focused upward, thanks to the reinforced walls that survived a fraction of a second longer than the rest of the complex. They, and most of the reinforced roof, were vaporized along with everything inside and on the surface. Some of the outer sections of the roof were blown upward, and pieces of it would later be found ten miles from the blast.

The entire complex was reduced to a fine suspension of radioactive particles that clung to the hundreds of tons of earth and rock as it rose in an immense fireball. With the southeast wind, the fallout would blanket the towns of Mahabad, Ardestan, and scores of small villages as far as Naein.

Chapter 50
Natanz

Three-quarters of a mile from the center of the blast, Sergeant First Class Ebrahem Ahmadi stood in the doorway of his checkpoint guardhouse. The only vehicle he had seen since coming on duty at nine that evening was a diplomatic sedan whose driver refused to identify his passenger. Director Engeta had called ahead and cleared this car and its passenger, so he had let it through.

He lit a cigarette, stood in the open doorway and blew a puff a blue-gray smoke into the night sky. Both his legs snapped as the ground wave raced across the surface. As he fell, a brilliant flash of light blinded him. Now lying face down in the dirt, the blast wave hit, lifting and throwing him sixty feet from the shack. He was paralyzed, but still breathing when a twenty-ton section of the steel-reinforced concrete roof landed on him. He was the last of the seven men at the facility to die.

Twelve thousand miles above the Earth, a Block III GPS satellite passing over Saudi Arabia recorded the explosion. The silicon photodiode detected the distinctive bright, double flash. It was not the only satellite that noticed. A Russian GLONASS and a European Galileo also saw the flash, and the three satellites downloaded the information immediately.

Colonel Richard Dempsy was the Commanding Officer at the

Air Force Technical Applications Center headquartered at Florida's Patrick Air Force Base. He was in his office reviewing the schedule for a training seminar when an alarm sounded on the main floor. As he reached the first console operator, another alarm sounded two stations to his left.

The operator on the console said, "Sir, there's been a nuclear event in Iran. A Block III GPS is indicating a ground burst. Give me a second, and I'll have the coordinates."

From his right, another operator confirmed a seismic event somewhere in the Middle East. This system would take a few minutes to narrow down a specific location, but the last time it sounded, the North Koreans had conducted a nuclear test. Several phones rang at once, and then the colonel's own cell phone vibrated on his belt.

"Sir," his sergeant said, "it's Natanz, their enrichment facility."

"Jesus! I think Israel just eliminated their nuclear problem. Get the Pentagon on the line and also NORAD in case they haven't seen it themselves."

Darioush Amiri sat on the balcony of his parents' apartment on the outskirts of town, enjoying his last cigarette of the night.

His meeting with Engeta had been a smooth one this time, but tomorrow would be a different story. Just this morning, he found a fault with the new software program, something as simple as the weapons' internal clock, but with Engeta, nothing was simple. Tomorrow when he had access to the mainframe, he would try to isolate the problem and correct it.

The apartment sat on top of a rise overlooking an old three-hundred-acre pomegranate farm with a view of the Karkas Mountains. It was midnight and the full moon sat just above the horizon, giving him a spectacular view of the foothills to the northwest.

It was a peaceful moment. The small town was quiet, and he watched as a light breeze blew the smoke from his cigarette out into the night.

Then a silent white flash lit up everything he could see. For a moment he thought that lightning had struck somewhere nearby, but the flash didn't fade; instead, it intensified. He had to look away, and saw his own shadow on the wall behind him. The brilliant white on the wall changed to yellow and then orange, and he looked back towards the ridgeline and watched the fireball eighteen miles away.

Then the ground shook, and he heard his mother's china teacups rattle in the kitchen. The lights came on, and she stepped outside, clutching her robe and looking at the roiling fireball.

The dull sound of the explosion reached them next.

"Wake up Father. We need to leave right away." Looking at the rising mushroom cloud, he felt the slight breeze in his face and knew they had to hurry.

There would be no speaking to Engeta tomorrow.

Chapter 51
Hicks

Putting her headphones on the desk, she thought about the voice. It had been with her since the sixth grade; always there, always guiding her, and always right, and now it was back. She had listened to the tape even through the dark times when it seemed her world was falling apart: her diagnosis, her father's death, and her mother's last fight with dementia. Then with just her father's tape she had made deputy director, one simple step away from the Ivory Tower.

The Risperdal had kept the voice away for two days now, and she took one every morning as she rode the elevator to her floor. The side effects were mild compared to Thorazine, but it did affect her sleeping, and today she was feeling it.

The phone calls started the moment she entered her office, and she dismissed each, including the director's personal cell phone. If she answered his call, she would have to tell him the truth, and there was the possibility he would try and take over the investigation.

No, this is mine, you pompous ass.

She was walking on thin ice. She should be upstairs briefing him right now, telling him everything—it was protocol—but it would also leave her with no leverage. She stared at the headphones again, wondering why she had trusted the tape for so long. Even now, she had the urge to restart the file just to listen to her father again. Her father, just like the voice, had never been wrong. But the two often conflicted; how could they both be right?

She felt a sharp pain between her eyes, the beginning of a headache. She took two Percocet, swallowed them, and closed her eyes hoping the pain medication wouldn't react with the Risperdal.

Twenty minutes later, she could feel the drug working on her pain. "It feels glorious," she said to the darkened room.

Then she thought of her interview with Robert Croft. He was hiding something of course, she was sure of it. Had he found a quantum computer on the ship, was he briefing that damned general right now, or was it all a ruse? Who had actually seen this unbelievable thing?

None of it's true, Marjory. There never was a ship, and that's why Croft eliminated the two scientists.

"You're wrong this time," she said.

Something was there, some form of proof, but Croft was hiding it from her, maybe for his own personal gain.

It's this new medication, Marjory. You're not thinking clearly. Stop taking it!

"No, it is working. Stop trying to confuse me," she said.

Is it really, Marjory?

She opened her eyes as she heard thunder and thought a storm must be brewing, but it was someone pounding on her office door. She looked at her watch and saw two hours had slipped away since taking the Percocet.

The door was locked, and on the other side her assistant looked terrified.

"I was worried about you, Director Hicks. There has been an event in Iran, and the director is en route to the White House. He has been trying to reach you, and he sounded angry."

"Thank you. I'll call him right away."

Two hours gone, and now the director was on his way to the White House without her. Maybe it was the Risperdal after all. Maybe the dammed voice was right.

An event, Marjory. Now he's going to the White House without you.

No doubt he wants to bolster his importance with the president and all his generals. That bastard Scott will probably be there too. I told you to never trust that man, Marjory. He has friends in every corner of Washington, and he knows too much already.

"Shut up!" she said aloud.

As she thought of the retired general, she remembered the MP working with Croft on the missing pilot and his ship and called Price.

"Price," she said once he answered. "I need that MP major's cell phone number ASAP. Do you have it?"

"I believe so, Ms. Hicks. Give me a moment."

"Just text it to me when you have it, and I mean right away."

Moments later, she had the number and called the major.

"Major Flórez, this is Deputy Director Hicks of the NSA. Do you know who I am?"

"I've heard the name, Ms. Hicks."

She heard the slight as the soldier ignored her title. "I have spoken to your superiors on the incident at the White Sands Missile Range, and I am the one now in charge of this debacle. Do you understand that?"

"Yes, ma'am. How can I help you?"

"You are to cease all contact with Croft and his people immediately. You work for me now. Do you understand that as well?"

"Yes, I do."

The tone of his voice changed, a trace of condescension. No doubt he didn't appreciate a woman being his direct superior. It thrilled her.

"Cancel whatever you were doing. I want your full attention on locating this pilot if he even exists. Use everything at your disposal and report only to me, and only by voice, nothing in writing. Are we clear?"

"Yes, ma'am."

She ended the call, then looked at the half full bottle of Risperdal and shook them all in the wastebasket. The green, three milligram tablets were now scattered uselessly with the documents she had just shredded. It was hard to see them sitting there, useless. What if she needed them after all? One by one, she fished them back out of the trash and put them in her Altoids tin.

That's another mistake, Marjory

She ignored the voice this time and thought of taking another one to shut the voice down, maybe once and for all, and then her office phone rang, a call from the director's personal cell.

"Yes, Director," she said casually. She was still angry, not just from talking with Flórez, but for all the interruptions, including this one from her boss.

"Listen, Hicks, this is the last time I want to tell you to answer your phone when I call. I am still waiting for your report on whatever the fuck is going on in New Mexico, and now I hear two civilians may have been killed out there. What the hell is going on, Marjory?"

"Two civilians are missing, Director. I was sitting here preparing my report to you when you called. I'm sorry I missed it, sir."

"Marjory, two hours ago there was a nuclear event in Iran, possibly an attack by Israel. I need to know my deputy director is on top of things while I'm meeting with the President in Washington. Are you?"

"Yes, sir. I am," she said, not hearing the slur in her words.

The line went dead. Slamming her phone on the desk, she closed her eyes again.

Chapter 52
Croft

Croft sat at the head of another gray metal table in the base's commissary. Everything was gray in the Army; the only other option, a beige-brown color was just as bad.

Fischer sat across from him, staring at a cold, uneaten fish sandwich. Under the fluorescent lighting, Fischer's face looked ashen, accenting the dark circles under his eyes.

"I met with him last night," Croft said.

Stephens looked up, but said nothing.

"He's calling himself Sandy Walker, but it's not his real name."

"You met in person? Dammit Bob, you're going to end up in Leavenworth."

"I know, that Hicks woman scares the hell out of me, but she pissed me off too."

"What about the pilot, does he know what happened to Jon and Carol?"

"He's not sure, but he said there is little or no chance they survived."

Fischer looked back at his plate. "I have to know. I can't just walk away from this now. The ship is gone, Jon is gone, the investigation is over, and I have no answers."

Fischer was livid, the muscles in his jaw spasming. He told him everything he could remember about the meeting.

"I wish I had answers, Emil, but I don't. I submitted my retirement paperwork an hour ago and I don't think they'll court martial me, it will draw too much attention and that's the last thing they will want. Leaving will make it easier for everybody."

"So now what?"

"Well, I'm heading home to pack. I'm driving to Albuquerque to look for a place to live and get my mind off this thing. Sara's parents used to live there, and I always enjoyed the city. I'll keep in touch, but for now, I've got to get away from this before I go insane."

The drive back to his apartment led him past the damaged hangar. He saw the ragged hole in the roof and the entrance now blocked by barricades and crime scene tape. Getting away was probably what he needed. This was all a failure in his eyes—the first loss of someone under his command. He would never be able to close this file. Someone else would do that for him.

His bed was just as he'd left it, covered in stacks of clean clothes, the few extra linens he owned, cheap towels, and toiletries. An empty olive drab duffle bag and two of the suitcases Sara bought just before their honeymoon lay open on the bed waiting for him.

There were so many memories in this room. Good ones, bad ones, and now it didn't feel like home. Just a place to store his things and sleep.

As he put the first stack of clothes in the duffle bag, his cell phone rang. "Yes?"

"Colonel, it's Burton. I know Bowman is back in command, but I wanted you to know the base has just been put on alert, DEFCON 3. Something serious in Iran is all I know."

"DEFCON 3, Jesus! Thank you, Lieutenant, let me know if you hear anything new."

Something big in Iran! The base hadn't been at DEFCON 3 since the Cuban Missile Crisis and that was before he was even born, and now there was nothing for him to do. It was a helpless feeling being relieved of command and by Friday, he would be unemployed.

DEFCON 3, dammit! With a cold beer, he switched on the news hoping to see something involving Iran.

There was nothing but politics and commercials. Bored and frustrated, he closed his eyes and thought of Sara which led to the dream. Dreams had become easier to remember recently and he recognized the dress she had been wearing in the last one: a purple sundress—she loved that dress. In the dream, they were walking in London, the last stop on their honeymoon. Then he thought of Stephens and Vones, then the pilot, Sandy Walker.

"Trans-Data" he had said. A founding member. He laughed and thought of himself in a suit and tie behind a desk.

"Not in this lifetime, my friend," he told the muted television.

Give me until Wednesday. Well, tomorrow was Wednesday, and if he didn't hear from the man, he would call Flórez and tell him everything. It was out of his hands now.

He could live off his pension comfortably and if things got tight, he could find work somewhere. Tired of living on drab military bases, he was going to look for a country club in the suburbs as he once promised his wife.

Lost in the thought of moving, he didn't notice the grainy video playing on the television. Then he sat up realizing he was looking at the mushroom cloud of a nuclear explosion. He ignored the anchor and watched the video taken by someone in a town called Arisman, southeast of Natanz in Iran. The bright, unmistakable mushroom cloud was rising behind a mountain range.

It was like watching the old nuclear test videos he had seen hundreds of times over his career. The video was probably taken with a cell phone that was having trouble focusing on the cloud. The person's hand was shaking, but there was no mistaking what had happened. The top of the cloud was losing heat in the upper atmosphere, but it was still a seething dark red mass as the video ended.

"Holy shit!" he said and turned the volume up.

"This just in," the anchor said. "The Israeli president denies any involvement in the attack on Iran's nuclear facility. The president said his forces remain on high alert only as a precaution for a possible Iranian counterattack. There is still no word from Iran. We've been told there are widespread power outages, and some electronic devices are not working, possibly due to an electromagnetic pulse or EMP, a byproduct of a nuclear explosion. I must point out that these are speculations so far. There has been no official word from our president, but the White House has scheduled a briefing for eight o'clock tonight."

"Something big in Iran," Burton had said. Well, now he knew. He stood and walked back and forth in front of the television as the image played repeatedly. This was the first aboveground nuclear detonation in decades, and this was big.

This will be one of those moments, a flashbulb memory seared into my brain for life, like the day of the September eleventh attacks in New York, or the morning the Challenger exploded during liftoff in Florida.

On September eleventh, he had been in the base commissary eating breakfast when a sudden hush came over the soldiers in the room. "An accident at the World Trade Center," someone said. "Clear skies; how could a modern airliner hit a building in clear skies?" Then the second plane hit, and shouts of anger erupted. "That was no accident!" someone yelled, then the Pentagon was hit. Silence was replaced by screaming and shouting. Men and women were ready for action. Anything was better than sitting in a cafeteria. Some were furious, others wept. This would be very similar. It was horrible, but you couldn't stop watching.

"Give me until Wednesday," the pilot had said, and he wondered if it was a coincidence.

Chapter 53
Six

Driving back to Santa Fe, his eyes darted between the road ahead of him and the rearview mirror expecting to see Flórez behind him. He was having second thoughts about having driven to Clovis. I could have sent the signal from anywhere. Why Clovis? It was one of the few places Flórez knew of, and he may still be in the town looking for him. But something told him it had to be Clovis, another premonition perhaps.

He pushed paranoia aside and watched the mundane scenery through the window. In his lifetime there had been plenty of death, but he had never seen it up close, much less caused it.

I pressed the damned key. What happened?

If his program worked, how many people died, did they suffer, and how many more will soon perish from the fallout?

How many mothers and fathers will die like my parents?

The thought of death reminded him of the two men in Chicago, and his stomach cramped. He pulled off the road just in time to heave up the single bite of the sandwich. He looked at the mess and then heaved again.

The heaving and the ache in his bowels felt like they would never end, leaving him on his hands and knees in the swale. Dust and grit battered his face as traffic raced by ignoring him. He looked at the desert sand beneath him and thought of Susan. Susan would have stopped to help a stranger.

As the cramping eased and strength returned to his legs, he got back in the car and pulled into traffic. His shirt, soaked in sweat, clung to his skin and the cold air coming from the vents gave him chills. It had all seemed so simple, so logical, so sterile. Now he realized the magnitude of pressing that dammed key.

What had he done to his past? He thought of Two and wondered what she would be doing now. Was she still alive? Was it possible that her time line was still occurring and running parallel to his?

Driving passed the Trans-Data complex, he looked for Flórez. There was no sign of him or the military; not a single car or truck was in the lot. He continued west and chose a Courtyard Inn, parked the Explorer and went inside.

A crowd of guests stood silently in the hotel lobby in front of a television, and he saw the word Natanz on the screen. Something had happened after all and he felt his stomach twist again. He didn't want to see it yet, not like this and not with all these people around him.

Drained physically and mentally, he got a room. Exhaustion, his cramping stomach, the desire to shower and sleep were competing with his need to know what he had done in Iran.

The small refrigerator in his room was stocked with water and miniature bottles of alcohol, and he grabbed the closest, a Jack Daniel's Tennessee Honey, twisted the top off and drank half the bottle. He grabbed several more and sat on the edge of the bed.

He had never had much of a taste for hard liquor. He had tried vodka once at a graduation ceremony and had not liked the taste. He stripped off everything but his underwear and turned on the television.

In the center of the screen, stood an empty podium with the seal of the White House, behind it stood two US flags. In the bottom corner, a grainy video of a mushroom cloud rose, and scrolling underneath that, "Nuclear Blast in Iran. US armed forces on alert."

The text repeated itself several times as he drank the remains of the first bottle, savoring the rich taste of honey. The aroma and the alcohol took the edge off the dread of what he expected to see next.

A man walked to the podium and he drained the second bottle, dug his fingernails into the rich leather of the recliner as if bracing for the impact of a collision.

"The President of the United States and the Secretary of Defense both strongly deny any US involvement in the events that occurred hours ago in Iran, and we condemn the hostile act of any nation responsible for today's attack. We join the rest of the world in prayer for the people of Iran." The man left the podium without taking questions.

His briefing was followed by an earlier recording at the UN building in New York. Iran's UN Ambassador, Ahmed Khoshroo stood a few feet in front of his Russian counterpart as they held a news conference.

"As I stand here this evening, many thousands of Iranians are dead, and many more are dying. Just after midnight in Tehran, a nuclear bomb was dropped on the peaceful city of Natanz. Israel and its ally, the United States, have long threatened to destroy our attempts to develop peaceful nuclear energy, and they have apparently followed through on their threats. We condemn the Zionists and all their allies in the West. We ask for an immediate UN investigation and the punishment of all those involved in this massacre. Our armed forces are on full alert, and we will have our revenge."

The ambassador continued speaking, but Six stopped listening. "Revenge," the man had said. He had made things worse, and now the world was at the brink of a war that never happened. Millions had died in his time line, and now it was possible that millions would die again, only this time, he alone was responsible for their deaths. *I have to fix this!*

The laptop came to life, and he uploaded files he had saved over the last few days. The two warheads in Israel were safe for now, but the Iranians would soon discover what he had done. He needed to tell someone where they were, but who?

And where is the other warhead?

It has to be on a ship. The huge propane tank was too big to get through security at an airport, but going through a major seaport would be easy. Wherever it was, it was still off-line, and he set an audible alarm to let him know when it tried to reconnect with its mainframe.

He was asleep long before the uploads finished. The sun had set, the desert sands were cooling, and there were three Jack Daniel's bottles, two Patron XO Cafes, and a Fireball all empty and in the trash.

Chapter 54
Atlanta

At the CNN headquarters in Atlanta, Grace Holloway sat in the producer's chair in the control room. In front of her, a dozen technicians sat at their consoles, controlling and cueing video and audio clips for the next hour's news. The glass panel in front of them showed the current feed from the New York, Washington, and Los Angeles control rooms. A separate screen off to the side was the CNN International program.

She was grateful to work on something other than the tensions developing in the Middle East and Europe. After scanning the printout of the hour's scripted news, she saw the next few guests were in their chairs, waiting for their interviews.

Ashley Santiz, anchor for *The Legal Opinion*, was next, and both the anchor and her guest were cued on split screens. The guest, Marlon Davis, a gun control activist from Chicago, was fighting with his earpiece. A technician had stepped over and was trying to secure it when the fifteen-second countdown began.

Viewers in their homes watched as Santiz began.

"Good afternoon to all of you on the East Coast, and good morning to those of you joining us from the rest of the country. We have continuing coverage on the crisis in Iran, but first we will speak with Marlon Davis in Chicago."

As the anchor introduced her guest, the screen split and

showed Davis with his finger in his ear, struggling with the earpiece. Behind him in the background, the old Sears Tower, now called the Willis Tower, loomed over busy traffic in downtown Chicago.

The man missed the cue when his earpiece slipped out, and Holloway cursed. She watched him on the monitor as he tried to force it back in his ear, then the image was replaced with another one showing two men walking past a row of twelve white canisters.

"What the hell is this?" she asked. She heard a similar outburst from the crew behind the camera, then she heard people shouting on the control room floor.

"Someone's hacked our feed!" Holloway yelled to her assistant.

"I apologize," Santiz told her viewers. "We seem to have lost Mr. Davis. I hope we'll get him back in a moment. Let's take a short break."

But there was no break, and the image of the two men expanded to full screen. Holloway recognized the men as the current and former presidents of Iran. Occasionally, other men, dressed in lab coats, came into the camera's view.

The video was in black and white, there was no sound, and several minutes into the footage, another man came into view. Holloway did not recognize him. As the video continued to roll, the newcomer walked the two presidents to the nearest canister, lifted an access panel, and pointed to something inside. The men smiled, and he replaced the panel.

At the bottom of the video feed, there was a date and time stamp, it was December 12, 2024 21:25 Natanz #5. Then the screen changed to a different room. The date stamp was the same, but this camera identified it as "Natanz #4." This room was larger than the first and was occupied by hundreds of stainless-steel centrifuges. The video switched again to the original room with camera number five. There were only six of the glossy white casings now and six empty cradles. The black Emblem of Iran, its four crescents and a sword, were painted on the sides of those remaining. The time stamp on this video was June 24, 2025 23:58:39." As the seconds counter reached fifty-five, the image on the screen vanished, leaving the gray-white snow of static.

The CNN feed returned to Ashley Santiz, who looked confused, then she realized she was back on the air. She started to say something, but the CNN logo replaced her image and then cut to a commercial.

Brian Cafferty wasn't having much luck at Fox News in New York either. All their equipment was working correctly, but every attempt to cut into the black-and-white video failed.

One commentator stared at the screen and said, "God, I hope those aren't nukes. Look at the date."

"Brian, what time did the first reports of the attack on Natanz come in?"

"Just after midnight their time, a few minutes after that last video ended."

"Holy shit! I think that was them getting hit."

At the Pentagon, the Secretary of Defense, Robert Polink, and his aide watched the recorded CNN news video for the second time.

"Definitely nukes," Polink said aloud. "Nothing else would make sense. That third guy is Director Engeta. He's in charge of their nuclear program. No way to be certain that they're armed and ready though. In the first video, those last six aren't hooked up. You can see a computer ribbon cable plugged into each of the first six. I'm not sure, but I'd say the first six are farther along, maybe even complete. In the second video from that room, the first six are missing and the last six are now connected to that console. Whoever uploaded this video must want us to know that's important. The video ends the instant we monitored the explosion."

"Sir," his aide said, "we have the data from the two drones we sent out over Natanz. The 'sniffer' picked up an isotope that doesn't match anything we have on file, and I think we have all the current reactor signatures. It's possible it could be something new from China, maybe India, but nobody else is producing new material. Personally, I bet it's Iranian, and it's probably from one of those right there," he said, pointing to the monitor.

"I think it's possible that this was some type of Iranian accident, not a strike by another government. An accident, or maybe sabotage. Wait, are we missing something here?" Polink asked. If the explosion took out those six nukes, where are the other six?"

The Secretary of Defense heard his printer come to life, and he waited for the machine to finish.

"Holy Mother of God!" Polink said, holding the page, "Listen to this, 'There are six more warheads. Two are in Israel at the following coordinates. Three are in Tehran. The final one is missing and possibly on its way to Washington, DC.'"

"Get me someone from logistics, and see if the Israeli liaison is still in the building, and I want to know how someone hacked us and sent this to my personal printer!"

"Sir, I'm hearing the White House also received the same information. It's being seen all over Washington."

Chapter 55
Haifa, Israel

David Haim and his assault team were in the ready room at five in the morning. Awake now since the news of the Natanz event, they were watching a replay of the Israeli-Egyptian soccer game when the Red Phone, the direct line to Mossad's command center rang.

"Haim," he said, and then listened. "Understood." He hung up and turned to his team.

"Full gear and in the ready room in five minutes."

At 5:16 a.m., their brown delivery truck pulled out of the nondescript two-story warehouse and headed toward Haifa on the Coastal Highway. The captain listened to the radio traffic on his earpiece as headquarters relayed updates from the drone. The warehouse was a one story, windowless building with a single roll-up door surrounded by a standard eight-foot chain-link fence topped with razor wire. No guards or security personnel were visible in the drone's high-definition video.

Haim listened to radio traffic from the second team already in place at the Ramat Aviv Mall: "Two LP gas tanks," someone said. "One is showing heavy gamma radiation. The other is minimal and appears to be full of LP. No sign of surveillance, although there are plenty of security cameras in the parking lot."

Haim's sniper team made their way to the second floor of a warehouse across the street with a clear view of everything but the back of the target building.

"It looks clear, Captain. No movement, and no visible surveillance."

The entry team used a Halligan bar to pry open the front door. The two lead penetrators cleared the small office as two more broke off and cleared the rest of the building.

"All clear!"

A single flatbed trailer sat in the empty warehouse, and Captain Haim walked around it, filming both the trailer and the two red, white, and blue LP gas tanks strapped to the frame. The trailer itself looked like a common, well-used flatbed. There was no license plate, but a serial number and an Egyptian registration plate were riveted to the frame. The tanks themselves appeared new and smelled like fresh paint. The camera streamed it all back to someone in headquarters, and he was told to secure the perimeter and wait for instructions.

"Secure the building, four in front, two in the back, and bring the truck around to the front. Adina, you and Johnny stay on your post until we get relief. Radio if anything moves." Two clicks on the radio told him she understood.

He was told it would take fifteen minutes to get the techs there from Negev. He sat on an old plastic milk crate and leaned his Galil rifle against the wall, listening to the sounds of the seaport two blocks away. He looked at the two tanks and wondered if he would live long enough to see the flash.

Chapter 56
Six

Light streaming in through the curtain meant he had overslept. It was after nine in the morning. He splashed hot water on his face, dressed, then picked up the suitcase, the laptop, and his bag of soiled clothes and rushed out of the room.

Eric Ridge had recommended an office manager, and the man was due to arrive at Trans-Data in twenty minutes. With everything he owned in the Explorer, he raced to the deserted parking lot, arriving with ten minutes to spare.

Pacing in the office, he was nervous and needed coffee but he had forgotten to buy the machine. News on his laptop was all about Natanz, and things had worsened. A video showed a gaping crater in the open desert. Another showed the damaged town of Natanz itself, the camera panning over hundreds of bodies in the downtown streets.

"That can't be possible," he said aloud. "The town is too far away to have been so affected."

Then he watched as a fleet of Russian warships cruised in the Mediterranean Sea, military bases around the world were on high alert. A war was imminent. In his mind, missiles were already in the air, bombs were falling, buildings collapsing and dead bodies littered the streets.

"What have I done?"

Typing furiously on the laptop, he wished he had put the telemetry suit on, it would be quicker but it was packed away. He spent the previous night uploading programs and videos that should have eased tensions. They should have been delivered by now. What had gone wrong?

He needed more time, but Flórez could be seconds away and the first warhead could already be in Washington.

Can I program the laptop to disable the warhead on its own?

He pictured a government agent searching the laptop, prodding its files, interrogating him, torturing him, and then remembered the beacon—no one could crack its memory! He accessed it, wrote a new program and uploaded it. The beacon acknowledged and signed off.

The Earth's future was now in the hands of a satellite the size of a basketball.

"I'm missing something," he said.

Croft! If something does happen to me, Croft should know about the beacon. He started to call the colonel and saw Susan's text.

I will be in Albuquerque this afternoon. Meet me there for dinner if you can. Hilton Gardens.

The text had come in two hours ago while he slept. He read the text again. It meant she wanted to talk, but was it a positive thing, or was she ending it all and wanted to do it in person?

He grabbed his keys—and saw a man standing outside the glass door. Flórez had finally found him. He froze, unable to move—the man smiled and waved.

The man looked nothing like a soldier. There was a boyish smile, he wore a two-piece suit and Oxford shoes. The office manager.

"Good morning, Mr. Walker. I'm Dustin Torrence. Eric Ridge sent me over."

Chapter 57
Flórez

Flórez watched a young man in a suit enter the building, then put the binoculars on the seat. It was a combination of both luck and experience that led him to Trans-Data. One of his aides found a hit on a Sandy Walker through a real estate transaction, and it was an odd one—an abandoned office complex far from the business district of Santa Fe.

From this distance, the man looked too young to be the pilot. But there was a Ford Explorer already in the parking lot, and the Saguaro Inn manager had mentioned a dark-colored SUV, possibly a Ford.

He picked up his phone and saw he had missed another call from Croft, the third one this morning. He debated calling his old friend back, but he was working for Marjory Hicks now, and she had made it clear that Croft was no longer in the loop.

He called her number again and listened to the recording. "This is Deputy Director Hicks, leave a message."

"Ms. Hicks, it's Flórez again. I think I have the man you're looking for."

There was a lot going on in Washington with the attack on Iran, but finding this guy, if he was what Croft thought he was, was also important. There were two MPs on their way from White Sands, but they were still two hours away. Hicks had said to keep everything low key and on a need-to-know basis, so a helicopter out of Cannon Air Force Base was out of the question.

The door opened and two men walked out into the sunlight. Through the binoculars he watched them speaking, then walk around the building and out of sight. One of them was the young man in the suit; the other was dressed casually in jeans and a pullover shirt. The man from the future. He laughed at the way it sounded. He wasn't sure what he had expected to see, but this guy looked *too* average. He did look like the man in the bank's video however, but at this distance it was impossible to tell.

Seconds later, they came back into view and shook hands. He studied the older of the two men and then called Croft. As he waited for an answer, both men got in their separate cars and headed for the gate.

As Croft answered, both cars came through the gate and split up with the Explorer heading southeast.

"Shit! I'll call you back," Flórez said, tossing the phone on the seat. He was too far away and could lose the man in traffic. One quick turn on a side street, and it would be over.

The Explorer did turn, and it was gone.

"Shit," he repeated slamming his fist on the console. He hit the gas no longer caring if the pilot saw him. At the next stop sign, he had to gamble. Was the man heading to the interstate, or back into town. He turned right towards the interstate, accelerated and found the Explorer in front of him at the next light.

The light changed and both cars accelerated on the entrance ramp for southbound I-25. With the Explorer safely three cars in front of him, he called Croft. "I have your guy."

"Where are you?"

"We're southwest bound on I-25, he's a couple hundred yards in front of me. I'm not sure where he's going, but we're coming up on the Santa Fe Municipal Airport. If he doesn't exit there, he's probably going all the way to Albuquerque. Bob, I have to tell you, the NSA has cut you out. Hicks will crucify me if she knows we even spoke, but I can't get in touch with her, she's tied up with the nuke in Iran. I don't give a shit about what she wants, what do you want?"

"Tristan, be careful with this guy. I think he may have been involved in that."

"Are you serious—Iran? How the fuck is that possible?"

"I think he's trying to change history as he knows it, and he may not be done yet."

"I gotta hang up, Bob. I'll try to keep you posted if I can."

The Explorer passed the small airport and kept going. Keeping a car in between him and the pilot, he tried Hicks again, and this time she answered.

"Director Hicks, I have the man you're looking for in front of me on I-25, possibly heading to Albuquerque."

"Take him into custody immediately Major, and call me the moment you have him. It's chaos here at the moment."

"Ms. Hicks, Croft thinks this guy had something to do with Natanz. I shouldn't say more on the phone until we speak face to face."

People were shouting in the background, but the director was silent for a moment.

"You spoke to Croft?"

Before he could answer, she said, "Croft is not to be involved in this, Major. Was I not clear? Take the man into custody right now and call me the moment you do."

There was a click, then silence on the other end.

"Fuck you!" Flórez shouted into the silence.

With a small truck between them, the Explorer was cruising at just over the speed limit. Hopefully, he was going all the way to Albuquerque, and he would never see Flórez until it was too late. If his timing was right, his backup would be in place before they reached the outskirts of the city; the fewer people who saw the stop, the better.

He settled in for another hour of driving when his own brand of chaos happened right in front of him.

Chapter 58
Six

Traffic was light on the interstate, and most of it was heading in the opposite direction. Six listened to bits and pieces of conversations from random nearby cell phones and CB radios the truck drivers chatted on. Once he thought he heard the name "Croft" and listened for a few minutes before giving up and turned on the Explorer's radio.

His telemetry suit was folded neatly in the suitcase behind him. It had been days since he'd worn it, and his ability to transmit and receive without it continued to strengthen.

The next sign said "Santa Fe Municipal Airport," and as he passed it, he saw a small airplane sitting at the end of the runway, its propeller spinning and two people sitting inside. One of the two spoke into a microphone, and he heard a man say, "Cessna forty-four Sierra ready for takeoff." Someone acknowledged, and the small plane began to move.

The outside temperature gauge said it was ninety-six degrees. It would be warm tonight, just like the night in Clovis and he pictured Susan dressed as she was on their first date. What a perfect evening it had been. This date would be very different; he knew it, and there was nothing he could do about it. He tried to force a premonition, some hint of how seeing Susan would go, but there wasn't anything to feel, just an empty place somewhere in his chest.

He looked to his left and saw an elevated train track running parallel between the north and southbound lanes, and he imagined the train running next to him, huge clouds of white steam bellowing out of its engine, then remembered they would be running on diesel fuel, still it would be fascinating to see one.

His phone chirped in the seat next to him, informing him that the program he had uploaded earlier was finally decrypting in several places across the East Coast. Hopefully the escalation developing in the Middle East would ease once everyone saw the Natanz facility for what it was.

Ten minutes later and ten miles closer to seeing Susan, a road sign informed him he was approaching Alamo Creek. He hoped he might see a river, but all he saw were a few stunted trees and more scrub as he crossed over the bridge. There was a brief sensation of movement and a blur as something moved towards the left side of the windshield, and then silence.

Chapter 59
Flórez

Fred Thompson had been on the road now for ten hours. He might have had a chance to save the rig had he been more alert, but when the left front tire blew, he was late in reacting. His twelve-year-old Freightliner pulled hard left as he hit the brakes, which locked the rear wheels of the trailer behind him. The tractor swerved toward the concrete bridge ahead, and Fred yanked the wheel back to the right, causing the trailer to jackknife. He watched through the passenger-side window as the back of the fifty-three-foot-long Fruehauf trailer and its load of twelve tons of rebar began its slide to the left, then he felt the cab lift, and he saw only blue sky.

As the cab overturned, the trailer broke free and its momentum carried it over the elevated tracks. Then, like the cab, it too overturned, and its load of rebar broke free from the straps securing it.

The two SUVs following Fred Thompson's truck swerved, trying to avoid the overturned semi and sideswiped each other before coming to rest in the median.

Fred regained consciousness listening to the sound of someone pounding on his windshield. Disoriented and unable to open his eyes, the sharp smell of diesel fuel caused him to panic.

One eye was swollen shut, and the other one was covered in thick blood, causing his eyelashes to stick to his cheek, but he could see well enough to know the truck's cab was on its left side. Two women were looking through the windshield, and one wearing a red dress was hitting the glass with her shoe while the other spoke on a cell phone.

"You need to get out, the truck is leaking!" the woman with the shoe in her hand shouted. Both women looked down at the spreading pool of diesel fuel and backed away. He took his seat belt off and slid down, landing on the driver's door. It was awkward trying to stand, and as he reached up for the passenger door, pain shot though his arm like an icepick. His left arm was bent just below his elbow and was definitely broken.

The passenger door handle was in reach, but at two hundred twenty pounds and with only one arm, there was no way he could pull himself up. He tried kicking out the windshield, but there wasn't room to get enough power into the kick. He looked around the cab, unstrapped the fire extinguisher, and hit the windshield with it a few times. The glass cracked but wouldn't give.

"I can't get out!" he screamed, looking at the diesel fuel now pooling around his feet.

Flórez watched the southbound tractor trailer swerve, then the cab flipped on its side, sending its cargo through the landscaped median and into the southbound lanes. Clouds of vegetation and dirt flew everywhere, obscuring his view of all four lanes of traffic. The small truck he had been using as cover was braking hard now, and both he and the truck came to a stop short of the bridge.

Several dozen bundles of the steel rebar were blocking all the southbound lanes, and there was no way to drive around them. There was no sign of the pilot or his Explorer.

On foot, he ran forward past all the dust and debris, trying to get a glimpse of the blue SUV. Had the pilot avoided the accident, unaware of what had happened behind him?

He was breathing hard now, and he could taste the oily diesel fuel in the air. He turned toward the wrecked truck, close enough now that he could see the driver and the women trying to help him. The fire started slowly, then it reached the fuel puddled under the cab. *Whoomph!*

It blew a woman in a red dress off her feet and away from the flames as oily black smoke and fire engulfed the cab. Fortunately, the inferno obscured the sight of the man inside, but Flórez was close enough to hear him screaming. He watched helplessly, then turned and walked back to the median while trying to block out the sickening sounds of the dying man.

The fire was spreading onto the tracks and the heat was getting intense. He turned to look at the two women. The one in the dress was kneeling on the ground in tears, her hair singed in spots and both her knees scraped raw. The other was standing unhurt but motionless, watching the fire.

"Did you see what happened?" he asked.

She turned and saw his uniform. "I called the police just as it caught fire. I spoke to the driver," she said, looking at the cab. There was no sign of the driver now, just the swirl of orange flames and the heavy black smoke.

"I think you're in shock. You should sit down by your friend."

"I don't know her. She was in the other car." She pointed at two SUVs a hundred feet down the road.

She looked back at him, and he saw her eyes focus as if she was seeing him for the first time.

"It looked like he just lost control. He swerved and it flipped over."

"Did you see any other cars? Did you see a blue Explorer on the other side?"

"No, I didn't. All I could see was the truck."

Flames were eating at the dried grass in the median now, adding gray smoke to the roiling black cloud rising from the truck.

Hicks was going to be pissed.

He called his team and told them to expect the Explorer in the next forty minutes if it continued all the way to Albuquerque. *If.* There were a dozen places he could go, but with luck, they'll see the Explorer and grab the pilot.

The wind shifted, and the smell of everything burning forced him back across the road. Standing next to a bundle of rebar, he saw a large section of dark metallic blue sheet metal. He turned it over and saw the chrome embossed emblem—Ford.

Following the debris field and gouges in the asphalt, he made his way down to a shallow creek running under the bridge, and there sat the silent overturned Explorer. It would have gone unnoticed for hours with all that was happening above it.

He inched his way down to the creek and found the driver upside down and still strapped into his seat, his head just a few inches out of the water running through the broken windows. The deflated airbag hid most of his face. Moving it aside, he got his first good look at the man.

Blood from several deep gashes and lots of smaller superficial cuts dripped freely into the flow of water. He watched it run out the passenger side and into the sunlight, creating a rainbow of colors as it mixed with gasoline and oil leaking from the engine.

The pilot was breathing but unresponsive, and he let him hang in his seat. If his neck was broken, he could kill the man trying to save him. He chose instead to sit back and watch him breathe. As long as he could see the man's chest moving, he would wait.

Most of the SUV front end was crushed, and the passenger side of the windshield was missing. The other half was shattered but still hanging in the frame. The front passenger seatback and tailgate were also missing, and he saw them in the creek along with a bundle of rebar.

It wasn't hard to figure out: a bundle of the steel had broken free of the trailer and passed through the Explorer's windshield, taking out the passenger seat and the tailgate and probably giving the driver a glancing blow on the way out.

Sirens were approaching, EMTs he hoped. There was nothing they could do for the truck driver, but they had a living victim down here.

For the third time today, he rerouted his team, hoping they could get to the scene and help him sort things out. He needed to make several phone calls, and he knew there would be a shitstorm once he notified Hicks.

He sat on a damp stone and called Croft first.

"Bob, you're not going to want to hear this." He told Croft what happened and promised to keep him advised, then called Hicks. "Director Hicks, there's been an accident." He explained all that he could, and she asked no questions.

"Stay with him. Keep him isolated, and call me when you know where they'll take him. I'll take it from there."

The EMT truck arrived first, and a young lieutenant made his way down the bank.

"He's alive, but I was afraid to move him," Flórez said.

The lieutenant said nothing but checked the driver first and then the damage to the Explorer. "That was a good decision, sir."

A second paramedic made his way down to the creek and said a pumper had the fire under control.

The lieutenant said, "Okay, I need a backboard and a head restraint. Have dispatch start Life Flight. We'll extract him through the windshield once we stabilize his head."

"Where will Life Flight take him?" Flórez asked.

"Saint Vincent," the lieutenant said.

Flórez made two more calls and waited.

Chapter 60
Tehran

"How is this possible?" President Rouhani, said watching himself and Katami walking past the warheads. His Minister of Intelligence was most likely dead, and this technician was probably wishing Rouhani was too.

"I'm not sure, sir," the technician answered. "The system that stored the security footage was destroyed in the blast. That system was isolated from all outside sources. Someone inside Natanz must have uplinked the computer, a saboteur perhaps, but the computer runs a self-diagnosis several times a day. It should not have been possible."

"Well, there I am. The whole world is watching me on CNN. Don't tell me what should have been."

Rouhani had never agreed with the Ayatollah's plan. Eight months prior, he advised against it, "We have everything to lose and little to gain," he had said. "The world will condemn us when they discover the truth."

"But Allah will reward us," the old man replied.

Halfway through his meal. he got the summons he had been expecting.

The Ayatollah had not aged well, he thought. Maybe it's the stress of the last few days. His black lungee turban hid most of his hair, but his thick wiry eyebrows and beard were solid white.

The old man looked up and finally acknowledged him. "Tell me, Hassan, who is responsible for this destruction and the humiliation of the Iranian people?"

"Sir, we have no evidence of what happened at Natanz. We must assume that either Israel or the United States launched an attack. The other possibility is that either one of them infiltrated the facility and detonated one of our own warheads. All the evidence was consumed. There is nothing left to examine."

"Explain the videos that are still being shown around the world."

"I have no explanation, sir. I have the best people available investigating what we can. As you know, Minister Katami is missing and presumed to have been at Natanz with Director Engeta."

"What were they doing there at that time of night?"

"I don't know, sir. They may have discovered a security breach. There is no mention of their meeting in any of their emails."

The Ayatollah stood and made his way to the inner door. "Leave me. That is all for now."

Chapter 61
Croft

As Croft drove through the base's final security gate, a black Chevrolet Suburban was approaching from the opposite direction. Behind its tinted windows, he saw two people in the front seats. Was Hicks back for more blood? He accelerated and headed toward I-25 and Albuquerque.

Tomorrow, he would turn the car in to the motor pool, along with a few issued uniforms. He would keep his dress uniform though as a memento of thirty-one years of service.

A realtor was meeting him at the Ladera Golf Course at two, and he wanted to arrive early to see the clubhouse. How often had he told Sara that once he retired, they would live in a country club and rub elbows with the rich folks? The memory made him smile, and he forgot about the pilot for a moment.

In the course's clubhouse, he ordered a margarita and wondered why Sandy Walker was on his way to Albuquerque. He still had questions for the man, and being relieved of duty left him no way to find answers.

Fox News was on the TV above the bar. The president was speaking, but without the volume and no closed captioning, he was forced to read the banner scrolling on the bottom of the screen: *"USS Dwight D. Eisenhower aircraft carrier strike group passes through Suez Canal. US Navy-led Task Force 50 arrives in the Gulf region."*

Behind the president, he saw General Polink standing to his left and another man he thought may be the NSA's director on his right and Hicks was right behind him.

So she's not at the base, well, that's good news, he thought.

His cell phone rang and it was Flórez again.

"What? You can't be serious. Will he live?"

Croft jumped off the stool and paced through the empty clubhouse. "All right, Tristan, I'll try and make my way to Santa Fe and meet you at the hospital."

He paid his tab and headed for the parking lot. His phone rang again, this time it was General Scott.

"Bob, I know where you are. Meet me near the clubhouse. I'm almost there."

A light gray HH-60 Pave Hawk from Kirtland Air Force Base orbited over the practice putting green, sending golfers scrambling into the parking lot. It set down on the green, its wheels sinking into the soft grass up to their axles.

The door of the Pave Hawk opened, and General Scott waved him in. Lifting off, it ripped big chunks of sod out of the turf.

"How are you going to explain this?" Croft said, looking around the Pave Hawk's cabin.

"I still have a few friends—and I may have mentioned your name. I was at White Sands meeting with your soon-to-be ex-boss. The NSA and the FBI are involved now I'm afraid. Hicks will probably be leaving Washington soon and coming out here, so I wanted to beat her to it. I love pissing that woman off. On a serious note, she thinks you and Fischer are conspiring to obstruct her investigation. She thinks the ship is a hoax, that there is a foreign government involved, and you are either part of it or being played by them."

Except for the whine of the turbines and the rotor, both men sat in silence for a minute, then Croft said, "My name couldn't have gotten you very far."

Scott laughed. "Okay, so I was bored sitting around White Sands, and I wanted to see this guy in person."

"What's Hicks going to say?" Croft said.

"She'll be furious, but I don't work for her. Anything new from Flórez?"

"They transported him, but nothing since then."

Doctor Nelson Young made the first incision just above the navel and cut upward toward the breastbone. This was the tricky part, trying to avoid slicing through the bowel which would lead to a massive infection if the patient lived, but the internal bleeding would kill him first if he didn't find the source quickly. Several times now, his blood pressure had dropped to zero, and he had been transfused with whole blood twice.

"What's the patient's name?"

The surgical nurse glanced down at a chart tie-wrapped to the operating table, "Sandy Walker, thirty-two years old."

"Okay, I found it. A small puncture to the suprarenal aorta, a lateral aortorrhaphy will take care of it for now; we'll have to graft it later. There is another tear right there; clamp that please. We'll get to it next if he survives that long."

He was working as fast as he could, but the blood just kept coming. Now his rubber-soled booties were slipping in it.

"Okay, this one is holding, but he's still losing blood from there," he said, pointing to another artery. "How's his pressure?"

"Up a little, forty over twenty, but I'm having trouble reading the monitor. The signal drops out like there's a bad connection. Everything looks okay though. I'll swap it out for another one as soon as I can."

The doctor looked up at the monitor and sure enough the image was pixilating, flashing random colors before returning to the patient's vitals. Keep a close eye on it and let me know if it drops anymore."

As he worked on the damaged aorta, the team heard and felt the vibration from another helicopter landing on the pad above them. This one louder than the last.

"We may need to call in another trauma team. I can't stop on this guy; I figure another hour and a half at least."

The nurse looked over at her intern. He nodded and went out the door.

The intern pulled off his soiled gown and gloves and spoke to the nurse behind the desk.

"Doctor Young said to call in another team for the incoming victims. We have our hands full with this patient. What is it anyway?"

"It's not Life Flight; it's the military. They called in a landing clearance just before I heard them approach."

The intern took two steps at a time up the stairwell and saw the huge Sikorsky lift off as two men walked through the automatic doors. One was dressed in a full uniform, ribbons covering most of the left side of his chest and the other man was wearing plaid pants and a golf shirt.

The noise from the departing helicopter died down enough for the uniformed officer to speak as they descended the stairwell.

"I'm General Scott, this is Colonel Croft. We're here to see a colleague just brought in, Sandy Walker."

"Yes, he's still in surgery. Come with me. You can't see him of course, and I need to get back in there myself. There is another soldier here somewhere; I think he went to make some calls. You can sit here and wait." Scott nodded and the intern went back inside the OR.

Croft could see several of the trauma team through the small glass window, but he could not make out who they were working on. Frustrated, he turned and sat on a couch as Flórez came down the hallway.

"Tristan, anything new?"

"Director Hicks says she has a medical team en route, unknown ETA. And of course, she said this is strictly a need-to-know case. I told her I called you, and she's one angry woman."

"Sorry, Tristan. Maybe the general can help you out of that mess."

"Ha!" Scott laughed. "We're talking about the Deputy Director of the NSA. We're all probably screwed."

The three of them sat quietly looking through the glass section of the doors, wishing they could see more—when the lights went out.

"Now what?" Croft said

When the emergency lighting came on, Croft looked at Flórez bathed in dim red light. "They're going to be running tests on him soon if they haven't already. That may not be easy to explain. Any suggestions?"

"I was thinking the same thing," Scott said. "What is there that we can say? If they come out asking questions, I'll tell them it's classified and to keep their mouths shut until Hicks' people get here. Just a bluff, really, but they won't know. Then it will be her problem."

"I don't relish the idea of facing that woman right now." Flórez said, looking through the glass at the pilot. All the monitors that had been active moments before were dark, and panicked nurses and technicians were struggling to get their equipment back on line.

Somewhere above them, they heard the thrumming sound as the generator started. Then the lights in the hallway and trauma room surged, flickered, and then steadied.

Doctor Young felt sweat running down his forehead as the lights flickered again.

"Alright, calm down, everyone. Forget the monitors for now and help me keep this man alive! Just use a cuff and give me his pressure every thirty seconds. His heart is beating—I can see it right there—we don't need a monitor for that."

Another drop of sweat ran down his forehead, and the nurse caught it.

He stepped back and looked down at the patient. "Okay, this seems to be the last tear. I'll sew this up, and I think we're done with the bleeding. Blood pressure?"

"Fifty over thirty, still rising."

Holding up the X-rays in the flickering light, he counted, "Looks like five, six—no, make that seven broken ribs, three on the left and four on the right. No punctures to the lungs. Looks like a fractured pelvis too. I'm not sure what these shadows are on his spine, maybe something in his clothing during the X-ray."

"He didn't have a shirt on when they brought him in," the nurse said.

The lights surged, dimmed, and steadied again, and jagged lines and spikes scrolled across the few monitors still working.

"Is there a storm outside?" the doctor asked.

"I don't think so. It was clear when the second helicopter arrived."

"Well," the doctor said, holding the X-ray up to the light, "get an orthopedist on call. Let them know about the pelvis." He stepped back from the table, admiring his work.

"It's going to hurt like hell when he wakes up—if he lives through the night, that is. Let's close him up."

Croft was on his feet the instant the door opened.

"Doctor, what can you tell me?"

"He's alive. Many people with his injuries would be dead by now, but the next few hours will tell. There was some unusual brain activity, but both of our EEGs are malfunctioning now. I'm going to have an MRI and a CT scan done before he heads to recovery. Are you family?"

"No," Croft said, looking at Scott, "just colleagues. He has no immediate family."

"Well, it will be a while before you can see him, if and when he comes to. I hate to be blunt, but I want to be honest."

The three men looked up at the ceiling as the steady vibration above them announced the approach of another helicopter. A minute later, several men in suits walked through the door and addressed the general.

"General Scott, I'm Special Agent Bouie, FBI Albuquerque. I'm here to assist until Deputy Director Hicks and her team arrive. Also," he added, looking at the doctor, "Major Danko from Fort Carson and a team of surgeons are en route, ETA about an hour now. Doctor Young, I understand you were a Marine Corpsman in Afghanistan?"

"Yes, I was. But this is my patient. We have everything under control here. Why are you bringing in an outside team?"

"This is a classified matter. I'll need you and your staff to keep any details and all reports of this man to yourselves."

"But there will be a lot of our staff monitoring his recovery. That will be difficult." He looked at Croft and then back to Agent Bouie. "I saw some type of shadowing up and down his spine. I thought it was just a defect in the image. Is there anything I should know?"

"I can't say, Doctor. The surgical team on its way here now will assist you during his recovery."

Croft thought there would be little *assisting* and more like taking full control once they arrived.

Doctor Young was frustrated but nodded and said, "The internal injuries were severe, like I said, and the repairs are very fragile. I'm inducing a coma to eliminate movement for forty-eight hours. If any of the sutures or grafts come loose, he could bleed out before we could stop it. If he survives the next forty-eight hours, he will be out of the woods."

"Agent Bouie, I'm Colonel Croft," he said, extending his hand.

Bouie ignored Croft's hand but nodded, "Colonel, I'm sorry, but I have orders that you and General Scott are not to be on the scene. Ms. Hicks has asked me to escort you both from the hospital. We will take it from here."

Chapter 62
Aurora, Colorado

Marjory Hicks looked through the mirrored glass as the two women worked on Walker. The fluorescent tubes above the pilot pulsed a few times, like the man's heartbeat was affecting them. The pain throbbing in her head, synced with the lights and she reached impulsively for the Altoids tin in her jacket.

Getting the man out of Santa Fe had been a disaster, one she would have to deal with once the news got back to the director, but for the moment, she had to focus on the man behind the glass, Sandy Walker.

The women were talking, and she turned up the volume on the intercom. The static through the speaker pulsed with the lights, and it *did* sound like a heartbeat.

"Genetic engineering?" one of them asked. "Some type of experiment?"

"I don't know any more than you do, Britt. Just keep him sedated."

"It's been three days—four if you count the time at Saint Vincent's."

"Just do it! They want him sedated until they know if he caused the accident."

"If we keep upping the dosage, we'll kill him," the woman said, glancing at the mirror.

"Do you want to end up like the Life Flight team?"

"He was in an induced coma, how could he have had anything to do with that?"

Britt pointed to the flickering lights. "All I know is what I've overheard. The helicopter lost power and its pilot had some type of seizure. That is all I heard. They're lucky any of them survived. They say he's causing these electrical problems too so they want him sedated. Just keep him under until they tell us different."

The lights flared, brighter this time and shattering glass from one of the fixtures rained down behind them.

"I'm adding another two CCs," Britt said adjusting the flow on the IV. The pentobarbital was already suppressing the man's ability to breathe, and now he was on a ventilator. "Call maintenance and have them clean this up."

As the drip increased, the pulsing lights steadied, the static faded and the pounding in Hicks' head eased.

"This isn't right," Marjory heard one of the two say. She watched the anesthetist make notations on the chart, and both left the room. As the door closed, she went in and stood over him.

He looked harmless lying on the bed. Most of the facial cuts were healing, and others were still stitched, but not too bad for a man who had wrecked not just his car but survived a helicopter crash. He looked peaceful as he slept.

She didn't want him to sleep, she wanted him awake. Awake, and more importantly, talking. She needed to hear his voice.

"You're in my head, aren't you Mr. Walker?"

She thought of shaking him awake, but she feared him too. Just standing over him gave her chills. Part of her wanted the man to die, right here. She could wrap this whole mess up and be done with it.

"Just fucking die," she screamed.

You need to control yourself, Marjory, the voice said. *He can't help you if he's dead.*

The door opened, and the anesthetist came back into the room. "Is everything okay, Director Hicks?"

"Of course everything is okay. He's out, isn't he?"

The woman glared at her and closed the door.

"No, I don't want you to die, Mr. Walker," she whispered this time. "You're my golden ticket to the big office with the view."

The man was important only if he lived. She just needed him to speak. A twenty-four-million-dollar helicopter was destroyed, most of its crew injured, and the pilot may still die. They would pull the plug soon, then she would have to explain that to the director. To salvage the situation and turn it into something useful, Sandy Walker needed to talk.

"You're the key, Mr. Walker."

He knows who you are, Marjory, and he wants you to fail.

The man's face twitched and the monitor next to him went dark, she flinched and backed away.

"You can hear me!"

She looked at his face. Without the lacerations and bruising he could be attractive, but this man was trying to ruin her career.

She leaned in close and pulled at one of the stitches in his eyebrow. The light flared and feedback screamed through the intercom.

"Damn you!" she said.

She hated Colorado, hated being stuck on this damn base and hated him.

The inquiry would begin any day and she would have to explain to the director who this man was and what he might be. Fortunately, the shit had hit the fan in Iran. Lucky for her; not so lucky for Mr. Walker though.

He moved, clenching his fists as if he heard her thoughts. She backed away and almost tripped. Her last dose of Risperdal was kicking in.

She left when the lights began to pulse again and found the doctor from Walter Reed in his office.

"Doctor Williams, I'm not sure your sedation is up to the task, is there anything new I should know?"

"If you or I were on the other end of that IV we'd be dead, Director."

"All right, so what's next?"

"The scans are getting more difficult to read, those we can read show scar tissues already reinforcing the work Doctor Young did in the OR. He's a very good surgeon, but he's not responsible for the healing. It looks as if the repairs were done ten days ago rather than Wednesday night. That's if we can trust anything in that room right now; all this electrical interference is centered around him."

"Doctor," she said softly, "I don't give a shit about his health. I want to speak with him. That is your job. Don't let him die, and find a way to neutralize whatever it is he is doing. You said when you signed on to this project you understood that. Are you reconsidering now? If so, I can make other arrangements for you."

"I'm trying to tell you, he needs to be taken off the pentobarbital soon. If we keep him on it, it will have adverse effects on him — permanent effects."

"I hear what you are saying, Doctor, but I want to be clear. This patient may never walk out of here. It all depends on what we learn in the next few days."

"I'm just giving you a clear picture, Ms. Hicks."

"Do I need to remind you who I am, Doctor? No? Good. Continue. What else do we know? The artificial systems — tell me about them."

"Yes, the shadowing Doctor Young referred to: this is most remarkable, and it is what I think is affecting the electronics around him. Look at these X-rays taken the day of the accident. He turned his laptop around, and she saw two images. The one on the right was taken this morning. As you can see, they are significantly different."

"I'm sorry. They look the same to me."

"Look here at the brain. This webbing now completely encircles the parietal lobe. That's how we receive and process information. And here," he said, pointing, "the thalamus, it sorts and processes all the signals from the body to the brain and vice versa."

"Biology 101 was as far as I got at Princeton, Doctor."

"I'm sorry. I believe this artificial system acts as an amplifier and an antenna. It allows his brain to receive and process electronic signals and, more importantly, to send them out as well. Look here at the size of the one running along his spine, it now reaches all the way to the coccyx," he pointed to the tailbone, "and it's almost doubled in its thickness."

"Doctor, all I want to know is how we can bring him out of this coma and not lose control of him. I don't want him to be able to manipulate anything."

"Well, we should do it quickly. I think it's the coma that is affecting the growth in this system. He's unconscious and this system may be trying to compensate for the lack of consciousness."

"You think he's dangerous?"

"I wouldn't want to be on his bad side when he wakes up."

Chapter 63
Croft

Croft sat at the bar of the Sage Hotel and Suites trying to put the pieces together. The first ER nurse wouldn't talk to him. Another he recognized from the trauma room said Sandy Walker was transferred to ICU after his shift ended. But no Sandy Walker had ever been to the ICU according to the head nurse. Worse, the hospital's administrator said there had been no Sandy Walkers admitted in the last twelve months.

I'm up against the power of the NSA, and making people disappear is what they do best.

Hicks had clamped down tight on anything and everybody that had encountered the pilot. Even Doctor Young wouldn't return his calls.

He'd called Scott and asked him to look into it. That was yesterday, and now even Scott was avoiding him.

He paid his tab and drove to Saint Vincent's and parked near the ER entrance and waited for the doctor to come out.

"Doctor Young!"

The doctor turned away when he recognized him, but Croft was quick.

"Just a question, Doctor, and it will never get back to anyone. Where is Walker, and what happened to him?"

"You know I can't talk about it; you were there when the FBI warned me."

"What happened to him?"

"They took him the next morning, another big helicopter, I heard. That's all I know."

"You don't know where?"

"No, and that's it. I would stay away, Colonel. I saw one of them sitting in the lobby earlier. They're watching us all."

He let the doctor go and sat in his car, looking for surveillance. Maybe they were on the roof with a scope or parked in one of several panel trucks in the parking lot. But he was sure the doctor wasn't lying; the NSA was watching.

He started to call Scott again and looked at his phone. If the NSA wasn't listening to his calls, they may be listening to Scott's, and then he knew why Scott wasn't answering.

He texted him anyway. "General, let's play some golf soon." Scott couldn't play golf, but he could take a hint.

Chapter 64
Colorado

Blackness. Total blackness. He saw nothing, felt nothing, and heard nothing. He should feel fear, but even that simple emotion was missing. Something was wrong, something bad, but he couldn't think. *Where am I?* He tried to hold on to the thought, but it drifted away. *Am I even alive?*

It was anesthesia—he was drugged just like he had been so often in The White Room. He let go of all thought and explored the darkness around him. He was not in a complete void; someone was nearby, at least two people speaking. Their words were random and incoherent. Then they stopped and coldness crept up his arm and into his chest. He was losing consciousness again, but someone was close, standing right over him. He felt anger, hatred and …

Chapter 65
Hicks

"He's fully under now," the doctor said. "The EEG will only work when he's this deep. When the lights begin to flicker, we know we need to add to the drip."

It had been two more days, and she would not wait any longer. "With your permission," the doctor said, "I want to sever one of the smaller artificial nerves in his back to see what effect it would have and to take a piece for examination."

"Can we just cut the main pathway at the base of his neck?" Hicks said.

"He will lose his abilities permanently."

"So be it, Doctor, my patience is over. What good is he if we can't have him conscious?"

Through the glass, she watched the surgical team prepare. The single light fixture above him was steady and the EEG monitor showed waves moving across the screen.

Williams stood over the pilot, then looked back at her through the glass.

What the hell is he waiting for? "Just do it!" she screamed.

He made the first cut in the middle of the pilot's spine just deep enough to expose the nerve, and she thought the light above him brightened. It must have because Williams looked up at it too and said something to the anesthetist.

Hicks edged closer to the glass. She wanted to see everything, but she was not going in there. She was already nervous and worried the excitement and anticipation could bring out the voice.

Williams moved back over to the pilot and peeled away another section of tissue. This time there was a definite flash of light and Williams and the two women backed away from the table.

"More fentanyl, Brittany. Another ten units, please," she heard through the speaker.

"Ms. Hicks, you can see what's happening. He is reacting to everything I do now. We are on dangerous ground here. I can increase the dosage and maybe kill him, or we may suffer the same fate as the helicopter crew. I'm asking you to make the decision. Either we stop now, or I medicate him to the edge of death and continue."

Do it! the voice said.

"Do it, Doctor. Finish it."

"Ten more, Brittany, and ten milligrams of propofol too." He looked back at Hicks and nodded.

She watched him step back to the table and slice away another section of flesh.

This time, the lights went out completely. Someone screamed, one of the women. In the red glow of the emergency lights, she saw Williams collapsed on the floor, and both his nurse and the anesthetist were on their knees. The screaming continued, and in the glass's reflection, she knew she was the one screaming.

She recoiled and backed away from the window until she hit the far wall and collapsed, then the lights came on.

"He's dead!" someone screamed.

Was Walker dead?

No. He had killed the doctor and now he was in her head, exploring.

"I can feel you trespassing in my mind, you bastard!"

Still on her knees and shaking, bile rose from her stomach and burned her throat.

"Ms. Hicks!" Someone shouted.

Chapter 66
Six

The silence was comforting, free from his own pain, anxiety and fear. It wouldn't last, even now as the anesthesia wore off, he sensed someone close, maybe more than just one. He felt their fear, it was cold and edgy. A woman spoke, her words running together and slurring as if she was speaking a foreign language.

"We are on dangerous ground here," a man said.

His senses were betraying him. He tried to smell, to feel something—anything! Then he saw himself and wanted to scream. He was hovering over his own body looking down from above. He was face down, just like in The White Room as a hand holding a scalpel sliced into his back.

The hand belonged to an older man, long white tufts of hair stuck out of a purple latex glove and blood smeared the man's index finger as the scalpel worked its way down his spine.

My blood. My spine.

He knew what the man was thinking, almost as if the thoughts were his own. Then he felt a woman's thoughts also, and there were others. He tried to see them, to turn the man's eyes, but the vision stayed centered on his back.

The woman and a third person were in a conflict, arguing and he tried to listen, but the conversation was too chaotic.

A four-inch-long incision opened along his spine, and as the gloved fingers parted the flesh, he saw the braided metallic nerve. Small black filaments were visible, spreading out from the main nerve and disappearing between his vertebrae.

The scalpel sliced deeper, and through one of the hair-like filaments. A flare of pain blasted through his consciousness. He saw his body jerk as the gloved hand parted the skin again.

Like pulling a weed from soft earth, he latched onto the man's thoughts, to his consciousness. *The man doesn't care if I live or die.* The image changed, he saw the helicopter circling his ship and then Klaatu falling in the old black-and-white movie.

Reading the stranger's thoughts was similar to Wi-Fi, so he sent a powerful signal of his own. The last thing he was aware of was the shriek of a woman screaming.

Chapter 67
Hicks

She was freezing, confused, nauseated, and now someone was shaking her. She tried to stand, but her legs felt like rubber.

"Ms. Hicks!" It was the anesthetist. "Can you hear me?" the woman screamed.

"I'm not deaf, you idiot."

She finally had the strength to stand.

"Where is the doctor?"

"Doctor Williams is dead!"

The doctor's body lay crumpled in a fetal position against the far wall. The pilot was face down strapped to the table, the incision along his spine still open and a pool of blood had formed in the small of his back.

"What about him?" she asked. "Is he alive?"

"Yes, heavily sedated. There have been no more incidents since ... since Doctor Williams died."

"Shouldn't someone close that?" she asked, pointing to Walker's back.

Her head ached. A migraine, like none she had ever experienced. Pulling out the Altoids tin, she shook out two Risperdal tablets knowing she had been right for saving them, then swallowed both along with two Percocet. She would be out of pain meds in a week at this rate. *Then what? Where and how do I get a new prescription in Colorado? Too many of the wrong people will ask questions.*

"Clean this mess up and get the doctor out of there."

She had thirty minutes before the side effects would be too obvious to explain. Stumbling down the hallway, she made it to her temporary office and locked herself inside.

The opioids from the pain medication kicked in and took the edge off the migraine. She took out the headphones and put her feet on the desk and listened as her father began.

"Who in the world am I? Ah, that's the great puzzle."

"It's just me and you, Alice. Just me and you."

The two-hour long recording ended, and the turmoil in her head had eased enough that she put the headphones back in her desk and sat up. What had happened? What had she felt just before the doctor dropped?

It wasn't *something*; it was *someone*. She had fought with a voice in her head all her life. She could usually control it; she understood it. But this was different. She could feel someone pulling the very life out of the doctor.

She thought of the Life Flight pilot somewhere down the hall, lying in a coma, and knew what had happened. It was no seizure; it was Sandy Walker!

I wouldn't want to be on his bad side when he wakes up.

Chapter 68
Six

He listened. Something had changed and it felt similar to waking from deep sleep after a mission. He had heard a voice, or maybe a conversation happening somewhere nearby but all he heard now was his own heartbeat, slow and steady.

At least I can hear that.

He tried to speak, but there was no sound, and he couldn't tell if his mouth and tongue were moving.

His heartbeat was loud and it was all he had, so he focused on the sound and imagined it was a clock. He timed the beats and counted the minutes. Ten minutes, then twenty, and then he heard the voices again.

"He's awake. I'm sure of it."

"How can you tell?"

"Look at these new peaks. Beta waves are off the charts. He's thinking."

"Should we put him out again?"

"Yes, restart the drip. Add another .05 mgs of Nembutal per minute. Quickly."

"How long has anyone survived in there?"

"One of the Gitmo guys lasted twenty-five days."

"Jesus, that's some cruel shit right there, Conners."

"Better him than us."

He felt the cold in his arm again, starting at the wrist and working its way up to his shoulder. There was an IV line in his arm. As the Nembutal took effect, even thinking was difficult. *What happened?*

The last thing he could remember was driving to Albuquerque. Then he remembered the dreamlike experience in The White Room.

He listened as long as he could, hoping the men would speak again, but if they did, he couldn't hear it. Eventually, even the sound of his heart faded, and there were no dreams this time.

The two men looked at the EEG scroll across the machine until the transient peaks subsided and then looked through the plate glass at the tank below them.

"He's out. Call the deputy director and tell her he's burning through the sedatives faster. Tell her he won't live another twenty-four hours."

The technician looked at the sensory deprivation tank on the floor below and wondered who the man was. "A Black Project," the deputy director told him. "Keep him sedated and monitor his EKG and EEGs in between the other examinations," she had said.

Four times now, the man had been taken out of the tank and wheeled away to other parts of the lab. He had no idea where they had taken him, but he knew that several CT scans had been taken, and he had seen two of the scans. Laced throughout the man's spine and into much of his brain was an intricate web of fine wire-like threads, and they were increasing in size and length with each new scan.

As if the man in the chamber knew what he was thinking, the EEG spiked, setting off an alarm, and then returned to normal.

Chapter 69
Susan

Susan stood in the aisle as the engines on the Airbus spooled up. She had dreamed of this moment and now she couldn't wait to get off the plane.

It had been two weeks since he failed to show. Two weeks and not even an apology. *Why won't he at least return my call?*

She held the seatbelt demonstrator and braced herself as the plane pushed back from the gate. *How many times do I have to show them how to use a seatbelt? Who doesn't know how to fasten one?*

A small boy with bushy red hair sat in front of her, the only passenger paying attention. The rest of them had their faces turned away, some annoyed by the demonstration. She knelt in the aisle next to him. "Thank you for listening, young man."

Three and a half hours later in Seattle, she sat with the rest of the crew as the van drove out of the airport's parking lot.

"Are you alright, Susan?" The senior flight attendant said from the front seat. "You seem distracted today."

"I'm worried about a friend. Nothing serious."

It was serious. She tried his phone again. This time someone answered—and it wasn't Sandy.

"Who is this?" a woman asked.

"Who is this?" she asked in return. "Is Sandy there?"

The woman didn't answer. She listened to silence, then a faint metallic click and the woman asked, "Is this Susan Matthews?"

She ended the call and looked up, hoping the panic on her face wasn't obvious. The senior flight attendant was still watching her. "Let me know if I can help," she said, turning around.

Sandy was in trouble, and maybe his attorney had answers. She tried to remember the man's name—Eric something, and what about Robert Croft?

If Sandy was in trouble, Croft could be behind it all. Sandy has good reasons not to trust the military.

The van stopped and she was soon sitting on the edge of the bed in a hotel room searching for attorneys in Santa Fe.

There were three attorneys named Eric and she dialed the first one, only to hear a woman's voice saying the office was closed. It was 5:30 in Seattle and 6:30 in New Mexico. She dialed the next two anyway and recognized Eric Ridge's voice on the last one and left a message. "This is Susan Matthews. We met in Chicago. Please call me."

She hated this hotel. It was nice, better than those Midway put her in, but she loathed it just the same. With her face buried in her hands, she felt the tears slipping between her fingers. She had lost him, and now she didn't care where—or when—he had come from.

His story at the Copper Penny had stunned her; it was so far-fetched she refused to believe it. She had left angry, but sitting in her apartment, she put the pieces together and knew it was true. All she had wanted from him was honesty—he had given it to her—and she left him for it.

"He's from the future," she said aloud, listening to herself. She repeated it several times, hoping the words would make it more believable.

Dressed in sweats, she made her way to the hotel's gym and found a treadmill with a view of the seaport. A brightly colored cruise ship drifted silently out from the pier and made its way north into

Puget Sound. She watched thoughtlessly as it sailed out of view and ran until her legs cramped.

Sweat ran down the center of her back and her right knee ached. She had run five and a half miles missing two calls and a voice mail from Eric Ridge.

"Ms. Matthews, we must speak immediately. Call me at this number as soon as possible."

His message sounded urgent. Grabbing her towel, she left the gym and headed toward the elevator, listening to the phone ring.

"Ms. Matthews. I have been trying to find you, and your employer was not very helpful."

"I'm sorry. I've been flying a lot the last several days. Mr. Ridge, I'm worried about Sandy. Have you seen him?"

"No, I'm afraid I haven't, which is why I must speak with you in person immediately. When and where can we meet?"

"I'm in Seattle now and tomorrow evening I'll be in Denver."

"I'll meet you there. You have my cell number now. Call me the moment you land."

"Mr. Ridge, do you know Robert Croft? He is a colonel in the Army. He may know where Sandy is, but I don't know how to contact him either."

"I can't speak on the phone Susan, but we will speak later."

Twenty-four hours later, she came out of the jetway in Denver and Croft appeared at her side.

"Keep walking and don't look back. Someone is probably following you. Mr. Ridge will pick you up just outside the arrival gate. Susan, how much does this attorney know about Sandy Walker?"

"I don't know what he knows."

"Let's keep it that way for now. Head to the exit and Ridge will be waiting for you there. I'll meet you outside." And then he was gone, mixed in with the flood of passengers making their way down the terminal.

"Someone may be following you!" She couldn't help but look back

now. Half the people in the concourse were staring at her, or so it seemed. She thought of the woman answering Sandy's phone and looked at a brunette woman walking fast in her direction and waited, wanting to confront her. She wasn't going to let anyone intimidate her now, but the woman passed her never looking back.

The walk took forever, but she finally stepped out into bright sunlight, and a silver Nissan pulled to the curb.

"Jump in!" she heard Ridge say.

Croft was in the back seat, and the Nissan pulled away, joining a long line of cars leaving the airport.

"What's happening? Where is Sandy?"

"Colonel, tell her what you know."

Croft told her everything about the accident, starting with Flórez's first phone call.

"Susan, they said he was near death when they brought him in. I was there while he was in surgery. The doctor told me if he made it through the night, he would probably make it. Then the next day, he was transported by air to a military hospital in Colorado, and I heard the helicopter went down. According to my friend in Washington, the pilot and the patient were killed."

"Oh my God, what have I done? He was coming to see me!"

They drove in silence until Eric parked in the Hyatt House parking lot and then the attorney said, "Let's go inside. There's more you need to know."

The three of them sat on a rooftop terrace. A stiff wind blew in from the Rockies, and she shivered, wishing she had brought a jacket.

"Susan," the attorney said, "Colonel Croft said not to ask you any questions, that Sandy has something the NSA wants, but he can't talk about it. But I am his attorney. And there is an attorney-client privilege. I need to know what is happening."

She looked at Croft, and he shook his head.

"I can't tell you, Mr. Ridge. I don't know much either."

"Eric," Croft said, "the NSA doesn't always work within constitutional boundaries. They will tell you they do, but trust me, they don't. The less you know, the better you will be. I'm not sure they even know you yet, but they are watching me."

"I tried calling his phone yesterday. A woman answered, and she knew my name."

"Your name was probably on the caller ID," Ridge said.

"Maybe, but someone has his phone, and I had the impression she was waiting for me to call."

"I'll bet I know who that was," Croft said. "Which means she is aware of both of you. I'm surprised they weren't at the airport."

"Well, the reason I needed to speak to both of you is this: The morning of the accident, Sandy called me and told me that if anything happened to him, to expect an email. I asked Sandy if he was okay, and he assured me he was. He sounded good but something was worrying him.

"Seven days later I got that email and knew something happened. There were several attachments, and one of them was a will. In the will, he named Mr. Croft as the executor, which is why I contacted him, and you as the beneficiary."

"I'm in his will?"

"Yes, Susan. He left you everything, including Trans-Data."

She had been with him in Chicago but had left not knowing the details. She knew he had hoped to start a small business with the profits of his processor and call it Trans-Data, but she had rushed off for training with Delta, and he hadn't mentioned it since.

"Okay, so what do I need to do? Do I need to sign something? And what am I supposed to do with it?" she asked, looking at Croft.

"Whatever you want," he said.

"I'm sorry, I'm at a loss here. I don't even know what Sandy's business does."

"At the moment," the attorney said, "it's not doing anything. You should read the document. Besides the normal legalese, there are several pages of instructions, more like suggestions, for both you and Colonel Croft."

"Why you?" she asked Croft.

"I got an email too. One of the things it said was, 'Help Susan if you can.'"

"No text for me though," she said. "I haven't spoken to him since that night at the Copper Penny. I was so angry. I ignored all of his calls, and his last voice mail is still on my phone. "I'll leave you alone, Susan," he said. 'Thank you for everything.'"

She broke down crying and buried her face in her lap.

"Susan, none of this is your fault."

"I know, but it still hurts."

"So, what now, Colonel?" she asked, drying her eyes.

"I say we go back to Santa Fe and take a look at Trans-Data," Croft said.

"I'm supposed to fly to Philadelphia in the morning."

"Susan," Eric said. "Once you sign this will, you will own Trans-Data. This morning it was worth twenty-five million dollars. Do you really need to fly to Philadelphia?"

"You don't believe it," Susan said as the attorney drove away.

"Believe what?" Croft asked.

"I can tell you don't believe he's dead, or that it was a helicopter crash that killed him. I can see it in your eyes."

"You're right, I don't believe anything when it comes to Marjory Hicks. She's the Deputy Director of the NSA, probably the most powerful, most deceptive organization in America. I don't want to get your hopes up, Susan, but it doesn't make any sense. I mean, his death makes sense—the first crash was horrible, I heard—but I spoke with Doctor Young the next morning. He was afraid to speak to me at first, but just as he left, he said, 'I think your friend will be okay.'"

She listened, but she was fighting a losing battle with her emotions. The colonel mentioned death and described the crash as if it were some abstract event. She turned away and looked at the snowcapped Indian Peaks through the window.

"Anyway," he added, "I tried to check on him again later that same day and was told there was no patient by that name. I guess I pissed a few people off, so one of them walked me upstairs. There were two patients in the ICU, and even the staff had changed. It's as if the name Sandy Walker had been scrubbed from the hospital's records, and everybody that treated him has been transferred.

"I confronted the ER doctor again a few nights ago. I think the NSA has him really rattled, but I got him to tell me the FBI agents flew him out right after his surgery, and he was very much alive.

"So, Susan, why would they transfer him? I think this Hicks woman wants him under her control, somewhere out of the public eye. She's obsessed with this whole project."

"But the helicopter crashed. Your friend said so."

"It's true, but it was a civilian Life Flight helicopter, probably belonging to the NSA. It was en route to Buckley Air Force Base. The NSA has a station there, the Aerospace Data Facility, and Marjory Hicks is still there right now. That crash was two weeks ago. Why wouldn't she have returned to Maryland with everything going on in Iran? She should be up to her neck in what's happening over there."

"So do they think Sandy is involved in that?"

"Oh God, I was hoping you wouldn't ask."

"What? Tell me. Is he involved?" she asked.

"Susan, you remember the picture of Washington we found on Sandy's ship? I think Sandy may have caused the explosion in Iran. He mentioned he was going to do something big, something that would change history as he knew it, including the destruction of Washington."

"You can't be serious? He's one man, he's not some kind of secret agent. He was thousands of miles away!"

"Susan, think back to what Sandy is. You know it's possible."

"I don't want to believe any of it."

"I don't want to believe it either. I've tried for two weeks to find out what happened to him, and I've gotten nowhere. I'm a civilian now, maybe even less. People I used to go to for information won't even speak to me now. But I haven't given up yet, and neither should you."

Chapter 70
Andaman Sea

Jacksonville

Captain Jazayeri was on the bridge of the *Andaman Sea* several hours before dawn. He loved moments like this, breathing in the salt air, the ocean swells lapping against the side of his ship. He looked up at the stars shining brightly above him. It was an omen, a sign of good fortune.

Other than the stars, there was nothing else to see. He was too far from the main shipping lane and didn't expect to see any traffic. Things would change by dawn, but sunrise was four hours away. He checked the GPS, and he was right where he wanted to be. It was a perfect end to his part of the Ayatollah's plan.

Soon he would be rid of the death waiting in the forward hold. He looked towards the hatch and imagined the power hidden inside. He didn't fear it, but he wanted it off his ship just the same.

Back in the bridge he checked the radar, it was clear, and the communications console was still powered down. With the Wi-Fi and satellite systems off, there was no way the crew could contact shore. Mahamoud Madine had insisted on this: "Some lonely sailor will try to contact his lover, and the Americans will discover our plan."

Five hours later and forty miles from the coast of Florida, the radar operator pointed to the contact on the screen. "About sixteen miles astern and overtaking us," the operator said.

Jazayeri got the binoculars off the hook and stepped out onto the bridge wing. Looking aft, he was trying to find the contact, but the haze obscured everything on the horizon. He returned to the radar screen and saw the contact was closer.

"It's fast," he said. *Forty miles, twenty-one knots.* The captain did the math in his head. "That ship will overtake us before we reach port."

Only a warship was that fast. He scanned the horizon again and saw it—a Ticonderoga-class missile cruiser—and it was heading right at them.

"Riza, wake the crew. Allah has sent us company."

He thought of increasing speed, but that might look suspicious. Then he saw the cruiser turn slightly away, most likely to pass him on his starboard side.

On the western horizon, the top of a high-rise condominium appeared in the haze. *Close enough.* The ship was fifteen miles from shore, and the cruiser was now two miles behind him. "Riza, slow to ten knots, switch on the communications console, and contact the harbor pilot."

Twenty-five miles from the Florida coast, Ensign Ashley Singletary was bored. Since her shift began at 2300 hours, she had seen nothing on the *USS Vicksburg's* radar but a blank screen. Then near the end of her shift, a slight flicker of a contact on the edge of the screen caught her attention. She looked at Commander Beyer. "Contact fourteen miles dead ahead."

Ensign Pete Cainas swung the heavy Optex 20x120mm binoculars on its pivot and focused on the small light on the horizon.

"Looks like a big cargo hauler. No flag or name yet; still too far away. Should we hail them?

"Not yet," Beyer said, "It's almost seven; I'll wake the captain."

Captain Edmunds stepped onto the bridge, and Beyer briefed him on the transport ahead and their ETA to port. Looking at the ship through his binoculars, Edmunds saw the hull was light blue and shipping containers of all colors were stacked on its deck. The radar operator said the ship was now four miles ahead and twenty degrees to port, cruising slightly slower at twenty-one knots.

As the cruiser closed to just a few miles behind the freighter, Captain Edmunds said, "Slow to twenty-one knots and turn ten degrees to starboard for clearance. I don't want to be too close, and we're early anyway."

This was the *Vicksburg's* first deployment in the Atlantic, and he wanted a smooth ride into port.

In a stationary orbit over Texas, Six's beacon received the upload from the weapon onboard the *Andaman Sea*, searched its programming, determined the ship was within safe parameters, and transmitted a signal of its own.

Jazayeri looked toward the skyline and saw the port entrance. As he did, a small keypad in a container deep inside the cargo hold came to life, and six digits scrolled across the LCD screen. Then the keyboard, the container, and the rest of the ship and crew vaporized as one hundred and forty pounds of enriched uranium detonated in a six-thousand-degree Fahrenheit fireball.

Edmunds turned to his radar operator just as the bridge filled with a flash of brilliant white light, blinding him and most of the fourteen crew members on duty. Then the shock wave blew out the forward windows, knocking him and one helmsman into the rear bulkhead.

"God damn it!" Singletary heard behind her. She looked back and saw Beyer kneeling over the captain.

"He's dead," Beyer said.

Most of the bridge crew she saw were down on the deck—some on their hands and knees, blinded by the flash; others stunned by the shock wave.

She looked forward and saw a wall of water thirty feet high racing toward the ship.

"Starboard ninety degrees!" Beyer yelled, but there was no one on the helm, and the console was dark like the rest of the electronics.

"Brace for impact!"

The ship's gas turbine engines were unaffected by the blast and were pushing it forward at twenty-one knots and into the first wave. The huge wave hit the *Vicksburg* at a thirty-degree angle, and for a moment, it was on the edge of capsizing. The ship rocked hard to starboard just as the next wave hit, almost as violently as the first, and a spray of water came through the windowless bridge, soaking them all. Blood and salt water swirled around Singletary's feet.

There was a moment she thought the ship could still capsize, but the cruiser eventually settled, still racing toward the expanding fireball. Singletary was close enough now that she could feel the heat coming through the open bridge.

"Cainas," Beyer said, "comms is down. Run to the combat information center and tell them to turn the ship ninety degrees to starboard and slow to ten knots, then get a corpsman up here."

Beyer stepped over the captain's body and out of the bridge to inspect the damage. The canvas cover had ripped free of the five-inch gun, and a one-inch diameter antennae cable swung freely across a port bridge window. Looking aft, the main antennae array had broken free above the bridge and hung over the side of the ship.

The Sikorsky SH-60 Seahawk at the rear of the ship hung in the support rigging of the landing pad, its tail rotor dragging in the sea, creating its own wake. As he watched, another cable broke free, and the twenty-eight-million-dollar helicopter went over the side. As the Seahawk sank, he felt the ship slow and begin a turn to the north. Another quarter of a mile and the ship would have penetrated the blast radius, which had stopped expanding outward and was now rising into a deep blue sky.

Ensign Cainas, out of breath and bleeding from lacerations on his face, stumbled back into the bridge.

"Sir, we contacted Jacksonville Naval Air Station on the VHF radio.

It's the only communications we have. Two Seahawks are inbound. ETA: two minutes!"

"Is the pad clear?"

"No, there is debris all over the pad, but I have people clearing it now."

"What about the communications and our intercom?"

"Should be up in a few minutes, still just VHF ship to shore."

"Okay, thanks, and Cainas, have someone check you out as soon as it calms down."

"Yes, sir."

He needed to get a report to Command soon, but he would not use the VHF with half the Jacksonville population listening in. Jacksonville NAS knew of the explosion, that the *Vicksburg* was damaged, and that there were casualties. Other than knowing the explosion had originated from the container ship, he had little to add.

Retired New York City police officer Jessie Norman sat on his ocean-front terrace, enjoying the early morning sunshine. He had the crossword out and had filled in the first clue when a ship's horn sounded.

On the twentieth floor, he had a spectacular view of Jacksonville Beach. A tall sailing ship was making its daily run southbound along the shore. Farther out, two oil tankers sat at anchor waiting their turn to enter the port.

He penciled in the last word, *minaret,* and pushed the puzzle aside. The sun's light on the terrace changed. Its normal hue of light yellow, brightened to a shade almost blue, like a welder's torch.

Offshore, a second sun rose out of the sea, enveloping the first one.

"What the hell!"

It was painful to look at, and he turned away. The street below him was bathed in brilliant, bleached whiteness.

Two nights earlier, he had watched Arnold Schwarzenegger in one of the *Terminator* sequels. The cloud he was watching was similar to one in the movie, but this one was worse; this one was real, and it was right in front of him.

He stepped back from the rail in shock, and for a second considered there had to be a reasonable explanation for what he was looking at—a new movie perhaps, or a dream? Pain medication had given him nightmares like this.

Midway between the cloud and the shoreline racing at the speed of sound, a wall of compressed air raced toward the beach. It was easy to see, not only because of the disturbance it had with the water's surface, but the compression turned the humid air into a visible vapor.

Grabbing the railing, he braced himself as it hit the building, rattling his French doors and setting off dozens of car alarms below. It blew his potted geranium off the table, its clay pot shattering. As he picked it up, he thought about radiation and fallout.

Can a shock wave carry radiation?

A loud crack echoed off the surrounding buildings as the sound of the explosion raced in behind the shock wave. It was nothing like the dull thud of an artillery round. He had been close to artillery in Vietnam, and this was different, like a rifle shot at close range.

Below him, parents cried as they gathered up their screaming children and rushed off the beach, dodging broken cabanas and overturned umbrellas. Screeching tires and the sound of two cars colliding added to the cacophony on the street below. The street, empty and serene minutes ago, was filled with cars and trucks all trying to get to the bridge and onto the mainland.

There was chaos on the beach, but the ocean appeared calm, boats still moving along the shoreline seemingly unaffected by what was happening on the horizon, or on the shore. He looked farther south and saw the sailing ship listing to starboard, its sails shredded and rippling in the breeze.

He looked down again, and then back out to sea. It was shocking how high the mushroom cloud had risen. It was white now—vaporized sea water—and not much different from the cumulus clouds up and down the coast. Only its terrifying shape gave it away.

His building shook again, he could feel the vibration through his slippers. Gripping the iron railing, he prepared for another blast, but two gray helicopters raced overhead toward the cloud. As they thundered over him, he looked out to the horizon and saw the tiny speck of a ship, just a gray dot close to the cloud.

Washington

"What do we know?" the President of the United States asked.

"Sir, we believe the nuke was onboard a ship named the *Andaman Sea*, sailing under the name *Dena Ann*. Its last port was Oran, and it's owned by Sombra Shipping Limited in Panama. However, Sombra is saying the ship is in dry dock in Syria.

"And how do we know this?"

The NSA director interrupted. "Sir, one of our sources in Israel contacted us moments after the explosion. He sent this photo of the *Andaman Sea* as it was taking on cargo just before leaving Tartus, Syria. The man you see on the bridge is Saleh Jazayeri, a captain in the Islamic Republic of Iran Navy. His last command was the frigate *Moje*, and the man next to him is believed to be a nuclear specialist from Natanz."

"And you trust this source?" the Secretary of State asked.

"He is a senior officer of the Mossad. Yes, I trust him," the director said.

Tehran

President Rouhani sat alone on the second floor of the Sa'adabad Palace when the main door opened. Two uniformed captains of the Islamic Republic of Iran's Army came through and into the dining area unannounced.

"How dare you! What is the meaning of this?" Rouhani demanded.

"You are under arrest by the order of the Ayatollah. Do not resist or you will be restrained, sir."

He stood, saying nothing and allowed them to escort him out into the hallway.

"You have failed your people, Hassan," the Ayatollah said. "We entrusted you with the very weapons intended for the destruction of the infidels. Now one of those weapons has exploded off the coast of the United States. At every opportunity, you failed. You have embarrassed and humiliated us all. You will be detained pending a trial by the Supreme National Security Council. President Madine will oversee your duties until there is a new election."

President Madine, he thought. How quickly they've replaced me.

While Sandy Walker lay unconscious in Colorado, six hundred miles away at Whitman Air Force Base, things were very different. Twelve B-2 Spirit stealth bombers rose into the night sky, and by dawn, the last of them crossed the border of Georgia.

It was Deborah Hilou who fired the first shot. The petite Israeli Lieutenant was cruising over Iraq at four hundred fifty knots when her weapons operator picked up the first air-defense radar. Her briefing included information there were no Iraqi air defenses along her route and operational radars were most likely ISIS fighters using systems stolen in the fall of Mosul.

As she selected the new AGM anti-radiation guided missile, her threat warning went off. A Russian-designed radar was locked onto her aircraft.

Her missile ignited and slid off the rail, accelerating to fourteen hundred miles per hour and locked onto the radar dish twenty-six miles ahead.

Aati Haman saw Hilou's F-15 and the rest of the incoming Israeli strike force on his early warning radar fifty-five miles away. He was helpless until the first aircraft reached the thirty-mile limit: three more minutes. Terrified, he heaved himself out of the seat and watched the targets creeping across the screen. Finally, the Fan Song radar locked onto the lead aircraft and he toggled the fire selector and listened for the sound of the launch, but the only sound he heard was the hum of the cooling fans.

"Gendeh!" *Bitch!* he screamed at the console.

Aati had never fired an actual missile, but he knew instantly that the launch failed. Grabbing the checklist on the console, he went over each procedure. He had only been a cadet when he and his superiors abandoned their post at Mosul and surrendered to the advancing ISIS militants. Most of his classmates and superiors had been executed that day, but Aati and several other cadets were spared. His classroom training in using the Russian Guideline missile was the deciding factor that saved his life.

He repeatedly jabbed his finger on the firing switch until Hilou's missile hit the radar dish outside his trailer.

A fragment of her warhead sent shrapnel into the closest missile, igniting its solid fueled booster rocket. It ripped free from its trailer losing two of its stabilizers, and shot skyward, tumbling end over end until it impacted two hundred yards away.

Hilou watched the uncontrolled missile and targeted the command trailer with a single five-hundred-pound bomb. The smart bomb's guidance system flew it to within its twenty-one-foot accuracy profile and it detonated in the dirt outside Aati's trailer.

When it struck, Aati was sitting at the control panel which absorbed most of the shrapnel. He was thrown out of the far end of the destroyed trailer and lay face up looking into the night sky, unable to hear the Israeli strike force heading east into Iran.

Rouhani was asleep when his bed shook. Sitting up in the dark, he heard the command center explode several blocks away. He was in the guest quarters at the government Senate Building, a room just big enough for a bed and a small bathroom with a toilet and sink. The room smelled like old sweat and urine, but he knew his situation could be much worse. He turned on the desk lamp and watched fine particles of dust floating in the light.

Above him, someone was running up a flight of stairs, then the wailing of an air-raid siren pierced the silence. His room had no windows so there was nothing to see and other than the siren, there was nothing to hear either. He sat in silence brooding, feeling his bed shudder as targets were hit farther away.

The guards came for him at noon the following day. He stank from perspiration, and his suit was wrinkled and covered in dust. Even so, he held his head up and walked out of the room with the same two captains, down the long hallway and back to the Ayatollah's residence. He knew that in the next few minutes, his life was about to change.

"Hassan! Good afternoon. Have you eaten?"

"Yes, thank you."

"The Americans and the Israelis have made us pay dearly for Mahamoud's mistakes."

Mahamoud's mistakes?

"I have sent him to Syria until things stabilize here. We have suffered greatly, but we will persevere until we have eliminated these Godless heathens from the Earth. I need you to retake command. The Americans have made many demands; you will see to them. We will appear meek in the faces of our enemy until we are again able to strike. Do you understand?"

"Yes, I will start immediately."

"Then go. Inform me of your progress."

Rouhani looked out the window as the driver made his way through piles of rubble and saw the remains of the command center. It was happening just as he predicted: the Americans will know everything, and soon Iran will become a pariah on the world's stage.

Chapter 71
Hicks

Hicks switched off her television. The NSA's headquarters in Fort Meade was a madhouse. She didn't need to be there to know, she could feel it. Analysts poring over a flood of data coming from Iran; others trying to link the *Andaman Sea* or the *Dena Ann* to the Jacksonville nuke. History was being written, a nuclear event off the coast of the United States—and she was a thousand miles away. "Everything is happening in Fort Meade, and I'm stuck here in this shithole!"

It was your own doing, Marjory, the voice said. *Your greed and ambitions have ruined you, and wasn't I the one who told you to stop taking the drugs? Look at yourself; you're a mess.*

The pen in her hand snapped, spewing black ink across her desk.

She saw none of it; her mind was focused on the man down the hall; the pilot of a UFO, a man from the future. "What a load of shit," she whispered, her teeth clenched in rage. She would break the man and be rid of the damned voice, but first she needed him and the voice to know she was in control.

You've gone too far this time. The doctor's death is what will destroy you.

"Fuck you!" she screamed in the empty room.

She swallowed her third Risperdal tablet of the day and listened to her father's voice again.

"Have I gone mad?" The Mad Hatter asked Alice.

"I am afraid so. You're entirely bonkers. But I'll tell you a secret," Alice said. "All the best people are!"

"I am going mad," she mumbled and threw the headphones across the room.

The pills were already making her drowsy. Her arm weighed fifty pounds, and she could barely keep her head upright. She looked at the headphones lying on the floor and remembered her father's last words: "Good night, Marjory."

For twenty-five years, she had listened to those words. They were all she had left of him. They were her anchor, and they had worked … "for twenty-five years," she screamed.

The voice she had ignored for so long was dominating every part of her life. Now even the cocktail of drugs couldn't keep it silent, and their side effects were impairing her decisions. She was no fool. She knew if this didn't end today, she would be ruined.

She stood, steadying herself with the desk and felt the tremors in her arms and legs. Reaching for the door, she saw the ink stains on her hands.

"What the hell!"

On her desk, she saw the broken pen laying in a pool of black ink.

"Fuck this!" she said and stormed out.

In the chamber's control room, the two medical technicians looked up at her and then at the stains on her hands and her jacket.

"What are you looking at?" she asked.

"Nothing, ma'am."

"What's his condition?"

"He's sedated and stable. This is his twenty-third day."

"Wake him up."

The junior tech didn't move. She looked down at herself and saw a disheveled woman. Her expensive beige suit, covered in small black dots, smears of ink around both pockets of her jacket, then saw she was barefoot.

"Ma'am, are you okay?"

"No, I am not okay! Do I look okay to you? Get out! Leave us!" she said, and the junior man ran out of the room.

Alone now with the one technician, she looked through the glass into the room below. The sensory deprivation chamber looked like an oversized black coffin covered in a gold fishnet, a thick bundle of wires and tubes snaking their way across the floor. It was a carbon fiber–reinforced capsule designed to eliminate the body's ability to sense anything. It had always been the last resort in breaking a terrorist.

After the doctor's death, they shielded the tank with several layers of copper mesh, creating a Faraday Cage to eliminate radio waves from entering or leaving the tank.

"Can he hear me?"

"With the mike on, he'll be able to hear everything in this room once he wakes. It will only take a minute for the Nembutal and Diprivan to wear off; he burns through them fast."

"How will you know?"

"We hardwired his telemetry feeds into this console: pulse rate, respiration, and brain activity. He's in deep sleep now, but look, you can see these peaks beginning now."

She wasn't interested in his machine. She could feel him down there, stalking her. Or was it schizophrenia's game? Which voices were real? She thought for a minute, remembering Price in her office, then the smug French woman, and now this man.

"Mr. Walker, I know you can hear me!"

She waited, her face pressed up against the glass. The voice was quiet now. *Good. He's afraid.*

"You're sure he can hear me?"

"I'm not sure, but he won't be able to answer you. He's in a gel; his jaw is encased in it, he's intubated and wearing a mask. It's part of the deprivation experience."

"Damn it! I want to hear his voice! I need to know if it's him!"

"What—what are you saying?"

She looked at the tank below her and waited for the voice, that goddamned voice that always knew when she had made a mistake. *It's him; it must be him!*

"Leave me," she whispered. She turned and looked at the technician. He hesitated, then was all too eager to leave.

The door slammed shut. Now she was alone with him.

Sitting at the technician's desk, she thought back through the last three weeks. *What have I done, and how can I fix this? This man can give me the break I need. My ticket to the big chair and the room with a view. I can't fail now.*

A team had finally been assembled to investigate the helicopter's crash, the injury to its pilot, and now the doctor's death. She'd been vague when she described Croft's investigation and downplayed the major's theory of the ship and its origins. But once they started digging …

From the future! What bullshit! The ship is gone if it ever existed. And now the man in the tank was trying to destroy her career.

"I know you can hear me, you bastard!"

She stood and looked through the glass at the tank. The shakes had ended and the voice was quiet, so she walked barefoot out of the room and down the steps to get closer.

The pod, or the tank, or whatever they wanted to call it, sat alone on a tile floor. The copper mesh glinted in the light and looked like spun gold. She ran her fingertip across the mesh, imagining she could penetrate its magical barrier and feel the man's thoughts.

"I could open this and kill you right now."

Do it! the voice commanded.

The voice startled her, and she thought the technician had come back into the room. She looked up at the control room, she was still alone.

"No, I won't do that. It would be too obvious, but an accident would work. An overdose maybe."

She was arguing with the voice out loud now, knowing it was another step down the ladder of insanity.

"There would be an autopsy, and it would be difficult to explain!"

She had to think. She had made so many mistakes already and she would not make another one.

"Are you awake in there?" she put her ear to the gold mesh and listened, but there were no sounds. "Soon my friend." she whispered to the black coffin, and walked out.

Chapter 72
Six

He could feel a woman's presence.

"He can't hear you, he's in deep sleep now," someone said.

"Mr. Walker, I know you can hear me!"

The tinny sound of a woman's voice came through a speaker right above him. Its wiring terminating in a diagnostic system in another room.

"Mr. Walker!" The same woman, but angry now.

"Leave me," she said, and somewhere a door closed.

He was alone, listening to the hiss of static through the speaker. Then he felt a presence, someone was close to him, and the woman spoke again. "No, I won't. That would be too obvious."

She was right next to him, whispering to someone.

"Are you awake in there?" she asked.

A new electronic signal penetrated the darkness, it was weak—it was her cell phone.

"Soon, my friend," she said. Her presence faded and the sound of a door slamming came through the speaker.

Numbing silence. Those brief sensations along with the taste of hope were ripped away. The last vestige of the woman's anger lingered, and then it too was gone. But her phone!

The small fragments of the phone's software, corrupted as they were opened in his mind. The phone belonged to Marjory Hicks, a meaningless name, but one name in her contact list was not—Robert Croft.

If only he could get her close again.

A door opened, a tinny sound, then shoes scuffing on a hard floor. The man had returned—and the speaker's circuit was cut.

Hicks

"Yes, Director Hicks, he's under now. I've increased the drip another ten percent. His heart stopped for a minute and I thought I would have to yank him out, but it's beating again real slow. I want you to know, Ms. Hicks, his liver and kidney functions are dropping. He could die in the next few hours or, at best, later tonight."

"I understand. Thank you," she said.

She looked in the mirror and saw what had frightened the technicians. The ruined suit, black ink smeared across her face and streaks of it in her matted hair. "And where the fuck are my shoes?"

You can always buy a new suit, the voice said.

"Goddamn you." If she could control the voice, she could ignore it too if she chose, let it fade until it was simple background noise.

"If only I had some Thorazine, I could turn it off completely. This new stuff is weak."

A trace of drool ran down her chin as she spoke. She wiped it away with the sleeve of her suit, leaving a new black smear that reached from the corner of her mouth to her right ear. She looked like a circus clown, and laughed at her reflection.

"Just one more day, Margory and I'll be on my way back to Maryland."

Her phone rang.

"Jesus Christ!" she said, looking at the caller ID. "The god damned director."

"Yes?" she said, praying the single syllable word was clearer and stronger than it sounded in her head.

"Marjory, is everything okay out there? I'm hearing things. What is going on?"

Here we go, the voice said.

"Sir, everything is fine. I sent you a report on the incident with the helicopter. Last I heard the pilot was recovering. What have you heard?"

"I've heard a lot that wasn't in your report. Doctor Williams is dead, for one thing—that's a pretty big omission—and who is this man you have in custody now?"

"We're not sure who the man is, I'm still tying up some loose ends from the incident at White Sands, and this guy was involved."

"The news media mentioned a fatality on the helicopter, and it wasn't explained in your report."

"Just a cover story, sir. I can explain it when I get back—hopefully tomorrow."

"I want a detailed report by the end of the day, and not some bullshit like your last report. I want to know why you have had a man in a deprivation tank for almost three weeks. Christ, Marjory, get him out of there. Are you insane?"

"He will be out this afternoon."

"I want that report tonight, Marjory—a full report!"

The line went dead. She stared at the phone as if it had betrayed her. She squeezed it as hard as she could, hoping to hear the screen shatter in her hand—the pain would be a welcome alternative to what she was feeling now—but all she did was bruise her palm.

She called the technician. "Wake him. I'm going to clean up, and I want to speak with him when I'm done."

"You just had me dose him again!"

"Was I not clear? Wake him!"

The shower felt good. She turned the hot water on full and scrubbed the ink off her fingers until her skin was raw and the water ran cold.

She dressed in her favorite navy blue suit and stared into the mirror. This suit meant serious business, if she was going to speak to this bastard, he was going to know he was dealing with a serious woman.

She was fully in control now, but she listened to the tape one more time.

"... and how she would feel with all their simple sorrows, and find a pleasure in all their simple joys, remembering her own child-life, and the happy summer days."

Six

Six was swimming in a deep blue lake. The water was warm, like bathwater, and the air was crisp, like Paris in spring.

This is a dream, or a false memory. I have never been in a lake in my life.

He learned to swim in a pool at school and did laps every day in the station's gym, but he had never been in a lake. A muscle in his leg cramped, and he turned toward shore. The water thickened and the shore, once so close became a blur in the far-off distance.

The cramp worsened, both legs ached as he struggled in water that had cooled, now a thick and slimy paste. Slipping below the surface, he gagged as the gelled fluid filled his lungs.

"Mr. Walker, are you awake?"

He looked up trying to see the surface, reaching for the woman calling his name, but there was no surface and no light this deep. Then the blackness reminded him of where he was, and knowing brought him back from the edge of death.

She was back, her voice coming through the speaker again.

Then a man's voice: "I'm going to bring you out of the tank, Mr. Walker. It's going to be very bright. Keep your eyes closed until I tell you."

His voice changed. "I just want to warn you, Ms. Hicks," the man whispered. "No one has ever been in the tank this long, or with the amount of drugs we've used, so prepare yourself. Permanent side effects are almost assured."

"Just open the goddamned thing!" the woman shouted.

A servomotor whined behind him and he felt a change in air pressure, then movement. The movement started with a jerk and it felt like someone hit him in the chest with a hammer. He couldn't breathe—he was drowning again.

"Jesus Christ, I was afraid of this!"

Hicks turned away from the tank and saw the technician punching buttons on the console as a scroll of paper unwound from the machine.

"What's wrong?"

"Panic attack, probably, but his heart is too weak. He's going into cardiac arrest."

She smiled and looked back into the room as an amber block of gelatin rolled out of the tank on casters. She could see his form through the translucent gel, and a portion of his face was visible; the rest was obscured by a mask.

"Okay, his heartbeat is steady now, but still weak."

"Shouldn't you go in there, maybe take the mask off?"

"Give him a minute for the diazepam to settle him down, then we can talk to him through the intercom. I'm not going in there if he's angry and end up like Williams."

"Mr. Walker," he said into the microphone, "I have the illumination down as low as I can make it. I'm going to come in and remove your mask. It may be difficult for you to speak at first. Also, should you try to harm me, I've set your IV to dump a lethal dose of potassium chloride into your veins. It will kill you if I don't return to disarm it. I'll begin in just a minute. Again, keep your eyes closed."

She grabbed his arm as he turned to leave. She mouthed the word "no."

"This man scares me, but it's just a bluff."

The man was encased in translucent gel, unmoving and as silent as the voice in her head. She watched from the safety of the control room as the technician removed Walker's mask. He was intubated, a clear tube in his mouth and a smaller one in his nostril.

"This may be uncomfortable, Mr. Walker. I'm going to remove the tube from your throat so you can speak. Speech will be difficult. You've been intubated for some time now."

She couldn't hear every word. Opening the door, she stood on the landing at the top of the stairs and still couldn't hear. The technician was whispering to him now.

"Speak louder dammit, I need to know what you're doing."

The man ignored her and she took a few steps closer until the smell reached her. Stifling the urge to puke, she covered her face with her hand as the tech slid the tube out of his mouth. Dry heaves caused her to slip and fall. Grabbing the railing, she steadied herself and took another step closer.

She had to hear his first word. She had a dozen questions and he was going to answer them right now!

Two more steps and she heard him take his first breath, a deep raspy sound.

"That's better," the technician said. "Small breaths please, Mr. Walker. I'm going to get some ice chips to soothe your throat, I'll be back in just a moment." He looked over at her and nodded, making his way to the stairs.

"He looks better than I expected. The ice will help and maybe he can get a few words out. Don't be surprised at anything he may say. I'd be shocked if he's still sane enough to speak at all."

The smell was awful this close. If she had been forced to breathe this putrid air for three weeks, she'd be insane too.

"These are ice chips, Mister Walker," the tech said as he returned. "Suck on them for a second before you try to speak."

The man didn't move. His chest was obscured by the gel, but she could see the vein in his neck pulsing with a heartbeat. Then his jaw moved, slowly at first and he opened his mouth.

"Sure, just a few. I don't want you to overdo it. I'm going to remove your head restraints now. You may feel some pressure."

With a scalpel, he cut through some of the gel, then pulled and the amber block separated. A film of clear plastic covered his hair and forehead and the tech sliced it away. The man opened his eyes, and stared at her.

He didn't try to talk or move, but his eyes were locked on hers.

She took another step; she could touch the tank if she wanted to, but there was something about the thing and its gold mesh that she wanted to avoid, that and the stench inside it.

"Mr. Walker, do you know who I am?" she said.

His eyes were the deepest blue, but not in an attractive way. They were the blue of a gun's barrel.

"Stop! Don't look at me like that," she said. "Answer my question."

He didn't answer.

"Can you take away the rest of this mess he's covered in?"

"Of course."

It was quick. Once the scalpel cut an inch into the gel, it was easy to pull apart, and then she saw him completely. He was nude, except for the clear wrap that protected his skin from the gel.

A catheter ran from his penis into a fitting underneath the table he rested on. He shivered and his breathing quickened, but his eyes stayed focused on hers. If he was embarrassed, it didn't show.

"He's cold, she said."

"I don't have anything to cover him."

"Well get something!"

The tech left, and she was alone with him.

Kill him! the voice said.

Their eyes locked in a battle for dominance, and she would not lose, not to him or anyone.

Kill him! the voice repeated.

He looked away, and she knew she had won. "You're no superman; you're just a man. I'm Marjory Hicks, Mr. Walker. Walker, is that what I should call you?"

Six

The transmission was complete. Six looked at the capsule and the copper mesh and knew why he could not link with anything before. But he was out of it now and could feel and read everything around him. He took a deep breath and looked at her again.

She was Susan's age but looked older, not physically, but mentally, as if she was worn out. He felt her rage build, then retreat, only to build again. She was fighting something internal, and he could sense something or someone else in the background.

"Wh—" he choked on the simple syllable, it felt like swallowing shards of glass. "Why are you so afraid of me? What have I done to you?" He tried to raise his head but couldn't move.

He moved his fingers and felt the plastic wrap on his thigh. Feeling his leg was a start, and he tried to move his head, to follow her as she walked out of his view.

She laughed. "Why would I be afraid of you, Mr. Walker? Look at yourself."

He tried again, but he was still too weak. He closed his eyes. The light hurt, and he didn't need to see her anymore. He felt and sensed everything he needed to know about her.

"You are afraid though," he said, "and you're afraid of the voice in your head. You're afraid you might one day become that person, aren't you, Marjory Hicks? I just listened to the audio file on your phone, Alice in Wonderland. I've read that story, are you Alice?"

He opened his eyes and saw the look on her face, a grimace that pulled her lips tight. Her teeth were clenched and her hands were opening and closing like claws. Her hatred smelled like decaying plants—then he heard the voice.

"Kill him now before it's too late!"

She ran at him and reached for his neck as the door upstairs opened. The technician appeared at the top of the stairs holding a blanket.

"Ms. Hicks!" he yelled. "What the hell are you doing?"

Her grip loosened and she backed away, still staring at him. The tight tendons in her neck slackened, and her face returned to the woman he had seen a moment before, but the hatred still seethed beneath her skin.

"Ms. Hicks, there's a phone call for you in your office. It's a Mr. Price and he says it's most urgent."

"It's Deputy Director Hicks, you asshole," she said.

She turned and left, the anger following her like smoke from a chimney. He could move his head now and watched her climb the stairs, leaving the technician alone in the room with him.

"Mr. Walker, I'm sorry about all of this," he said, glancing at the control room. "This is all I have to cover you. As your metabolism burns off the rest of the narcotics, you'll feel warmer. I'll start removing this prophylactic sheeting … if you're ready."

The technician stepped back in anticipation, waiting for his approval. The man's fear was palpable. He nodded, the bones and cartilage in his neck popped like snapping twigs.

"Who is she?" he asked.

"She's the Deputy Director of the National Security Agency, Mr. Walker."

"What is wrong with her and what has she done to me?"

"I can't answer your questions. She is a very intense woman, as you just saw. You have been in this isolation chamber for over three weeks … ever since Doctor Williams' death."

"Did I kill him?"

The tech stopped cutting through the thin film, his eyes moving toward the empty control room again.

"I'm afraid you did."

"Was he the one who cut me? I had a dream, a vision that I was in a hospital and someone was cutting me with a scalpel."

"I wasn't there, but I heard that's what happened. The doctor collapsed and died. There is no cause of death yet."

"Don't fear me." He tried to lift his head again, finally able to look at himself. He saw he was naked and noticed the IV port in his elbow.

"Why can't I move?"

"That is a side effect of the drugs used to keep you sedated. They aren't designed to keep anyone under for more than a few hours, but we kept you in this chamber for fear you would kill us all. No one could figure out what happened to Doctor Williams, but we knew you were the cause—your abilities, if you know what I mean."

His fear had come true: the dreams of the hospital, of being imprisoned, experimented on, and tortured. It was all true.

"Price, what is it?"

"Ma'am, you asked me to call you if anything new came up. The satellite is transmitting again, and someone is communicating with it."

"Who, can you decrypt it?"

"It's not encrypted. It's using a simple binary code now. Everyone can read it."

"Okay, what is it transmitting?"

"Ms. Hicks, it's a cell phone text message. It says, 'I'm in a room with Marjory Hicks. Help me.' The message originated from your phone."

"It's Deputy Director Hicks!"

She ended the call, so infuriated with Price, she hadn't listened to him. Then it hit her. "My phone," she said, pulling it from her pocket.

Message sent

The phone buzzed in her hand—an incoming call from the director.

She couldn't speak, she could barely breathe. The phone, buzzing like bees, slipped from her fingers and crashed onto the tiled floor, shattering the glass screen.

"Margory?" It was the director's voice. The screen showed his official photo dressed in his black suit, the Stars and Stripes behind him.

She wanted to laugh, looking at him through the cracked glass, the cracks spreading like spiderwebs.

With the spiked heel of her Dior shoe, she stomped on it. Again and again, she pounded the phone until the case broke open and the battery flew out. She smashed it too until gray smoke and yellow flames shot out of it like fireworks. She backed away and turned her anger on the case, stomping on it until the heel of her right shoe broke off and flew across the room.

"But I don't want to go among mad people." The voice said, mocking her.

"Oh, you can't help that, we're all mad here. I'm mad. You're mad."

"How do you know I'm mad?"
"You must be, or you wouldn't have come here."

Six

Her screams were distant but getting closer, a sharp painful shrill. The technician backed away as the control room door flew open.

"Do not interfere and stand as far away as you can," he whispered to the tech.

Her footsteps were uneven, she was limping and still wailing as she came down the stairs. The anger and hatred had changed, now they were tightly focused on him like a laser. She was going to kill him.

The technician ran to the far side of the room, collapsing in the corner, his hands pressed to his ears,

He could lift his head enough to see her now. One shoe was missing its heel, and she wasn't alone. She was in a rage, but a man was controlling that rage.

Her hands were around his throat faster than he could have imagined. They were strong, digging into his flesh. Her face, inches from his was locked in that same grimace. Her teeth were bared, the shrill deafening and her warm saliva pooled on his chest.

Behind him, the technician screamed. He focused on the voice in her head and took hold of it. It was difficult, like trying to grasp something slimy, the harder he squeezed, the more it tried to slip away.

Kill him! Kill him!

He could see her sickness—a gray-green tumor, pulsing in her skull. It smelled like rotting cheese.

Hicks' fingers dug deeper. He couldn't breathe and he was losing consciousness. He pulled again at the raging voice. It was her father's voice, the same voice in her recording and he wondered what the man had done to her to break her so thoroughly.

His vision narrowed and all he could see was her face now. Spittle raining down on him as she screamed, the tendons in her neck stretching so tight, he thought they would snap.

Just kill him, Marjory! Kill him now!

Her face was at the far end of a long tunnel, and the technician's screams grew distant. He was losing this battle. He was tired and wanted it to end. But he also wanted to live, to see Susan one more time. He pulled hard, felt something snap, and passed out.

The technician kneeled over her, his finger on her throat feeling for a pulse. Her heart was beating, but weak and irregular. He ran up the stairs, two steps at a time and called for help looking back through the glass at the man below.

Hicks was convulsing now, but he couldn't help her. He could not go back down the stairs. He had felt something down there, something evil and it had touched him. He sat down and realized he had shit himself. He wept until his young partner rushed in.

"Go help Hicks," he said.

"No fucking way! Look at her, I'm not going down there."

Somewhere far away, a door slammed and they heard heavy boots running down the hall, lots of them.

Soldiers in combat gear and EMTs rushed into the control room. Two soldiers went down the stairs and knelt next to Hicks. The senior officer, a lieutenant, looked at Six and the isolation tank.

"What the hell happened to this man?"

"She … she tried to kill him."

EMTs put Hicks on a gurney and carried her out.

"Look at me," the lieutenant said. "What have you done to this man, and what is that?" he asked, pointing to the tank.

The technician looked at the tank, and he knew he and Hicks and everybody else had crossed a moral line.

"I can't tell you anything. It's classified, just get him out of here. Revive him, whatever, just get him out of here."

Chapter 73
Susan

Croft drove and Susan got her first look at the Trans-Data complex.

"It's bigger than I expected. Where is everyone?"

There were office buildings, warehouses and a few smaller buildings scattered around several acres of open desert.

Eric Ridge and another man stepped out of a car parked at the closest and largest of the buildings.

"This is it, Susan. Just the four of us, five including Sandy."

The attorney smiled and opened Susan's door.

"Welcome both of you," he said. "Susan, Robert, I want you to meet Dustin Torrence. Sandy hired him on the morning of the accident. He's your office manager."

"I haven't been back in the last several days," Torrence said. "Mr. Walker must have ordered a lot of office equipment and furniture. It started arriving the next day, and I did what I could to organize everything. Eventually the shipments stopped coming though, and I locked the doors."

Susan walked in, took a deep breath of cool air, and cried. Monet's *Le Pont Neuf* hung over the receptionist desk. Wiping her tears, she touched the canvas, her fingertip tracing the outline of a wet street in Paris.

"Dustin, did you pick this one out?"

"No, that one was already here. He left the rest to me.

In Sandy's office, she sat in his chair hoping it would help connect her to him, but she was disappointed—it was just a chair.

The three men watched her and said nothing as she leaned back, swiveling the chair from side to side and looking at the artwork on the wall. She stopped and looked at one painting and walked over to it.

"I picked out the art," the young man said. "I was trying to coordinate everything with the Monet, it seemed important to him. It's a dreary painting, unless you know what to look for. I find it vibrant now, the muted colors help you focus on the people strolling along the river Seine."

"You've done well, Dustin," she said.

"He was in a hurry that morning. I think he was heading to Albuquerque."

"I hope he was." She remembered her anger when he didn't show, the memory haunting her now. "So, what am I to do with all this?" she asked Croft.

"His text mentioned the two of you continuing his work, but I don't think he was referring to computers," the attorney said.

She pulled open one of the desk drawers and found a dozen external hard drives. "Faster-than-light propulsion" was written on the first one.

"Mr. Ridge, Dustin, can I have a minute alone with Mr. Croft?"

Croft picked up the hard drive and read Sandy's handwritten label. "Sandy said Carol Vones's research had led to the development of faster-than-light travel. With her death, maybe he wanted to create what she couldn't."

"Or maybe he wanted us to," she said. "What do you think, Colonel?"

Croft didn't answer. "Jesus Christ!" he said, looking at the text on his phone, then at her. "I think this text is from Sandy."

Then her phone vibrated.

"I'm in a room with Marjory Hicks. Help me," she read.

She launched herself out of the chair, knocking the hard drive off the desk. "Who the hell is Marjory Hicks?"

"She's the NSA woman I was telling you about. He is alive, Susan, I knew it!"

She stood and read the text again. "Help me!" Chills crept up her arms and the back of her neck.

"Damn it!" Croft said, working the keypad on his phone. "I can't get through to anyone."

Eric Ridge burst through the door. "Look at this text on my phone!"

Croft nodded. "Our phones too."

Chapter 74
Walter Reed National Military Medical Center

Croft and Susan followed the director of the National Security Agency as they walked down the hallway, Susan's heels clicking softly on the linoleum tiles. Two military police officers rose as the director approached the door.

She looked through the glass and saw him. Sandy's bed was raised and oscillating around a pivot point like a carnival ride—tilting him left and then right. He was intubated, and she could see a machine pushing air into his chest. He was surrounded by monitors and more machines with flashing lights. *So many wires.*

"The doctor is not optimistic. He says no one has ever endured what Mr. Walker went through and lived," the director said.

"Why? What did he do to deserve this?" she asked, but the director ignored her question.

"Only a handful of people know who and what he is, Ms. Matthews. Most who do, are in this room. Your friend in there—Six, or Sandy Walker, whatever we decide to call him—is responsible for what happened in Iran and everything else that followed later. In theory, he may also be responsible for saving many lives in what could have been an attack on Washington.

"What has been done to him was horrific, but right here in the United States, a doctor is dead and a pilot is in a coma, and then there is Marjory Hicks."

"What about her?" Croft asked.

"She's in the next room. She'll probably be discharged in the next day or two. She doesn't remember anything. Since she was a child, she has suffered from schizophrenia, and we never knew.

"Her father was a decorated Army officer. He served in Korea as a combat medic and later as a psychiatrist, helping veterans returning from Vietnam. The pressures must have gotten to him, and he committed suicide when Marjory was eleven. Somehow she managed to keep her illness hidden."

"What's going to happen to her?" she asked.

"She's already tried to resign. She says she can't remember anything involving your friend Mr. Walker and didn't recognize his name. She also says the voices that have troubled her for years are gone. I think whatever happened between them has changed her. Maybe he was battling her illness in the end. The report the technician in Colorado filed is incredible, if it's all true. I think for now it's best for all of us if we keep her close by."

"What about Sandy?" Susan asked.

"We'll keep him here at Walter Reed unless someone objects. The NSA will pick up the tab, but he is free to leave when he recovers."

"If he recovers," Croft added.

"Yes, if he recovers. The doctors here don't know what to make of your friend. Only two of them have access to him, and they are both military and know that everything about Mr. Walker is classified.

"I'll need you to sign a nondisclosure form also, Ms. Matthews. If he is a man from our future, I'm sure I would be one of many that would like to sit down and talk with him, but we have done enough to the man, I think. I hope he lives, and that one day he will want to talk to us. Until then, I don't suppose you'll have a problem with all this going away, Ms. Matthews?"

She looked at Croft, and they both nodded.

"I want to sit with him alone for a few minutes."

Croft walked to Marjory Hicks' room. The door was open, she was sitting up and watching TV. She looked at him. "Can I help you?"

She was different. The cold stare was gone and her voice had lost that hard brassy sound he remembered. She didn't have a clue who he was.

"No, ma'am, I'm sorry to have bothered you."

"Do I know you? I'm Marjory."

He considered saying yes, but remembered the directors' comment, *'I don't suppose you'll have a problem with all this going away?'*

"No, ma'am."

He walked back and joined the director and saw Susan holding Sandy's one free hand. Staring felt intrusive and he looked away.

"Let's get some coffee, shall we?" the director said.

"Colonel Croft, there are a lot of missing pieces in my puzzle. I know it was you who sent the text that alerted the Mossad to the nukes in Tel Aviv and Haifa, but do we know for sure if Sandy Walker is responsible for Natanz or the nuke off Jacksonville?"

"Yes, I sent the text, but to your last question, I honestly don't know. I met the man once in a bar and he never mentioned anything about Natanz. He was just afraid and wanted my help."

"Afraid of what?"

"He was afraid he would be captured, tortured, and imprisoned before he was finished. And his fears came true, didn't they?"

The director ignored the barb and asked, "Finished?"

"Again, I don't know. I do know the picture of Washington was important to him. All I can say is I trusted him. I trusted him, and look where he is now."

Susan came out of the room, her eyes a little redder than when she went in.

"Ms. Matthews, I hope Mr. Walker fully recovers, and I'm sorry to have met you under these conditions," the director said. "I hope to see you both again soon."

Chapter 75
Susan

Three weeks passed with no changes in his condition, and she was growing tired of the sympathetic looks from the nurses.

Croft had hired Emil Fischer to develop a plan for a genetic engineering lab in one of the Trans-Data buildings. Several of Jon Stephens's coworkers also signed on, and the first building was dedicated to both Stephens and Carol Vones. Trans-Data now had fourteen employees.

In Washington, DC, she and Croft walked down the National Mall to the Lincoln Memorial and looked back at the Reflecting Pool.

"I wanted to see this," she said, holding the photo.

"This is where he stood, right here where we are standing now," she said, comparing the picture to the landscape. "I've seen this view a hundred times over the years, and it will never look the same to me now."

It felt like any other photo, glossy on one side and dull on the other, but she knew what she was holding.

The young boy was Sandy, and he was holding his mother's hand. Although the picture felt new, she knew it was ancient, and that some several hundred years from now, the photo would never be taken.

The two silently looked out toward the Washington Monument,

watching the tourists enjoying a peaceful autumn day, not much different from the few people in the picture.

"Let's head back. I've seen enough."

"Walk with me a minute," Croft said.

He led her along a path through a grove of trees, then past the three bronzed soldiers standing vigil, then the two of them stood in front of the massive black granite wall of the Vietnam Veterans Memorial.

Croft stopped in front of Panel 22 West and touched one name.

"Who was he?"

"My uncle. He saved my father in Vietnam and I never got to thank him. I come here when I can, just to tell him that."

She looked at a few names and put her hand on the cold granite. She looked down the length of it, seeing the mirrored landscape reflecting off its surface.

"So many names," she said. "Do you think Sandy will live?"

"Maybe. He's survived so far, so I think he has a chance. I worry he may pull through only to be a cripple, or worse. Let's just hope for the best."

Chapter 76
Six

He hoped this dream would never end. He was with her, holding her slender hand and touching her deep red nails with his fingertips, her thin gold ring reflecting the sunlight.

This was the dream he'd had all his life, from his first days at the Institute when he learned his parents had died. But he knew this dream would be different.

He saw the changes, slowly, as his viewpoint pulled away. The woman was still holding his hand, but they were in the white room now. He looked down and saw that the woman was Susan, as he knew it would be. He looked at himself now and knew he was dying. He saw her tears on his hospital gown and tried to speak to her, to ease her pain, but he knew she wouldn't hear him. *How ironic. In all those years, and in all those dreams, she comforted me when I was suffering, and now I'm trying to comfort her.*

His view continued to change, and he could see Croft at the window watching her and knew the colonel would help her. It was their destiny, perhaps.

Then he was flying, not in the blackness of space, but over a green patchwork of fields. Looking down, he saw farms with tiny people and tiny animals working the land.

He glanced back, not wanting to leave her, but she was gone. Looking around, he saw he was not on a ship or plane of any kind.

He was flying as if he had flown all his life, bird-like, soaring wherever he wanted. Ahead were snowcapped mountain peaks, and he felt the cold air rushing up from them. Steel blue rivers led to a vast ocean, and he saw whales blowing huge plumes of vapor into the air. He inhaled deeply, and he could taste the salt.

He turned and headed back over the land. The smell of salt changed to citrus, and below, there were green fields of orange groves stretched out as far as he could see.

He flew higher now, as if the sky above was calling him. The fields and the animals were now too small to see, but the sky kept calling his name.

"Six," he heard. It was a familiar voice. "Six, I'm here," it repeated.

It was the void, the intelligence he had felt a long time ago, the one that had doomed his ship. He tried to speak to it, but it was too far away.

Higher and higher he flew, and the deep blue turned into the blackness of space. The smell of citrus was gone, and he looked up and saw there were no stars.

"Sandy," he heard a voice say.

Chapter 77
Susan

She held his hand and felt him go. She thought she had prepared herself. She thought she was ready.

"His organs are shutting down, Ms. Matthews, I'm sorry …"

As he slipped away and the monitor alarms sounded, she wasn't ready.

"No!" she said to the empty room.

She touched his face and remembered the candlelight in his eyes at the Yucca Grill, so deep and full of life. She looked now into his half-open, lifeless eyes and whispered his name one more time.

"Sandy."

She put her head on his chest, hoping she could smell his scent—smell it and remember it—but all she smelled were the scents in the room. She sobbed, her tears soaking his gown.

On a December morning in one of the coldest winters in New Mexico's history, five men and one woman stood on the steps of the Trans-Data headquarters in Santa Fe. Susan stood behind Croft, hoping he would block the freezing wind as the office manager took the picture.

She hung the photo in the lobby next to the only picture ever taken of its founder. She had thought of cropping the Coyote Deli's menu out of the picture but left it as it was.

Both pictures would be reproduced and moved several times over the many years until they ended up in Trans-Data's Atlanta headquarters. There, a small boy on a school field trip separated from his classmates and looked at the blonde woman in the picture.

"Come along Six, your parents will be waiting."

He ignored the instructor, staring at the picture and memorizing the faces. "I know you," he said. "I know you all."

Final Thoughts

As early as I can remember, I was fascinated by science fiction. I watched the original *Buck Rodgers* on a B/W television. Then came *Lost in Space*, and as I got older, *The Day the Earth Stood Still*, filmed in 1951.

The first book I ever bought and read cover to cover was Robert Heinlein's *The Moon Is A Harsh Mistress*. I was hooked and in the next several years I read everything Heinlein wrote.

I've read all the old classics and eventually I turned to fantasy with novels like *The Wheel of Time*, horror like *Salem's Lot* and military thrillers like *The Hunt for Red October*. Today I read just about every genre, both fiction and non-fiction.

When I retired, I knew I wanted to write and my first attempt was this novel, originally titled *Six*. Early critiques made me realize I had a lot to learn about creating a story worth publishing.

I shelved Six for years as I wrote my memoir, *Who I Am: The Man Behind the Badge,* As the memoir was being published, I began a crime series starting with *Lieutenant Trufant.*

I never forgot Six sitting in my hard drive. Once *Lieutenant Trufant* and its two sequels were finished, I reworked *Six* several more times until I felt it was worthy of publishing, and I hope you agree that it is. As you read this, I'm working on the rough draft for *Echo Two*, a sequel to this story.

To the future my friends,
Jeff Shaw

About the Author

Jeff Shaw served as a police officer for twenty-four years in South Florida and began his memoir, *Who I Am: The Man Behind the Badge*, soon after retiring. He is the award-winning and bestselling author of *Lieutenant Trufant*, the first book in his Bloodline trilogy; followed by *LeAnn and the Clean Man* and *Broken*. He has also written numerous short stories and most recently his science fiction thriller, *Echo Six*.

- Award-Winning Finalist in the Autobiography/Memoir category of the 2021 International Book Awards.
- *LeAnn and the Clean Man*, once ranked #3 on Amazon's International Thriller list.
- *Echo Six*, runner-up for Killer Nashville's Silver Falchion Award 2022.
- *Hans*, runner-up for the Terry Kay Prize for Fiction 2020

Now a full-time writer and resident of Ellijay since 2007, Jeff is a member of the Atlanta Writers Club, The Blue Ridge Poets and Writers, and Sisters in Crime. He and his wife Susan live in the north Georgia mountains.